PLAYING WITH FIRE

Catalyst Trilogy Book One

TIMOTHY DIAMOND

Playing With Fire

Author: [© Timothy Diamond]

National Library of Australia Cataloguing-in-Publication entry

Creator: Diamond, Timothy author.

Title: Playing with fire / Timothy Diamond.

ISBN: 9780994263100 (paperback)

Series: Diamond, Timothy. Catalyst trilogy ; bk. 1.

Subjects: Historical fiction.

Dewey Number: A823.4

Publishhed with the assistance of www.loveofbooks.com.au

"Catalyst"
By Timothy Diamond

"Catalyst":

/'katalist/n – 1. A chemical agent that causes catalysis

2. A substance (e g an enzyme) that changes especially increases, the rate of a chemical reaction, but itself remains chemically unchanged.

3. Somebody or something whose action inspires further and usually more important events.

As defined by: The Longman Pocket English Dictionary

First published   1986

Third Impression 1987

ENDORSEMENTS

The narrative of this novel is rich in colour and action. The life of young hero Tom Davis moves spontaneously through the pages, with author Timothy Diamond's unique style of writing and creative presentation. The author gives us food for thought between war and peacetime activities. The book is suitable for both genders, and especially Ex-Military personnel will enjoy this novel.
F.E.Louttit - BBAdmin - CWRRSM Chief WRAN Radio Supervisor (Retired)

The author's style is unique in the way the story flows with humour and action, yet still moves at a good pace. Books one and two were great, and I am lookiong forward to reviewing number three.
J.L.Galloway - Correspondent, US Military Affairs Consultant, Co-author 'We Were Soldiers'

A fine read, I like your style.
C.E.Moore - Director US Military Archives, Washington DC

ABOUT THE AUTHOR

"Timothy Diamond" is a pseudonym for my real name.

I grew up in the provincial town of Rockhampton in Central Queensland, and the exploits of my hero, "Tom Davis," are loosely based on actual events in my own life. (Hence the pseudonym)

My story is original and exciting; it contains elements of young love, teenage rebellion, family conflict, corruption, war time experiences, and espionage, a book that could rival the works of Clive Cussler and Ken Follett.

The Catalyst Trilogy is my first full length work of fiction. However, between 1988 and 1994, I wrote multiple articles and reports on recreational diving that were published in *Scuba Diver Magazine* and the *Gold Coast Bulletin*. I also wrote the feature article 'The Round Trip' for *Yachting Australia* magazine in 2009.

ACKNOWLEDGEMENTS

To Diane, without your insistence, patience, putting up with my all night sessions, first draft editing, and cover design, and even waiting for household chores to be done, this book could not have been written. Thank you, I love you.

Ralf B: for 30 odd years, you gained snippets that hinted at some of the things I had been involved in, you suggested that I write a book, well now it's all out there; I hope you enjoy the full story in the right sequence. To change Spock's dialogue a little, "you have been, and always will be, my 'best' friend".

Diana Mason: for keeping an eye on my health, and helping me function.

Sean Gills: for keeping me sane, and helping me function as well.

Martin Devereaux: for keeping my hands working to pound the keyboard.

Tennille: for keeping the hair out of my eyes, and stopped my pulling it out.

Julie McGregor, my Publisher: for her patience, and all the help.

GLOSSARY OF
TERMS & ABBREVIATIONS

Military or 24 hour time is used in this book, expressed in hundreds. 3pm+12hrs would be 1500 hundred. Each time zone is given a designation in the phonetic alphabet GMT is expressed as Zulu time.

Distance is measured in both old imperial measure, and also metric. Even though we changed to the metric system in 1964, some people and places still use the imperial system.

Non Military

Core Subjects – school curriculum subjects that were mandatory, English, Maths, History, Geography, and Science.

Exam Results – were measured in the old system like the US giving, A, B, C's, instead of the now popular OP score system.

Fag – smoke

six of the Best – the number of caning strokes

Sin Bin – penalty time out box

Non Compos – unconscious, or nearly so

Beer Brands – XXXX, VB

Hooter, whistle, or bell – to sound the end of playing Time

Insync – synchronised

Merlot – type of red wine

TAB – booking system for goods

Telecom – Telstra's old name

Shunter – railway job position

Hush Money – Payoff, blackmail

Cop Shop – police station

MC – Master of Ceremonies

Turkey – derogatory name, meaning idiot

Arvo – slang for afternoon

JP – Justice of the Peace

PA – Personal Assistant

Trick Cyclist – Psychiatrist

Dances – Pride of Erin, progressive barn dance

Card Games – Euchre, 500, Bridge

Freo – Fremantle

Southpaw – left hander

PNG – Papua New Guinea

Z's - sleep

Military Terminology:

ADF – Australian Defence Forces

RAAF – Royal Australian Air Force

APC – Armoured Personnel Carrier mines/grenades

Anti-Personnel Devices –

Cong – VC irregular soldier's

Combat gear –ammo belt, back-pack, guns

Claymores – Anti- Personnel Mine

Cam Blanket – camouflage nylon Blanket

Comm's – communication (radio)

Charlie – enemy troops, VC, or NVA

Cherry Beret – military police (slang)

Corps – branch of army i.e. Signal Corp

Corp Training – specialised to Corp

Civvies – someone outside the army

Conflab – conversation

Dark Green – area of dense jungle

Dry mess – eating mess, no alcohol

Extraction – taken out of area

FSV – fire support vehicle, armed APC.

Fatigues – name given to daily work wear

Green Machine – slang name for army

GCHQ – General Command Headquarters

Herc – Hercules transport plane

H.E. – High Explosive

Heavy ordinance - explosives

2IC – second in charge

Ingram – sub machine pistol

Intel – Intelligence

Insertion – move into area

Kit – belongings

K.I.A. – killed in action

LZ – landing zone

LUP – layup area for sleep and food

Lance Jack – lance corporal

Lance Corporal – rank above private

Mag/Magazine – ammunition container

M40 – sub machine gun

M16 – US armalite assault rifle

M79 – grenade launcher

MP's – Military Police

NTR – Nothing to Report

Nogs – derogatory name for enemy

NVA – North Vietnamese Army

NCO – Non Commissioned Officer

NATO – North Atlantic Treaty Organization

OR's – other ranks, below sergeant

OC – Officer Commanding

OP – operation

Prone Position – laying down on belly

Q Store – Quartermaster store

Reveille – wake up time, non-wartime

RPG – Rocket Propelled Grenade

RSL Club – Returned Servicemen Club

Recce – reconnaissance

RAR – Royal Australian Regiment

SOP's – standard operating procedure

Sarg/SGT – short for sergeant

SLR – Self Loading Rifle

Shrapnel – bits of metal from a blast

Spook – Spy

S.A.S. – Special Air Service

Slopes – derogatory name for enemy

Suppressor – silencer

Sterling – gun maker

Sigs Mess – signal corp mess

SRT – Special Response Team

SSM – Staff Sergeant Major (stores)

SR10 – short range radio (500mts)

64set – long distance radio

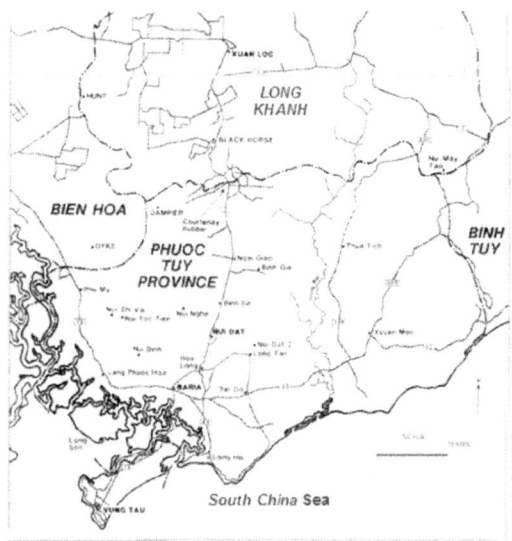

Phuoc Tuy Province

From 1966 to 1971 the Australian SAS Squadrons were based at Nui Dat and mostly operated in the area covered by this map, however from time to time would do special operations in other regions. Missions were conducted throughout Phuoc Tuy Province and across the border into Bien Hoa, Long Khanh, and Binh Tuy provinces. The border and mountain areas were generally covered with extensive areas of thick jungle, hence the saying "a walk in the dark or long green". While the areas around the villages and towns were usually cultivated, either with rice paddies or rubber plantations.

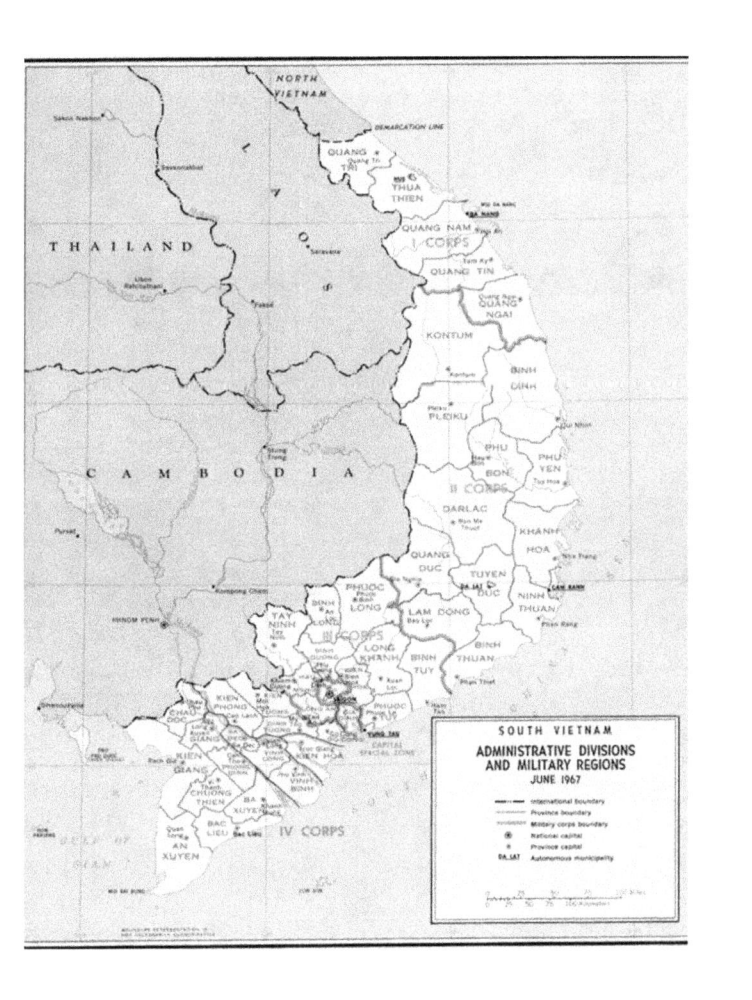

SOUTH VIETNAM

ADMINISTRATIVE DIVISIONS
AND MILITARY REGIONS
JUNE 1967

- - - - International boundary
———— Province boundary
∼∼∼∼ Military corps boundary
⊛ National capital
⊙ Province capital
DA LAT Autonomous municipality

CHAPTER 1

Jill was twenty-five and drop dead gorgeous. At five-four with long black hair and perfectly formed firm breasts, she was a knockout. I, on the other hand, was an arrogant and rebellious twelve-year-old with a razor sharp mind and a constant hard on. She was the teacher, I the student. My offer to walk her home from school on a warm summer day turned into a torrid three month coupling of finely tuned bodies and minds. This became the catalyst for a chain of events that took me across continents, changing both me and the world in which I lived.

I was the last one to walk into the room, and I swaggered in, supreme and confident in the knowledge of my place as top dog in the natural pecking order of things. At the start of the year, the four bullies in our class of twenty boys and two girls had fallen under my fists and fighting ability. Since then, everyone looked to me as their leader. I stood about five-six and had hazel eyes that could become quiet piercing at times. My black hair was uncombed from playing football at lunch time, my the top three buttons of my uniform shirt were unbuttoned, which showed off the width of my shoulders and my lean body. My shorts were snug around my hips, and my socks were down. I took my seat at the back of the room without even glancing at her. I finally looked, and I was gone. I instantly decided that I wanted to make her mine.

I was born into an aristocratic family that immigrated to Australia in the 1950's. My father had married my mother while still in the forces after World War II; he worked most days as a department store manager. My mother also worked, but not because she had to; she did it to improve her social standing, and so she wouldn't have to look after us kids. She was intolerant, and anything we did wasn't good enough, and if we ever did anything wrong, her temper knew no bounds. Unlike most mothers, she was not the kissing and cuddling type; she seemed uncaring.

I was the oldest of five, and we must have inherited genes from both of them, because I grew up smart. At times I found I could run rings around everyone with my intellect. Most of my early childhood was spent in a quiet country town on the main highway midway between Brisbane and Townsville, where you had to grow up tough or suffer the bullying of peers. So I grew up strong as well as tough. And if I wasn't involved in some fight or other mischief at least every second day, well, I was having a quiet week!

Going to primary school in the 60's was boring because I found I knew more than my so called teachers. I couldn't wait to get to high school where I might find something that would present a challenge. Wrong! The hardest thing going into grade eight was choosing which courses to take, a no brainer really. An academic course that was meant to be the hardest, as you probably guessed that was the one for me.

In those days you had eight subjects to complete. Six were core subjects, and the other two were electives. Of course, we had different teachers for the various subjects. Some were good and others were, as I saw it, a waste of space. No, I'm not going to tell you what Jill taught, so forget it!

How did things start? Ok, well, Jill came in to take over for our regular teacher, who was leaving. The first time I saw her, I was gob smacked. Christ, what a body. Anyway, I was having a bit of a problem grasping an idea, so she came over to help me through it; once I caught on to her way of thinking, what I had been trying to grasp was easy. Her class was the last for the day, so as everyone made their way out, I lagged behind to see if she needed any help.

"Thank you....?"

"Tiger miss. Tom Davis really, but people call me Tiger."

"Well, thank you, Tiger. I've got all this stuff to get home, but I didn't bring my car in today."

"Too easy, miss. I'll carry it and walk you home, if you'd like?"

She looked at me and said, "Ok. All my stuff is here, and I

don't live far away. Since it's after hours, call me Jill."

On the way home we talked about school, subjects, and what was going on in the world. At one point, she told me that she was amazed by the intellect in someone my age and asked, "Are you sure you're not a twenty-five-year-old in disguise?" We both had a bit of a laugh.

All too soon we arrived at her place. After putting her stuff down on the coffee table, she asked me if I'd like a cold drink; I accepted, and we both had a coke. With the cokes finished, I said, "Well, I suppose I'd better get going." I made a tentative move to kiss her goodbye.

She moved her face so that kissing her cheek turned into a kiss full on the lips! What was going to be a peck on the cheek became a very passionate kiss; our arms wrapped around each other tightly.

What happened surprised both of us, but we did not let go of each other. We kissed passionately again, and this time I let my hand leave her back and caress her right breast. She moaned and held me tighter to herself (it would have taken someone who was brain dead to ignore my hard on).

After our embrace, she took me by the hand and said, "Come." She led me into her bedroom. We started to kiss again. As we kissed, I slowly started undoing the zipper on the back of her dress, while she unbuttoned my shirt. I stepped out of my shoes. I unhooked her bra, and as soon as her nipples touched my bare chest, she moaned again. When we let go, she slid back onto the bed and I undid my shorts and let them slide down, jocks and all, and moved to the bed to remove her undergarments. She made this easier for me by arching her back and lifting her backside so I could slide them off. I joined her on the bed.

During the next passionate kiss, I moved over her and she guided me into her and said (or was it shouted?), "Now!"

I entered her as deeply as I could go, and she moaned in ecstasy as we made love to each other for the first time. After what felt like fireworks going off repeatedly, we lay in each other's arms holding on to each other. Shortly after, we talked about how this shouldn't have happened but made arrangements to see each other the next afternoon. And thus started our love affair!

I was late getting home one night, (don't know why), so my mother had to have her say. Me being me, I came right back at her, which started one hell of a Barney between me and the oldies. It ended with me telling them I was sick of the crap and was going to move out, which naturally started round two. I got the, "Think you can make it on your own? Where do you think you're going to live? You're too young to get a job" speeches. Now, all these points made sense, of course, but I wasn't going to let them think they had won, so off to my room I went. I packed a bag with some clothes, a spare school uniform, and told them I was leaving. I got the "You'll be back" routine, and as this was being said, I walked out.

Ok, so now what? I thought to myself as I walked along aimlessly. I found myself close to Jill's place, so I figured, what the hell, why not? I headed there to see her and tell her what had happened. She was a bit surprised but happy to see me again so soon after leaving earlier. We kissed quite passionately after she closed the door, sat down with a cup of coffee and a coke, and I told her the story while she was cuddled up in my arms on the couch.

Her initial reaction was one of shock, but she told me that I could stay with her, and we would talk more about my other options later. We cuddled together, listening to some music, then went to bed for the night. I found sleeping the whole night with Jill curled up in my arms for the very first time very enjoyable and decided that I could very easily get used to it.

Over breakfast, we discussed the plan for the day. Jill was going to take her car to school because she wanted to get me my own set of house keys, and I would do what I always did and walk to school. Rather, I would go back to the family house and grab my bike, then go to school, I thought this would be the better option, so after giving her a long kiss goodbye, she gave me the spare back door key and I did just that.

When I left, I was feeling good and well with myself; of course, as life has a tendency to do, I got a sure kick in the ass. As

I arrived in the yard at home, Dad was doing his usual car check prior to leaving for work. He right off started with the questions: "Where had I spend the night? What was I up to? How did I intend to live?" And on it went. So, as you can imagine my bubble had been burst, which put me in a really good frame of mind to start the day, and the day just got worse as it continued.

When I arrived at school, I threw my bag on the rack outside homeroom and went down to the oval where some of my mates were kicking a football around. I went through the usual pleasantries and joined in. When I got the ball for a kick, it went a little off skew and smacked this kid Joe fair on the side of the head. Well, that really kicked it off! He came over and started calling me names that I can't repeat, so I told him to fuck off and shoved him backward. He came back with a swing (fool), I blocked and punched him in the stomach (no other option really, he was nearly six foot!). As he straightened, someone warned us that a teacher was heading our way. "Shit!"

Off to Jack Robertson's (the principal) office we went. After receiving six cuts on each hand each, Joe and I met and agreed that this was not over and arranged to meet down on the riverbank right after school to finish it.

I went back to my mates to let them know what had happened, and bummed a smoke off Brownie (there's always one, isn't there?). Halfway through my fag, guess what? I got sprung by our maths teacher. Back to Robertson's office. Now Robo had already given me six, so he told me to be back right after last class for another lot. Oh brilliant! Now I had two appointments that afternoon. Ok, I could handle this. I saw my first appointment (Joe) nearby as I left Robo's office, told him that I would be there, but maybe a little late due to the second appointment. Would this day get any better?

Answer: no. It didn't get any worse, either, though. During the day we had a period that I was looking forward to because it was Jill's class. After class was over, I hung back so I could tell her that she may arrive home before me because of an appointment that could take a bit of time. What? You didn't think I'd tell her the real reason did you? Do I sound like an idiot? Don't bother answering that!

Ok, the appointment with Robo. He proceeded to give me the lecture about smoking, to which I replied that this was a bit rich coming from him as he was a smoker himself. At least he agreed with me, but because it was on school grounds, he had to uphold the rules, so another six of his best on each palm and away I went. Shit! Now I had a fight to go to and I couldn't close my fists properly.

During my bike ride down to the riverbank, I clenched and unclenched my hands, hoping to be able to close them into fists without too much pain. When I arrived at the usual site, it seemed as if half the school was there. My usual crowd of mates joined me, and I said, "Let's get on with it."

As Joe and I were squaring off, I was playing for time. I considered the problem of how to really hit him in the face when he was so much taller than I was. He asked if I was ready, to which my reply was no. I proceeded to tell him my dilemma. I told him I really didn't want to kick him in the balls to bring him down where I could get at him. I spotted a small mound not far away and asked him if he wouldn't mind going over there so I could stand on the mound and we could get amongst it.

Now here's where the hilarity starts. He actually agreed! So to the mound we went and started the fight. I dodged his first couple of swings, blocked the third, and then let fly with a brilliant right that caught him on the side of the jaw. The noise I found out later was heard all the way to the back of the crowd. Naturally, he went arse over tits. As he started to get up, I planted a left on the other side of his jaw for good measure and a hard uppercut to the point of the chin. That was it: lights outs for him and not a mark on me, but, by Christ, my palms were really throbbing.

After a few moments, he started groaning and waking up. I went over and helped him up and asked if he was ok. He replied that he was ok and we shook hands. I said, "Better luck next time."

His reply was quite funny. "Not against you. You're too fast and hit like an express train." I took this for the compliment it was supposed to be, and we became firm friends after that.

Now I had to get ready to face the music from Jill. I hoped she only knew about the morning episode and not the smoking one, and especially not the fight. No such luck! When I got to her place, she was waiting for me. The first thing she did was look me up and down and walk around me looking at my head and arms. She wrapped her arms about me and said, "Thank God you're all right. I was so worried I almost came down to stop that stupid fight you'd gotten yourself involved in. Let's have a look at your hands." She promptly took my hands in hers and studied them, commenting, "Good, no damage. Are your palms sore?"

Christ, she knew about that as well. "No," I replied. "Not now. How did you know about that?"

"Don't forget I'm a teacher. Of course, I'm bound to hear things about students that were in the shit for this or that reason. Naturally when your name comes up I take interest without trying to be too obvious, which I'm starting to find hard. So yes, I know about this morning, AND about you being caught smoking. Also, I overheard a couple of the kids talking about the fight being arranged before you told me you'd be late, so let's hear the whole story. How come you're not hurt?"

We sat on the couch with her leaning against me and my arms around her. I proceeded to tell her the whole story whilst absently playing gently with her lovely breasts, tracing all around them with my fingers and running my fingers over her nipples.

Later that night as we were getting dinner ready (yes, she was teaching me how to cook, something I'd never thought I'd do, but Christ am I thankful for those early lessons now), we started to broach the subject of the predicament I found myself in with my family. After I told her I wasn't about to give in, we started firing ideas off each other about what I could do. Eventually it was decided that I would try to get a part time job so I would have money coming in to live on. She was adamant that I shouldn't give up school, and that I should at least stay until I sat the junior exams in year ten. Because of the promise I made to her, I did just that.

7

That night we talked a lot and made love to each other, and settled down to sleep afterward. With Jill cuddled in my arms as usual, two thoughts went through my mind. The first was rather pleasant; she was actually teaching me how to make love with a woman. I was learning how to respond and interact with them. We had discussed women in general, the way they reacted differently in given situations. To give you an example, in foreplay, different sorts of strokes on her back would make her arch as if wanting more, or a stroke on the neck would draw a pleasurable shiver. I learned how to look at a woman to make her feel as if she's the only person in the room and that you're interested in her alone during a conversation. The second thought was much more disturbing. I began to realize that our affair or relationship (whichever you care to call it) would not last and would have come to an end. I realized I was learning to be independent, and even though I hated to admit it, our age difference would become a factor in the future. No living happily ever after for us!

Over the next couple of weeks, we laughed, we talked, and if I had a problem with school work she would help me find the answer my way. I also got better at cooking.

One afternoon after school I was walking down the town's main street and saw a clothing shop with a sign in the window for an assistant. I went in to see if it was for a male or female. It was for a male, so I spoke with the person in charge of the shop and applied for the job on the spot. The only stumbling blocks were my age, where I lived, and the hours I could work. Mr Petersen (the owner) seemed ok, so I told him the story, although I told him I was boarding with one of my teachers. He considered my application; deep in thought, then looked over at me and said: "You seem to me to be someone trying to make your way in the world despite hardship, so I'm willing to give you a go. Go to school and be here by 3:30 ready to start. I will need you until 5:30 each week day and from eight until one on Saturdays. You will be paid the normal junior wage. "Can you manage that"?

I said I could, and it was agreed that I would start the following

Saturday, when he would start showing me the ropes.

I went home to tell Jill the good news, and we kissed and hugged happily. Over dinner, Jill let me have some of her wine. She showed me how to tell a good wine from one that's not so good, thus started some lessons on wine and liqueur appreciation over the coming weeks. You know, the only thing that spoiled what we had together was our age difference, which meant we couldn't go out in public holding hands or putting our arms around each other. I also couldn't show off my girlfriend to my mates or shout to the world, "This is MY girl"!

We got into a routine. Go to school. Go to work. Come home. Do my homework with Jill by my side (she would always tell me that I astounded her with my intellect, and wondered how I was so smart, like I was twenty years older than I actually was). Help cook dinner, talk or watch a bit of TV, then off to bed and make love. Then do it all again the next day. Believe it or not, this suited me, and we were content with our lives. Then the axe fell!

It was a Friday afternoon, and I came in from work to find Jill holding a letter in her hands and crying uncontrollably. I rushed over to her, took her into my arms, and tried to quiet her sobbing. I asked her what was wrong. She told me between sobs that she had some good or bad news depending on how we looked at it. Instant thought, shit, she's pregnant!

I said to her, "Well, we can work this out together when you calm down and tell me what happened. Go and wash up and I'll pour you a wine, grab a coke, and we'll sit down and you can tell me all about it."

When she came back after composing herself, she held out the letter and said, "Tiger, you need to read this."

The letter was from the Department of Education informing her that the position in Brisbane she had applied for now had a vacancy and asked if she was still interested in taking it on. I asked what it was all about, and as it turned out, the position it referred to was one she had applied for shortly after getting her teaching degree. The position was at one of the colleges in Brisbane, where

9

she had lived with her parents. At that time, there had been no vacant positions, so she had put in for the one in our town and got it. But this prior application had remained on record, which meant she could transfer to this position at the end of term in a month. She had talked about wanting to go back to Bris during our previous chats, so now we really did have a problem.

We had never discussed breaking up before, so I guess this was as appropriate time as any. We talked about moving down to Bris together, but we both knew that wasn't going to work for many reasons. I had no wish to move down to the big smoke; plus we would be under the public spotlight much more in the city. It was decided that I would need to either think about going back home or look for somewhere to live so I could carry on with school and work.

We would try to spend as much time together before parting. As you can imagine, this wasn't an easy conversation to have, and our emotions got the better of us at times. So talk was interspersed with crying and holding on to each other, and neither of us got much sleep that night.

At work the following Saturday morning, a bloke came in who looked quite familiar. While talking to him, we discovered that we had lived next door to each other in the days when our families were living in Ascot in Brisbane. It turned out that Pete was looking for a flatmate. I asked how much rent he was after and where he lived, so we made plans for me to visit him after I finished work that afternoon.

When one rolled around, I jumped on my trusty iron steed (bike) and pedalled to Pete's address, which wasn't all that far from work. He showed me around the place and the room he was letting. It had a bed, desk, and wardrobe, so we sat down and I told him of my predicament. I was still going to school and having to work part time and needed somewhere to live because the place where I was staying would only be available for three more weeks. We started about talking rent and my share of the electricity costs. After doing some quick calculations, I realised I would still be left with about sixty-five percent of what I earned each week. So, yes, it was a done deal, and I could move in early the following month. Now I had a place to stay taken care of. I went home to let Jill know what I had arranged. She was happy for me but sad as well.

The next three weeks went by all too fast, with arranging her moving and our school lives. I took most of my meagre possessions to Pete's, only keeping a spare set of gear that I could carry in my school bag.

We spent our final night together, clinging to each other as much as we could. I asked her not to stop when she drove off in the morning or I was likely to break down in public. We made love as if there was no tomorrow (which there wasn't).

I could have smashed the alarm clock when it rang loudly the next morning. She didn't want to move and neither did I, but it had to be done. We had our final embrace and kiss in full view of anybody who was watching, I opened the car door for her, and as she got in I could see her crying. One last kiss through the window and she drove away without looking back, just as I had asked her to do.

That was the last time I ever saw Jill. I had loved her without reservation. She had been my mentor, my teacher, and my first love. Jill had been my saviour and the person who changed my life forever.

CHAPTER 2

Over the next few weeks I wasn't good company for anyone, as I withdrew into myself. I was missing Jill. I was angry with myself, and her. I blamed my problems on her for leaving me, and questioned myself about not going with her. The only outlet I had available to me was either getting into fights, (that worked for a while, because I could release my pent up anger by pulverising someone), or some other form of mischief. One of those pranks had the whole town in an uproar. I'd gotten hold of a massive supply of bubble bath, and one night went and poured all this stuff into the town's prized coloured fountain in the middle of town. The bubbles and soapy water went everywhere. The grass, footpath, and surrounding roads were covered with frothy water. The fountain spewed out bubbles and soapy water for days. There was no colour though, because the lights were buried under the foam. "Christ." It took the best part of a week to clean-up, and all I really got out of it was a couple of giggles. Not worth the trouble after all!

One night Pete and I were talking, and he told of numbers that could be used in phone boxes (Pete worked for telecom at the time) for free calls. He told me how to get the phones to ring themselves, and that they would continue ringing until someone picked up the phone. "Bullshit!" I said, and he replied "Go see for yourself then."

So I went up to the corner phone, lifted the handset, dialled in the four digit code he had given me, and replaced the handset. Sure enough, it started ringing. I let it ring while I thought to myself "This was handy to know." I then went into the phone box and lifted the handset; no tone was heard so I put it down. When I got back to the flat Pete told me he had heard it ringing from across the street. "Cool," I thought. The other number he gave me was to make free calls. The only difference was that instead of hanging up after dialling the four digit code, you followed it with the number you were going to ring and waited for it to connect

Anyway, even these distractions, though adding to my knowledge base, didn't help. I seemed to be on auto pilot. Then one day, the lights came back on, but the anger was still there. Naturally, I was at school at the time, so someone was going to cop it! I disagreed with the answer our maths teacher, Mr. Cochrane, had given us, and voiced my opinion by telling him his answer was wrong.

To make matters worse, I got up from my seat, went to the blackboard, wrote in the correct answer, and drew a ring around it. I turned to him and said, "If you're going to teach it, then at least get it right!" to the cheers of my classmates.

He ordered me out of the classroom and told me to wait for him outside. While I was outside, I thought I may as well have a smoke, and proceeded to light up. Next minute Cochrane flew out, grabbed my smoke, threw it on the ground and said, "Get down to the principal's office and wait for me there. I'll be down soon."

As I walked into the school office, Robo was coming out of his and asked what I was doing there, so I told him. He looked up and said, "Not again! Ok. We'll wait till he arrives before we go any further."

I didn't have to wait too long before Cochrane arrived. We both went into Robo's office where we were directed to sit while he closed the door. After returning to his desk, Robo asked Cochrane why we were here. To give him his due, Cochrane kept to the facts without embellishment (so despite the circumstances, he was starting to earn my respect).

Jack then turned to me and asked "Why did you decide it was necessary to point out the mistake in a manner that disrupted the class, and then break the school rules by smoking?"

My answer was, "Because the so-called mistake was so obvious that half the class would have seen it. If something is supposed to be taught, it should at least be done correctly! Not haphazardly, so that the answer given to the class is wrong. As for the smoking, I got bored being outside."

Robo appeared to think things over, and then said "Well, you owe Mr. Cochrane an apology for a start, Davis. Then I'm going to call your parents in and we'll have a chat about this."

When I heard this I instantly jumped in and said, "Ok. I apologise to you, Mr. Cochrane, for my behaviour."

I then faced Robo, and asked if we could talk in private. Robo looked over at Cochrane and asked if there was anything else. Cochrane accepted my apology and said "No, there was nothing further," so Robo asked him to close the door on the way out.

He then looked at me, and said, "Ok, out with it!"

Now I considered Jack to be a fairly reasonable person, and told him of my situation (omitting all reference of Jill and our relationship, for obvious reasons). I also told him why I really blew up in class, because I felt that the situation was due to pure incompetence on Cochrane's part, and that he was useless as a teacher.

Jack just looked at me, and said: "My God, Tiger, you've been fending for yourself for the last four months? You're smart enough to know better. I would have helped, or are you THAT stubborn?" My reply was simple and to the point. I looked him in the eye, and said "Yes. Now I've got a science class. Can I go?" He just shook his head and said, "Yes, ok, off you go."

Of course, after the science class that I was late for, the usual gang wanted to know how I got on after being hauled off by Cochrane. I told them that I was able to get off the hook, and let's see what happens in the next maths class. As we made our way to the next period, talk centred on the upcoming football match. A couple of us were playing in the game against North Rocky High, now only about two weeks away.

Well, that little episode with Cochrane and Robo brought me back into the here and now. I started to realise that I had to change my attitude as I still had a lot of growing up to do. I guess that change was noticeable, because when I got to work that afternoon, Mr. Petersen said (or was he being sarcastic?)" "It's good to see you back again. Are you ready to work?"

With a laugh, I replied that I was. He said "You know Tom, if you do have some troubles you are quite welcome to talk them over at any time. I was young once, you know." With that, we both laughed, and he started to show me some of the new stock that had come in that morning.

The day of the footy match rolled around. We had home ground advantage, which turned out rather well for us. Anyway, I was on the wing and my opposite number would have been about a year older and six inches taller than me. His name "Skeeter Johnson," and from first glance I knew we were really going to lock horns. Sure enough, from kick off it was on. The ball went to Skeeter, and I took him with a flying tackle around the midriff and promptly received an elbow in the neck for my trouble. I thought to myself, "Ok, if you want, two can play that game." The next time he got the ball, I dragged him down with a head high tackle, and a smack in the mouth for good measure. I ended up with the ball and we had the turnover we wanted, but I was taken down around the ankles. After playing the ball, I stayed with play. After the next tackle the ball was passed out to me, and off I went. Skeeter came rushing at me; I only needed to get past him and the full back. As Skeeter came at me, I used an elbow block, brushed him off, side stepped the full back, and the try was mine. As we were walking back to our half of the field, Skeeter came over and said: "Think you're pretty good, don't you, arsehole?" Of course, me being me, I replied: "No, I know I'm good!"

As the game progressed the battle between us got more heated, and during the next tackle, he smashed me with an uppercut as I was about to play the ball. This was absolutely the last I was going to take. As I finished playing the ball, I let go with a right to his stomach and then smashed my left into the side of his jaw with as much power I could give it. I was rewarded with the sound of breaking bone as he went down and out. Needless to say I was sent off, and the team had to play one man down for the 10 minutes sin binning I'd been given by the referee.

While I was in the sin bin, a note arrived from Skeeter with his phone number on it. He asked me to give him a call in a couple of days. I put the note into my bag and started to concentrate on the game. By the time I got back on the field, the score was level, and North Rocky had the ball. There was only enough time for one more play, (here's where the home ground advantage comes in) and Skeeter's replacement had the ball. As he got to just over the half line mark, he was on course to pass over a very slight rise and fall in the ground. It was not really noticeable, but running full tilt, the quarter step rise and fall made for disastrous results. Anyway, I struck him at the same time as the rise wobbled him, which meant the ball went loose. I scooped it up, reversed course for our try line, and went off full tilt, shrugging off tackles as I went. I scored and won the game.

Yeah. Ok, instant hero! Anyway, after we went off and got changed, I was joined by my mates. They wanted to know why it took me so long to unload on Skeeter, and how much damage did I think I'd done? I told them about hearing the bone crunch after I hit him. I showed them the note he had sent to me, and asked what they reckoned about that? One of them, ever the optimist, said "Looks like you're about to have another fight on your hands, and this guy is quite a bastard. From what I hear, he fights dirty and will use anything in a brawl." My reply to this news was, "Great! That's all I need, I'll wait and see what he wants in a couple of days."

That afternoon when I arrived at work, Mr. Petersen congratulated me on my win. When I corrected him, and said that it was a team win I had only played a part in it, his reply rather took me back. "Not the way I heard it. It's all over town, you know, how you hospitalized that thug that was picking on you all the time!" "Oh, shit," was my reply. "I really don't need this sort of attention. How do I duck all this?" "Don't worry about it Tiger. It'll all blow over in a couple of days, and people will have something else to talk about."

While we were talking, someone came into the store, but I hadn't looked at him until he came to the counter. As I was about to ask if I could help, I looked up. Oh fuck! It was my father. I turned

16

to Mr. Petersen and said "I'll be out back." I saw his quizzical look and walked off.

As I left, I heard Mr. Petersen's, "Sorry sir, can I help you?"

"No, I'd rather talk to my son, if you don't mind," my old man said rather angrily.

On hearing this, I returned to the shop and stated that anything he wished to say could be said in front of Mr. Petersen.

The old man said "I've known you've been working here for a while, that you still go to school, and are still causing trouble!"

With this, Mr. Petersen went to interject. The old man held up his hand to cut him off, and said, "Its ok. I'm not here to argue. I just want to find out what this one thinks he's up to."

I replied, "Yeah, well I have my own place, a job, I still go to school and I'm surviving, something you didn't think I could do. Anything else you want?"

His reply was, "No, not right now. Just wanted to know that you're ok, and to let you know you can come home any time you wish. Just let me know, and I'll square things with your mother."

With that, he nodded at Mr. Petersen and walked out. I went back to our conversation as if we hadn't been interrupted, but Mr. Petersen asked what I was going to do. I told him, "I'm not sure, but will think about it later."

A couple days later, I came across Skeeter's note again, and decided to call him. I mainly wanted to see if he was looking for retaliation. Did I need to get ready for a full on brawl or not? After I got to the flat that evening, I went to the phone box, and called the number. Skeeter came on the line, sounding a bit muffled. I said who was calling and asked why he was so muffled." He replied that I had broken his jaw." Oops! Ok, now I thought he would be wishing to finish what we had started. However, he asked if we could get together to talk over a deal of some sort to do with playing footy." So I told him I probably couldn't see him till either Saturday afternoon or Sunday, because of work." He said this was fine and gave me his address. We arranged to meet on Saturday at 2 pm, at his place.

The following day at school, I met up with the guys, and told them of the conversation I'd had with Skeeter and about the meet with him on Saturday. A couple of them asked if I wanted back up, because he could be setting me up to get hospitalised by his mates. Cripes! That one hadn't occurred to me! The more I thought about this, the more I thought it could be a possibility. Anyway, as Saturday rolled around, I shot home after work and changed into an old set of clothes. If I would be fighting for my life, I didn't want to do it in a good set of clothes that cost hard earned cash. Now, Skeeter's place was on the other side of town on the way to the local meatworks. Was this a possible omen? As I got near his area, I really started taking note of who was around, just in case there was going to be an ambush after all. When I got there, he was waiting on the front steps. I looked around, and he asked what the matter was?" When I told him what had been going through my mind, he laughed and said "I wouldn't fight near home anyway. The cops know the place too well. Come on in."

As we went in, he started to explain the reason he wanted to see me. He thought I was too good a player to be just playing amateur school footy. He asked if I was interested in making money out of it."

"How?" I asked, and he proceeded to tell me that he played 'A' grade for the 'Raiders' (one of the local teams), and he could probably get me in if I was interested. He then told me he made fifty bucks for playing a game when the team lost, seventy if there was a draw, and one hundred for a win. What else was there to say, but "I'm in." He made a phone call to his coach while I was there, and his coach said that he'd be there in half an hour. The coach arrived and, true to his word, Skeeter gave Coach Dixon an unbiased view of the way I played football. He said I played hard and fast, and that I wasn't afraid of taking on big solid guys either, as I was the one who broke his jaw.

Dixon's comment was "So you're THAT Davis. I've heard of you, a real scrapper. Are you really up for this? You'll be going up against some really big and older players!"

"I told him I was. He looked at Skeeter, then at me, and then said: "Ok, but I can't put you into the line-up straight away, so I'll put you into reserve grade first and see how you develop. Is that ok with you?"

My reply was, "Will I get paid?"

He told me the rates for reserve grade players; thirty dollars for a loss, forty for a draw, and seventy five for a win. This was very good money, so I told him I was ready to take it on.

He shook my hand and said "Good.

Then to Skeeter, "Well done. See you both at training on Thursday night. I'll leave you to let Tom know all the details," and with that he left.

Well, I thought to myself, playing something I enjoyed, and being paid for it. Cool! So Skeeter filled me in on where training was being held, and when, and what to bring, after which I left. Well, much later I found out that Skeeter had been paid one hundred dollars for my recruitment, and didn't say anything, or share any of it, "The Bastard!"

At training the following Thursday night, I learned that the reserve grade trained with the 'A' grade side. Skeeter was there, but not training because of his jaw. After training, everyone made their way down to the Railway Hotel for drinks. At the bar I ordered a beer, (well I tried!) but Bobby, the barman just looked at me. He ended up giving me what he said was called a 'lime, lemon, and bitters'. Skeeter laughed, I gave him a sour look and enquired about his jaw.

He said, "I'll be right to play again in a week or so."

I said "Sorry about that."

He laughed it off with, "No worries, it was my own stupid fault. Here's to Saturday," and we clinked glasses.

The next Saturday, I played my first grown up game of football, and it couldn't have gone any better. We won. I scored twice, so I was well pleased, and picked up seventy five bucks into the bargain! I just wish Jill had been there to see it, and share in my triumph.

Apparently, someone new coming into my life had been watching me, not that I knew it at the time! I only played two more games in reserve grade (both wins). At training the following Thursday, after the third game, Coach Dixon asked if I was ready for 'A' grade yet? "Yep," was my immediate reply? I trained with 'A' grade that night, with Skeeter on the opposite wing. This really didn't seem to gel; I'd rather have been on the same wing. I put this idea to Coach Dixon down at the pub later that evening, and he agreed to put me on the outer wing, with Skeeter next to me.

Sunday was the 'A' grade playing day, so we all met at the pub (unofficial club house) and got into the team bus to go up to Brown Park. When we got there, I had our runner go and grab me a program book, as this was the first time I had ever gone to this sort of event. While I was in the change room there was time to have a look at it, and my name was listed as debuting in the team! I was elated to see it there, and showed Skeeter.

His reply was a blasé "Yeah, get used to it. Now get your head focused."

The side we were playing were the team score ladder leaders, and considered tough to beat. I guess someone should have told them that, because when we got on the field, we carved them up. The combination of both Skeeter and I worked like a treat. When we had the ball he'd keep the big guys off me. If it looked as if I was in trouble I'd send him a quick pass, and vice a versa. Then in defence, our whole team was ferocious. The score in the end was eighteen zip in our favour. Wow, what a game, especially considering that they were going to be tough to beat!

When the self-congratulations and hijinks were over in the change room, we piled into the bus and headed down to the pub. Amid all the cheers, we made our way to the bar. Bobby our barman came up to me and I asked for a beer.

He looked at me the way he usually did, and with a chuckle said "Sure why not? You deserve it, XXXX or VB?"

"VB thanks," I replied.

I was grinning like a Cheshire cat. Yes! I'd finally made it into the adult world.

Speaking to Skeeter glass in hand, he said to me "Looks like you've got an admirer," and nodded towards the door. I looked around to see a brunette about my height, nice figure, staring at me with a smile on her face. I went over to her and said "Hi, I'm Tiger, can I get you a drink?"

She replied "Barbara, just an orange or a soft drink thanks. I'm not allowed to drink alcohol yet."

I laughed and said "Neither am I, but I get away with it. Be back in a minute..."

She had found a table when I got back with the drinks, so I sat, and we started chatting. I asked, "How come I'm lucky enough to be in the company of such a beautiful girl?"

She laughed and replied "Luck," and laughed again. "Plus I haven't been able to take my eyes off you since I first saw you play, a few weeks ago." (Remember I said earlier that someone had been watching me!) "Well, here's to luck then," I said and we clinked glasses.

When she finished her drink, I asked if she would like another. To which she replied "No thanks, I'm just waiting for my father over there, talking to one of his workmates." Just as she finished saying this, he came over and asked if she was ready. She introduced us. His name was Ray Finlay (and boy, he was big). Barbara said she was ready, and got up to go. I quickly asked "Can I call you sometime??" As I asked this, her father, with a surprised look on his face, just shrugged his shoulders. Meanwhile she had written her phone number on a drink coaster, passed it to me, and smiled. I nodded and they left. I just stood there watching them go.

CHAPTER 3

Well, during the next few weeks, life was hectic. Football on Thursday night and game day on Sundays. School and work every week day, plus work on Saturday mornings. Finding the time to spend with Barbara, Oh yes, I had contacted her, but she wasn't allowed to go out with me until I had met her parents. We settled on talking to each other over the phone and a couple of minutes in person prior to and after the Sunday games. Barbara was sixteen and had left school the previous year to go nursing. She had no problem with my age, as I had been upfront with her about what I was doing (no she didn't know about Jill) with my life.

Over a Wednesday night phone conversation, Barbara and I arranged for me to go to her place, and have dinner with the family. Then either her mother or father would drive us to the pictures on Saturday and pick us up afterward. At work the following afternoon, I was having a conversation with Mr. Petersen about football, and he asked me "Tom, what are you going to do if you get injured in some way?"

This took me back a bit, as it's something I'd never thought about, and I told him so. He then said "Well, do think about it, and it might pay to write up a list of people to contact if something really goes awry." My reply to this was that I would.

"Oh, by the way, I'll be available to work over the holidays if you want me to." "Good, good I'd like that. I'll tell you something else I enjoy the conversations we have when you're here. They keep me young."

Saturday had finally arrived, and I was due at Barbara's at five o'clock. Her house was up near the hospital where she worked. It would take me at least half an hour to pedal up to there, so I got ready and left at four thirty. As I approached the door, was

I apprehensive? Shit yeah! Ray opened the door. He shook my hand and told me to "Come in" as he closed the door behind me. He said "Right this way," and with that I followed him into the lounge room. I spotted Barbara on the couch already dressed to go out, and her mother (I assumed) sitting in one of the armchairs.

Ray said, "Well, I suppose introductions are needed? Tiger, this is my wife Betty, Betty ... Tiger..."

With this, I walked across the room, shook her hand and said, "Hi, how are you?"

She replied, "Fine, and you I hope? Please sit."

I went and joined Barb on the couch. As I did, she put her hand in mine and gave it a gentle squeeze. Ray had parked himself in the other armchair, and Betty asked "So, is Tiger a nickname or your real name?"

With this, Ray laughed and Barbara said "Oh mother, his name is Tom, Tom Davis."

Ray interjected and said "He's one of the best pair of wingers that the 'Raiders' have had for a long time, him and that Johnson fellow." At this, I just smiled and said "His name's Skeeter, and yeah, we do ok..."

Betty, not to be denied, asked "So Tom, what do you do?" Well, by now I had decided to play it as it came, so replied "I go to school, have a part time job, and play football.," Betty looked a little confused, so I pushed it a little more by adding, "I'm thirteen, three years younger than Barbara, and no longer live at home, if that was going to be your next question. Barb and I have already talked about this and she doesn't have a problem." I think that I had thrown her a bit, because she looked around and couldn't come up with another question. Ray then asked "Do you think the 'Raiders' can win this season??" "Yes, if we keep playing the way we have been," I replied. Betty asked which movie we were going to see, so I said, "The new Clint Eastwood movie (a spaghetti western, I can't recall which one)." Shortly after that, we were joined by Barb's younger brother and sister. No, I can't recall their names." Then we went into the dining room to have dinner.

During dinner both Barbara and I copped a bit of ragging from her siblings. After dinner, Ray drove us downtown to the theatre. He said "I'll pick you up about eleven," before driving off.

Finally, we got to have some alone time. While the movie played there was a lot of kissing and cuddling, with as much foreplay as we could get away with. I was stroking and fondling her breasts and nibbling her neck and ears. She was stroking and rubbing my crotch through my strides, which left us yearning for more. However, it would be sometime before we would have the opportunity to get into bed and make love to each other. But if nothing else, we were out together. Ray was waiting when the flicks came out, and drove us home. He then asked me if I needed a lift, because he was heading off to work. I told him it was ok, and I had the bike, so we watched as he headed off. I then I gave Barb a long passionate tongue kiss goodbye and I headed for home.

The next day I headed for the pub and our lift to the game. We had to win this one to be in the quarter finals and things were going well. Half way through the second half we were in front by a good margin. I was about to score again, when I heard a yell from Skeeter, "Tiger, watch out!" Just then, one of the oppositions' front rowers grabbed me by my left arm and gave it an almighty, excruciatingly painful jerk; intended to bring me down. I was spun around, and hit the outer goal post with the side of my head. Luckily the post suffered no damage. I on the other hand, was knocked out cold for the first time in my life. No lights on and nobody home. The rest of this is second hand knowledge, so please bear with me."

Apparently, I was so far out of it, that I was carted off to hospital. Barbara had a screaming match with team officials about a possible concussion and broken shoulder, and then she travelled to the hospital in the ambulance with me as well! While I was being assessed in emergency, Barbara went home to get ready for her night shift. I didn't know any of this at the time, as I was still non compos. I came to after half an hour and was told that I was suffering from concussion, and my arm had been dislocated. My arm had been attended to while I was still unconscious. The upshot was that I would be staying in overnight, until reassessment the next day. Ok, but bugger that, I just wanted to know if we'd won! My question was answered a little later.

I was taken up to a ward from emergency. I must admit I was still a little groggy, but I discovered later the ward that I was in was where Barbara worked. Soon afterward I had my first visitors, Skeeter and Coach Dixon. Yes, we had won, but Skeeter had finished the game in the sin bin after I went down. He had gone over to the forward and started beating the crap out him, before being hauled off. Learning this, I turned to him with a smile and said, "Thanks mate, hope he wasn't too much of a handful."

His answer "He didn't stand a chance."

Coach Dixon just shook his head laughing and said "You two," then asked "So what's happening?"

I told him "It's only mild concussion and I should be out of here tomorrow, so yeah, I'll be at training."

He laughed and said, "Good. We'll see you then. Oh by the way, you'll probably need this." He handed me one hundred bucks, then left.

Shortly after, while I was in a light doze, a nurse came in and lifted my hand to take my pulse. I opened my eyes, saw Barbara, and asked, "What are you doing here??" She laughed and replied, "This is my ward, so I'll be looking after you."

"Cool, that's a bit of luck," I replied.

Then I asked "Could I make a phone call?"

She replied "No, but I can make one for you. Who to? What about? What's the number?" I asked her to phone Robo and inform him that I wouldn't be at school in the morning and why.

She said "Ok. I'll sort it out for you, but I better keep going or I'll be in trouble. I'll pop in as much as I can," and with a quick kiss on my cheek she left to carry on her work.

Just on dark I had two more visitors, my mother and father. They asked me how I was. I told them it was only minor, and I'd be out again tomorrow. That's when the old girl said "Well, don't you think that it's about time you stopped all this foolishness, and came home where we can keep an eye on you??"

This started my temper rising, and the tone of my reply bore that out. "No, and if you are prepared to listen, without interruption, I'll tell you why." I received an affirmative nod, so I continued. "The reason for this so called 'foolishness' is because you tried to totally control me. You would never listen to what I had to say, and if I didn't conform to your way, you'd get dad to try and beat it into me. Well, I'd finally had enough and I left. So for the last nine months I've made MY own way, and I'm surviving, probably better than you expected. If I come home it will be when I want to and not before!"

My voice started to rise as I was saying this, and my mother retorted by angrily waving her hand around the room. "You call this surviving? Your father and I could go to the law and make you come home."

Now! She'd gone too far. My voice dropped down to a deadly chill, as I said "I'll only disappear again, but if you want to, (I shouted) try It!"

Before any more could be said, Barbara came rushing in, and asked "What IS going on?"

I replied, "Nothing, Sweetheart. Oh, by the way, these are my parents. Mum and Dad, this is Barbara my girlfriend, and tonight also my nurse."

Ever hear the phrase, silence is golden? Well, at this stage it was priceless and comical, as they tried to grasp that idea! Barbara said "Hello. But I'm not pleased to meet you at this moment. Sorry."

Dad then piped up and said "That's quite alright. We understand, and (with a bit of iron in his voice) this is not the time, or the place for this, we'll go."

He gave me a nod, and turned the old girl (who was still looking furious) by the shoulders and marched her out.

Barbara then looked at me and said "I heard most of that down at the nurse's station, are you alright?"

"Yeah sure," was my reply.

Then she asked, "Are they REALLY your parents?"

"Yep, now you know why I don't live at home."

"Ok," she replied, and then told me that she had spoken to Robo for me. The doctors usually did their rounds about nine in the morning, so I would probably get out about ten. She said to go around to her place, as she would wait up for me and get her mum to drive me home. With that gave me a kiss and said she'd better get back to work, and I settled down and went to sleep.

As expected I was out of the hospital just before ten. I walked around to Barbara's place and Betty answered the door.

She said "Hello Tom, are you ok now? Barbara told us what happened."

My reply was "Fine, thanks Mrs. Finlay. I was asked to come around as soon as I got out."

"Come in. Barbara fell asleep waiting, I'll go wake her up," she said.

I replied "No, don't do that, what I could do with is a decent cup of coffee."

She said with a laugh "Of course, come through to the kitchen and I'll make you one." "There you are," she said as we both sat down to have a cuppa.

"Thanks" I said as I put a couple of sugars in. While we were chatting, Barbara came in rather sleepily, kissed us both and said "Good morning." Betty made her a cuppa. While this was being done she asked how I was. Over her coffee, she asked Betty if they could drop me home, which wasn't a problem. Just then, I realised my bike was still at the pub, so I said, "Thanks, but I'll have to go down to the pub to get my bike."

Betty then said "That's alright Ray left the back seat down in the wagon, so it'll fit in." After our cuppas, Barb got changed we all got into the station wagon, and headed to the pub.

When we arrived, I got out saying I wouldn't be long, and walked into the bar. Bobby saw me walk in and said. "Hey Tiger, good to see you're in one piece. If you've come for your treadly, your coach was going to drop it at your place." Thanking him, I told him I'd see him on Thursday and went back to the car. I explained that it was already at my place, so we went home with me giving directions to Betty. She pulled up and I said to both of them, "This is the first time you've been here. Would you like to come in??" They both said they'd love to, so I opened the door for them both and with an exaggerated bow said, "Follow me, and I'll put the kettle on." As we went up the stairs, I noted that my bike was indeed there. I opened the door saying "Go right in, make yourselves comfortable, or would you like the ten cent tour?" Which I gave them, silly really, considering I hadn't made my bed and the place needed tidying up. I apologised for the mess, and they both laughed as I said, "I shouldn't have given the cleaner the day off." I enquired "Coffee all round, juice or soft drink?" As we drank our coffees, Betty asked "What are you going to do for the rest of the day?"

I replied, "Well, first off, I'm going to clean this place up, and then will probably go into work early. I'd like you to take my girl home so she can get some more sleep." As I said this, Barb leaned across and gave me a kiss on the cheek. Betty said with a chuckle, "Tom, you can rest assured that will be happening." After the drinks were finished, I walked them down and opened the door for them. Barb told me she had two more nights to go. She told me to ring after that, gave me a kiss, and slid into the car. Betty also gave me a kiss on the cheek and said she was starting to like me, but not to hurt her little girl." Well, that was a surprise!

True to my word, I gave the flat a cleaning up, had a shower, got changed into my work gear, and rode into work. When I arrived at work Mr. Petersen looked surprised and asked, "Did school get out early, because it's only two o'clock??" So I told him what had happened and that I hadn't gone to school due to not being released from the hospital until that morning. After assuring him I was ok, we got on with some work. We chatted about different subjects such as football, Barbara, my parent's visit to the hospital and what had transpired, and whether I'd done enough study for the end of year exams which were coming up soon. Every now and again he'd ask me to solve a math problem for him, or we'd talk about history and geography, so in a way he was helping me with keeping my studying up and on track. He would at times recount some of the things he had done in his younger days, or we would talk about world events and what was happening behind the headlines. We speculated about why events in out of the way places like Borneo and Vietnam could have ramifications in Australia, and what form they could take. In a way, he started to teach me things that weren't in textbooks. How to never take anything on face value, and to look for the true meanings behind things or events. The most important thing I learned was to never take one side of a story as gospel without hearing both sides, and to make my own decision about what's true. He imparted this wisdom without actually him or me being aware of it. To us at the time, these were just topics of conversation.

The next morning, I went to the school office and asked to see Robo, just to assure him that I was fine and back on deck. I also needed to find out what the end of year exam dates were, so I would have a clearer picture of what time I would require to be ready for them. As it turned out, he also wanted something from me. The teachers at school were having a tipping competition, and the bugger wanted some inside information about which team had the best chance of winning the premiership, cagey bastard! Well, with a smile, what else could I say, except "Put your money on the 'Raiders', and here's fifty to put on for me, otherwise I'll turn you in, you old bugger." I then asked him what the odds were, and he replied "Less of the old, and eight to one." "Good, that's four hundred and fifty you'll owe me, when we win," I said with a laugh as I walked out of his office.

Friday rolled around, and that night I rang Barb. While we were talking she asked I if she could cook dinner for me the following night at my place." My instant reply was a resounding "Yes!" Then she told me that Betty would drop her around and pick her up again later. "Mind you, I have things on my mind other than dinner," and we talked about these other possibilities. I knew she couldn't say too much, because other people were listening to her end of the conversation. After the phone call, I went back to the flat and asked Pete what his plans were for the following night. He said he was going out west for the weekend, and wouldn't be back till Sunday afternoon. This worked in well, and I told him why I had asked. He laughed and said, "Don't get into too much trouble." He asked "Do you still want another driving lesson Sunday night?"

"Of course," was my reply, and we watched a movie before I went to bed.

After work the following day, I rang Betty to see if she knew whether I needed to get anything for that night without Barb being aware. She laughed and told me, "You're a treasure, and no, don't bother getting anything." I gave the place the once over, had a shower and waited for them to arrive at five thirty. When they pulled up, I went down and helped Barb bring up whatever she had brought, and asked Betty if she'd like a drink before heading home. She replied, "No thanks, Tom, you two have things to do. I'll see you later." I walked her out, opened the car door for her, and as she got in she said, "No monkey business, mind!" Then off she went. I raced back upstairs where Barbara was waiting for me. She came to the door as I closed it, and put her arms around my neck as mine went around her. We kissed passionately, after which she suggested some music while she started dinner. I put on an LP by 'Gary Puckett and the Union Gap' then went up behind her and put my arms around her. She turned to give me another long kiss, and said with a smile, "This won't take long, and then we can eat and do whatever." I said with a smile "I'll take the whatever, please." We both laughed, and she started cooking dinner. I went and sat on the lounge, listened to the album and then changed it when it was finished, to a Roy Orbison album. Just as I sat down again, Barb came and joined me. She placed my arm around her shoulders and snuggled into me. She leaned her head back for me to kiss her, which I did, and told me dinner would be about ten minutes. As I started to lightly bite her neck, she moaned and kissed me on the face, then said "Stop, wait till we've eaten." Silly girl. She didn't she know I'd already started eating!

After a tasty dinner of Shepherd's Pie we started some heavy petting on the couch, which quickly escalated into a rather intense, erotic passion that moved us into my bedroom. I proceeded to undress her, all the while kissing her, and moving my hands very gently over her breasts, stomach, firm buttocks and inner thighs. Barb started to moan with pleasure, and moved convulsively against me, as she frantically removed my clothes as well. Now both naked, we slid in unison onto the bed. I started to explore her lower body very, very gently with my fingers, while licking and in turn gently sucking the nipples of both breasts. She in turn was firmly stroking my engorged erection, and kissing and lightly biting my neck. Eventually it all became too much for me, so I moved over her as she opened her trembling thighs. As I entered her firmly, she gave an ecstatic moan, and her fingernails dug into my back as we began to move together. After thrusting and moving as one, her whole body convulsed, and with a low groan of pleasure as she had an orgasm. As she went into her orgasm, I felt a surge of adrenaline-like pleasure as I came as well. All too quickly it was over, and we lay there wrapped in each other's arms for quite some time, locked into position. Our breaths were ragged and in sync, as we inhaled each other's breath. Finally, when we were able to speak, with me still inside her, she said "God, that was wonderful, and worth the wait." I could only agree with her, and said, "It would be even more wonderful if you could stay the night." Unfortunately, that wasn't possible.

After we had showered together, dressed, and cleaned up the place, I made us both coffee. We spent time on the couch with her lying down with her head on my lap. We talked while the radio was on in the background. We both agreed that we needed more time to be together on our own, instead of her parents being in the way or catching us out. We could not see any way around that for the time being. After a while, there was a knock on the door. Betty was standing there when I opened it so I asked her in. "Hope dinner went well, but I'm here to take Barbara home," she said. I replied with a smile "Ok, but you could leave her here if you wish." Barb laughed, but somehow I don't think Betty got the joke. I asked "Would you like a cuppa before you go?" Betty said "No thanks, and you need to get some sleep, aren't you playing tomorrow??" "Indeed I am, and no doubt my favourite nurse will be there," I said glancing at Barb. "What about you, Mrs. Finlay?" I enquired. She replied "Make it Betty, and no, Ray's working, so I'll be looking after the other two. I suppose we had better get going then," and with that started to head to the door. When we got downstairs I said "That was a lovely dinner, Sweetheart," and gave Barb a kiss. She laughed and said, "Yes, it was nice wasn't it?"

"Sure was," I replied as I opened the door. She slid in and Betty got in, we all said goodnight, and off they went.

The game the following day was hectic and a hard one, but we won. That put us into the semi-final, so two more games to go before the season wrapped up, hopefully with our team as the winners. At the pub, Ray called in to find out if we had won, and after leaving work, bought me a beer, shook my hand and said "Well done, now win the next ones. I've got to head home but I'll see you later, no doubt."

CHAPTER 4

We won the next game fairly easily, now for the Grand Final. We had two training sessions that week, Tuesday and Thursday. On Friday at work I asked Mr. Petersen if he would do me a favour. He said, "I'm fairly certain I could. What, can I do for you?"

"I would like you to go to the local bookie. If the odds are more than three to one against the 'Raiders', put a bet on the final for me, please." He seemed to consider my request for a moment then said, "Tiger, you know I'm not a betting man. Give me about five minutes, and then I'll go." He then asked, "How much are you prepared to lose, if it goes wrong?" I pulled one hundred out of my wallet, and replied "We won't lose, that's how much I'm sure of it," as I gave him the hundred. "I'll be back in a while," he said, as he left the store.

Mr. Petersen came back about fifteen minutes later all excited. He said "Tom, apparently your team isn't expected to win at all! The odds were ten to one. I'll keep your bet with mine and collect on them next week." Stunned, I just stared at him speechless. He saw my look and said sheepishly, "Well, to prove my faith in you, I placed five hundred on as well."

"Shit!" Was all I could say for a moment, I continued with a laugh, "Can we get back to work now?" Mr. Petersen laughed as well.

Later that night, I was speaking to Barbara on the phone. She told me that she would be at the game on Sunday and at the pub with Ray afterward. After that, she would be on nights until Thursday morning, after which she had four days off. She said we could probably get together again during those days off and told me she'd see me Sunday.

Ok, game day, and we were up against the toughest, and dirtiest team in the competition, 'Easts'. In the change room we all went about our preparations in a quiet businesslike manner, far from the normal way we prepared. Coach Dixon gave us his pep talk, and told us that if we stuck to the game plan, watched out for each other, and played the way we usually played that we would be the premiers. He finished by raising his voice and yelled, "Go out and take it to them!"

The first half was quite hard and the game seesawed. Skeeter's opposite number tried to take a swing at him. In the following tackle, he fell down with blood running from his nose, and it really had nothing to do with the knee in the face. That started a brawl that took at least five minutes to sort out, and just as we were about to resume play, the half time hooter went.

When we came out for the second half we really started to hit our stride, and played the way we usually did. All the jitters were gone, so down to business. They were giving us a hard time, and we gave as good as we got. When we got to within the last ten minutes of the game, the score was level and we had the ball. Skeeter took off full steam, with me right beside him. As he was about to go down under heavy attack by three defenders, he flicked the ball to me. I found an extra spurt of energy, going fast for the try line. I saw their full back coming toward me from the line, and as he started to crouch for the tackle, I only had a millisecond to decide on a course of action. Without anyone to pass to, I pushed into a dive, and pulled into a ball as I went over his head. I rolled down his back, and as my foot made contact with the ground, launched into another dive. I landed full stretch over the try line, and lay there laughing. The referee, flying up, looked at me, then looked at the field behind me, and blew the whistle for the try. As he did, the full time hooter sounded. The ref looked at me still lying there with a massive grin on my face, and said, "That was one of the most incredible moves I've ever seen. Well done" and put his hand out to help me up and shook it at the same time.

Next minute, Skeeter flew up and lifted me in a bear hug, yelling

"YEAH!" Then the whole team was around me, and I was hoisted onto a pair of shoulders, as we all went parading around the field. While I was up there, I spotted Barbara and Ray and gave them a wave and a smile. After a lap around the field, I was dumped head first into the ice water of the drinks barrel, and then lifted out, and I was still laughing. I was given a bear hug by Coach Dixon, and he asked "Where did you learn a move like that?"

Still smiling, I said, "I have no idea. I made it up as I went along, do you think it worked?"

He looked at me dumbfounded, shook his head and replied "Yep, I think so," and we both started laughing again.

This time, the change room was a far cry from earlier in the day. We were rowdy and boisterous as we changed and joked with each other. Coach Dixon came in and asked for a bit of quiet. He then said that he had some good and bad news, and this got everyone's attention. He went on, "Training Thursday night (we all groaned) will be here, and the end of season awards will be held in the function room upstairs." He stopped, we all cheered and then he continued. "Wives and girlfriends are invited," then with a smile said, "Please wear suits, guys." "Next item and this is important. Guys, there's no cash in your envelopes, fellas; they're all in cheque form. This is because instead of the usual hundred, it was decided that if you'd won, you'd be paid five hundred for this game, PLUS one thousand dollars as a bonus!" Well, we all erupted cheering while he started handing out our envelopes, with a smile on his dial. After they'd all been handed out he yelled, "TO THE PUB!" And we all trooped out to the bus.

The bus pulled up outside the pub, and everyone was waiting. An almighty cheer went up as the door opened. When I got to the door, another massive cheer erupted again and Barbara flew up, threw her arms around my neck and kissed me full on the lips, rather embarrassing really, in full view of everyone! Anyway, I held her and said, "I need to see you and your father when we get a minute." I kept my arm around her as I headed for the bar, all the while receiving slaps on the back or shoulders. Barb went to find Ray, and as I got to the bar, I looked enquiringly at Bobby. Smiling, he put the glass he'd just poured in front of me and said, "It's on me." I flashed him a smile and nodded sideways to Skeeter. Bobby laughed and said "Yeah, him too," and poured another beer. With that, Skeeter laughed, and as Bobby went to pour someone else a beer, we clinked glasses and both said "Cheers."

I downed mine then went off to find Ray and Barbara. As I got to them, Ray passed me a glass and said "I found out you drink VB as well." We raised our glasses to each other, and said "Cheers." He enquired, "You wanted to see us?"

"Yes Sir. May I have the honour of having Barbara accompany me as my date for the awards dinner on Thursday night?"

He laughed, shook my hand and said "Of course. Betty and I'll be going, so we could pick you up."

I replied "Great, thank you sir."

"Now stop calling me sir. It's Ray to you, Tiger."

Barbara grabbed me by the neck and kissed me, so I said "Hope you've got a pretty dress, Sweetheart?"

"You betchya," she replied.

The next morning I awoke with a heavy head, and figured that I was suffering a hangover (first ever, not good). All my mates were waiting to congratulate me as I pedalled into school. A couple had been there, so my last dive became the topic of conversation, and they wanted to know how I managed it. Just after the morning break during our fourth period, the school PA system came to life. "Tom Davis, report to the Principal's office please." It was repeated three times. My mates looked at me, and I just shrugged as if to say "Beats me." I left the classroom and headed down to Robo's office. As I got there, the secretary, Janet, told me to go right in. When I got to Robo's door he directed me to shut the door and sit. As I did, he asked "Have you seen this?" and showed me the back of the local paper. There on the paper was a picture of me, stretched all mid-air, and the headline said" 'Raiders' win with desperate bid."

"God, the photographer must have been on the ball for that shot, and the headline couldn't have been more on the money."

"Shit! No," I answered, and he said "I didn't think you had. I was there, and the picture is marvellous. It really looked like that, it was pure joy to see you get out of what I thought was a disaster. By the way, I've taken the liberty of phoning the bulletin, and ordering two full sized colour copies of the photo, one for you and the other's for me. That ok?"

"Yeah, thanks," I replied.

Then he opened one of his desk drawers, said "Oh, by the way," and counted out eight fifty dollar notes. "Here are your winnings." He added another fifty "And there's your initial fifty. Thanks for the tip. You, Cochrane and I made a bundle..."

I looked at him and asked "Cochrane bet on me as well?" His reply gave me something to think about. "Yep! He thinks you're an arrogant smartarse, but he champions you as well."

"I'll be blowed," was all I could say.

Robo continued, "Anyway, you better get back to class and thanks again. I'll let you know when the photo gets here." With that, I picked up my four hundred and fifty and left.

Arriving at work that afternoon, I saw that Mr. Petersen had taken the back page of the paper and taped it onto the front window. I walked in smiling and Mr. Petersen came up to me smiling, and said "Hail the hero, Congratulations, Tiger!"

I thanked him and said "It was a hell of a game, but I'd said we'd win."

"But not without your last try, I wish I'd have seen it. Accept the glory, you've earned it."

"Ok," I replied.

"Now to business," he said. He went to the till, came over to me, and counted out eleven hundred dollars. He gave it to me and said "Go and put that in the bank right now; we'll talk when you come back." So off to the bank I went.

I deposited the winnings into my account, keeping the initial one hundred and fifty in my wallet, and then returned. While we talked I brought up the fact that I had to buy a suit for Thursday night. Mr. Petersen said "No, not just any suit" and then asked "Are you taking a young lady?"

"Yes," I replied.

He seemed to think for a minute then said "Hmm, yes, come over here and let's see what we can find you." He picked out one of the most expensive, but lightweight, suits in the shop! And said "Let's see how you look in this one," and ushered me off to the change room to try it on. After I changed, I showed him the end result. He grabbed his tape measure and came over, looked me up and down, and said half to himself "Hmm, shorten the leg and arm, take in here, let that out a bit, ok you can take it off, now but I need your measurements. Put your shorts on but leave your shirt off." I did as requested and Mr. Petersen took measurements of my shoulder width, chest, midriff and my hips, and asked my height. I wasn't sure, so we measured that too; five foot five and a half at that time. He then said "You know Tom, you have a very athletic build, very broad shoulders tapering down to a lean waist, muscular arms and legs, no fat, all muscle. I'd hazard a guess and say you're pretty strong, not at all like me, small and skinny except for the beer belly of course," he laughed. "You wear clothes that hide your physique when you should be flaunting it!" We both laughed. He continued, "We'll try this on again tomorrow after I've made some alterations."

I tried the suit on again the next day and it fit a lot better. Mr. Petersen made some more notes, and when I tried it on Wednesday, it fit like a glove. Then Mr. Petersen had me try on a pale blue shirt he'd already picked out, made a few notes, and selected a narrow tie the same black as the suit. He nodded his head and said "Sir's suit will be ready tomorrow afternoon." When I arrived on Thursday, the suit, shirt, tie and belt were in a bag hanging up. Mr. Petersen said "Tiger, sir's suit is ready for the ball. Not just any suit mind, but a tailored suit, with my compliments, at no charge!"

When I went to protest he held his hand up and said, "Tiger, take it son, with my thanks for all the fun I had walking into the bookies and seeing his face as I handed our winning bets to him for reimbursement. Now take it, go and get ready. Tell me all about it tomorrow. Oh, have some fun too!" I was close to tears; I knew the cost of the suit and shirt without all the tailoring he had done, so I gave him a grin and nod and headed home.

When Barb and her parents picked me up it was dark, so they didn't get the full effect of the suit until we were inside, under the lights at Brown Park. As I put my jacket on, Betty gasped, and Barbara said "God, you're beautiful."

I replied "Isn't that my line?" with a smile. Betty said it was a nice suit so I told them with pride that my boss, Mr. Petersen, had tailored it for me. Betty then asked "Is that all you under that?" So I took off the jacket and turned around for her smiling. "Cripes, you are built," was all she said as we moved inside.

We found a table and sat, and I saw my parents at another table with some of the club officials. I realised then that the company my father worked for was a major sponsor, and as general manager, of course he'd be there. He spotted me, leaned over to the old girl, and then she looked toward me as he rose and came over to our table. He excused himself to Ray and Betty, so then I had to do the introductions. He then said "Your mother and I have been talking, and we would like to have you come home for Christmas lunch at the end of the year, if you haven't made any plans yet."

Barb squeezed my hand and I looked at her. She nodded so I looked at him and said "Only if you invite both of us, Barbara and me."

He said "Alright."

"Ok, we'll talk about it later," I replied. With that, he got up, thanked Ray and Betty for the intrusion, and said he'd better get back.

Just as he left, the drink waiter arrived. Ray ordered Two VB's and a gin and tonic for Betty. When he looked at Barb, I interrupted by asking I if she'd like to try my old drink. She looked at her father and nodded, so I ordered a lime, lemon and bitters.

Ray laughed and nodded, and I then asked the waiter to bring the wine list back with him. As he left I asked Ray "You don't mind if I order the wine for dinner do you?" He looked at Betty; she nodded, and he answered, "Sure, go for it." So when the waiter came back with the drinks and the wine list, I perused the list.

Because the dinner was a set menu, mainly beef, I chose a nice Merlot, and asked that it be brought with an ice bucket so it could be lightly chilled. Just then Skeeter, glass in hand, gave me a slap on the back, so introductions were made all round. We all made a toast, "To the 'Raiders'," and then Skeeter went back to his table saying he'd catch up later. Dinner started to arrive, and once we were all served, I poured the wine for Betty. I looked questioningly at Ray; he nodded, so I poured his. I looked at Barb, and then looked at Ray and Betty, who said "Just this once." I poured a half glass for Barb and looked at Betty. She smiled and nodded, so then I poured my glass. When she tasted her wine, Betty stated, "Excellent choice. How did you know to have it chilled slightly?"

"An excellent teacher," was my reply with a smile, thinking to myself, "Love you, Jill."

The awards ceremony got under way after dinner, with different sized silver cups and medallions with envelopes attached. The first award was for the "Highest Attendance" for both training and games. It was awarded to me, so up to the podium I went to receive the medallion and envelope. I couldn't wait to get back to the table to see what was in the envelope. Well, bugger me; it was a cheque for five hundred dollars.

I showed Barb and she gave me a kiss and a hug, and moved her chair closer to me, so she was at my side. I gave Betty the cheque and asked, "Will you look after this for me, please??"

"Sure," she replied. The next award saw me back at the podium, "Best Recruit" of the season. This time I received a wine glass sized silver cup, and the cheque was for one thousand, which went straight over the table into Betty's purse. I was back up at the podium to receive "Most Improved Player," another cup to match the other, another cheque for one thousand into Betty's purse.

The next award was introduced by Coach Dixon; he announced "The next award is for the "Highest Try Scorer" of the season, and we have a tie for the first time, so the prize money has been split and both players receive this cup (holding up one of them). Ladies and gentlemen, Skeeter Johnson and Tiger Davis!" With that the whole room erupted into applause and cheers, and Barb grabbed my neck and kissed me, as I tried to rise. I met Skeeter half way up to the podium. Smiling, we shook hands, and proceeded with our arms about each other's shoulders, laughing all the while.

We received our cups, and another five hundred dollar cheque went into Betty's purse. Coach Dixon was back on stage and he announced "That the next award would be presented to the winner by the general manager of 'Stewarts' Mr. Des Davis. The recipient of this year's "Best Player" award will be taking home that monstrous cup on the table, have his name engraved on the club's perpetual shield, and a cheque for two thousand dollars. It was a forgone conclusion, and was cemented with one of the finest feats of acrobatics I've ever witnessed on the football field. This year's winner! Tom 'Tiger' Davis!"

Well, the place really erupted. As I stood up, Ray stood and shook my hand, Betty came around the table and hugged me, and Barbara threw her arms around my neck and kissed me, and didn't want to let go as I tried to move. While making my way up to the stage, I glanced in my mother's direction. She was smiling, crying and clapping all at the same time. On the stage, Dad shook my hand, passed me the cup (envelope taped to the inside) and then gave me a hug and said in my ear, "I'm proud of you, son." I turned toward the audience and held the cup aloft, smiling all the time, amid yells of "SPEECH, SPEECH."

I made my way to the microphone, and said "Christ! Thanks for this guys, not bad for someone my age huh? (Everyone laughed at that). But I'm only as good as the guys I play with, even if some of them are twice my age, the old buggers (more laughter). But seriously, they've looked after me and I'm proud to have had them on my side, and hopefully for the next couple, I think I've got maybe at least a couple good years in me yet (more laughter). Really, all I can say to you and them is thanks, and let's do it again next year!" I left the stage and slowly made my way back, amid handshakes and slaps on the back. As I passed Skeeter and his date, I said "Now, let's party." As I got to the table, the music started. I placed the cup on the table, passed the cheque to Betty with a mouthed "Thanks," took a long pull of my beer, grabbed Barb and headed to the dance floor.

The rest of the night was a blur, but I awoke the next morning with a massive hangover. I went down to the call box, told Robo's wife that I wouldn't be at school that day, and I'd see him Monday, then went back home to bed.

The rest of that year passed quickly. I sat the end of year exams, and was rather pleased with myself when the results came out, five 'A's, two 'B's and a 'C' in art. On the first Saturday in December, while up at Barbara's place, I was asked to join them for the holiday that was planned to coincide with Ray's two week break that started Christmas Eve. It was decided that I'd be picked up with my gear on Christmas day. Then both Barb and I would be dropped off at my oldies place for lunch, after which we would join with the whole Finlay family again for Christmas dinner, sleep there that night, and leave on Boxing Day for the coast.

One problem did arise, that being what to give Barb, Ray, Betty, and my oldies as Christmas presents. The younger siblings in both families were easy. Put some cash into cards, and they could buy what they wanted. I was thinking this over one day at work and asked Mr. Petersen for his advice, "Oh, that's easy. You and your young girl go shopping together for your respective mothers, and you might see something for young Barbara. As for your fathers, give me a minute," He then went into the front of the shop, and came back about ten minutes later. He had two cards, and gave them to me. On them was printed 'This entitles the bearer to his choice of suit, tailored to measure' and they were signed by him.

"My Christmas present to you, Tom," he said.

Tears welled up in my eyes and the words caught in my throat as I said "Mr. Petersen, I don't know what to say."

His usual comical look came onto his face, and with a twinkle in his eye said "A simple 'Thank you' will do."

I gave him a hug and said "Thank you."

He gave me a pat on the back, "You're welcome," he replied, then we let go of each other and we both looked a little embarrassed.

He then told me to arrange to go shopping with Barbara on Saturday as he was giving me that morning off. So I rang Barb that night, told her what he had done and arranged to go shopping on Saturday.

We found a couple of crystal sculptures we thought they'd like, plus I saw a gold necklace that would look good on Barb, so I made an excuse to go back and buy it. That was our shopping spree, presents, done and dusted, bring on Christmas day………

CHAPTER 5

On Christmas Eve, I phoned Barb from work, and arranged to meet at her place that night to wrap the presents and write out the cards. Over the phone we decided that twenty dollars in each of the youngster's cards would be enough and that I would have dinner up there with her family. So I made sure I had at least six twenty dollar notes in my wallet before leaving work. After wishing Mr. Petersen and his wife a merry Christmas, and assuring him I'd be back at work on the second Monday of January, I left to pedal up to Barbara's.

When I arrived there, I received a long embrace and kiss from Barbara. As we started inside, I held her back and asked if she would be adverse to us not giving out our presents until we got back from my oldies place." "Good idea," she agreed, and after a quick kiss and we went inside. Over dinner she asked her parents about our decision, and all agreed that it was a great idea, although her brother, Mark, and sister, Elizabeth, didn't share that opinion. Yes, I have remembered their names! While we were co-signing cards and wrapping, I said "You know, of course that goes for us as well." This was greeted with an "Aww" and a pout, but I held firm. After it was all done, after another embrace, I headed for my place to pack some gear for the trip away.

Betty and Barb picked me up at eleven, and after putting my gear into the back, I leaned in the driver's door gave Betty a kiss on the cheek, and wished her a Merry Christmas. She laughed and said "Get in, you cheeky bugger," so I got in the other side next to Barb. She gave me a kiss, and held my hand. I gave Betty my old address, and we left. When we arrived, I got the pressie bag out, and opened the door for Barb. Betty said "Just ring when you're ready, Sweetheart," so I cheekily replied "Ok." Betty just laughed and drove off. We went in and up the stairs and I rang the bell. The door was answered by my mum; she kissed Barbara on the cheek, saying "Come in, come in.," I brought up the rear, nodded and said "Mum," while I was trying to gauge her mood.

She moved off to lead the way, leaving me to close the door. As we got to the lounge she said "Barbara this is Lesley, (my younger sister) Gillian, (youngest sister) Johnathon, (younger brother) and Maxwell (youngest brother). Des you've met, and I'm Jean. Everyone, this is Barbara, Tom's girlfriend." After the intros, Dad leaned across gave Barb a kiss on the cheek saying "So glad you came. Pleased to see you again," He then put out his hand, which I shook with the respective "Son."

"Dad..." I sat down as I did, with Barb not letting go of my hand. She sat on my lap, and then John said "Saw your photo in the paper."

Barb let go my hand, reached into the bag, and pulled out a framed enlargement of the original that I had given her. She asked, "Was it as good as this one?"

Showing it to everyone before giving it to the old man, saying "Merry Christmas, Mr. Davis."

"Des thank you, very much," Dad said.

Barb replied "You're welcome."

With that, she turned to the others and said, "The picture is not nearly as good as actually seeing it happen. It was wonderful; your brother is truly magical to watch playing on the field." She gave my hand a squeeze as John asked me "Can you do it again now?"

"Nope, but it won me two thousand dollars when I did it!"

The old man commented with a laugh "I know, I signed the cheque."

Straight away I replied, "I DID notice that," and we all laughed.

Seeing Barbara had let the cat out of the bag, we gave out all the stuff in the bag except Mum's and Dad's. After hers was opened, Mum kissed and hugged Barb, as she placed it on the sideboard against the wall, and admired it until Dad was given his. He then handed it to her and gave me and Barb, both at once, a long hug murmuring "Thank you" while we were in his arms. After that, we all trooped into the dining room for lunch. The only dampener being the frown I received from the old girl when I asked to join the old man in a scotch and dry.

An hour after lunch, Barb and I decided it was time to make tracks up the hill, so I asked if I could use the phone, and explained our plans for the next week or so. The old man told us he'd drop us off, to save Ray or Betty coming out. I opened the gate to get the car out, and Barbara said her goodbyes.

Dad tossed me the keys from the top of the stairs with the comment "Bring it out if you can drive yet."

Grinning, I replied "Watch me.," I reversed out and spun the wheels to point up the hill, and I left the car running and waited for him and Barb to join me.

He then said "You know where we're going, so you drive." Grinning, I put up the arm rest; Barb slid into the middle of his new HR Premier and waited for me to get in, which I did at the same time as the old man. As I slid the column stick shift into drive, the old man warned me, "It's got a lot of power so take it easy."

All too quickly the drive was over, and as we climbed out, he came around to the driver's side and said "Oh by the way, Barbara has your Christmas present from your mother and I." Barb was nodding in the affirmative, and his parting comment was "Have a good holiday, you two." I thought to myself that when he got home, he was in for a tongue lashing from the old girl for letting me drive.

When he was gone Barbara showed me the card, and I read the note printed inside: "Ring this number and ask for Joe. He'll show you a selection of used cars. Whichever one you will pick, your mother and I will pay for. It may need some repair work, but I can help you with that, signed: your father." After reading this, I looked at Barbara. She was smiling, so I pulled her into an embrace, kissed her, and "Wow!" I exclaimed, and we went inside.

The present giving produced much the same results as previously, except now, it was time for Barb's necklace, which of course had to go on NOW! Barbara had got me a signet ring engraved with my initials. Yes, it went on straight away as well! We stayed curled up on the lounge listening to music until she had to give her mother a hand with getting dinner ready. Ray and I went outside with a couple of beers and we packed most of the stuff going with us the next day, and then went in for dinner. That night Barbara and I fell asleep in each other's arms on her bed, apparently Betty had decided not to wake us until morning.

Down the coast after the camp, and the tents had been erected. It was time to kick back, go swimming or walk the beach. During our walks along the beach each day, Barbara and I would search for a secluded dune that would afford us some privacy to make love to each other that night. We also went for a couple of night swims that culminated in making love in the water. At night, no matter what Betty tried, each morning we would always be found asleep in each other's arms in the wagon where I slept. In the end, both Ray and Betty gave up trying.

All too soon, our holiday came to an end, and so the second Monday in January I was back at work. I arrived at the same time as Mr. Petersen, and he said "Ah, Tiger, glad to see you. Did you have a good Christmas?"

I replied "Yes, thanks."

He then continued "I'll show you the opening up procedure and later I'll show you what to do prior to lock up.," He took in my quizzical look, laughed, and said "I'll explain shortly, let's open up first." We then went through what needed to be done prior to opening at nine o'clock. When we opened the shop, he told me he'd be back in a while and would tell me what was going on when he got back."

He came back after about an hour with package under his arm, and remarked "I think it's about time for a cuppa.," I went out the back and put the jug on, made us both coffees, then joined him out the front. As I placed the coffee on the counter he said, "Now

Tom, because I have you here now, I'm going to take advantage of that. On Wednesday, I'm going to leave the shop in your hands and take a holiday for two weeks. Tomorrow I'll show you how to do the banking, and then you'll know everything you need" I was about to interject, but he put his hand up to let him finish, "Also as of today, I will be paying you as an adult."

Well! I was stunned; barely thirteen, and drawing an adult wage. I was really at a loss for words, and I told him so. He replied "You deserve it; you're making your way in an adult world quite admirably. You're trustworthy and have a sense of honour; don't ever lose those qualities, and you'll be fine." Now, these are for you." With that, Mr. Petersen pushed across the package. As I pulled out a box from Telecom, he said "Just leave that one for the minute," so I pulled out another small packet that contained a set of keys on a key ring.

He said, "That is a set of all the keys you will need for the shop, including the safe key," and asked "Do you remember the combination?"

"Yes," I replied.

He continued "Open the other one now, it's a pager and we'll set it up for you." After setting up the alerts and showing me how to use it, he said "Now you can give people the number, they ring it, leave a message, you'll get the message, and you then ring them back if you need to. Let's do a test." He phoned my pager number from the shop phone and left me a message that he wouldn't let me hear. A minute later the pager started beeping. I read the display, and it showed the number that rang, then the message "Now get back to work." I laughed, as did Mr. Petersen.

That night I rang everyone I knew, what the hell. I wasn't paying for the calls, it took ages, but I gave them my pager number, and explained how it worked. A few of them knew, but others didn't. While on the phone with Barb, she told me that she would be on nights after Thursday for the following five, but said she'd page me now and again. Also while on the phone to Skeeter, we arranged to meet up at my place on Saturday afternoon.

The next day, I arrived at the shop just before Mr. Petersen. As I was about to unlock the front door I saw him walk around, so I waited for him. He said "Go ahead and open up," and as we were unlocking the back, he told me that he had brought his car in. He showed me where the back lane way came in, saying "If you ever want to leave your bike here instead of out front, you can leave it here near the door." As he was saying this, I noticed his car. It was dark blue with very nice lines. I remarked "I haven't seen a car like this before, what make is it??"

He smiled and replied "It's a Japanese Bellett GT.," After that, we went back inside and continued the opening up process. Later during the day, Mr. Petersen and I went across the road to the bank and I was shown the procedures and introduced to the relevant bank staff.

Back at the shop, Mr. Petersen explained that he was going to leave my pay envelopes for the following two weeks in the safe. As he finished telling me this, his wife Doris, dressed in a floral dress with a small matching hat, walked into the shop. After greeting me she turned to Mr. Petersen and asked "Eric, you haven't forgotten we have to pick up the plane tickets, have you??"

"No, dear," he replied.

She then said "Well, I thought I'd come with you."

He replied "Yes, dear, I'll just get my coat." He turned toward me and rolled his eyes upward, smiling over their normal banter and I found it very hard not to burst out with a laugh at his last expression. With a "Back soon, Tom," they left the shop arm in arm.

Upon their return, Mr. Petersen switched the jug on and we all had coffee. Over her coffee, Doris remarked to me, "Tiger, it was so good of you to offer to look after the shop so Eric and I could go away for a holiday, thank you." With a quick look at Mr. Petersen, and receiving an imperceptible nod, I replied going along with it and smiling, "That's all right, Mrs P, just have a good time." When she left Mr Petersen said, "Tiger, you know everything you need to run the shop, so instead of me coming in tomorrow, you'll be on your own. Remember that if anyone wants some tailoring, I'll be back after the Australia day weekend, and if you need anything my pager number is in yours."

Saturday afternoon Skeeter came over as arranged and showed me the car he bought the week before, a cream SV1 Valiant (the model with the spare wheel outline on the boot) that had a black roof. We hopped in and went for a burn. During the drive he said "Now I've got wheels, it's easier to get around. I was going to head out to the Kabra dance tonight, want to come?"

"You bet" was my reply.

"Well, I'll pick you up at six." I then told him about the note I got from the oldies for Christmas, and we decided we would go and have a look sometime in the next couple of weeks. I was ready and waiting as Skeeter pulled up that night. I got in and off we went. It felt good to be able to get out of town and have a few dances, generally have some fun. We arrived back at my place around one in the morning. Skeeter said he'd give me a bell next week and drove off. The following week Barb wasn't working so Skeeter brought his girlfriend and we went to the Bouldercombe dance, again another fun night. This remained the pattern over the next few weeks, except one day I received a page from Skeeter asking me to ring, which I did. He said "My mechanic will be available the following Saturday and do you still want to check out the cars??"

"I certainly do, I'll ring the bloke and arrange to see what he's got," I replied.

The following Saturday Skeeter, myself and his mechanic, Bevan, arrived at the car yard and I had a word with Joe (the owner). He showed us what was available, and my eyes immediately fell on a FC Holden, white with a chocolate brown roof and rear side panel trims. The column shift had been converted to a floor shift. Bevan checked it thoroughly lifting the bonnet, and then sliding under it, asked me to start it. He came out from under the car, and then checked the engine bay. He pulled a long screwdriver from his overalls, placed the end of the driver near each spark plug and listened by putting his ear to the handle. He did this with each plug then went along the tappet cover doing the same thing, then turned to Joe and asked "Can I take it for a spin?" While Bevan was away I went into the office with Joe and phoned Dad. I Told him I was getting a car checked over so he said he'd come down.

Bevan arrived back, and then the old man. I went through the introductions and Bevan said "Well, it's in fairly good nick, apart from needing a new exhaust. The gear box could do with an overhaul and it needs a couple of new tyres." If it was taken to his workshop I could work on it there on the weekends with him supervising me, and could be on the road after three weekends' hard grind." So the old man went over to the office, was gone for about five minutes, came back and said "Ok, the car would be delivered to Bevan's the following week after all the transfers were done."

He gave me a slap on the back saying "It's all yours, but no driving until all the work is done." He thanked Bevan shook hands all round, and left. We all climbed back into the car after shaking hands goodbye with Joe, Skeeter drove to Bevan's workshop. I thanked him and he said "I'll see you next week," and went inside. Skeeter and I headed back to my place, where we had a drink. We grabbed my good gear, because we were going to a dance just up the road from Skeeter's place that night.

That night at the dance, some turkey took exception to Skeeter dancing with his so-called girlfriend, and we got into a brawl facing this idiot and five of his mates. After ten minutes Skeeter and I were the only ones standing, but my shirt had been ripped and Skeeter had a cut on his cheek, so we went back to his place for a drink and got ourselves cleaned up. We then cruised around town for a while before he dropped me off.

Life seemed good. Back at school I was doing grade nine without any problems. The footy season was due to start, everything was fine at the shop, and I would see Barbara when she wasn't working. I'd pulled the gearbox out of the car and had stripped it down, replaced the second gear cog, and it was back together ready to go in. Skeeter and his girlfriend Joan, Barbara and myself were all meeting up the next Saturday night for the dance out at The Caves.

Betty dropped Barbara at my place at five, so we had time to jump into bed for some love making. It had been awhile, so as Barb had her second orgasm I came with her. Life was indeed good. After showering and getting dressed, Skeeter and Joan arrived while I was putting my shirt on. After a bit of small talk, we all got into the car. Joan and Skeeter were in front while Barb and I climbed into the back. There was a fair crowd out there as we arrived, and I spotted a couple of my mates from school as we entered to pay at the door. The opening dance was a Pride of Erin, followed by a waltz, then a foxtrot, after that there was a short break, so we adjourned to the pub next door.

Skeeter and I had a beer, while the girls had orange juices, then we went back to the dance. We were joined by my mates and I introduced everyone, then the next dance started a progressive barn dance. As I was about to change partners for the third time, my pager went off. I read the message as I was dancing, then stopped, and excused myself to the next lady and looked about for Skeeter and Barb. As I did the pager went off again, Skeeter, alerted by the pager tone, saw me standing in the middle of the dance floor, He left the person he was dancing with and came over. By now Barb and Joan had noticed I'd stopped and joined us, as I shakily handed Skeeter my pager. He read both messages aloud which said: "1/ Lesley hit by car get home now, 2/ up at hospital come quick" He exclaimed "Shit! Let's go…"

The drive from The Caves into town and the hospital took half an hour. We pulled into the emergency department and parked the car. We all went inside. As we entered, I noticed two uniform cops and two plain clothed detectives talking to dad. My mother was sitting down and crying. Barbara let go my hand, went and put her arm around her. As she did, Mum turned and continued crying on her shoulder. Joan went and helped Barb while Skeeter and I went over to see what was going on.

Cal Turner, the lead detective, knew both me and Skeeter from the pub, so he told us what had occurred. Sometimes referring to his notes, said "At about seven thirty tonight, Lesley was walking along and crossing North street between the two primary schools, when she was struck by a car. The driver has been taken into custody but it appears that he had been drinking. We're just waiting to see what her condition is before going to talk to him." Barbara had joined us as he was saying this, so said to me "I'll see what I can find out," and went through the doors into emergency.

She came back ten minutes later, glanced around and asked to talk to me outside. Skeeter told dad that we were going outside for a smoke, and I did indeed light up as soon as we were outside. Barbara then said, "There's no easy way to say this. Your sister is in a coma right now, Tiger; she may not come out of it! They're going to be taking her up to ICU shortly, but after that it's a waiting game."

As we went back inside doctors were talking to Cal and my father. He lurched and Cal steadied him, he then went over to Mum (I guess that they had tried to prepare him for the worst). Just then, Lesley was brought through on her way to ICU, and Mum and Dad followed. I turned to Cal as he was about to leave and asked "What's this guy's name?"

"I can't tell you that," he replied, so I said in my usual deadly quiet tone "Give me five minutes with him."

"Tiger, that's not going to happen, so please let me do my job." Then he and his partner and the two uniformed cops left.

Skeeter took me by the arm, and Joan and Barb joined us as we made our way to the ICU. I turned to them, thanked them for their help. I asked Skeeter to take Barbara home for me as I was staying, and asked him to collect me the next morning. I kissed Barb goodnight, and they left. I joined the oldies and sat down to wait.

The next morning Skeeter came back, and Dad said "Can you take Tiger home to get some sleep? We'll stay and ring if there's any change," so with that I left. On the way to my place I said to Skeeter, "Skeet, I want this bastard!" When he dropped me off he said, "Get some sleep, I'll see what I can find out. You have my word."

The following happened while I was asleep. Skeeter went down to the pub and found Ted Truscott, a cop that we knew, and said "Tiger's sister was run over last night! What can you tell me?"

Ted replied "Yeah, I know. I was the one that arrested him." Skeeter then replied "Good, I want his name and address."

CHAPTER 6

Skeeter arrived back at my place around three, and told me what he'd found out. Deciding that there was nothing I could do at the hospital, we planned a course of action. I went to make a few calls; the first one was to Barbara, to ask her to keep me informed about Lesley's condition. I also asked her to keep an eye on the oldies when she was at work, if she could. The second and third calls were to Robo and Mr. Petersen respectively, informing them that I'd not be at school or work for the next few days after telling them what had happened.

Back at the flat, I threw a change of gear into a bag, left a note for Pete, and grabbed my rifle, (a 2020 Savage with telescopic sights). I checked that the magazine was full, put another ten rounds into a pocket, and then Skeeter and I left the flat. As I put my stuff on the back seat, I noticed he had packed some food and his binoculars, but what really caught my eye was his shotgun. I looked at him and his comment was, "We've got short and long work covered now." I just nodded and we drove off.

As we drove along I asked him, "What about missing school?"

He replied "What the hell, I'm leaving at the end of the year, besides, mates stick together. Somebody else started this, but we're going to finish it!" We were heading toward the coast, but would be turning off to another township before actually getting to our destination.

We were getting close to a mate's parents' farm along the road, so when we got near I told Skeeter to pull in. They weren't there, but I didn't think they would have had a problem with what I had in mind. I told Skeeter to grab the shotgun as I pulled my rifle out of its case. We hiked up the hill at the back of the house and down the other side. I found a suitable position and said to Skeeter "I need to fire off a few rounds, to get used to this thing again."

Looking for a target, and spotted a tree three hundred yards away. Through the sights I saw it had a knot hole about half way up and fired. Result: a tad left. I made an adjustment to the scope and fired again. Bingo, nailed it, and then put two more right into the same spot. I turned to Skeeter and remarked "Ok, ready." He nodded then whirled, blasted a tree root to splinters, then we went back over the hill to the car.

We arrived at the address Skeeter had been given by the cop. The address belonged to the bloke who had run Lesley over. We pulled up the car so we had a good line of sight to his house.

The only time we left our position for the next three days was to get some supplies of food and drink, while waiting for a male to show himself. All the talking we did between us over this period cemented a mateship into a close bond. I was also determined, that should we get caught, I would take all the blame and try to shield Skeeter from the ramifications as much as possible. Even though he had had scrapes with law before, this one was going to be on my head alone.

On Wednesday, after four days of waiting, my pager went off, I read the message, then passed it to Skeeter, "It was from Barb saying that she was with my parents, and my sister had died" He asked "What do you want to do?" Close to tears I just replied "Let's go." We both remained silent the entire trip back to town. Skeeter drove to my parents' house. As we arrived I saw Cal Turner and his partner at the top of the stairs about to go in. I said to Skeeter "The law's here, I'll just grab my gear, you take off, and we'll catch up later."

He headed off while I walked in. Cal and his mate were on the veranda waiting to talk to the old man. As I went by them, I opened my old room and tossed the gun and my gear on the bed. Cal asked "Do I have to confiscate that?" nodding toward the gun case on the bed, "No," was my only reply.

Sunday arrived, and as I entered the pub with my footy gear, Coach Dixon asked "Are you ok? I can take you out of the line up if you wish?"

"No, I'd rather play, get my mind on other things, you know?" He then said "Sure. When's the funeral?"

"Wednesday at the crematorium, at ten," I replied and then it was time to get into the bus. The game was the first of the season, without too many incidents, "A bugger really, because I really wanted to hit someone."

After the game in the dressing room, Coach Dixon announced to the team, "Ok, everyone knows what happened to Tiger's sister. For those wishing to show support for his family, her funeral is being held at the North Side Crematorium ten o'clock on Wednesday." Back at the pub, the win wasn't celebrated the way we usually did. There were a lot of condolences that I accepted, but after a few drinks and a few words with Skeeter, I left.

The place was packed on Wednesday. Skeeter, Coach Dixon, and the entire team came. Barbara, Ray and Betty, and Mr. Petersen and Doris were there. He had closed the shop to attend. Robo was there, as well as a lot of my sister's school friends, and I guess a lot of the town residents. Her brown coffin was draped with flowers, and at the end of the coffin a framed picture of her had flowers all around it. Dean John Powell, the archbishop of Saint Paul's Cathedral, officiated at the service. Dad gave a speech, as did the principal of her school, Robo, and Mr. Petersen. When the service was closing, music was playing and people were crying as the curtains parted for the coffin. That's when the old girl really burst out crying; she'd sort of held it together until then. Afterward everyone made their way back to the Railway pub (Bobby had donated the use of the pub as the venue for the wake) for drinks. I was surprised really. All those people and alcohol, not one fight! "Just goes to show you, huh."

Two months went by and things had slowly returned to normal when my sister's killer went to trial. He was found guilty of causing death while driving under the influence. The sentence was one month's jail time, loss of license for eighteen months, and a thousand dollar fine. I went ballistic! With the ruckus I caused yelling at the judge, I'm lucky I didn't get locked up, too. I was ejected from the court room; outside I punched one of the cement columns, knocking chips out of it. Didn't do my hand much good either!

Close to the middle of the footy season, I received a pager message from the old man asking me to come around and have dinner and see them that night. So after work I drove around, said my hellos, and asked about the summons. The oldies were planning on taking a holiday, and I was asked if I would stay at the house while they were away. I said that I would as long as Barb could visit me there when she had nights off. Getting an affirmative on this, it was announced to the others that I would be living at home while they were on holiday. So the following week I temporarily moved back. In the meantime, I let Pete know what was happening and gave him the rent to cover my time away from the flat.

John was almost as good working things out in the brain department as I was, and while I was back home asked me what I had been doing while Lesley had been in the hospital. I told him, and also said "You're not to tell ANYONE that, understood?" He replied "Yep, sure."

A week later, after the Sunday game win celebrations, Barb came home with me. Just after nine, the oldies arrived home early and caught us having sex in their bed! Well, the shit the fan! The old lady screamed at me "What the devil do you think you are doing?" So I quite calmly replied "Well, what does it look like?" She just looked at me furiously, turned to the old man and said "YOU deal with this," and stormed out. He looked at both of us, and said "You two get dressed and come out to the lounge." As we reached the lounge, dad was on the phone. He said "Good. I'll see you soon," and hung up. The old man looked at Barb and said "That was your parents I was talking to, they'll be here soon." I suggest you two sit down and wait." It sounded more like an order than a suggestion. A short while later, Ray and Betty arrived. When everyone was in the lounge, Dad asked "So how long have you two been having sex together? And who started it? I don't want any lies." I gave Barb's hand a light squeeze and said "I did, and since about three weeks after we met."

Ray then asked "While you were on holiday with us?" Barb went to say something but I cut her off, looked Ray straight in the eye and said "Yes." Dad looked at Ray and Betty, and then said "I think we should all go into the kitchen and discuss this over coffee or tea." As I went to get up, he looked sharply at Barb and me, and barked "Not you pair. You can wait here until we tell you your fate." They then all went into the kitchen leaving us sitting there.

They all trooped back in after a while, and the old man looked at us and said "Well, it's been decided that there isn't much we can do to stop you seeing each other, mainly because you'd find ways to do it, if you wanted, behind our backs anyway. You, Tom, I can't control anyway. Should you wish to sleep together, we're not going to stop you, but you two had better be taking precautions. Ray will be making his rules, if you are up there, and you had better stick to them.

Here, it won't be in MY bed, and if it's at your flat, that will be if Barbara has been given permission to sleep over. So no more going behind our backs, understood?" We both agreed, and I then explained that it would only be now and again due to work, footy, and school commitments. All in all we got out of that fairly easily, but they were right, they really couldn't have stopped us in any case.

One Thursday night after training, I was sitting at the bar nursing a beer when in strode a couple of cops that were off duty. I watched as Bobby went through the routine of pouring them a drink. What happened next I had seen before, but had never really noticed until now.

After giving them the beers, Bobby just walked away without charging them. When he came over near me, I asked him, "Hey, Bobby, how come you didn't charge the cops? Do they have a tab or something?" Keeping his voice low, "I wish. No, the cops get free beers here, and that way I don't pay the usual monthly 'hush money' figure," he replied. He went on after seeing my quizzical look. "Ok, keep this under your hat and don't say a word to anyone. All the pubs in town get charged a monthly fee for the cops to look the other way, in regard to underage drinking and small fights. The money gets collected each month and they all get a cut, but most of it goes to the higher ups. So instead of paying the two grand each month, I give them free beers."

My curiosity was aroused, so I asked "How long has this been going on?"

"Ever since that new guy Lewis Trevors took over as the head honcho at the cop shop last year," he replied. Well that was a turn up, so again yet another piece of information went into my knowledge base, "Who knew if it could be put to good use at a later stage?"

The game on Sunday was tough going against the 'Easts' because we were getting close to the finals again, and it soon became obvious that Skeeter and I were targeted. Each time that either of us had the ball we would be fending off at least three opposition attackers.

During the second half, one bloke brought me down with a head high tackle, and gave me a punch in the eye while he had me on the ground. In retaliation, I got up, braced myself, and slammed my head into his face. This resulted in blood pouring from his nose. I said to him, "You'll think twice about trying to sucker punch me again, you arsehole." One of his mates went to try and grab me, but by then Skeeter was beside me with the referee. This incident caused the gloves to come off, and the game developed into a fight fest at every opportunity. So, yeah, it was a hard game, but yet again, we came out on top, and because of the loss, the 'Easts' were out of finals contention all together.

I was joined at the pub celebrations by Barbara, and she informed me that she could sleep over at my place that night. After leaving the pub I drove her home to get her overnight stuff, and we went back to my place after having dinner with her family. When we were settled back at my place watching the Sunday night movie, she asked "Tom, would you teach me how to drive your car?" I looked at her as she continued "I'm going to get my learners permit, but Dad's car is auto and yours is a manual so can I learn in yours?" I glanced over at Pete, he was a great help, and he just shrugged his shoulders. I said "Well, I don't have a licence, so I really can't teach you, but your father can use my car to teach you if it's ok with him." You can talk to him and we'll arrange something between us."

"Oh thank you, I'll talk to him tomorrow" she replied.

I said "Well, don't forget I'll be getting you home early, and I need to be at school by eight thirty."

She replied with a smile "Well, we'd better go to bed early, I don't want you being too tired."

So we said goodnight to Pete and went off to my room, where we amused ourselves with each other's bodies for an hour or so before drifting off to sleep.

As I was walking in the school gate after dropping Barb home, Robo, who must have been waiting for me, asked me to join him in his office. After we were seated in his office and coffee brought in by his secretary, Jack asked how things were going. Not wanting to beat around the bush I forestalled any small talk by saying, "I'm fine, now let's cut the bullshit. What's on your mind?"

"First off, I would like to say you have been one of the brightest pupils that I've ever had the privilege of meeting. Even though you've been a right pain at times, and setting you on the right path has been a challenge, I've enjoyed watching you develop into the young man you are today. All things come to an end, and next year I won't be here to help or guide you, because they're moving me on to another school. In all the time I've spent here, I've never been to a football game, out of school of course. Is it possible for you to get me a ticket to the Grand Final?" he asked me.

Even though this was getting quite emotional I replied, "Sure thing, do you want a ticket for your wife as well? I hope your money is on the 'Raiders' to win again?" "Yes, I'm betting on you guys again. To tell you the truth, I've always backed the 'Raiders', ever since we moved here, and, no, just me," he replied.

"Consider it done, you've been a good boss, Jack, and I'll miss you," I said. As we stood and shook hands and I left his office with tears clouding my vision.

That afternoon at the shop, I asked Mr. Petersen if he was interested that much in football, to which he replied "Oh yes, both of us are, but we haven't been to a live game for some time. Why?"

So I then asked "So if I could wangle a couple of tickets for the Grand Final, you'd be interested?"

"Good heavens, yes," he replied with a smile.

I said "Ok, I'll see what I can do, but don't say anything to your wife just yet, leave it with me." So the following Thursday night I had a word with Coach Dixon, and told him about Robo leaving. I asked him if it would be possible to get three passes to the members' box for the Grand Final. He replied "Yes, I can get them for you, but we haven't got there yet, you know," I simply said "We will, and we'll win again this year."

Ok, I thought to myself, that's the tickets taken care of. Now, for what I had in mind, I needed to pull in a big favour from my father. On Saturday morning it was quiet in the shop, so I asked Mr. Petersen if I could take half an hour off to see my old man. He just waved his hand in a gesture of "Go." It only took me five minutes to get up the street, and as I entered Stewarts Department store I spotted the old man talking to one of the floor managers. He saw me waiting and came up to me when had finished and asked "Is there something I can do for you?"

"Yes, there is. I need a big favour," I replied, "Ok let's go up to my office and you can tell me all about it," he said.

When we reached his office, he motioned me to a chair opposite his desk, and as he sat down he asked what it was all about. I told him about Robo leaving and the Grand Final passes I was trying to organize. Then I said "What I would really like to do is invite him and his wife, plus the Petersen's to the awards night, and was wondering if you could pull some strings and get me a couple of double invites."

"Well, they must mean a lot to you for you to come to me asking for help," he replied.

I answered "Yes, they do, and you're the only one I know who could be able to manage it."

"Do you realise that I'm not your enemy, just a father who wants the best for his son?" He asked.

So with a smile on my face said "Yeah, I now realise that." As I was saying this, he reached into one of the desk drawers. He smiled and said "These were going to a couple of my managers, but they didn't come last year, so it looks as if you have a better use for them," and handed me two double guest invitations to the awards night. "Thanks," was all I said as he handed them to me. He replied "I do want to see you get at least one try when you get into the final, though."

I replied with a smile "No worries on that score," and then left to go back to work.

Mr Petersen's eyes lit up as he read the invitation to the awards night I had handed him. He remarked "Oh my, Doris will be pleased. I'll have to get my suit aired out, and speaking of which, Tiger, you had better bring yours in. You look to have grown in the last year. Thank you for this."

Smiling, I replied "It's me that should be thanking you; I'll make sure there's room for you and Doris at my table. Oh, and I'm still going to be working on the Final tickets, so let's keep them secret for the time being."

The game the next day was a winner for us, and this put us into the Quarter Finals. Back at the pub, Coach Dixon handed me the three passes I had asked for. He clapped me on the back said, "Just you make sure we get there."

I replied "No worries, Coach."

The next day I arrived at school early, and went to the office and asked to see Robo. I was shown into his office and sat. I said "I think you may find some use for these, boss," and handed across both the Finals pass and awards invite.

I said "There is the proviso however, that your missus should be at the dinner."

He replied "Oh, she'll be there, even if I have to drag her along. Thank you, Tiger. Oh, by the way, do you want me to lay any money on the 'Raiders' for you?" With a smile on my dial I nodded and passed him one hundred dollars.

That afternoon I took my suit into the shop with me, and sure enough Mr. Petersen needed to alter it. By now I was five foot seven. Luckily, Mr P hadn't cut off too much last year, and it would still fit. "Oh, by the way," I said as I handed him the passes to the member's box "I hope you both enjoy the game, but please don't tell Mrs P yet, lets' keep it as a surprise."

"That we will, I'll put them in the safe," he said with a smile.

The next couple of weeks were hectic, what with football, school and an active social life with Barbara; we did however win through to the Grand Final.

During Grand Final week, Doris came into the shop just prior to closing on Wednesday night. I took advantage of her being there and asked what she would be doing on Grand Final day. She replied "Oh, nothing special. We might get to watch the game, if they televise it again." As she was saying that, Mr P had been at the safe, so I asked "Well, wouldn't it be better to see it live?" I gave her the passes that Mr P had handed to me behind my back.

"Oh, thank you, Tom," she said as she hugged me, tears of joy running down her face.

The Final that year wasn't as brutal as the previous one, but it did have its moments. Late in the first half, Skeeter had copped a cut on the cheek from a misplaced boot, and had to go off and have it attended to. While he was off, one of our front rowers, Dean, who worked as a shunter in Ray's gang, took his place. We were close to scoring when he was tackled, flicking the ball to me as he went down. Just as he yelled "Go, Tiger!" I saw him get a knee into the side of his face. As the last defender was about to go for a tackle on me, I slipped underneath him and took a full stretch dive over the line to score. As the try whistle blew I headed back to Dean to see how he was. When I got to him he was sitting up, so I asked "Are you ok?"

He replied "Yeah, just a little groggy."

"Well, let's get you up, we can't have you sitting around all day," I said as I helped him up. We both laughed as we headed back to get ready for the next kick off, which didn't take place because the half time hooter sounded.

As we came back on for the second half, Skeeter took his usual position as we waited for the kick-off. I asked with a smile "Are you ready to go to work yet?"

Smiling also, he replied "Yeah, lets' carve them up," and we both laughed. After that, Skeeter scored once and I scored again. The game progressed easily after that. We were ahead by six points when I got the ball again. With Skeeter at my side we (that was for us) trotted toward the try line. Looking around, I saw no opposition worth worrying about, and my inner sense of honour and fair play kicked in. I flicked the ball to Skeeter, saying "Go finish it," and started to slow down.

After the try whistle sounded, we made our way back to the half way line to start again, and as we were waiting the full time hooter sounded. Yeah, the 'Raiders' had made it two in a row and we started congratulating each other. The following celebrations in the dressing room, and back at the pub, were very loud and boisterous, and lasted for days. The awards dinner was put off until Friday night instead of the usual Thursday night, but no one seemed to mind that change.

CHAPTER 7

Friday night I was picked up by the Finlay's again. When we arrived at the function room we chose a large table. We left room for Skeeter and Joan, Mr. and Mrs. Petersen, and possibly Robo and his wife. Shortly after seating, Skeeter and Joan arrived followed by Mr and Mrs P. I made the introductions all round and we all sat again. As we did, the drinks waiter arrived. Ray asked everyone what they would like and ordered, then finished with, "And bring back a wine list for Mr. Davis, please." Skeeter laughed, and Betty said to me, "Well, you made such an excellent choice last year, dear, how about you do it again?"

"Ok, I'll give it a go," I replied. She then proceeded to tell the others how well the wine complemented the meal last year. As she was doing this, I spotted Robo and his wife arrives, so excused myself and went over to him. I said "Jack, I saved you both a spot at our table if you wish."

He replied "We'd like to, however, I've been invited to join the club officials at their table."

Looking around, I said "No problems, it's over there. You know my parents, catch up later maybe?"

Coach Dixon was at our table when I got back; he and his wife were going to join us. He was in the middle of telling everyone that he wouldn't be the MC tonight, because of a special guest. I had a pretty good idea who that was going to be. As I glanced around the table, Joan reached for her drink, and I noticed an engagement ring on her finger. I looked quizzically at Skeeter, who knew I had seen it, and he nodded his head. He leaned across and said "Yeah, well, I thought it was about time, and she wants to get married anyway."

"Congratulations, but just make sure she doesn't go giving

Barb any ideas," I replied, and shook his hand. Everyone was getting on quite well, and the conversation and joking only ceased as the dinner started arriving. I was complimented once again on my choice of wines. Skeeter was the exception, asking "How can you drink that stuff? Give me a beer anytime."

I replied, laughing, "Let some culture into your life, buddy," and that triggered an all-round discussion on different sorts of drinks. After dinner was finished, the club chairman took the stage to announce and introduce the MC for the night, and as I had guessed, it was Jack Robertson.

Robo took the stage and started with his speech, "Thank you ladies and gentlemen. I'm here tonight at the invitation of one of the most gifted and worst students I've dealt with. (Laughter) Thank you, Tiger," gesturing toward me as people started applauding. After that he continued, "I would assume that he let the cat out of the bag to the club officials, and that's why I was asked to officiate tonight. For those that aren't aware, I've been transferred to Brisbane next year, so this is my last year here." Applause followed this remark and laughter after his next comment, "I suppose that will make some students happy and relieved." Ever since my wife and I arrived in town twelve years ago, I've been a 'Raiders' supporter, and will continue to be so. We would also like to thank you for all your support over the years, and we'll miss you all, thanks everyone." As he finished, everyone gave him a standing ovation, and when the noise started to die down, he raised his hands and continued "All right, let's move onto why we're here, the first award..."

The first award I was called up for was again "Highest Attendance." It was again followed by "Most Improved," then "Best and Fairest Player." As usual, all the cheques went into Betty's handbag, and the table was getting a fair collection of silverware thanks to both Skeeter and I. Skeeter was called up again to receive the "Highest Try Scorer" award. Bugger! He pipped me by one. Then it came to "Player of the Year," and I was called up once more. My acceptance speech was as follows, "Thanks again

67

everyone, but as I said last year, this is not only for me but the whole team. A lot of folks didn't think we could make it two in a row, but we have." This comment received tremendous applause and cheering. As it died down I continued, "I would like to take it one step further. Next year we're going to try for something that hasn't been done yet. So Jack, (looking around at Robo) get your bets on early, because it's three in a row next season!" With this comment the place erupted into cheering and applause. Above the din, I held up the cup and said "Thank you again, one and all." Back at the table, there were handshakes and kisses all round, and the cheque joined the others in Betty's bag. Not a bad haul all up; with the game money, cheques and the side bets I'd made, my bank account would be over eight thousand dollars richer.

The next morning, after a very late night and a lot of alcohol, Mr. Petersen and I were definitely feeling hung over, so our coffee consumption was up quite a tad, and our conversations rather subdued. We talked about the previous night, and how much fun he and Doris had, how my studies were progressing, and then told me of a trip he and Doris were thinking of taking over Christmas. He asked "You wouldn't mind looking after the shop again, would you?"

"No, by all means go ahead and make your plans. I hadn't planned anything for Christmas anyway, so go ahead and have some fun," I replied.

"Thanks, Tom," he said.

In the last week of November, I sat the end of year exams, but I had to wait until the first week of December for the results. During that week I was summoned to Robo's office. As I was shown in he said "Ah, Tiger, come in. Sit down." After I was seated he asked, "Have you given much thought to what you are going to do after you leave school?"

I replied "No I haven't, but I'm pretty sure I won't be sticking around town, there's a bigger world out there, who knows?"

"Well, if you went on to university with your brain and the right education, you could do anything you wanted. I guess from the expression on your face, that's the last thing you want to hear? Ok, well, please think about it. Now then, your exam results are here," and held up a bunch of papers. He then continued "Your results are the best in the entire school, 'A's in all subjects; you should be very proud of yourself. Congratulations," and reached across and shook my hand. "I probably won't see you anymore, so take care; it's been a pleasure to know you."

"The same to you, boss, and don't forget that bet," I replied. I got up and shook his hand for the last time. It was a hard thing to say goodbye to Jack Robertson; he had been a good friend.

That Friday, because I didn't need to be at school and Barbara had the day off, I picked her up. We drove all over town doing our Christmas shopping, and then went back to her place for dinner with the family. During dinner it was arranged that I pick Barb up after her shift on Christmas Eve. She would spend the night at my place. We would see my family Christmas morning, then drive down to the coast and re-join her family for dinner. We would stay with them for the few days holiday we had, then she would stay at my place until the family came back to town after their holiday.

The next morning Mr. Petersen and I talked about Robo's departure, and what would be happening over the Christmas break. Over our mid-morning coffee he said "Well, I've got everything up to date and made up your pays for the next few weeks. After this morning I'll be on holiday til the second Monday in January. Oh! I've also put a Christmas card in the safe for you."

I replied "Thanks, Mr. Petersen, you two take care, have a safe trip, and wish Mrs P a Merry Christmas for me." Two days before Christmas Eve I pulled one of my pay envelopes from the safe, along with Mr Petersen's card. It contained a cheque for five hundred dollars, and the note on the card read "I knew you wouldn't accept this if I were there, so have given you this bonus for services rendered in cheque form. Merry Christmas from Eric and Doris." The cagey old bugger, so that's why he left it in the safe. So when I did the banking, I deposited the cheque into my account.

Everything went as planned and without any dramas over

the Christmas/New Year period. It was just a matter of getting through this year and I could then leave school. Until then, I had been marking time. I really had to start thinking about what I was going to do in the future. At that time I still had no idea about what I was to do with the rest of my life, so these thoughts were never far from my mind. I knew however, that I wasn't going to stay in this town longer than was necessary, due to my intellectual capabilities outstripping most people I came across. I was like a round peg in a square hole. The culture of people in this town, apart from a few exceptions, was narrow and small minded. They were happy doing the same thing over and over. They were happy in their cowboy town rut, never wanting to move ahead and experience life.

A couple of weeks after school started, I was driving home from work one night, and as I was going through an intersection, Bang! I was slammed into by another car failing to give way. Both cars ended up across the intersection. The front of my car smashed into the cement column between two panes of plate glass window in the Holden Showroom. The other car sailed right through the window on my left and into a new Premier on display, showering glass everywhere. Because of the noise generated from the crash, Dean John Powell came rushing over from St. Paul's across the road. He helped me out of my car, and then we went to see what the other driver's condition was. Shit! He was unconscious and a cop, a high ranking one at that, judging by the pips and insignia on his uniform. We both noticed by the smell that he reeked of booze. "Oh great! Now the shit is really going to come down on me! Would you assume that he's drunk, Father?" I asked.

"Yes I would, and he hasn't given way like he should have. Ah! That sounds like the ambulance now." The ambulance arrived, followed closely by the cops. I told the ambulance attendants that "I'm Ok, but check the other guy."

As one of the attendants said "Ok, but we'll check you out in a minute," the cops approached me and asked "What happened?"

So I said "I was coming up the street and out of nowhere this guy slammed into the middle of my car, then with a side and forward motion I've ended up here, and he sailed through the window."

Just then, the first ambulance officer came up and said, "We've got to check this one out, the other one is in there passed out drunk," indicating inside. When the cops walked away I asked for his name and contact details saying, "I've got a feeling I might need them for later," so he passed me a card with his details. Just then, one of the cops exclaimed "Oh shit! This is Chief Inspector James, the deputy commissioner!"

"Christ!" said the other one.

"Well, we better do this by the book," and with that came back to me. Out came his notebook and he said "Ok, let's have your story again," and started writing. After he had finished he faced Dean Powell and asked "Were you a witness, Father?"

Dean Powell answered his questions and he wrote down the answers as he went. He then faced me and asked for my licence, so I asked "Aren't you going to put the bag on the other guy first, he's as drunk as a skunk?"

He turned to Dean Powell and said "You can go now, Father." He didn't move. The cop turned back to me and said "Well, I know Chief Inspector James doesn't drink. Now show me your licence please."

"That's crap! I'll remember you said that" I replied.

"And so will I" interjected Dean Powell, after he asked for my licence again. I said "I don't have one, I'm only fourteen."

He said "Right, we'll be taking you to the station, and charging you with driving without a licence, underage driving, and failing to give way."

"What!" Both Dean Powell and I exclaimed together, as he started putting me in handcuffs.

He said "Right, into the car," and as he opened the back door of the cop car, I was pushed in. I said, "Father, can you call the old man, please?" and he nodded an affirmative. As we drove to the cop shop one of them remarked "Christ, you're in a shitload of trouble now, Davis."

At the station I was put into a cell. Shortly after that four big cops came into the cell, each carrying a phone book. One of them said "Now you're going to forget all about Chief Inspector James being drunk, or you're going to have some accident damage you didn't realise you had." I knew that I was about to have the crap beaten out of me, but decided to go down fighting.

I said, "I'll only speak to detective Cal Turner, and as for that other prick, you can fuck off!" With that, I started to shape up as the first one took a swing. He caught me in the ribs, but I nailed him with a left to the jaw. I dodged the next couple of blows, smacked one cop in the eye, and broke the nose of another one. The number of blows coming my way and too many assailants was taking its toll on me. However, I knew they daren't mark my face, I didn't have that the same restraint, and my temper was on over boil, so I was able to land a fair amount of damage on them. I bloodied noses, ears, lips, teeth, and blackened eyes. As one went down, I kicked him in the face and broke his jaw. Another one grabbed me from behind, so I pushed backward ramming him into the bars, while kicking out at one coming toward me. I turned and smashed the head of the one that had grabbed me into the bars again, and by now there was only one left standing. I was spent, but shaped up to continue.

As I was doing this, there came a ferocious roar from the doorway into the station. As I glanced around, I saw the old man come racing into the cell block with the original two cops who arrested me and the desk sergeant hot on his heels trying to hold him back. They took in the scene; three cops down and bleeding with ripped and bloodied uniforms; the discarded phone books, my shirt ripped but still hanging on me, and me barely standing but ready to keep going. Dad reached me as I was about to fold, held me up, and in a voice laced with so much menace and fury that I'd never heard from him before, ordered the desk sergeant "GET ME YOUR STATION COMMANDER RIGHT NOW!" "Yes, Sir," was his only reply.

When the station boss arrived, the old man and I were seated in another empty cell with the cell door open. He took in the scene, and asked "What the HELL has been going on here?" The desk sergeant told him why I was there; the old man took over then. "I arrived to see what was happening with my son, and heard a fight going on in here. I tried to get in here as those two tried to stop me," indicating the first two standing against the wall. I then took up the story. "These four came into the cell to try and convince me that I was mistaken about Chief Inspector James, but I wasn't having any of it. This is the result," waving my hand about. He turned to the Sergeant and said "Leave those four in there and lock the door, I'll be speaking to them later."

He then asked "Has this young man been officially charged yet?"

"No, sir," was the reply.

He continued "Good, he won't be. Find him a clean shirt."

Then he turned to us and asked "If you're up to it, would you join me in my office please?" When the Sergeant came back with a clean cop shirt, I put it on after discarding my ripped one and we followed the station boss to his office.

After we were seated in his office, he introduced himself as Inspector Harry Oxford, and said "Tell me the whole story of how this came about," looking at me. So I told him the whole story and finished with telling him about my witnesses (Father John and the ambulance attendant) about James' condition. "So considering he was in the wrong in the first place, I will be looking for compensation, or I will not only scream to the media, I will bring a law suit against James and the police force."

He replied "Hmm, I see. Ok, well, I've decided that you won't be charged with any offence, but I can't do anymore at this stage until I talk to Chief Inspector James in the hospital. I'll be going up there when we are finished. I will have to speak to my boss Senior Inspector Trevors, so I suggest we reconvene this meeting at ten o'clock tomorrow morning. How's that sound?"

I glanced at the old man and he nodded, so I said "Ok, but I would like detective Cal Taylor present during our talks, as he's the only honest cop I know. Maybe you, but I'll reserve judgement on that for the moment. Ten o'clock tomorrow then." We got up and left. On the way back to my flat, I asked Dad "Do you still have that pocket cassette recorder?"

He replied "Yes. Why?"

I said "Good. Now tomorrow, please let me do the talking and don't be surprised at what comes out, just trust me. I know what I'm doing." When we got there, I said "Thanks for the lift. I'll see you at work about nine thirty and thanks for all of tonight. See ya."

The following morning Cal was waiting at the front door of the cop shop when we arrived and said, "I've been told that you've asked for me to be present at a meeting with the higher ups. Care to fill me in?"

Dad let me do the talking, and I filled him in about what was going on. Then said "I asked for you because you seem to be an honest cop, and not mixed up in what's going on, but also what I'm about to do comes down to blackmail. Are you going to have a problem with that and arrest me later?"

"Thanks for your vote of confidence, and no problem with me, I'll just be there as a silent witness only. Let's go in," and with that led us up to Senior Inspector Lewis Trevors' office. Along with Trevors was Harry Oxford looking rather tired. As we all sat, Trevors said "Harry has told me about last night's events, and I agree with his decision. No charges will be made against you, Tom, and the deputy commissioner will pay for your car to be repaired. We can put this whole thing to bed, if you agree not to talk about it."

"What did he think I was stupid or something?"

"Not so fast" I said "First, my car is a write off. Secondly, four of your cops tried to beat the shit out of me. Thirdly, you want me to stay quiet about it. Well, no deal, until you meet my demands."

"You're in no position to make demands, son," Trevors interrupted. I held my hand up for silence. I continued, "Don't call me 'son'! I'd commit suicide if you were MY old man! Now my demands! One, Twenty thousand for a replacement car. Two, I'm issued with a Drivers Licence with my birth year back dated to nineteen fifty. Three, I become a protected person as far as any cop in this town is concerned. Not so much as a traffic ticket in the future! Now I need a smoke, so Dad, Cal and I'll go outside while you consider my demands. We will come back in ten minutes." With that, I indicated to Dad and Cal to head out. As we got outside the cop shop Cal said to Dad "Christ, your boy's got guts. Unbelievable." Looking at me as I lit up he said "And yep, that was pretty much blackmail in there," with a smile on his face. Grinning back at him and the old man I said, "It's not over yet. I still have a trump card I may have yet to play. If I do, you'll know it just don't have a heart attack when I do. Ready?" With nods of agreement we headed back inside.

Back in Trevors' office we re-seated ourselves. I looked across at Trevors and asked "Well?" He looked back at me and said "I can only get you ten thousand to replace your car."

I thought about this and drew it out mainly to piss him off, then said "Done, as long as I get the cheque before I leave here."

He replied "Done."

He continued, "Your licence will be issued to you before you leave."

"Done," I said, and he went on, "Now as regard to protected status, I can't give any orders to that effect."

So I replied in a hard tone "You can and will, because I know all about your little protection racket concerning all the pubs in town. I have Statuary Declarations from most of the publicans in town and your Internal Affairs Department in Brisbane would have a field day with that information. What's the going rate.... two thousand dollars a month?" Well, I thought poor old Lewis was going to have a coronary, he'd gone all purple. Cal had leaned forward with a perplexed look, and the old man coughed (from laughter?). Harry went white as I dropped that little bombshell!!

I sat back smiling and waiting for everyone to gather their

composure. Trevors mumbled "Ok, done."

"Good, now for my last demand," I said, "We'll all go into an interview room, and put this deal on tape."

"Done," Trevors agreed.

So we all moved into an interview room. Two tapes were inserted into the recorder and turned on and the following recorded: "Deal struck with Tom Davis in the presence of Senior Inspector Lewis Trevors, Inspector Harry Oxford, Detective Sergeant Calvin Taylor, Mr Des Davis and Tom Davis. Tom receives ten thousand dollars as replacement for his damaged vehicle, an open Qld Drivers Licence, year of birth to be back dated to nineteen fifty, and from this date to be considered a protected person by members of the Central Qld Police Precinct. All of this will be considered to be null and void should any person involved in this interview divulge the contents of therein to any outside party."

When we had finished the recording, I leaned across the desk, ejected my copy, and placed it into my shirt pocket. Trevors took the other copy. As we were leaving the room, Trevors said to me, "One day, Davis, I'll get you for this!"

So I replied "No, you won't Lewis. Should anything untoward happen to me, the Statuary Declarations and this tape will go to the Internal Affairs Department. Now be a good boy and go write out my cheque. I'll be along to collect it as soon as my licence is typed out."

Within ten minutes I was standing outside the cop shop, thanking and shaking hands with Cal Taylor. I lit a smoke, and asked him "Are you going to be alright after this?" Smiling, he replied "Oh yes, they don't dare touch me now. I know too much." As we walked away the old man asked "Where did you get that info?"

So I just said "I told you to trust me, which you did, and I said I knew what I was doing, and I did," then asked "Tell me, Dad, feel like a coffee?"

CHAPTER 8

While we were having coffee, the old man asked "How did you get all those Statuary Declarations?"

I replied "I've only got three. From Bobby and a couple of his mates. I ran a bluff, and Trevors folded. I've still ended up with a cop shirt." We both laughed at that. Then he asked "When are you going to look for another car?"

"As soon as possible. I'll give Joe a ring and see what he's got, but I've still got the bike. The only problem I have is what to do with the wreck. I'll ring round the wreckers and see if they want it, not that I'll get much," I replied. After coffee I went into work. Mr. Petersen was concerned after I told him what happened, but told me to do some ringing around from the shop phone, and that he'd give me a lift home after work.

The first call I made was to the cop shop to find out where my car had ended up. Apparently, it had been taken out to the Gracemere wreckers, which was six miles out of town. My next call was to them, and I told them that I'd see them in a couple of days. Then I rang Joe at the car yard, and was told he had a few that might suit. Next I called Bevan and asked if he could spare the time to have a look at a car for me. It turned out that he could, so I gave him the shop address, and arranged for him to pick me up and we'd go to the car yard together. At Joe's car yard he showed us a Ford '66 XP Fairmont Futura, with wide polished drag mags. It had bucket seats, a 'T' bar auto shift, heavy duty diff and gearbox, and an extra fuel tank for long range driving. Bevan and I took it for a spin. "Handles well, brakes are good, and lovely to drive, want to try it?" He pulled over and we switched seats. As we did, he had lifted the bonnet and said "Perfect, you know that any Ford V8 would bolt straight in here. As long as you had an auto flywheel, put in a 2" exhaust system, lower it, an inch all round, possibly a new paint job, and you'd have a mean pearler of a car." I drove back to the yard, and it was heaven to drive. When we got there I asked Joe about the car's history. He said "Here's where you're lucky. It's only had one owner and he put in the long range tank and the mag wheels because he's out the other side of Alpha. We traded it two days ago for the latest model; I'll let you have it for six thousand." We negotiated on the price and shook hands on five thousand cash. We finalised all the paperwork that he would lodge first thing in the morning, and the car would be detailed and ready for me by eleven. Bevan drove me back to work and I said to him, "Thanks for that, I'll be in touch in a day or so." We shook hands and he took off.

I filled in Mr. Petersen when I got back, and he said "Fine Tiger stay on your normal start time if you need, but what about school?"

I replied "Well, I'm going to stay off for the rest of the week due to my crash injuries." He just raised his eyebrows and we both laughed. The next day I walked downtown to the bank and withdrew the five grand I needed, then went across the street to the shop and had morning coffee with Mr Petersen. After that I jumped on a bus that went past the Ford yard, got off and walked in to Joe's office. I paid him and he gave me the rego papers transferred into my name and two set of car keys. As we went outside, he swung his arm at the car and said "There you go, Tiger, all yours. Try and take better care of it this time," and we shook hands laughing. When I drove out of the yard I headed towards Gracemere and the wreckers.

When I arrived, I went inside the office, and the guy at the counter asked "Hey, aren't you Tiger Davis of the 'Raiders'?"

More or less used to my notoriety by now, I replied "Yep, is the boss around?" "Matt, you're talking to him," he said.

I continued "My car was brought in the other night, because of a prang."

"Oh yeah! The FC, come with me," he replied as he led me into the yard. "Well, there she is, probably not worth fixing, but the parts are worth salvaging." This was the first time I had really looked at all the damage, and had to agree with him. I asked "Ok, how much is it worth to you?"

He replied, "Let's go back inside and I can work it out for you." As we headed back inside, I spotted a V8 sitting on one of the work benches and asked "Is that thing out of a Ford?"

He glanced at it and said, "Yep a 351 blueprinted phase 4, from out of a GTHO we got in last week. Nice huh?"

"Hmm," was all I replied. In the office, after looking at some paperwork, he said, "Well, the cops are picking up the storage fee, so I can offer you five hundred for yours. Rather non-committedly I asked, "That V8, how much do you want for that, best price for a cash sale, if it's in good nick?"

He replied "Oh, it's in top nick, nothing wrong with it, to you six hundred."

Thinking this over, mind you, I'd already made up my mind. I asked "Ok, let's do a deal. Make the motor five hundred, throw in an automatic flywheel and delivery, and I'll give you my car. We go outside to the motor, take a photo of you and me shaking hands. You get the photo blown up, I'll sign it, and you can get it framed, and hang it here, what do you say?"

"Deal." he replied and held out his hand, and we shook to seal the deal. So while he went off to find his wife to take the photo, I rang Bevan to let him know about the motor and what it was, and that it would be delivered to his workshop that afternoon. After the photo was taken, he told me that the motor would be delivered within a couple of hours. I gave him my pager number, and said "Call when the photo is ready and I'll come back and sign it for you." On the way back into town I called into Elders Auto spares and bought a new stereo system, a good pair of spotlights, and a venetian blind for the rear windscreen. I waited a couple of hours for them to be installed, then drove into work. The next morning I drove over to Bevan's workshop. He came out and said "Motor's here, and it's a beauty. Want to hear it?"

Looking pleased, I nodded and replied "Hell, yeah!" We went

in and the motor was sitting in a cradle. We attached starter cables to a battery, poured some fuel into the top of the carby, and Bevan touched the cables to the starter motor. The engine roared into life, "Oh, yeah!" I exclaimed, once the fuel ran out. Bevan then said "If you can stay and help, we can take out your old motor and have this one in by this afternoon."

"Let's get started," I replied with glee.

By two o'clock we were done. The V8 fit like a glove, and looked spectacular sitting in the car. We then went next door to the muffler shop, and he had a word with the boss when he came over. With nods of agreement, it was indicated to me to drive the car around. As I drove it in, I was guided onto the hoist, and I shut it down. He looked underneath when the hoist was up, and said "Well, I can do you a two inch system, but only in stainless steel, put a 'lukey' in the middle here, and a couple of resonators right at the back. Should give you a real cool note, and cost you about two hundred all up."

"Done," I replied.

He then said "Ok, well, I'll get started on it now and should be ready by ten o'clock tomorrow." So we headed back to Bevan's and he said "I can give you a loaner til tomorrow," and showed me an old Hillman Minx. I then asked "How much do I owe you, buddy?"

He replied "On the house mate. I've made a good deal of money betting on the 'Raiders' since you and Skeeter have been playing together, so I probably owe you, but the lowering blocks will cost about forty dollars." The next day I paid for the exhaust work, the car sounded lovely, and Bevan and I had the lowering blocks all in by one o'clock. As we were leaning back on a forty four gallon drum of fuel looking at the car, Bevan remarked "You know a paint job of British Racing Green would set those mags off nicely."

I asked "Know a good painter?"

"Shall we go for a drive?" He took me to a Panel Beater's two blocks away and we talked to his mate Jeff, who suggested the roof and rear windscreen support panels be white, and the rest of the car painted a metalflake British Racing Green. It would cost me another two hundred and be ready the following Monday, so we left it with him and walked back to the workshop. I hopped back into the Minx, thanked Bevan, and headed to work.

On the Monday morning I went to school, and straight to the office. I asked Janet the secretary "What's the new guy like? What's his name?"

She replied, "His name is Ian McPherson, and he's an arsehole, do you want to see him?"

"I guess I'll have to front him sooner or later, so yeah if I can, thank you," I said. Janet used the intercom, and told me to go through. "Ah, Davis, I've been waiting to see you. According to your file, you don't live with your parents. You made quite an impression on my predecessor, and top of the school in your exam results, and so do you mind telling me why you haven't been in classes for the last week?"

Still standing in front of his desk, I said "Well, sir, most of the teachers here would have known, as word get around this town pretty quick, that I was involved in a car prang, and I've been recovering from injuries."

He replied "I think that's a poor excuse to have time off, and you're just being lazy. What do you think of that?"

Now this guy was really pissing me off, even if he was right, so as I took my shirt off and yelled at him "I suppose all these bruises are just imaginary too. Now I don't have to be here, I just came to the school as a courtesy, to let you know in person why I hadn't been here. I also have to see my doctors later this morning, so I won't be here for the rest of the day either. So what DO YOU say to that?"

"Hmm, it seems that what's in here about your temper is true. Put your shirt back on. I apologise for calling you a liar," he replied. Just to put him in his place, I said "Accepted, but if I take time out there's not a thing you can do about it, because I can blitz any exam you set. Now I'll be going, good day," and walked out.

After this set to, instead of staying for the first two periods as I was going to do, I went to the car and drove to Bevan's workshop, dropped off his car, and walked to Jeff's panel shop. My car was waiting and it looked spectacular. I paid Jeff, and as I was about to leave my pager sounded. It was a message from Matt at the wrecking yard, letting me know the photo was ready for signing. I decided to drive out there after I'd seen Bevan. Bevan thought the car looked great, and I must admit I thought the same. I thanked him for all he'd done and we worked out that for all the expense, the car really only cost me five thousand six hundred all up, so I was well in front. Now, off to keep my word. I put a cassette into the stereo and headed out to Gracemere. When I pulled up, I left it running and popped the bonnet. As Matt walked out he asked "Is this yours?" I nodded and he continued, "It's beautiful." As I lifted the bonnet, he said "Oh, man, with that in there you've got the hottest and fastest car in town." After shutting it down and closing the lid, we went inside and he showed me the enlarged photo. I pulled a sharp pointed marker out of my pocket and signed, "To Matt, and the gang, the best for parts, Tiger Davis," and said "There you go, as promised, now you can get it framed and hung up."

He then asked "Hey, Tiger, what are the 'Raiders' chances this year?" I answered "Well, the team is going all out this year, because we want to do what no other team has done and win three in a row, and you can bet we'll do it." I left after having a coffee with Matt and his missus, and headed back into town.

I knew that Barbara had the day off, so I headed to her place, pulled up and went inside to knock on the door. She and Betty beat me to it, coming outside while I was halfway to the door. Barb saw the car and said "Wow, is that yours? It's fantastic!"

Betty asked "We heard about the accident, are you ok?" About to answer her, Barb gave me a squeeze and I winced, which Betty noticed. "Yes, I'm ok. Just a little tender still. I'll tell you the whole story over coffee." As Betty made the coffee, she told me what she had heard. Apparently I drove into the Deputy Commissioner of Police and ran him off the road. Laughing as I heard this,

82

I took out photos of my car that Matt had taken and given to me, and showed them to Betty.

"Look at these as I tell you the truth about the accident and how it occurred." I told them both exactly what happened and why it happened, then told them of the attempt to change my mind about James' condition in the cellblock. They couldn't believe that it could happen, so I once again took off my shirt and they saw the blue and yellow bruises. Betty asked "Good God, and that was a week ago?" I nodded and told them about getting a cop shirt to leave the station in, so she asked again "Did you report it?"

I answered "Yep, and it's all been taken care off, but I've been organising a new car so that's why I haven't been up before."

Immediately Barb asked "Can we go for a drive?"

Looking at Betty and receiving a nod I replied "Just as soon as I finish my coffee."

Betty said "Well, if I miss you when you come back, come up for dinner tonight after work, Tom."

"Love to" I replied. Then out to the car we went. I opened the door for Barb, then went around got in and turned it over. Barb said "Ooh that sounds mean," so I told her about the new motor as we drove off. We headed to my place to amuse ourselves in the bedroom for a couple of hours before returning her home and going to work. Ray was home when I got there for dinner. He handed me a beer and the photos, and said "I've been told the story by Betty, here's to winning another one."

The next morning, I rang the school and informed Janet that I wouldn't be there until next week, mainly to piss off McPherson. Then I went to work, arriving at the same time as Mr Petersen. "Good morning, Tom. Into work today?" he enquired. I told him I was, "So where's the new car?" I indicated it two parks up and he said "nice" as we walked up to it. I handed him the keys and said "Go ahead take it for a spin."

When he got in and turned it over, he said with a beaming smile "Oh, yes." I said "Just watch it, it's a V8, I'll go ahead and open up." When he arrived back, he was smiling from ear to ear and said "Thank you. So quick and responsive, a real pleasure to drive, would leave my GT for dead, well done, Tom."

During our morning coffee break, I told Mr. Petersen of my run in with the new principal, plus my doubts about my future. He asked "What do you want to do?"

I replied, "Well, I really have no idea. I just don't want to keep going to school to do grade twelve, just so I can go onto university for more school work. It's boring! And there's got to be more to life than being stuck in this town for the rest of it?" He nodded, seemed to chew over what I had said, and then started to tell me of his past:

His father was a scientist, and his mother did alterations for a local tailor. They lived in Norway prior to the outbreak of World War II. When he was sixteen, the German army invaded; they escaped Norway and made it to England. Mr. Petersen enlisted in the Army, and drove tanks during the rest of the war in the Middle East and Europe. After the war, he left England and came to Australia to work on the Snowy River Scheme, then became a horse Breaker. He met Doris, who was working as a cook on a local cattle station, and eventually they married. He had made enough money from horse breaking to open the shop here, and because he had learned to sew from his mother, he was also able to offer a tailoring service.

After he told me this, he said "Yes, there is another life outside of this town, and some, like you, need to explore it. I was like you when I was young, and due to circumstance I was able to see the world outside of my village. Tom, you are the maker of your own destiny. You have the potential to do great things; all you have to do is take the first step. Decide on a course of action and don't let anything stop you. I'll help and advise you as much as I can, but when all is said and done, you have to make the choice. You could think about any of the armed services, you only need to enlist for three years now, that's always an option."

I thought about that conversation a quite deal over the coming months, and at the same time subtly sounded out other people's opinions. I did know that if I was going to leave town at the end of the year, or early the year following, I'd have to start making some preparations for my departure from town. The first thing I would need was my Birth Certificate for identity reasons. Of course I already had my licence, if needed I could always claim an error in regard to the year of birth. So one day while talking to my father, I subtly suggested that perhaps it was time for me to look after my own paperwork, and he agreed. A day later he came into work and handed over my Birth Certificate, with the warning that if I lost it, a replacement could take months.

Early in March, just prior to the football season starting, our landlord needed to do some repairs to the flat and give it a new coat of paint. He would need a couple of weeks to get the work done. This wasn't a problem because Pete would be working out at Emerald for the next four weeks, and I could temporarily move back home for the time it would take to get done. After speaking to the old man, it was decided that I would move back in over the weekend. Pete would be in Emerald, so the landlord could start on the Monday. Two weeks later on a Friday night, Skeeter and I took off for a shooting trip up at a property near St. Lawrence. When Skeeter dropped me off, as usual I left the rifle out of its case on the bed to be cleaned later, and then asked the old girl if there was anything to eat. Well, that sparked off an argument, along the lines of me treating the place like a hotel. She went on and on with the snide comments, and how I didn't care about anyone in the family except myself, and how much of a disappointment I had turned out to be. I let her rant and rave without really arguing back much because I'd heard it all before. Then she said, "You couldn't even be here when your sister was dying, you were too busy having fun, and off gallivanting with your mates!"

Even though my temper hadn't really risen prior, that remark was enough to make me explode. I started mouthing off and didn't hold back, even when I saw her go white as I unleashed my fury in the shape of verbal abuse directly at her. As I continued, I heard a barked command "ENOUGH! Now stop." I turned to see the old man standing at the entrance to the pool room with my rifle in his hands. I turned toward him, and as I did, noticed that the safety catch was off. I sneered at him, and said "Or what? You're going to shoot me?" Then I placed my hands on my hips, and with concentrated venom in my voice stated "You'd better make the first one count, otherwise I'll kill you barehanded!" Just then my brother John leaped out of the pool room, pushed the barrel up, and the gun fired sending a round into the roof.

While everyone was stunned, I grabbed the rifle, ejected the magazine, unlocked the bolt to clear it, put the safety on, and then threw it onto the lounge. At the same time John told the oldies exactly what I had been up to during the time my sister was in the coma. As they both looked at me, I said, "Right, now I'm going to pack my gear, I'm going to my place, and I won't be back!" While I was packing, my mother came into my room and said "Tom, I don't know what to say."

I replied "Good, then don't say anything." I finished my packing, put my gear in the car, retrieved my rifle and left without saying anything.

Back at the flat, everything smelled of fresh paint, so I opened all the windows, and started to clean my rifle. Just as I was putting it away in its case, I received a message from Barb stating that she'd be down in an hour, and could stay the night. When she arrived, she asked me to give her a hand getting changed. I don't know about the getting changed part, but I did help with getting her clothes off. After we had made love to each other and were laying back spent, I said to her "That we needed to discuss something important," and she replied "Ok, what do you want to talk about?"

I explained to her all the thoughts I had about what I wanted to do, and about leaving town at the end of the year or early next year. My doubts about what I wanted to do and where, and what we would do about our relationship, and finished by asking her to think about these things, and to let me know her thoughts in relation to what I had explained to her. She agreed that there was a lot to think about, and we would need to have some more in depth conversations as time went on, since it was inevitable that I would be leaving.

A couple of weeks later I was glancing through Mr. Petersen's morning paper, and noticed a recruiting ad for the Defence Forces. I had a detailed look at what was being offered, the requirements, and how to apply for an information booklet and application form. I cut out the ad to take home, as I had decided to send away for an information package. What the hell, it couldn't hurt! Later that night, back at home, I read the ad again. The requirements for identity purposes were listed as a Drivers Licence. That wasn't a problem. A Passport or a copy of my Birth Certificate, both of these would present a problem. I didn't have a Passport, and my Birth Certificate didn't have the same date of birth as my licence. I would need to change my Birth Certificate somehow.

After the game on Sunday, I got to have a quiet word with Skeeter at the pub. I filled him in about my plans for making tracks out of town at the end of the year. I told him I was considering joining the defence forces, but to do that I would have to falsify some documents, and asked "Do you know of anyone who could possibly do some forgery?"

He replied "Well, as a matter of fact I do. It'll cost you, and I'll arrange a meeting at my place. I'll let you know when."

CHAPTER 9

Two days later I received a pager message from Skeeter, telling me the meeting was set for six the following night, and to bring everything with me. Before leaving for school on Wednesday, I made sure I had my Birth Certificate in the glove box, because I would head for Skeeter's place after work that afternoon. When I arrived, Skeeter and I had a beer while we waited for his mate Colin. He asked me "Can I get a copy of your licence to doctor, because I still haven't got one?"

I replied "Sure, no problems, I was going to suggest that anyway." Colin arrived and we all sat at the dining room table to discuss what I required; two copies of the original Birth Certificate, and three altered copies, an altered copy of my licence, and an altered copy of my licence with Skeeter's details.

After looking at both licence and Birth Certificate, he said "The licence isn't going to be a problem, and we've got a big new copier that does things in colour at work. What I can do is do the unaltered copies for you, plus do some copies for me to work with, and Skeeter can pick up all the normal copies from me tomorrow arvo. Then I can work on what needs doing, and the altered copies should be ready in about a week."

Then I asked "How much will the job cost?"

Colin thought for a minute or so then replied "Seeing you're a mate of Skeeter's, seventy five bucks should cover it."

"Ok, done" I replied. After Colin left, Skeeter and I talked for a while, and he said "I'll bring the documents to training tomorrow night, and thanks for arranging the licence for me." Shortly after that I left.

The next day while I was at work, I phoned the British High Commission in Brisbane and asked for an application for a British

Passport to be mailed to me at the shop address. That night after Skeeter had given me the originals and the straight copies I requested; I asked him if he had An Australian Citizenship Certificate. After he told me that he did, I asked him to pass it onto Colin to copy and change into my name, with the issue year as nineteen sixty. He replied "No worries, I'll get it done." A week later, I was back at Skeeter's, sitting at the table with him and Colin. Colin produced the fruits of his labours; three changed Birth Certificates, An Australian Citizenship Certificate in my name, and the drivers licence in Skeeters' name. I compared the original Birth Certificate with the forgeries. Colin really did classy work, and they were perfect. I paid Colin the seventy five dollars I owed him plus gave him an extra ten dollars for the extra Citizenship Certificate he made for me. Now I hoped I had all the documentation I needed, all I had to wait for was the applications I had sent for to arrive.

Early the following week, the information and application package arrived from the Defence Forces, and two days later the passport application. After opening and reading the information from the Defence Forces, I decided that if I was going to join the Air Force, I'd need to stay at school and complete senior level. That put me off the Air Force; I really couldn't see myself in the Navy, so probably the Army offered the best choice due to the numerous branches one could decide on. However, I would sound out Mr. Petersen, seeing he was in the Army in England. The best thing was that I didn't have to make my mind up at the time. The requirements were the same for all, I just made the height requirements, and the Identity documents that I would require were Birth Certificate, Driver's Licence, and Citizenship Certificate or Passport, so the forgeries Colin had done for me would cover these bases.

At work the following day, I got Mr. Petersen to help me with the passport application, and then went across to the bank and had the manager countersign the application and photos as a JP. Back at the shop, I enclosed an unaltered copy of my Birth Certificate and it was ready for sending off. Then I asked Mr. Petersen about his days in the Army while he was in England. After he told me some of his tales about those days, he remarked "Ok Tom, you don't ask something without reason, so what are you up to?"

I replied "Well, you know how we've been talking about what I could do with my life, and I sent away for an information pack from the Defence Forces. It arrived the other day and I've been reading through it, and sort of made up my mind about trying for the Army." He looked at me with a small smile and said, "You might have a problem with your age." So I told him that I could possibly get past that. The initial enlistment was for three years, but if I didn't really think it was for me, I could apply to leave it after six months. He said to me "You better bring it in and we'll go through it together, just to make sure you're not getting in over your head."

I took the information pack into work the next day, and he went through it with a fine tooth comb, turned to me and said with a laugh "Sounds good. Pity I'm too old, otherwise I'd probably give it a go myself, but what interests you?" "Well, the transport corps looks interesting, there are three branches of that; air, land and water. That could be interesting, don't you think?" I replied. He looked at the booklet again, and asked "Yes, it does, but do you think it that would hold your interest?"

So I replied, "I'm not sure, but I'll never know unless I give it a go."

He said pensively and with a bit of laughter, "You're right on that score, you'll never know about anything unless, as you say, give it a go. You've come a long way from when I first met you Tom, and if you decide to go I'm going to miss you a great deal."

"Well, I'm not gone yet! Let's get some work done," I replied laughing. His statement about missing me gave me thoughts about some of the things, and people, I would miss in town. "Is this kept others brain dead, and in the cowboy town rut?"

At school the next day, I saw Janet in the office and asked "Could I do a photocopy of a couple of documents please?"

"Sure, I'll show you how to use it," she replied, and I copied an altered Birth Certificate and my Licence. While at the office, I found out that Janet was a JP, so asked her to sign the photocopies as true copies of the originals. She looked at me and said, "This isn't your true date of birth?"

Without answering her question exactly I just said "Well, they are true copies of the legitimate originals, aren't they?"

Hesitantly she replied "Well, yes." "So there isn't any problem, is there?" I asked. She replied "No. I guess not," and as she moved to her desk and started writing and signing them, after she was finished, I gave her a smile and thanked her.

That afternoon at work, Mr. Petersen and I went through the application forms and filled them in; then over to the bank again to get the manager to witness my signature. Back at the shop, I popped the forms and photocopies into the return envelope and Mr. Petersen said he would post them off on the way home.

On the following Sunday, after the teams fifth successive win, we were down at the pub. I was watching Skeeter as he talked to one of the other players; he was still just a smidge taller than me, his unruly sandy coloured hair all over the place (didn't he ever use his comb?), and he was getting deeply tanned being out in the sun with the rail gang. His physique was a mirror image to mine, and I knew that he was almost as strong as I was. As I took this all in, I started to think that if it hadn't been for a simple shared interest in football, we would have probably ended up being sworn enemies, ready to fight each other at the drop of a hat. Instead, we had turned into best mates who backed each other to the hilt, and shared each other's secrets that would never be divulged to anyone. We had both gone out of our way to help each other at times, and I started to think about how much I would miss him when I left town. He came over and said "You're looking thoughtful, anything wrong?"

"No, mate," I replied, and told him about sending the application off. I told him that I was thinking about the people and things I'd miss when I did eventually leave town. After hearing me out he said "Well, you ain't gone yet, and it's your shout, let's have another beer."

A couple of weeks later, I had a chat with Cochrane prior to our maths class and asked him "Who was taking care of the bets for the footy tipping competition now that Jack was gone?"

"I can, why?" He replied, so I asked "What are the odds on the 'Raiders' winning again?"

He said, "Thirty to one, only because three in a row has never been done before. Mind you, I've of got a hundred on it happening, mainly because of you."

Thinking this over and doing some quick calculations, I said, "Ok, tomorrow I'll bring in five hundred to lay down, if that's alright?" I think I shocked him a bit but he agreed. That afternoon, prior to going into work I called into the bank and withdrew one thousand dollars from my account, which left me a balance of nine thousand eight hundred and sixty. As I walked in the shop Mr. Petersen asked "I heard you pull up, where've you been?"

I replied "I had to go to the bank and get some cash, how you feel about a walk to the bookies'?" In answer to my question he went to the safe, counted out five hundred dollars, and then closed it again. He asked "How much do want me to lay on for you?"

"Five hundred, same as you, oh, and please let me know what the odds are when you get back," I said with a smile. He replied, also with a smile, "Go the 'Raiders', I assume," with his usual mischievous laugh.

When he arrived back, he had a smile beaming all over his face, and told me that the odds were twenty five to one. With some quick calculation, I worked out that, on those two bets alone, I stood to make twenty seven thousand five hundred! Nothing to be sneezed at over all, so that really put a smile on my dial as well. While we were having a coffee, he put his hand up and said "Oh! I almost forgot in all the excitement, this came for you in the post this morning." He leant over to the end of the counter, produced an envelope and passed it to me. It was from the British High Commission, and inside was my passport! Valid for ten years, the enclosed letter explained the rights I had as a British citizen and a list of addresses for all the High Commissions in other countries of the world. That Thursday night at training, I asked Coach Dixon to get me another couple of members box tickets for the Grand Final and a double invite to the awards dinner for Mr. and Mrs. Petersen. This seemed fitting as it was going to be my last season.

A few weeks later, as I arrived at work, Mr. Petersen handed me a foolscap size envelope from the Department of Defence. I opened it and we read the contents together; it stated that my application had been received, and I was requested to attend the main recruiting office in Brisbane for aptitude and medical tests. These would take place over a three day period within the next month. If I couldn't make it, I would have to wait for the next intake assessments during the following year. Included in the envelope was a return travel certificate for the railways and a room and meals voucher at the Peoples Palace Hotel on the corner of Ann and Edward streets in Brisbane, which were two doors away from the main recruiting office. We both looked at each other and Mr. Petersen asked "Do you think you can get the time off from school and football?"

"Yep, I'll take the day off from school tomorrow and book my travel, probably come into work early, and let you know how I get on."

The next day I went down to the train station to book my travel to Brisbane and back. I booked a sleeper on the south bound Sunlander that left town at four pm on Sunday, and would put me in Brisbane at approximately ten o'clock on Monday. I then booked a sleeper on the northbound Sunlander for the following Friday. It left Brisbane at four pm and arrived in town at ten on the Saturday. So I would only miss one game and a training session, and a week at school. While I was at the station I rang Barbara's to see if she was on or off. Betty answered and told me Barb was at home till four when she went to work, so I told Betty I'd be up shortly. When I arrived, I went inside and over a cup of coffee let them know what I had been up to and about the trip to Bris. When Betty asked "You're too young, how did you manage that?"

I replied "I found a way around the age barrier, but I guess I'll have to wait and see if it works or not. I'll know more when I get back." After coffee was finished, Barbara told me she wanted to talk to me in private, so we went to her room. As soon as the door was closed she said "So you're really doing this, are we going to break up now or later?"

"Barb, I told you that I would be leaving this year or early next, as for breaking up I have no wish to do that until I know for sure. I'd like us to continue, but it's up to you. Keep in mind though; we don't get to see each other as much these days, what with work and all. Do YOU want to part now or later?" I said. She replied "Later, much later," and I said "Fine, how about a kiss before we both go to work?" Well, we had more than a kiss, and it was quite satisfying for both of us, then I had to keep going. I said goodbye to Betty and headed for school. At school I informed Macpherson that I'd be away in Brisbane soon for a week or so, in case anybody missed seeing me around, then left to go to work.

When I arrived at work just after midday, Doris was in the shop with Mr. Petersen. As I walked in, she said to me "Hello Tiger, would you care to explain to me what you and Eric have cooked up that's got him chuckling all the time?" A little taken back I glanced at Mr. Petersen who made a money counting gesture, immediately worked it out and answered "Well, I'm not sure what you are talking about Mrs P. Maybe it's about the Grand Final and award night tickets I'm trying to arrange for you two; I told Mr P about it yesterday."

"Oh, well, thank you, Tom, we'd love to come to both. Eric really can't get up to much without me finally finding out,"

With that, she came over to me, gave me a kiss on the cheek, and continued, "Thank you again; you're such a sweet young man."

She then left the shop with, "I'll see you at home, Eric." With a much relieved expression on his face he said "Thanks, Tom, hopefully that'll put her off the scent for a while. Now what's this about tickets?" I told him about the tickets I was trying to arrange, and then said "You do know she'll find out about the bets; she always does."

Laughing, he answered "Yeah, I know, but your remarks about

the tickets will put her off for quite a bit, I think.," Laughing as well, I agreed with him, then told him about the travel arrangements I made. I asked "Are you sure the week away is ok for you?"

"Of course, dear boy, no problems, and I'll consider it part of your holidays, so you'll still be getting paid." I thanked him, and then went out back to put the jug on.

Thursday night I asked Coach Dixon "What time is our game slotted for on Sunday??" "Ours is the main game, so we'll probably get onto the field about two. Why?"

"Well, I have to be on the Sunlander down to Bris at four, and I won't be getting back til the following Saturday, so I'll have to miss Sunday's game and training next week. I'll be able to play the game Sunday week," I answered. He said "Hmm ok, I'll take you out of the line-up this week and put you in for Sunday week, but don't forget we're gearing up for the quarter finals soon. Like you, I'd like to get three in a row, just to stick it to this town, and show them it can be done.," While saying this he had a smile on his face. Later at the pub, I told Skeeter that Dixon had taken me out of the line-up for Sunday's game, and why. He shook my hand and said, "Well, good luck, and take care of yourself down in the big smoke. Remember I won't be there to watch your back, and call as soon as you get back."

Then I replied "I will, oh, get a bet on the Final down soon, the odds were twenty five to one the other day, and I threw five hundred on."

He laughed and said "Already in for a grand, pal," then we both laughed and raised our glasses to each other. That night when I got home Pete was still up, and seeing this was one of those times that we had time to talk to each other, I filled him in what was going on with my life, including the trip to Bris. It was arranged that I would leave the rent for the next three weeks in the usual place, and he'd take care of it while I was away. He informed me that I'd better not be gone too long, because he didn't want to lose the money he had also put on the 'Raiders'.

That Sunday, instead of getting ready to play, I was packing a travel bag and my documentation to take to Brisbane. That afternoon, as I was about to put my bag in the car, I received a pager message from Barbara, and it read "Take care while you're away, love you, Barb." Now that was the first time either of us had used the 'L' word, and really not a good time to start as I saw it, especially as we would have to part company sooner than later. I drove down to the pub and arranged with Bobby for me to leave the car in the pub car park while I was away. I took my bag into the bar with me and sat to have a drink; close to leaving time I would just walk across the road to the station. As I was having my drink, I asked Bobby if the game had started, knowing he would have it on the radio in the back. He told me it had and was nearly half time and the scores were level. After another beer, I told Bobby I'd see him in a week, grabbed my bag and headed across the road to the station.

The rail trip to Brisbane was interesting but long, and I was quite happy to have had a sleeper. When I arrived in Brisbane at Roma St station, I went to the ticket office and checked my return was all in hand. They even gave me the sleeper cabin number and car number. After getting directions, I headed outside to the cab rank, climbed in the first one, and told the driver to take me to the Peoples' Palace. Two minutes later I was there, damn I could have walked if I had known where I was. It was only three blocks away from the station. I checked in and was given my key. My room was on the third floor; it had a bed, wardrobe, fan, and window (that had a good view of the brick wall of the next door building). The shower and toilet were communal and two doors down the hall.

After putting some stuff in the wardrobe, I went and had a shower, dressed into some clean gear, went down to the office to find out what time and where the meals were, then headed out to do some exploring.

I left the entrance, turned right, and headed down Edward St. The building that my window faced was also where the main recruiting office was, and I thought to myself "Well that's fine. I'm virtually next door so I don't have far to go." I went into the recruiting office, saw the main desk and went up to speak to the person there. After I announced my arrival, I was told to be there at eight thirty in the morning, and then someone would take charge of the group I was assigned to. After that, I left to continue the exploring, and continued down toward the main part of the city.

At the bottom of the hill, I passed Adelaide St, had a quick glance up and down, and decided I'd continue down Edward St. I looked at the cross streets, passed Queen St, then Mary St. and Margaret St, eventually coming to Alice at the bottom. In front of me was the botanic gardens; through the trees I could see the river, so I went into the gardens and followed the path which lead me to the river, which was across from some cliffs. Ok, all very interesting, but I was on a fact finding walk not a nature ramble. Following it brought me to another path leading back up towards the city, so I took it and came out of the gardens on the corner of Albert and Alice. There was a real big hotel called the Park Royal. Ok, it was big, but royal? Really, someone was full of themselves. Continuing up Albert I came to Festival Hall which, to me, looked like a movie theatre. A block up was Queen, which looked like one of the main streets. I continued up one side to the end near a bridge, and then went back down the other, ending up back at Edward Considering there was a pub on the corner, and I thought I wouldn't stray too far with the exploring, so went in for a drink.

Well, the first thing I noticed was that there was a woman serving at the bar! Then I realised something I'd forgotten; I was in the big smoke. This could pose a problem for me. Even with ID saying I was over eighteen, twenty one was the legal age for getting a drink! How fucking ironic! At (supposedly) eighteen I could join the forces and fight for the country, but couldn't legally buy a drink! How stupid was that? Oh well, I was here now so I'd give it a go anyway. I pulled up a pew at the bar, and waited to be served. The barmaid came up and I asked for a VB. She said "Sorry, honey. You look underage to me," so I passed across my licence, she looked at it, and continued "You're still underage, honey." Becoming really pissed off, I replied "So I can fight a war, but not get a drink?" She replied "Ok, just this once," and grabbed a pot glass, poured my drink, and with a wink told me the price. She put the change on the bar, and said "I'll let you have a few, but if you see any cops walk in, scarper!" I thanked her and she moved off further down the bar.

After having a couple of drinks, and with a wave to the barmaid, I left, headed back up to the hotel, went up to my room and read a book to kill time. The book I was reading was 'War and Peace' and it was one of the books I had to do an essay on for the English exam at the end of the year. Finishing off after three chapters, I went downstairs to the dining room for dinner. I ordered the mixed grill, as it sounded as the lesser of the two evils, the other being bangers and mash. Well, the steak was tough and nowhere near as good as home, plus to my mind someone needed a cooking lesson. After finishing what I thought a truly less than satisfying meal, I had a shower, set the alarm for six thirty and read for a bit before going to sleep.

CHAPTER 10

The next morning I was up, showered and dressed, and grabbed all the documents that were requested. I then went down for breakfast. It couldn't really be called breakfast, because it looked as if the previous night's dinner had been reheated with eggs (I couldn't tell if they were supposed to be fried or poached.) The only difference being there was juice, cereal and bread for toasting available. However, I did decide to eat a reasonable amount, because I wasn't sure if we would be getting a lunch break. After I had eaten, I read the front pages of the local paper just to kill a bit of time, and then went outside to have a smoke. As I was smoking, I drifted next door to the recruiting centre, and waited for them to open up.

After it opened, I sat down and leafed through some recruiting pamphlets while waiting and other guys filed in and did the same. Eventually a Captain came and addressed us, and told us that we would be split into two groups of ten. The first group would be having medicals, while the second group would do the aptitude testing, and the procedure would be reversed the following day. There would be a lunch break of an hour at twelve, and we would finish around three thirty each afternoon. He then called out the names of group One which would do the medicals first. I ended up in that group. All our requested documentation was handed over, checked to make sure it was all there, and put into manila folders with our name. These also had numbers on them. I learned later that the numbers were to be our serial numbers from that time on.

We then trooped through the door into the inner workings of the centre. This was followed by interviews by a doctor, one by one. After the interview, the medical continued with checks on height, weight, eyesight, hearing, colour blindness, and the list goes on. Suffice to say it was very thorough and took til about three, including the lunch break. For the lunch break, most of us went back to the hotel where we were all staying, and sandwiches were ready for us. There was time for a couple of smokes before the afternoon session. At the end of the day, we were finished before group Two and we all went off to do whatever to fill in time until dinner. I went off down to the pub, and thankfully the same barmaid was working, so I was able to get a couple of drinks and have a smoke in relative peace.

I was feeling a little lonely and seriously contemplated using the phone number I had for Jill's parent's place to see if we could meet up. But because I had matured, I realised that you can't go back. We had our time and moved on with our lives, and without trying to sound cold or callous, Jill was like the Gene Pitney song, "The Girl Belonged to Yesterday."

Having had a couple of drinks, I headed back to the hotel and did some more reading before and after dinner. The next morning was a repeat of the day before, except Group One was sitting the aptitude testing. It was pretty straight forward stuff; maths, English, history, and science. Every now and again they threw in a tricky one with instructions that had to be read all the way through without shortcutting, otherwise you'd blow it. For example, you might have four pages of written instructions, get to the last one, and it would say "Just write 'done' on your answer sheet." From what I heard later, a few of the guys had short cut and solved the problem without reading all the instructions. Idiots! It took them a lot longer that way. Then the psychological tests, with correct word, shape association with time restrictions, how do you feel about questions, tick and flick, multiple choice questions, and on and on. After the lunch break, we had face to face interviews with psychologists for ink blot association tests. They also asked some, what I thought, were really stupid questions. I think I upset the guy doing mine, because after an hour of this shit, I was getting a tad pissed off at the stupidity. He then asked me "If you were in the desert and a battleship started firing on you, what would you do?" Did he think I was absolutely stupid? So I immediately answered back "Get my submarine and sink it!" Well, his reaction was unexpected; he looked up from the papers on his desk, leaned back in his chair, took off his glasses and asked "Where did you get the submarine?" I replied testily "The same fucking place you got the battleship," He just looked at me and said "That's all for today, you can go now." I got up and asked "What happens tomorrow?" and he replied, "Everyone has face to face interviews, just wait in the foyer to be called, and send in the next person please." I thanked him and left.

It was three fifteen when I left the centre, so I went down the road for a drink. The barmaid, Sheila, was on, so no problem getting a drink. I took a long pull of my beer and then lit up. I wondered if I had screwed up by letting the trick cyclist (psychologist) get to me with his silly questions. As was about to finish my second beer, I spotted a cop walk in the Queen Street door, so I legged It out the Edward street door and headed back up the hill to the hotel. That night at dinner, I sat with a couple other guys from my group, and was asked if I knew what we were doing tomorrow. I informed them about the face to face interviews and what we had to do in the morning when we got there. After that I headed upstairs for a shower and some more reading before sleep.

Next morning, we waited to be called, and because four guys had been called one after the other, I assumed that there were four interviewers, which would make things go a bit faster. I was called in at nine thirty by the original Captain from day one. As he seated himself, I was directed to the seat in front of his desk, and I waited until he had finished reading some of the stuff in my manila folder which had gotten thicker than when it started out. He sat back and said "Well, Davis, your test scores are well above average, and apparently you really impressed one of the psychologists with your answers. What branch of the Army interests you?"

"Most likely transport, Sir, but it's still a toss-up about which branch," I replied.

"Have you ever considered applying for officer training?" He asked, "With your scoring, you'd have no problems."

I thought about this for a minute and asked "What are the down sides, Sir?" he gave a little chuckle and said "Apart from the school being in Victoria, there's three months of intense training, and learning to become a leader, but the biggest down side is that you can be posted to any corp or unit, so there's a lot of moving around."

I thought it over and said "No, I don't think it would be for me. It would feel as if I was jumping a queue, and if I decide the Army isn't working for me, it would probably be harder to give it away."

"Well, yes it would. I have noted that I asked you about officer training, and that you have declined, so should you consider it in the future, the availability is always there, and do you have any questions?"

I asked, "Yes, Sir, what happens now?"

"Right, well, we fill out all your paper work, you are sworn in, you sign the Official Secrets Act, and this will be the first of many times that you'll do that throughout your career, if you are accepted. Then, what will happen is you'll receive a letter in the next month or so stating if you've been accepted or not. What will follow that will be a movement notice to report to either back here, or further south. The training intakes usually start every three months, so the next intake will be late November." He then passed over a card with a number on it (the same number as on my folder) and said, "This is your service serial number, from now on you will be required to know it off by heart, so don't lose it. Are you ready to proceed?"

I replied "Yes, Sir."

At eleven thirty I was finished, after signing a whole heap of forms, and swearing the oath of service. With a handshake the Captain said "Congratulations. You shouldn't have any problems with acceptance, you're through with this section of the process, and enjoy the rest of your day, Davis." So off to the pub I went. After Sheila had brought me a pot, I sat at the bar enjoying the drink and a smoke, contemplating what to do with the rest of the day.

After a couple of beers, I went back to the hotel for lunch. While there, I met up with some of the guys that had been in either of the two groups, and four of them were leaving after lunch to head to their respective homes. After handshakes and congratulations all round, I went upstairs to do some reading. Well, at least with the time away, I was getting through what I considered a very tedious book to read, and by now I was more than half way through it. While at dinner that night, I met up with the remainder of the assessment intake and found out that some had passed and the others hadn't. But hey, they had given it a go. Plus it probably put them out of contention with regard to conscription, which looked like happening the way the current federal government was talking. After breakfast the next morning, I enquired about when I had to vacate my room, and was informed that I would be required to vacate the room after the lunch period, which was fine by me. I could make my way leisurely to Roma St station to await my train north. So after opening time, I made my way to the pub I had been frequenting, and took my place at the bar. As Sheila placed a pot in front of me, I said "Sheila thanks for being so understanding, this is the last time I may see you, after this I'm headed back to where I came from, so I just wanted to say thanks for your patience, and understanding. Cheers," and raised my glass to her. She replied "Well, thanks Tom, and you be safe wherever you're going. How long before you take off?" So I told her "about lunch time" and she replied, "The next one is on the house, you take care, wherever you're headed, love."

Over the next hour or so, with drinks and smokes, I contemplated my life from this point on. Sure, I would miss people. The town- I wouldn't miss. Maybe what I could do would make the world a better place, (Christ, how presumptuous was that thought?) Would I be able to stick to my own moral code of doing the right thing? I suppose the answers would come over time. I could only hope that I would never lose sight of those morals, whatever may eventuate. Shit, thinking like that could really do your head in, and instantly become a candidate for a white wrap around coat. Fuck! Wake up, Tom! About half twelve, after four pots and a dozen smokes, I gave Sheila a salute and headed back up to the hotel, had lunch and a couple of coffees to clear my head, then went up to my room to pack. I went down to the office to check out, and left. After a ten minute stroll, I arrived at the station, found the right platform, then settled down to read and smoke while waiting to board the train north to home.

Waiting around doing nothing tends to bore the crap out of me, because I'm used to being active, so after an hour of doing nothing except read, I gave the book away and started to walk a couple laps of the platform. I was taking in the sights and smells of diesel engines, rail tracks going everywhere, and the coming and going of suburban trains. During my wander, I noticed that I wasn't the only one waiting; a few travellers were scattered along the platform, and one caught my attention. A cute brunette wearing a blue shirt and jeans, shorter than me by an inch or so, slim with a nice looking body. As I walked by she got my attention by asking for a light. As I flicked my lighter into life, holding it cupped for her to light her smoke, I caught a good glimpse of her nicely rounded breasts as she leaned towards me. I introduced myself, and she told me her name was Debbie, and she was heading up to Cairns for a holiday. So I told her where I was going, and I also told her which cabin I was travelling in, and left her with an open ended invitation to join me in the club car, once we were under way north. I thought to myself that if she accepted my invitation, it could be an interesting and less lonely trip. Shortly after we finished our cigarettes, the train pulled up to the platform, and it was announced over the PA, that people could board if they were ready. The departure time was just under an hour away, and after helping Debbie onto the train with her luggage, I retrieved mine and boarded.

In my cabin, I checked out the amenities, and from experience knew that the bunk could sleep two, settled myself, and then headed to the club car. When I reached it, I was informed that it was officially closed until the train started the trip, so I made my way onto the platform for another walk and smoke. As I walked, I was glancing sideways into the train, and in one of the sitting cars I spotted Debbie settling herself in. With a smile, I thought to myself that after a couple hours of sitting up like that, she would probably take up my invitation, and could very well end up in my cabin for the night. It would be too tempting to miss out on, and it couldn't be perceived as cheating on Barbara as we were already going to break up anyway, so I wasn't breaking my own inner moral code of honour between right and wrong.

Four o'clock on the dot the train sounded the horn and started to move, slowly at first, as it moved into a tunnel it gathered speed. After passing a few suburban stations, it slowed for a while, and then gathered speed again. I watched through the window as we went through some of the suburbs, and then made my way to the club car. Seated at a table, I again watched the suburbs roll by. Just as I was about to finish my beer, I saw Debbie come into the car from the other end. She saw me and came and sat down. As she did, I asked if she would like a drink. After coming back with the drinks, she asked "Would you like a game of Euchre while we talk?"

I replied "Sure, what are the stakes?"

She laughed and replied flirtingly "Well, that's something we could talk about."

I laughed also and called "Spades," she passed and said "Let's play for who pays for dinner, loser pays."

"Done," I replied, as I took the points for a march.

While we were playing, the conductors came through, and we gave them our tickets to clip and continued our card and flirting game. Very shortly Debbie moved seats so she could sit beside me, instead of opposite. While I was getting us another round, she dealt the cards. When I got back, we continued playing both games. As I took the first game, we both lit up and she leaned closer to me, with one hand on my leg, and as she blew out a stream of smoke. I turned towards her and gave her a kiss, which was returned with enthusiasm. I then returned to dealing the next hand, and she said "Ok, I'm paying for dinner, now what are we going to play for?"

With a smile on my face I replied "How about breakfast?"

Smiling and being coy, she asked "Where? Shall we go to your place or mine?" Laughing and going along with her, I replied "Well, it would have to be my place, it's got a bed." As I was saying this I had leaned into her, and our heads were against each other. Her only comment was a longing "Hmm."

Just as we were playing the last hand in the second game, which I was about to win, an announcement came over the on board PA system, stating that the dining car was open and ready for service. I looked at my watch the time was six o'clock already! Time flies when you're having fun. Debbie put her arm around my shoulder, her head against mine, gave me a kiss on the cheek, and stated "Well, I'm paying for dinner and breakfast, what do we play for after dinner?"

I laughingly replied, "Why don't we discuss that over dinner?" She laughed and said "Sounds good, but first I have to go to the little girls room."

As I let her out from beside me, I whispered "Don't pee long," and she got the word play straight away, laughed, and said "Don't go away."

When we arrived at the dining car, we were served by the staff at a table for two; menus and the wine list were at the table. After deciding what I would have, Debbie told me what she would order. I said "Well, seeing you're paying for the meals, I'll order and take care of the wine." As I reached for the wine list, I found what I thought would go with our meal, and then spotted something else on the list, I asked "Are we going to have desert?" She said "Naturally." When the waiter got to our table, after ordering both meals and dessert, I asked the waiter to keep the food and drinks bill separate. I then ordered the wine for dinner, a sparkling red cavelli, and sabra liqueur, to go with dessert. When the meals and the wine arrived, she sampled the cavelli and remarked, "Hmm lovely, you really know your wines." We both had cheesecake for dessert, together with the sabra. "Excellent," Debbie said. "I was almost on the point of orgasm, that liqueur is exquisite." She then asked teasingly "Ok, what are we playing for with our next game?"

106

I replied with a laugh, "Your body, of course."

She laughed and asked "Well, where are we going to play?"

Smiling, I replied "My place?" She just smiled and said "Naturally. Let's go."

As I closed the door to my room, she put her arms around me. I turned to her, and we had a very long and passionate kiss. As we finished our embrace, she said, "Forget the cards, you win, you get me for the night." and started unbuttoning my shirt. Luckily the bed had been lowered. I switched on the small bedside light and turned off the main cabin light. I reached for Deb, pulling her into an embrace, undoing her buttons, and removing her shirt, as our tongues started exploring each other's lips and mouths. I unclipped her bra, and slowly ran my hands down each arm to remove it. After our kiss, I gave her a slow, small bite on the neck, she responded with a groan. From her neck, I bent over and gently took one of her breasts in my hand. I kissed it and gave her nipple a light lick; by this time she was groaning heavily with passion, and couldn't undo my strides fast enough. I helped her, and at the same time undid her jeans. Then butterfly kissing her abdomen as I lowered myself to slide her jeans all the way down and off, as she slowly lifted first one leg then the other. At the same time, I shrugged my strides down over my hips and stepped out of them.

During another long embrace, we lowered ourselves onto the bed, and I gently slipped her pants off. She moved further onto the bed, while slipping off my jocks, with her hands gently caressing my hips and bum. In the process, I started caressing her vagina, with a couple of my fingers moving firmly and knowingly inside her moist vagina. Receiving an instant moan while our mouths were still locked in a torrid tongue kiss, she tightly gripped my erect penis. As I slowly inched my hand up her back and sides during our continual kiss, she moaned, pleaded and begged "Please take me." So I slowly moved over her and penetrated her in one smooth, firm and sure deep movement. As I went very deep inside her, she gasped, shuddered and moaned in ecstasy at the same time. As I moved to gently lick and suck her nipples, she cried out "Oh

God! I'm coming," and she did, in great convulsive shudders that rocked us both in orgasmic unison.

I let the shudders die a little, and turned while still inside her. She was now on top of me, but I controlled her movements, as she came again and again. I arched up into her yet deeper again, and kept her having orgasm after orgasm until I emptied myself up and into her with a solid spray of hot thick cum. This stimulated another massive orgasm, so much so she yelled out in ecstasy, and then collapsed down onto me, all the while wracked with shudders. After a while, the shudders died down and she was able to talk coherently she commented "Good God that was fantastic. That's the best sex I've ever had. Christ, you're good! Where did you learn that?" I smiled and replied "Just comes naturally, literally," with a wicked laugh. And I thought to myself, "Do women actually practise saying that compliment, or do they get into the sack with drop kicks that don't know anything?"

She asked if there was a shower in the cabin, so we both went in and showered together, a little cramped, but we made do. We then got back into bed again and she snuggled under my arm and right up against me, so what else could I do but get her horny again. Starting with light touches, then slightly harder strokes, that pulled us both into ecstasy land again. She whispered "Can we go again?" In answer, I rolled on top of her, and while sucking hard and deeply on her nipples, entered her again, and my liquid sprayed hotly into her accepting warm vagina again and again. That night she had enough orgasms to keep her going for a few years, before we finally settled into sleep.

After a hearty breakfast the next morning, we adjourned to the club car, and had another coffee while we smoked. With a mischievous smile I asked, "Want to play cards?" She replied laughing "Oh, God, not again!" However we did end up playing cards again as the world passed us by. A little later, one of the conductors was coming through the car, so I pulled him up, gave him my cabin number, and asked "Is anyone booked into my cabin after I have to get off?" He looked at his clipboard and replied, "No, not that

I can see."

"So, my girlfriend could use it to Cairns?" I asked.

Chuckling he replied "Yeah, sure, no worries, I just need your name and ticket number, miss." I thanked him, and he continued on his way. "Thank you for that, Tom, could you help shift my luggage, into OUR cabin?" So we went off to collect her suitcase and take it back to the cabin.

When we got there the bed had been made up. I put Debbie's suitcase away and packed mine up at the same time, then we sat there smoking and playing cards again. I was tempted to take Debbie again, but knew there wouldn't be enough time before the train pulled into town. As the train neared the outskirts of town, I got ready to go. I pulled Debbie into a long embrace, and said with a wicked smile "Thanks for your company, Debbie, hopefully we'll meet again." She replied "It's me that should be thanking you I've had a very memorable night. I'll not forget you for a long time, Tom, and thanks for the cabin." As the train pulled into the station, one last embrace, and I left the train.

Without looking back, I walked to the pub car park, fishing the car keys out of my pocket as I walked, and unlocked the car. I threw my bag into it, and then went inside to let Bobby know that I was back, and that I would see him tomorrow for the game. Back in the car, the rumble from the exhaust as I started it was comforting in a funny sort of way. Slipping into drive, I headed out of the car park and downtown; I would just get to the bank before it shut. I withdrew the five hundred that I would need the following Monday, and went across to let Mr. Petersen know I was back. I told him I would fill him in on Monday afternoon, and then headed for the flat.

CHAPTER 11

When I arrived at the flat, I made two phone calls. This was easier now as Pete had got hold of a phone from out of a phone box, installed it, and turned the line on. We still used the usual procedure, but without having to walk up to the corner. The first call was to Skeeter, letting him know that I was back. We talked for a bit and I told him I'd fill him in with all the details the next day. The second call was to Barbara's place. Betty answered and told me that Barb was working til four, which was fine, so I arranged to go up and speak with Betty at two; because there was something I needed her advice about. Then I unpacked and had a shower.

When I arrived at Barb's place, both Betty and Ray were home, so while Betty went to make coffee and bring a couple of beers, Ray let me know that the 'Raiders' had lost the game the previous week. When Betty had brought the coffee and beers, I said "I'm glad that both of you are here." I told them about what I had been doing, and the results of the Brisbane trip to the recruiting office. Due to this, I would be quitting football at the end of the season. Then said "My main problem is that I've tried to talk to Barb, and we've decided to carry on together until the last possible minute, but I don't know if that's really fair on her. That's why I need your advice." Betty asked "So you weren't thinking of doing something silly, like getting married?" "No, but Barb put that forward as an option, and I vetoed that, because we're both too young," I replied. Ray asked, "When is this likely to happen, Tiger?"

I said, "I'm not sure, but the intake usually takes place in early December, so I'll probably have time to finish grade ten at school. The footy ends before that, but I somehow don't think I'll be here for Christmas."

They both looked at each other, and then Betty asked "What

does Barbara have to say about this?" I thought about my reply and said, "She doesn't really want to break up, and I think she thinks she'll wait for me to come back. But that's the whole point; I may not come back to town at all!" I leaned forward and showed them the pager message Barb had sent then continued, "I was thinking of breaking it off after the awards dinner, without any clue as to how, but after reading that last week, I'm not so sure." I would like her to be there, seeing as this will be my last, but I do need your advice on when and how I go about it."

Betty asked "How sure are you of not coming back?"

My answer was quick in coming, "There's nothing holding me here, and there's a lot of world out there for me to explore, so, no I don't think I'd come back to live. Maybe a quick visit, to collect my car, but that would be all." Ray asked "You've made up your mind about this, and you're sure it's what you want?"

"Yes, sir, to both" I replied.

He and Betty looked at each other, and he said "Ok, we'll wait til Barbara's home, and then all four of us will discuss this and try to sort it out. This will hurt her, and we both know this is what you're trying to avoid, but it's going to have to be done and to tell you the truth, you have become part of the family, and we'll miss you."

Talk turned to general matters until Barb arrived home, and after she had given us all a kiss, she went to get changed then joined us in the lounge. She sat beside me, grabbed my hand and gave me another kiss, then said "Oh, it's good to have you home." Betty said, "Well, Barbara, Tiger's told us about his plans to leave town, now we would all like to hear some of your thoughts about how you feel about it, and any solution you may have thought of?" While she gathered her thoughts, she looked at each of us, and tears started to well in her eyes. Then she said, close to crying "I haven't been able to think of any, except, we could get married, but Tom's said 'no' to that, but I don't want to split up either." As she finished, she buried her face in my shoulder crying, and wrapped her arms around my neck. Ray, Betty, and I looked at each other worryingly, and then Betty said "I'll go get us all a drink, then we can talk this out."

When she returned with coffees for Barb and herself, and beers for Ray and I, Barb had stopped sobbing, but not taken her head and arms from around my neck and shoulders. Betty said "Barbara, honey, we know it hurts, but your father and I agree with Tom. Getting married is not the answer. We think that the weekend after the awards dinner this year, you and Tom can spend your final time together, before he has to go. It'll hurt you, but your father and I will help you through it." Ray was nodding his head in the affirmative, Barb finally unwrapped herself, and picking up her coffee, had a mouthful and said, "But I love him so much." Ray just replied with "We know, honey, we do too." "But we all have to do things we don't care to do, but they have to be done all the same. Now cheer up, and make the best of the time left. As your mother said, we'll be here to help." Now I was close to tears, as Ray made the statement about loving me as well, then I fully realised how many people I would actually miss.

Trying to make light of things, Barb gave me a punch on the arm, "Just don't go and get yourself killed, or I'll never forgive you." Trying to keep a fragile situation, I laughed and said "No way, sweetie." Hopefully the crisis was now averted, and talk turned to some of the things I experienced in Brisbane. That night I had dinner with the family, and spent the night in Barbara's bed. After breakfast the next morning, Barb came with me to collect my footy gear from the flat, and then we went to the pub, and onto the bus for the game. Skeeter gave us both a hug as we got on the bus, and said "About time you came back to work. Tell me all about it later."

As we headed out from the dressing room, Skeeter slapped me on the back and said, "Ready to carve them up!" I replied "Well, somebody has to, you didn't last week," and we both ran onto the field laughing. The result of the game was a forgone conclusion, what with Johnson and Davis back together again. We carved them up good, and the game won by thirty points. Down at the pub, celebrations were in full swing when Coach Dixon came over, shook my hand, gave me an envelope, and said "Good to have you back again, now we can move onto the finals without fear." Laughing with him, I said "Coach, um something serious, hate to say it, but this is going to be my last season." His look turned serious, and he asked "Does this have to do with your trip to Bris?" "Yes," I replied, and he said "Ok, we'll talk about it on Thursday night, meantime let me buy you a beer." He went off to the bar, and I looked in the envelope; it was the tickets I had asked him for. When he came back and handed me a beer, I said "Thanks for these," as I held up the envelope. "No worries, for one of my star players," he replied. A little later, I took Barbara home, gave her a goodnight kiss, and headed for the flat.

The next morning I headed for school and caught Mr. Cochrane as he was about to enter the school grounds. I asked "Are the odds still the same on the 'Raiders' winning the final, sir?"

"Yes, they are" he replied, so I gave him the extra five hundred I'd withdrawn, and then said to him "I'd double your bet if I were you, sir."

"Thanks for the tip, Tiger, see you in class," he replied.

Now to say I was anxious about getting to work would be an understatement. I was feeling real happy, maybe it had something to do with everything seeming to fall into place, and be right in the world. I guess a trick cyclist would have fun with a statement like that, but who really cares? When I got inside the shop Mr. Petersen was waiting, and he gave me a hug and said "Now, tell me all about it."

Instead of much work getting done, after coffees had been made, I started to tell him all about my trip; he interjected with a few questions, so I'd answer them, and then move on with my story. When I got to the interview with the trick cyclist, Mr P and I were laughing so much, there were tears running down our faces. When I told him about the battleship question, he asked me, "Well, what did you say?" So I told him what I had said. Well, that was it, he fell off the stool he had been sitting on because he was laughing so much, so I helped him up, and he said "God, I need another coffee." I went out the back and made us both another coffee, and when I came back, I said "Well, you haven't heard the best part yet. The following day, we had the one on one interviews, and I was asked, if I would consider going to officers school!" Mr P just looked at me and asked "Well, what did you say?" I told him what my answer had been, and he continued "It's always worth thinking about; if they consider you worthwhile, it's not something to sneeze at, now tell me the rest."

I told Mr Petersen about the rest of the trip, including my interlude with Debbie. He just looked at me and said "Well, you're only young once, so what else has been happening?" I brought him up to date with what had been occurring since my return, and then gave him the envelope from Coach Dixon. As he looked at the contents, I said "Now, it's up to you to keep Doris off my back, I'm not going to be in the middle all the time you know." He laughed at that, and replied "Don't worry, Tom, these will keep her quiet. Thanks son."

On Thursday night, Coach Dixon called me across, and said "Ok, let's go have a little chat." We went over and sat down, and I told him about what was taking place in my life. He said "Well, I'm not going to ask you to stay, you've already made your mind up. All I can say is, you've made a difference since joining the team and you'll be missed, good luck, and there's always a place for you here, if it doesn't work out. But first, you promised a triple, so let's shoot for that, Tiger!" As I rose, he held out his hand and I shook it, and said "Thanks Coach, but can we keep this to ourselves for now?" He answered by nodding and saying "If we win this one, we'll be in the quarters, so get back to work," I replied "Sure thing, Coach!" After training down at the pub, Skeeter and I had time to get into a real heart to heart about what I was about to do, and I finished with the statement "Let's keep this between you, me, and Dixon for the time being shall we?"

Well, we made it through the quarters and into the semi's, next up was the Grand Final. The betting odds against the 'Raiders' winning took a dramatic dive, just as well most of us had laid our bets down early. The best odds anyone could get in the week prior to the final were two to one! At work one afternoon in the finals week, Mr. Petersen asked me to bring in my suit, so he could start on any alterations that may be required for the awards dinner. As I tried it on, we both noticed that the jacket was getting a little tight across the shoulders, and the sleeves were a little short, but the rest of it was still as good as after the first alterations Mr. Petersen had made over two years ago. When I had changed back into my normal clothes, Mr. Petersen said "Leave it with me, I'll soon have it altered." Just then Mrs P came into the shop all flustered.

While Mr. Petersen sat her down, I went and put the kettle on, and as I was coming back with coffee all round, I saw Mrs P take out a fifty dollar note. She tried to give it to Mr Petersen, saying "Eric, you have to go find a bookie, and put this on the 'Raiders' to win. The odds are three to one! We could make a hundred and fifty dollars!" As I put the coffees on the counter, Mr P and I looked at each other, then her, and started laughing. Mrs P just looked at us as if we were insane, and said "Don't you two realise that's a lot of money?" Mr. Petersen then said "Doris, my love, do you remember a few months ago when you thought that Tom and I were up to something?" "Yes," she replied, and he continued. "Well, at that time, both Tom and I had placed a bet of one hundred dollars each on this coming game. The odds at that time were Twenty Five to one!" I looked at him and caught an almost imperceptible frown, so didn't say anything about the extra four hundred we both had on. During this time Doris had been working it out in her head, and with a look of amazement, said "Oh, you both must think I'm mad." I replied "Not at all, Mrs P, but when I found out what odds were to be paid back then, we knew that the odds would come down fast, so I convinced Mr P to put our bets on then!" Doris then jumped up from her seat, hugged and kissed me and said "Oh, Tom, dear boy, just make sure you win!" I replied with a laugh "With you in the member's box, we don't dare lose!"

Sunday came around faster than I thought it would, as I was getting ready to leave the flat Pete wished me good luck and told me he'd see me down the pub after the game and buy me a beer, as he would be a little richer after the game. I laughed, then got into the car and headed for the pub, met up with everyone else, then onto the bus and up to Brown Park.

We were up against our old antagonists, the 'Easts', so we knew it was going to be a hard game, and right from the start it looked as if both Skeeter and I were in for some close attention. After about three tackles, I'd had enough of being a punching bag while on the ground, so told Skeeter what to expect. As the ball came to me, two of their forwards came hard my way, so I flicked the ball back to Skeeter, flung both arms out to my side and connected with them both with powerful back hand punches. This put one on the ground and the other wobbled off course. Then as Skeeter was about to be tackled, he flicked the ball to me, and I had a clear run to the try line.

When the half time hooter sounded, we were level on the score board, and in the dressing room, we were discussing the change of tactics that 'East' were using by hitting us with two man tackles. There was even a suggestion for us to change to their old rough-house tactics. While the discussion was taking place, I was doing some hard thinking about ways to get around these new tactics they were trying. Coach Dixon had come up with an idea that sounded good, and it could work; it was simply the same as a yank grid iron play. Of every player running interference for whoever had the ball. Some of the guys were dubious, but I thought it had merit, it would mean our five eight would have an offensive line in front of the ball carrier. After Coach Dixon had finished explaining it, I put my hand up and was given the floor. This sounded like the best time to break my news, so I said "Most of you guys have heard the rumours that I'm leaving town. I'm telling you that for once the rumours are true this will be my last season of playing, and therefore this is my last game. Like most of you, I have a fair few bets on the outcome, I have no wish to loose, plus we can do

116

something no other team has been able to do, so let's give this a go, and stick it to them!"

When play started in the second half, we tried this new tactic, and it worked like a treat. Then it was their turn with the ball and we reverted to our usual game of defending, but with an extra flavour of rough house, we really pounded them hard. During one play, Skeeter had the ball and I was by his side as two of their defenders came at us. I knew that Skeeter was going to pass to me, so I yelled "Keep it, but come my way." I then faked a trip and went rolling into the two that were almost on us, and brought them down as I went under them. I could just hear Skeeter laughing as he scored. We were ahead by twelve, but that was reduced by six, after they scored in turn. When we got possession again, it was very close to the end of the game. Even though we were in front, we needed a sealer to make it safe. We ended up with the ball, and as our five eight passed it out, it was off target, and too high, so as I ran to intercept I leapt into the air, and grabbed it. Just as a defender crashed into my midsection, he went down, and I used his body to cushion mine. Still on my feet, I sprinted for the line and grounded the ball across the try line, five feet down from the goalposts. The ball was kicked for the conversion, and the full time hooter sounded while it was in the air. We were awarded the conversion, and therefore won the game by twelve points. As congratulations flew everywhere, all I could think of was the shitload of money I had just made! So needless to say I had a grin from ear to ear.

After a victory lap by the team, we just ambled around while our supporters poured onto the field. Skeeter and I were sitting in the middle of the ground, getting claps on our backs, and a couple of kisses from girls bending over to do just that. Then I saw Mr. and Mrs. Petersen head towards us, so giving Skeeter a shove, motioned to get up. As we rose, Doris flung her arms around me, then Skeeter, kissing us on the cheek and thanking us. Mr. Petersen grabbed my hand and pulled me into a hug, saying "Well done, Tiger, what a history making note to go out on. Congratulations, my boy." Then

Doris was wrapped around my neck again, saying "We'll see you down at the pub, you beautiful boy." Feeling rather embarrassed, I looked at Skeeter, and he had a wide grin on his face. He put his arm around my shoulders and said, "Come on, let's go get changed."

In the dressing room, pandemonium reigned supreme; some of the guys were already half pissed, shouting and singing, some drinking in the showers even! As I was getting dressed, Coach Dixon came up to me, handed me the match fee envelope and said, "Congratulations, Tiger, I made sure they gave you a bonus. See you at the pub, for a drink." I opened the envelope, and the cheque inside was made out to the tune of four thousand. I gave a slow whistle as I did some quick mental arithmetic, including the bets I had on. I had made a grand total of forty six thousand five hundred in that one afternoon! Time to celebrate! On the bus back to the pub, Coach Dixon informed us that the awards dinner would take place on the usual Thursday night coming, and all the usual dress rules applied. He then said "I personally would like to thank and congratulate each and every one of you for your effort in being part of a history making team; and to Tiger, we'll all miss you, when you go. Now, first round is on me, when we get there!" There were cheers all round after his statement.

When we got to the pub there were people everywhere, but all of them made room for the bus to pull up near the front door. As the door opened, the cheers echoed throughout the bus. I followed Skeeter out, and Joan literally flung herself around his neck. I really didn't fare much better as I copped the same from Barbara. That afternoon, I don't think any player paid for a drink, they were being pressed on us left, right, and centre. Mr. Petersen and Doris were seated at a table with Barb, Ray, and Betty. As I joined them I was hugged and kissed by both Doris and Betty, had my hand shaken and hugged by Ray and Mr. Petersen, before Barb sat on my lap with her arm around my shoulders. I silently raised my glass in salute to all, and then took a well-earned long drink. As they were all talking about the game, I sort of zoned the conversation out and reflected on what I had helped achieve, how much

I would miss it all, and wondered if I had made the right decision. Then I thought about Jack Robertson, and wondered whether he had got his bet on, and a smile came to my face.

Shortly afterward, Pete came across with two beers. He handed me one and saluted me by clinking glasses, smiling all the while. I asked "How much?" His reply was quick an even bigger grin came to his as he said "Twenty seven thousand." I smiled as well, thinking that a lot of people had made shitloads of dough that day. As day wore into night, I got drunker, and then Betty got up and said "Well, we're going to have to go. Hope to see you all at the awards. Barbara, you stay with Tom and make sure he gets home safely. Goodnight all," then she and Ray left, followed soon after by Mr. and Mrs. Petersen. Skeeter and Joan joined us; he was probably as pissed as I was. I was also getting hungry, so I went to the bar and asked Bobby what food was available. After being told he'd send over some pies and sausage rolls, he passed me two pots and said "That's for you and Skeeter." As I went to pay him for the food, he said "No, Tiger, it's all on the house for you two tonight." After thanking him, I passed Skeeter his beer and informed everyone that some eats were coming soon.

After eating, I started to feel a bit better, but I knew I was still fairly pissed, so I took the car keys from my pocket and gave them to Barb. I told her "Looks like you get to drive me home, sweetie. Hope you'll be staying the night, because I might need a nurse."

She replied "Yes, I'm off tomorrow so I'll be staying with you."

"Good." I replied then asked Skeeter if he wanted another drink. Getting an affirmative, I headed to the bar and got two more drinks.

We left the pub at closing time, telling Skeeter and Joan we'd see them at the awards night. To tell the truth, I was so pissed by then, I even had trouble walking to the car, and just as well Barb was there to lean on. I passed out on the way home, and Barb got Pete to give her a hand getting me up to bed. She had the job of getting me undressed, and the last thing I recalled, I was wrapping my arms around her before zonking out.

The next morning I felt like death warmed up, and as if I'd been run over with a truck. I literally crawled to the toilet, and it seemed as if I was never going to stop peeing. Christ! I must have put away a shit load of booze. I felt a little better after getting rid of all that excess fluid, and as I went into the lounge, Barbara brought me a coffee. I grabbed it with shaking hands, and she cooked some bacon, eggs, and toast, then I finished with another cup of coffee and a smoke. After that, I felt a lot more human. It would have helped if the slight pounding in my head had gone away, but after four Bex powders, it abated, then disappeared, thank Christ!

CHAPTER 12

When breakfast was cleaned up, I sat down with Barb in the lounge and talked while we were both having a smoke. I enquired if she would be able to go to the awards dinner. She informed me that after she did two night shifts she would be having a week off before ten straight nights again. I then asked "Well, you know our last weekend is coming, do you want to go anywhere, or do anything special?"

She answered "Could we go down to the beach?"

So I asked "Yeppoon, Cooee Bay, or Emu Park?"

"Cooee would be nice," she said, and I replied "Sure, will we book somewhere? Or just go down and find a place?" It was decided that we would go on spec, and find a place down there. She would stay with me Thursday night after the awards, and we would travel down during the Friday morning.

After taking her home, I dropped by the school. It was lunch time so I would most likely be able to catch up with Mr Cochrane. At the office, after paging him over the PA, Janet asked "How did you get on down south?" Just as I finished replying "Everything went better than expected, thanks," Mr. Cochrane appeared. He came up to me, fished out an envelope from his pocket, and with a smile said "Tiger! This belongs to you, and thank you, ours were the only two bets on the 'Raiders'. I made a packet, only not as much as you, though!" Opening the envelope I looked at the cheque it was made out for the sum of thirty one thousand dollars. With a smile on my dial, I said "Thanks. I also need to tell you that I won't be in for the rest of the week due to family business," I lied. He told me that it was ok, but not to forget that the following week we would be doing mock end of year exams so that everyone had an idea of what to expect. After thanking him again, I left and headed down to the shop.

Arriving at the shop, I noticed that Mr. Petersen was looking a little the worse for wear, and asked, "Feeling a bit hung-over from last night still?" He just looked up and answered "I'm not as young as you. I'm older, and so it takes longer to get over it. When you get to my age, you'll wonder why we ever do this to ourselves, but it is fun doing it, all the same." All I could do was agree. I wondered how many times I would spend suffering hang overs; quite a deal I imagined. Then Mr. Petersen said with a weak smile, "I'm glad you're here. Now I can take a walk in the fresh air, and collect our winnings." He then went to the safe, got out the betting slips, and headed to the door saying with a smile on his face "This is going to be fun." Returning about a half hour later, he looked a lot livelier, and back to his normal self. I went and made a coffee for both of us. He counted out our winnings into two piles, with thirteen thousand in each. He put two thousand five hundred into his pocket saying "That's to show Doris." The rest went into the safe. While it was open I asked him to pass me one of the banking bags. I counted out five hundred, and put the rest of the cash into the bag. The five hundred went into my wallet, and I pulled the two cheques out, the one from the club for match fees and the other one collected from Cochrane, and they went into the bag.

Finishing our coffees, I asked if I could nip across to the bank. After depositing the forty six and half thousand, my balance came to fifty five thousand eight hundred and sixty. Christ, I was rich! Back at the shop, Mr. Petersen had me try on my suit. He'd done wonders with the jacket; it fit like a glove again. He looked it over, then had me do a couple of turns, and said "Yes that's ok, but try this one." He handed me a dark blue suit he'd pulled from the rack. I tried it on and it fit perfectly. It was light weight and made of the same material that my black one was. After showing Mr. Petersen, he asked "What do you think?"

"Great! It fits well," I replied.

He said "Yes I think so, now also here's a couple of shirts I've altered to fit you. You better go put these in your suit hanger to take home, and wear with the new suit on Thursday night." It took me a minute or two to realize that he had done all the work on the new suit, and was giving it to me. One suit, yes, but now another! That was too much, so I protested and offered to pay for the second suit. He said "Ok, if you're too stubborn to accept a gift, you can pay for the time tailoring it. Fifty dollars will cover it." I was overwhelmed, so to break up the tension and emotion I was feeling I said "Ok done, but I think you're overcharging me." We both laughed, and I put my arms around him and gave him a hug, saying "Thank you," to which he replied "You're worth it, my boy," and I noticed that he had a tear in his eye.

The rest of the week I'd go into the shop to open up, and Mr. Petersen and I would talk about many things, especially my thoughts about how I thought things would go in the future. During one of these discussions, I asked if I could leave my car in his care, until my return. The registration listed the shop as my mailing address. I withdrew two thousand from the bank, and gave it to him to cover rego costs while I was away, so even if I was gone for three years the car would always be ready for my return. Mr. Petersen would give it a run at least once a week, just to keep everything up to scratch. I also think he was a secret rev head, and would love to take it out. But it was all so I would have a roadworthy car upon my return. With an inner smile I let him convince me that was the case.

Thursday came around, and that afternoon we arranged for me to have the Friday off. I closed the shop half an hour early, and then headed home to get ready for the evening festivities. That evening I left the flat early, because I was going to pick Barbara up. When I arrived at her place, I had a quiet word with Ray and Betty about distributing some of my earlier silverware from previous award nights. It was arranged for them to bring last year's "Highest Try Scorer" and "Player of the Year," cups with them. These would go to Mr. and Mrs. Petersen, and any I earned from this dinner would go to their place for safe keeping, except for one that I had intended leaving with someone else. I then put Barb's luggage in the car, two suitcases for two days…honestly! Don't women know the meaning of 'traveling light'? As we were leaving Betty said "Tom, sweetie, I love the new suit," and here I'd thought no one had noticed. I replied "Thanks see you both down there."

When we arrived, I gave Barbara the car keys; after all I knew that she'd end up driving home. We then made sure that we had a table for ten. Skeeter and Joan arrived to join us, followed shortly by Mr. and Mrs. Petersen, then Ray and Betty. Betty took the bag she had, carried it to Doris and had a whispered conversation. Doris looked at the contents, her eyes going wide, then they both looked at me and I nodded my head. After that, Betty joined Ray. Doris had then spoken to Mr. Petersen, and he looked surprised. Doris then came around to me and as I rose, she wrapped her arms around me, gave me a kiss and hug, saying "Thank you, Tom, you're a darling." Smiling, Mr. Petersen joined her, shook my hand, and said "I'll take these down to the car. I wouldn't hear the end of it if I lost them. Thank you, Tiger." His look said and meant more to me. The drinks waiter came over and passed a wine list to me without saying anything. I laughed as I showed everyone the wine list. They started laughing as well, and then I called for the drink order. When he went off to get the drinks, I held up the list and asked "Dare I?" Receiving a unanimous "Yes," I ordered two of the same sparkling red cavelli I had got on the train, served in ice buckets. As the meal was served, I poured the wine, and as I lifted Skeeter's glass, he said "Not for me mate, I'll stick to this," holding up his beer. I replied "Come on, just this once try it, for me if nothing else." He nodded and I poured a little into his glass.

He tried it, and his look became a smile, then said "Nice, ok, fill it up." Everybody laughed and agreed it was very nice. I raised my glass in a toast saying "To all the people I'll miss the most, love you all." That's all I could say without getting too emotional. My toast was accepted, and I guess it had a dampening effect, because we ate in silence. I was thinking about how much I would miss them all. About half way through the meal, Skeeter said "I, for one, feel like I'm losing a brother. Here's to the best person I've never had to beat up, my brother, Tiger. Good luck mate." As I looked around the table everyone had their glass raised, some with tears in their eyes, others just nodding. I joined them in a raised glass, toasted, and the mood became lighter.

Shortly after dinner the presentations got under way, with Coach Dixon once more the MC. He announced that due to the team's historic win, all prize monies had been doubled for this year's awards. And because there had been no new players added to the team, there would be a new award, being "Most Valued Player." This would rank second only to "Player of the Year," with the prize money being the same amount. Following that announcement, the night proceeded with Skeeter being first up, receiving the "Highest Attendance" award, which tonight was worth one thousand. Dean was next up for "Most Improved Player.," He would most likely take over my spot next season as he was a very fast front rower who deserved his chance on the wing. I was called up for "Best and Fairest," and "Highest Try Scorer." After that there came a few more awards. Skeeter picked up two more, and it moved on to the new award. Coach Dixon announced "The "Most Valued Player," and "Player of the Year," will be going to the same person, so both awards will be presented at the same time. So Without further ado, the "Most Valued Player," and "Player of the Year," are awarded to, Tom 'Tiger' Davis!"

Well, as usual the cheering and applause echoed through the room, and as I got up I received kisses and handshakes from all at the table. I then made my way to the stage while acknowledging handshakes and slaps on the back. On stage, Coach Dixon was smiling; he shook my hand and pulled me into a hug, then stood aside as I was presented first with one cup, then the other by my father. He also hugged me and shook my hand saying "Well done, son." I took the envelopes out of each cup, placed them in my jacket pocket, and held up both of the massive cups by one of the handles on each cup. When the applause and cheering died down, I placed the cups on the table behind me, and approached the microphone to start my acceptance speech. "Well, I must say that I'm truly proud to win the inaugural 'Most Valued Player' award." I waited for the cheering and applause to die down, and continued. "By now, most of you know this, but for those that don't, this is my last year of playing football with the best team in town." There were some shocked murmurs in the crowd as I announced this, then I continued. "It has been an honour to play with this team for the last three years, and also to win 'Player of the Year' three times in a row, especially as each of those times we have won the premiership. To the club, my teammates, and all the supporters, I'll miss you all when I leave at the end of the year, thank you one and all!"

Applause and cheering erupted, and as I stood there, I glanced over to where my parents were sitting. My mother had a shocked look on her face, but was applauding slowly, as I assumed she was digesting what I had said. I then picked up both cups, as I had done before, noted which one was "Most Valued Player," held them up and made a slight bow to the room. I headed off stage, made my way to the table where my parents were seated, and placed the "Most Valued Player" trophy on the table. I said "You can keep hold of this one," turned, and headed back to my table. On the way I was congratulated, kissed, hugged and had slaps on the back, and words with some of the other players. Back at the table, everyone was either shaking my hand or kissing me. Being close to tears, I just indicated to Skeeter to join me, and we went outside and lit up. Seeing the look on my face, Skeeter embraced me in a hug and said "I know how you're feeling, pal. Take your time before you get it together, and then we'll go back." I just nodded and took a long drag of my smoke. After I had shed a few tears, and got myself together, we had another smoke then headed back to the table.

When we got back to the table, I took the cup for "Player of the Year" and passed it to Barb. I said "This is for you to keep and look after, all the others can be given to whoever you think, but this one YOU keep." She kissed me, saying in my ear "I will." Then I gave the "Highest Try Scorer" to Skeeter, saying "Keep this, and remember I can still beat you." We both laughed and toasted each other, then I passed the "Best and Fairest" to Doris, saying "I know you'll both look after this." She leaned over, hugged and kissed me, and said "Thank you, and remember we're only looking after them for you, dear one."

I turned to Ray and Betty and arranged to go up in the morning prior to leaving for the coast. Then after a round of toasts, Barb and I headed for the dance floor. After a dance with Barb, we went back to the table. I got Doris, then Betty, onto the dance floor, while Barbara danced with Mr. Petersen and her dad. Close to midnight Barb drove us home, and after getting out one of her cases, headed upstairs. I took the cheques out of my suit jacket and put them on the bed table to take to the bank before leaving for the coast. The cheques would boost my balance by a further twelve thousand, not bad for a night's celebration.

The next morning, we went up to Barbara's before heading downtown to the bank, and then we'd be headed for to the coast. Betty had the coffee on, while Barb put her dress from last night in the wash, and put the trophy cup in a glass doored cabinet in her room. I was telling Betty what I had told Barb about my silverware when she joined us. I told Betty that they were to keep whatever they would like, to remember me after I left town. After coffee, we left and headed downtown. While I went to the bank, she headed into the shop to see Mr. Petersen. I deposited the cheques and withdrew eight hundred and sixty, leaving a round figure of sixty five thousand in my account. Christ, I could've bought a couple houses with that! I joined Barb and Mr. Petersen for coffee, and then after telling him I'd see him on Monday afternoon, we left and drove toward the coast.

Arriving down there, we did a bit of a drive around, and then pulled into a motel within walking distance of the beach at Cooee Bay. During the afternoon we walked along the beach, discussing my leaving, and what she was planning to do with her nursing, and I asked whether or not she could ever saw herself moving out of town, and her own plans for the future. This discussion became the theme for the weekend, as talk would invariably revolve around these issues. That night we went into Yeppoon and ended up buying fish and chips for dinner. We walked around doing some window shopping before heading back to the motel. We watched a movie before making love to each other and then settling down for the night. To my mind, the sex we had that night, and during the rest of the weekend, seemed to lack a certain element. It seemed more mechanical than passionate. The joy we usually experienced just wasn't there. After checking out on Sunday, we went for a last walk on the beach, and the subject of my return came up. I told her that my chances of coming back to town and settling down were very minimal, or non-existent, and that if I came back to town, it would only be to pick up my car, and head off again. As she thought this over, she asked "So our chances of getting back together are nil?"

"As much as I hate to say it, but I guess so," I replied.

"So, you don't want me to wait for you to come back?" She asked, so I replied "No, I want you to enjoy life, and do whatever makes you happy. Don't waste your time waiting for me to walk back into your life, because it may not happen. I will always treasure what we have, and I will come and see you before I go, but after that, I don't know."

She cried a bit while embracing me, and I stroked her head until the worst was over, then we headed up to the car arm in arm. On the drive back to town, she sat right up against me, with her hand on my leg, and was silent until the half-way point. I think it really had sunk in, and she had been pondering. She must have made a decision, because with a little slap on my leg, she perked up, and became her usual happy, chatty animated self. When we arrived at her place that afternoon, after taking her luggage in, we had coffee with Ray and Betty, and I told them I would come and say good bye before leaving town. Shaking hands with Ray, we gave each other a nod, and Betty gave me a kiss on the cheek as she hugged me. Barbara and I had a long embrace and kiss, and then I left and headed to the flat. I drove with misty eyes; my emotions were going full strength, with guilt and remorse, leaving people I cared about, and I think regret was high on that list.

During the week that followed, I received my movement papers from the Army. I was to report to the recruiting office in Brisbane on the first Friday of December, and was allowed one suitcase and a carry bag. This worked out rather well, because I would just get my Junior Exam results a week before leaving. I showed Mr. Petersen the letter, and after reading it he said "You better go on up to the station and book the train, off you go." At the station, I booked a sleeper on the southbound Sunlander leaving at ten pm on Wednesday. It would arrive in Brisbane at four in the afternoon Thursday. Having done this, I went back to work and told Mr Petersen. He consulted the calendar, turned to me and said "That's only three weeks away, will you have enough time?"

I replied "Well, I start the final exams next week, and should get the results a week after that. A few goodbyes over a couple of weekends, shift some of my stuff back home, yeah, I'll be able to make it."

Then he said "Well, the Wednesday you leave, you bring your car home to my place, have dinner with Doris and me, and we'll take you to the station."

I replied "Well, it looks like we've got it all sorted."

That night I told Pete what was going on, and asked if he was ok with it. He told me it wasn't a problem, and that he would miss having me around. At school the next day, I saw Mr. Cochrane and explained my situation, and he thought that we both needed to go have a talk with McPherson. After explaining the situation again, it was decided that, instead of doing them at odd times over a week, I could do as many of the exams in one session as I could handle, then do the rest the following day. As soon as my exams were finished, my answers would be sent off straight away. I should have my results in ten days if I could start the exams tomorrow. I had no problems with this, so it was decided for me to start the exams first thing in the morning, in the vice principal's office.

At work that afternoon, I told Mr Petersen what I was up to and then explained that I needed to go have a talk with my old man. He told to go see him then and not worry about how long it took. Dad was in his office. I took a seat and then told him I was leaving town in a couple of weeks, that I was intending to travel light, and could I drop off the rest of my stuff at home. He informed me that it was ok with him, and to drop it off whenever I was ready. Back at school the following morning, I reported to the office and Mr. Cochrane informed me he or McPherson would be overseeing me during the exams. With that, he passed the first paper to me with the answer sheet, asked if I was ready, and I got underway. That day I did five of the eight exams, and to tell the truth, I was knackered. Down at work Mr. Petersen said "You look dreadful," so I told him why. He asked "How do you think you Went?"

I replied "I think I did ok, but it was draining doing that many in one hit." Then with a laugh he said "Well, look at it this way, you've only got three to do tomorrow, and then you're finished."

Laughingly I replied "Gee, thanks." We both had a laugh, and then a much needed caffeine hit.

The following day, I knocked over the last three exams before twelve, so I left after Cochrane told me he'd send me a page when the results came back and we shook hands. I went back to the flat, and sorted out what would go with me and what would stay. I decided to travel in my old suit, so my new one went onto the bottom of my suitcase. Having sorted that out, about half past one I rang Barbara's. Betty answered and told me both Barb and Ray were there, so I told her I'd be up in a little while, jumped in the car and headed up there. This was going to be my last goodbye to them, so I started to get a bit emotional as I drove. When I arrived, I told them what was taking place and about just finishing my final exams. I said "Well, this is really going to be goodbye. You've been very good to me you're like parents-in-law to me and always will be. I can't thank you enough, and I'll never forget you." After that we got emotional, so after handshakes and kisses, a long embrace and kiss with Barbara, and with a promise to call if I got back, I left with tears in my eyes.

Arriving at work, I was still wiping the tears out of my eyes. Mr. Petersen looked enquiringly at me, so I said "I've just said goodbye to Barbara, and the Finlay's." He just nodded and headed out the back to make coffees. When he brought them out, he motioned for me to wait, pulled out a bottle of scotch from under the counter, poured a shot into each coffee, put the bottle back, then we clinked mugs and drank in silence.

CHAPTER 13

That weekend, I moved most of my remaining stuff back to my parents' place, and sorted it out in my old room. As I was finishing, dad came into the room and I said "The only thing left in the car is the Savage rifle. It's all cleaned and oiled, and back in its case. Where would you like that, and the ammo?" He replied "You may as well put in your wardrobe. Will you give it to John, if I teach him how to shoot, and look after it?" Answering that it would be ok, he then asked "Do you know where you're heading, and when you're going?" "Yes, first to Brisbane, and after that... well who knows, and I'll be leaving Wednesday week." He asked, "Do you know what you are going to be doing, and what about your exams?" I replied "Well, I've done the exams, and should get the results sometime this week; I'll let you know when. As for what I'm doing, yeah, I do know, you might not like it, so you'll find out after I come back. I'll get the Savage, then I have 'goodbyes' to be said to some people." Going to the car I collected the rifle, took it back inside, and my father said "Take care and we'll see you later in the week. Come up for dinner." Shaking his hand said "Ok, I will."

After dropping my stuff, I headed over to the other side of town to Skeeter's place. Over drinks I explained what had been going on, and some of the regrets I had. He said "Tiger, you did what you had to do. Think of it this way, at least you're getting out, and I wish I could say the same, but I'll probably end up growing old in this shithole of a place." We then started reminiscing about how life had turned out for the both of us; the good times we had, and the bad times. He said "I can still remember the first time you came over here, you were as jumpy as a cat," and I replied "well, of course, arsehole, I was ready for one hell of a brawl, just goes to show, huh." We laughed about that for a while, then I said "And you still owe me half of my recruitment money you got. prick!" With both of us laughing, he replied, "Fuck off!" This triggered a whole lot more memories which we talked about, as we slowly got drunker. Over dinner, that Joan had cooked, Skeeter said "I know what? Next weekend will be your last in this burg, and you're now single. Next weekend you stay here, we have a party, you're going away bash. Joan will get some of her mates over, and let's see if we can get you laid again before leaving town." I agreed, and the party was arranged to start at six, and I'd get over there about four, to have some pre party drinks between the three of us. As the night wore on, Joan decided I was staying the night, demanding I give her my keys. She told me my bed was made up in the spare room. So after a few more drinks, we all went to bed.

The next morning after breakfast, we were relaxing over coffee and smokes, when one of Joan's girlfriends, Karen, turned up, and introductions were made. She was a cute blond, about five four, with a very nice and shapely body. Skeeter looked at me with a questioning look, and I returned it with a smile and a nod. Joan also caught this byplay, and knowing that Karen was definitely interested in me, invited her along to the party, saying that Karen could be my partner at the party if we wished. I said "Sure" and Karen said "Oh, I'd like that idea." After the girls went inside, Skeeter said "You bloody charmer, you can't miss with her," and we both laughed. Shortly afterward, I was about to leave. I went inside to tell Joan I was off, pulled Karen into a kiss and said "I'll see YOU, next week," and she replied "I'll be looking forward to that!" Nodding to Joan, who had been watching this byplay with a smile, I went outside to say hooray to Skeeter, then headed home.

During the week, I received a page from Mr. Cochrane saying my results were in, and could be collected from the office. Mr. Petersen told me to go and get them, and we'd look at them when I got back. After a quick drive, I arrived at school and went to the office. Janet told me that McPherson had them, and let him know I was there. He came out of his office with my results, and said "Well done, Davis, another good result, you topped the school again. Good luck in the future." I took them and thanked him, and with a nod to Janet, left school for the last time.

Back at work, Mr Petersen made the coffees, and then we opened the report. After reading it, I said "Damn, I blew it. I missed getting straight, 'A's by getting a bloody 'B' in science, Christ! What was I thinking?" Mr. Petersen said "Tom! That's an excellent result, don't beat yourself up, you were under a lot of pressure when you took those exams, you've passed with flying colours!" I must admit I was quite pleased with the results. After phoning the old man, I went home for dinner that night. Before dinner I gave my parents my results, which they thought were excellent. I was still a little annoyed by not getting straight 'A's, but what the hell, it was a pass after all is said and done. Over dinner the rest of my siblings were informed that I was leaving town, but didn't know when I'd be back. So a lot of questions were asked and answered, then after a scotch and dry, and a cigar with dad, the goodbyes were said and I left.

After work on Saturday, I headed home. On the way I called up to the pub, picked up a carton of VB, a bottle of scotch, and two bottles of dry ginger ale. Ok, supplies for the night fixed. I continued to the flat, and decided what I was going to wear out of the assortment of old clothes that I was going to throw away when I left town. I then showered and spruced up a bit, and, with nothing else to do, decided to head to Skeeters early. I arrived about three, so I was only a little early, and it would give the beer time to chill down.

Giving Joan a kiss on the cheek, and my car keys, we sat and had a drink of coffee, while she told us about Karen's reaction to being partnered up with me for the night. She had told Karen she could stay the night if she wished to, and that Karen had asked if she could sleep with me. We all laughed when Joan told us that her answer had been, "That would be up to Tiger." After our coffees and a few smokes, we ended up talking about old times again. Around five we were about to crack open a couple of stubbies, when Karen turned up. As she came up the stairs with an

134

armload, she asked Joan where she could put her stuff, so I cheekily replied "In my room, I guess." "That's being forward, isn't it?" She asked. I answered her with a smile saying, "No, just truthful," and smiling she replied "Ok, then." She put her gear in with mine, and then joined us for a drink sitting right up close to me. I did notice Skeeter's wink and Joan's smile as she did this.

Well the party went well. By that I mean no one got too pissed, and neither Skeeter nor I had to biff anyone. It wound down about twelve, but a good night all the same. During the party, Karen was all over me, and wouldn't leave my side, keeping other girls away. So yeah; it looked as if I was on a sure thing. This proved to be the case, as when we got to the bedroom, she couldn't wait to get me out of my gear, and into bed. After we had cleaned the pipes out for her a few times, I got the usual "You're awesome" compliment. ("I'm definitely sure, that women practise saying that compliment!") However, saying that, Karen was nice to snuggle up to. The next morning, after a further cleaning out, I walked into the kitchen and joined Skeeter and Joan. Both had smiles on their dials as Joan said "Well we heard that you were having a goodnight." "Yeah, it was ok," I replied with a smile.

When Karen came out looking well pleased with herself she and Joan made breakfast, then we all lazed around with our coffees and smokes, talking and taking things easy. After lunch, I started to get my stuff together, and put some in the car. I realised that the scotch and the dry were still there, so took them inside to Skeeter and Joan, saying "Keep this til I get back and we'll have a drink together." Then it was time to go, so I hugged and kissed Joan, Skeeter hugged me and shook my hand, and said "You take care of yourself, brother." I said goodbye to Karen, by giving her a kiss and hug, jumped into the car and headed down the street; in the mirror I saw them out on the street watching me drive away.

That Wednesday morning my last day in town. I said my "goodbyes" and shook hands with Pete, and told him I'd leave my keys on the table. It was a strained emotional parting. We had lived together for nearly three years, so it wasn't easy saying goodbye to a friend, confidant, driving teacher, and damn good flexible flat mate. After he left for work, I did my final packing, put my travelling gear on a hanger, sorted out what I would wear during the day, and what clothes I would keep. They would go into the car til my return, and then put the rest, an old pair of shorts and a couple of shirts, into the garbage bin. I took everything to the car, and went back upstairs for a final check around. I put my flat keys on the table, had one last look at what had been my home for the past two and a half plus years, and with a tinge of regret, locked the door and headed to my final day at work.

Mr. Petersen had come in early, so he had a coffee waiting for me when I walked in. He said "good morning, Tiger, I knew you'd be here on time, and I just got these made before you walked in." Smiling, I thanked him and we both enjoyed our coffees in silence for the first few slurps. Then I talked to him about my goodbye with Pete, and my strange reaction to leaving the flat and said "Without the house keys on my key ring, it feels naked somehow." He had a wry grin on his face and said "That's perfectly understandable, you've lived there for nearly three years, and it's the first place you've lived away from your home, and you're leaving it to move on. You'll get used to it the more you move around from place to place." We didn't have much work to really do that day, so would stop every now and then for some deep and meaningful conversation. Sensing my mood, he asked "Starting to get excited, and feeling regret at leaving at the same time?" "Yes and no, at the same time, does that make sense?" I asked in reply, "Perfect sense, I felt the same way when I left my original home country. Of course you know I've had some changes in my life, in the way of jobs and places I've been, and truthfully I still wonder at times how my life would have turned out like, if I'd have stayed. At times through your life, you'll probably think the same thing, as you get older, or if you have a tough decision to make. Just remember to be true to yourself, and you'll make the right choices." As he imparted this wisdom, I took it on board more than he or I realised.

After lunch, Mr. Petersen went over to the bank. When he came back, he called me over to the counter, and said "Now, Tom, I need to explain this to you. Don't even think of protesting, what's done is done. Now I've made up your pay, given you four weeks holiday pay, an extra week as severance pay, and I got it in cash so you will have ready money available to you." I protested that by saying "Well, I haven't earned four weeks holiday pay yet, I'll take the rest though." He replied "Ah, Tom, you and your sense of honour and honesty. Ok, put it this way. In all the time you've worked for me, you've only had about five weeks off in those three years. So yes, you are entitled to it. Put it in your wallet, and let's have no further argument about it." I put the cash- just over two grand- into my wallet. What with the money I already had in there, my wallet was fairly bulging. Not surprising really, as there was over three grand in it now!

Our discussions and questions continued throughout the rest of the day. We were drawing out our parting as long as possible, and when we closed the shop, for me it was the last time. I looked back for a few minutes, and Mr. Petersen must have sensed my mood and train of thought. He put his arm around my shoulder and said "Don't worry, Tom, it'll be alright, and so will you." After that, we got into my car and made our way to the Petersen's house. When we got there, Doris gave Mr Petersen a kiss, then came and hugged me saying "I hope you like pork roast, because we can't send you out into the world without a decent meal!" During this time Mr Petersen was making drinks for all of us, and as he passed mine I said "Thanks, Mr.-Eric." He smiled and said "Tiger, we worked together for years. You earned the right to call me by my first name a long time ago, I'm glad you've finally done so." I replied by saying "Well, then not only were you a friend, but you were still my boss, and due respect. You're not my boss anymore, as of half an hour ago, but a close friend." As I said this, I was smiling, but noticed that he had tears in his eyes, and Doris WAS crying. We sat down with our drinks while Doris rushed into the kitchen to look after dinner. When she came back, her eyes were dry.

Dinner was great, and I said as much, then we relaxed after dinner with a couple more scotches and cigarettes. We made small talk until, inevitably, it was time to go. During our conversation, I fished out the shop keys from my pocket, and passed them across to Eric. I took my pager off, "I almost forgot this," and passed it over. Eric said "No, that's yours. I gave it to you and you keep it. Besides, it's got our numbers in it, in case you might need anything." Shortly afterward it was time to go, we all headed to my car, and I passed the keys to Eric. He got into the driver's seat, I held the door for Doris, she slid into the back, and then I got in. At the station, Eric popped the boot and I pulled out my suitcase and travel bag. We made our way onto the platform after saying our goodbyes, with handshakes and a hug and kiss from Doris. They headed home, while I made my way, rather misty eyed, to the cabin and carriage number.

After I had settled myself in, the train began to pull out, so I thought I would celebrate my leaving town with a drink, and headed to the club car. When I got there, after ordering a scotch and dry, I watched the last of town go by with a raised glass, and then drank it down. As I ordered another at the bar, I looked around; the only others in the car were three women playing cards. Wondering to myself if I could get lucky again, I sauntered over, glass in hand, and asked if they needed a fourth player. I was asked if I knew how to play five hundred, and after stating that I did, the one that asked slid over and I sat down.

I introduced myself as the cards were dealt. The older ladies were Sue and Iris who were travelling together, and the other younger one was Ellen, who was my partner. I noticed that Ellen wasn't wearing any rings, and thought I might be lucky. I enquired if any of them would like a drink prior to starting the game. Ellen asked for a scotch, while Iris and Sue elected for beers. During the first couple of hands, I realised that Ellen could play and call well, and was a good playing partner. After the first game that we won, I ordered another round of drinks, and play went on. Iris and Sue won the next game. At the start of the decider, I was dealt a near perfect hand, only missing the joker. It was my first call, so I called six spades. Sue took it to six hearts, then Ellen called six no trumps. Iris took it to seven hearts. Thinking "In for a penny, in for a pound," I made a suicidal call of slam no trumps, not knowing what was in my partner's hand. I picked up the kitty, and as I did, I took note that Ellen was rubbing her ring finger. I gave her a quick smile, and threw out three hearts from my hand. I started leading out with my spade run, noticing that Ellen was throwing out her rubbish. After seven tricks, my spades were gone, and led out with a small diamond, which was taken by Ellen with the king. She then led out the ace of diamonds, and then the joker which she called a club, yes! Game, set, and match to us in one hand.

Just as we finished, the barman came over and asked if there were any last drinks, because he was about to close the bar. Iris and Sue were going off to bed, but Ellen asked for two scotches and mine was the same. I moved over to sit beside her, and she told me she was going to Brisbane for a nursing conference. I told her about Barbara and why we broke up, and then I told her why I was going to Brisbane and not knowing where I was going to end up. We then started some heavy flirting. Learning that she was in a seating car, and had been since Townsville, I then gave her, an open invitation to my cabin. I didn't give her any pushing; I was going to let her decide. But after our drinks were finished, she asked me to lead the way, and grabbed hold of my hand. Inside my cabin, the bed had been made up, and she remarked, "Oh, this is cosy," then turned and put her arms around my waist. We started kissing gently at first and then getting very passionate and hungry. After coming out of our embrace, she asked if she could have a shower. I opened the door for her and told her to go ahead. I put her clothes on the window table as she undressed and got the shower running.

I asked if she would like her back done, and she replied by saying "Be my guest," so I stripped and joined her in the shower, and we did more than clean each other's back, which involved some heavy petting and exploring hands. Drying each other off, we then climbed into bed and continued our explorations, and very soon she was moaning in ecstasy with each of my hand movements. I brought her to a climax before even entering her, and as her moaning subsided, I slipped over her leg and penetrated her as far as I could go. This brought a further moan of ecstasy and she started to move under me. I brought her to four more orgasms before flooding into her as she reached another orgasm, which elicited a cry of abandonment. As we lay there relaxing in each other's arms, I received the usual compliments before we settled into sleep, still within each other's arms. The next morning after showering and getting dressed, we joined Iris and Sue in the dining car, had breakfast, and then went back to the club for coffee and smokes and began playing cards again.

Having filled in a few hours with cards, we all went back to the dining car for lunch before continuing the card game, with drinks and smokes.

We continued playing cards until we started to pass the Glasshouse Mountains, which meant we were getting close to Brisbane. We decided that the game we were playing would finish our match that had kept us all occupied during the journey. Ellen called eight hearts, and I had a few good ones that would back her up. We won the hand and also the game. We thanked each other for the company and games, and then headed our separate ways to prepare for the run into Brisbane. Ellen came back to the cabin with me. When we were inside the cabin, I pulled her into an embrace, and as I was kissing her, ran my hand up her back which elicited a pleasurable moan. When we broke the embrace, I said "We have time for a quickie, if you're so inclined." She replied "The offer is very tempting, however I don't think there's such a thing when you are involved. You've made a dull trip very enjoyable, and I know now why your girlfriend didn't want to let you go, you're sensational!" During her comment I noticed that we were going through Caboolture. She continued "I suppose I'd best go and get my things sorted out," so I her pulled her into a last long embrace. She continued as we let each other go, "Whew! You're quite addictive. Thank you, for a very, very enjoyable and remarkable journey; I better go before I change my mind." With one last kiss, I opened the door for her, and she headed towards the sitting section of the train.

I tidied myself up, got my things together, then put my suitcase and travel bag on the seat. I smiled in remembrance, and thought to myself, well I did get lucky after all, and then watched the outskirts of Brisbane roll by. The train arrived at Roma St. Station at ten past four, and as it stopped I made my way casually to the carriage doorway, and onto the platform. Because I knew where I was this time, I decided to walk on up to the People's Palace. I checked in, went up to my room, and after a quick freshen up, headed out to the pub I had come to know. I greeted Sheila by name, and asked for a pot, and after three slow drinks, headed back up to the Palace to have dinner. The cooking hadn't improved at all, and after dinner I went up to my room and read a little before settling down for the night.

After breakfast the next morning, I repacked, checked out and headed to the recruitment office. I had a pleasurable relaxed smoke while waiting for them to open. By the time they did open, there was a bunch of us, all waiting with suitcases and luggage. As the office opened, a Sergeant came out and addressed us, "Ok guys, I just need to check who's here, then I'll tell you what will be happening" and with that called the first name.

Everyone on his list was there, so he continued to explain what would be happening. First off, a bus would arrive soon, we would board, and it would take us to Amberley Air Base, outside of Ipswich. Then after smoko, we would get onto a Hercules c-130, and be flown to Wagga Wagga Air Base. Then onto another bus and taken to Kapooka Army Barracks, where we would be doing our recruit training, and that we would get further instructions once there.

After the time it took to smoke another couple of cigarettes, the bus arrived, and we began our journey....and the next part of our lives!

CHAPTER 14

Well, the trip to Amberley gave me time to introduce myself and receive intros in return. We arrived on base, and were taken to the mess for smoko, and the quality of the food had me wondering that maybe I should have considered the RAAF after all! We then boarded the Hercules for our flight south. We got all the mod cons: aircraft to ourselves, except for our luggage and some supplies, these were packed into baskets that took up the width of the plane. The seats were really good, aluminium pipes fitted to the sides and floor, threaded with cargo netting straps, and seat belts? Well, what seat belts? The safety brief consisted of where the throw up bags were, and where the life jackets were kept. We wouldn't be over water, so probably wouldn't need them. The inflight movie was watching the crew work around the plane, and talking amongst ourselves or playing cards.

We landed in Wagga in the late afternoon, and instead of going on straight away, we had dinner in the mess courtesy of the RAAF. Well-fed, we awaited the arrival of the bus coming to pick us up for the short journey to Kapooka. As the bus pulled up, a Sergeant got off and addressed us. "Ok, listen up; as I call your name, answer, and move onto the bus with your case. What will happen tonight is you will move into your quarters, you will find bedding and a set of greens on your bunk. Reveille is at zero six hundred. Get up, make your bunks, then a platoon sergeant will take over, take you to breakfast, and then inform you of the day's activities. Are there any questions?" When no one spoke up he said "Good." and called us in alphabetical order.

The next morning our platoon sergeant, Sgt Lance Kendrick, made his way into our quarters, bellowing at us to form up, which meant standing at attention at the end of our bunks. He looked each of us over, and we did the same to him. He was in his mid-thirties, lean, about five nine or ten, with black hair and wearing a form fitting set of greens, compared to us standing there in our ill-fitting and loose uniforms. Shaking his head, and said "Just as well we're going to the Q store after breakfast," and then told us what would be happening for the rest of the day. This consisted of the Q (Quartermaster) store after breakfast, for issue of uniforms, belts, work boots, and full kits, and measurement for dress uniforms and shoes. Then we into the classroom for orientation lectures, and then haircuts before lunch. Then more orientation lectures, being shown where places were on base, and briefings by Sgt Kendrick; all this would end before going to the mess for dinner. We would then have the rest of the time off duty until the following morning.

After breakfast, off to the Q store we went. The first thing was to have our measurements recorded. This served two purposes; one the sizing for our Dress Uniforms, and secondly so we could be issued better fitting work greens. The very first thing we received in the production line style of issue was a large foot locker. This came in very handy for putting the ever growing mountain of gear issue into, and for transporting it back to the barracks. We were issued hats, belts, boots, field packs, ammo pouches, eating tins, utensils, webbing belts, and the list goes on. Even with the foot locker, all this stuff brimmed over, so it was really hard work getting all of it back to our barracks. Deciding this was going to be a bit difficult, I joined up with one of my fellow recruits, Mervin Baker. We got everything squashed down into the lockers, so we could sit one locker on top of the other, and then we lifted both together at each end, and started heading to the barracks building. Sgt Kendrick thought that this was a smart way of doing it and told us to proceed then return.

When Merv and I returned, some of the others had come out from the Q store, and had their gear issue standing in front of them while they were waiting. Sgt Kendrick called me forward, and asked "What's your name, soldier?" and I replied with, "Davis, Tom D serial number 02106688101, sir!" and he then said "Right Davis, don't call me sir. I'm not an officer, I work for a living!

Now explain to these others how you and your mate took your stuff back to the barracks." Replying "Yes, Sergeant," I then told the guys how Merv and I managed it. Kendrick then addressed them saying "Right, you heard the man. Now get to it and return smartish!" Kendrick had me explain how to get the stuff to the barracks to the rest of the guys as each new pair exited the Q store. Then we were allowed a smoke break while waiting for everyone to return. Kendrick then told Merv and I, to call him out of the Q store when everyone had returned. So when everyone was back, I nodded to Merv, and he called Sgt Kendrick, who came out and bellowed, "Davis, get them formed up!" Now, not having a clue as how to go about this, I bluffed my way through by having them line up three deep by seven in a line, facing away from the store. Merv and myself being in the front rank, Kendrick came to face us, and said "Sloppy, but reasonable. Now I'm going to teach you how to form up properly." Using Merv and me as the practice dummies, he continued, "From now on, anywhere you go on base, you march. Now, right turn straight ahead Quick March!"

Calling out the feet we should have been on, and getting us to swing our arms more or less dependent on the person, we learned the basics of marching. All the time teaching us how to turn and wheel properly, we made our way to the barbershop, and not just for trims. We all ended up with a number three crew cut all over, "So who said style was dead?" I thought to myself as I left the seat, feeling rather naked on top.

The next session was held in the classroom barracks, where we would receive all our lecture sessions. The first being an overview of how all our gear was to be assembled. Just as well we were given handouts, as it was a lot to take in. The next lecture was about the training we would get, and in what order. For example, all of the following week would focus on drilling, fitness, and our first time at trying the obstacle course. We were shown an aerial view of the base, which showed the different areas that we would be using. Most of this would come up in our walk around tour that afternoon, and then the different ranks within the defence forces, and how we should conduct ourselves when being approached, addressed, and leaving the presence of officers. Then we broke for lunch.

After lunch, as we were about to start the lecture, I raised my hand to ask a question, concerning the discussion that some of us were having over lunch. I was acknowledged and I asked "Sarge if we wanted to go for a drink, do we have to go off base?" Kendrick replied "Sorry to you all, my mistake, I forgot to mention this earlier, thanks for bringing this up Davis." He told us that all ranks had both wet and dry messes, dry being for meals, but the wet mess was for after work hours and was essentially the pub, with reduced prices. There were three mess rankings; the OR's (other ranks) mess, for all junior ranks, the Sergeant's mess, for sergeants and non-commissioned officers, and the Officer's mess, for all officers. The OR's wet mess only operated from four til ten pm every day. With that point taken care of, the lecture continued. It was about what weapons were in use within the defence force, and more importantly, which weapons we would be issued, and the different types that we would actually learn to fire! After the lecture, it was time for our walk, or should I say March, of discovery. With a "Take them outside and form them up Davis, dismissed!" We left the classroom, and formed up into ranks outside.

Leaving the classroom behind, the first tour was around the building lines, with the occasional halt for Sgt Kendrick to explain, or point something out, that we were required to know. Christ, this place was big! Just as well we were getting this tour otherwise I'd have never found anything, this place covered acres and acres of land! One of the buildings was the base dry cleaners and laundry; this was run by civilian contractors, and was where we could get any clothing alterations done, for a price of course. Most alterations were back on base usually within twenty four hours. Continuing our march, Kendrick showed us the base swimming and diving pool, the chapel, the base medical unit, the armoury, the base headquarters offices. We then moved onto the sports fields, the firing range, the explosives range, and last of all, the obstacle course. After explaining the course to us, he then had us walk the entire course, taking everything in, and then informed us that everyone had to complete this course every week, and was timed each time.

Kendrick then had us sit in a group. Allowing us to smoke, he explained that because the next day was Sunday, not much work was done. After the issue of stores to us, we needed time to put everything together, blacken and polish belts, shine shoes and boots, and generally sort our things out. We would be left on our own to accomplish this tomorrow, and that everything should be in proper working order come first thing Monday morning, when our training would begin in earnest. He continued by telling us to try each of our new uniforms on, and make sure that we were wearing the closest fitting clothes on Monday. There would be time given for us to get to the laundry and have alterations attended to, so that by the end of the week, we would at least look like soldiers. Also because we were in the machine now, we were expected to know military jargon. Most of these terms were in one of the handouts we were given earlier in the day. We were now soldiers, not civilians, as we were formerly.

He had one last thing to cover, so as we all lit up, he said "Now, in each platoon, there is usually a couple of members that show good leadership, and they are given an honorary rank in the platoon and are the go-to men, prior to coming to me, or any platoon sergeant. Are there any nominations, or do I pick someone?" Merv put his hand up saying, "How about Tiger Davis, Sergeant?" As Kendrick looked around, there were nods of agreement, and he asked "Anyone else?" There wasn't any, so he said "Davis, step forward." Feeling surprised and amused, I did as requested. He pulled out a Velcro Corporal's insignia armband, and showed me how to put it on. He asked "You know that big room with the desk in it, in your dorm?" I nodded and he continued, "Move your stuff into that room, Corporal. You're now my 2IC, any questions?"

As I replied, "No, Sergeant," he passed me another armband insignia for Lance Corporal, and said "Now Corporal Davis will be looking for a 2IC (second in command). I'll be leaving that choice to him and you. Ok, smokes out, and form up!" With that, we marched back to the barracks and were dismissed. We were on our own til Monday morning. After I had moved my gear into the private room, and sorted out what was going where, I asked if any of the guys would like to have a few drinks before dinner, and most of us headed to the wet mess.

Over congratulatory drinks at the mess, I learned more about the guys in my platoon; where they lived, and what they did in civilian life, why they joined, a few still had girlfriends, a couple were engaged, and one was actually married! They ranged in age from eighteen to twenty two. So, I was the youngest! Not that they knew that. We discussed what we thought of the green machine (Army), Kendrick, the Q store really caught a roasting, and what we had learned during the day. After dinner, I was back at the mess, and over a couple quiet drinks, contemplated the last few days. I was quite pleased with myself, in the army only two days and already a Corporal! Granted it was only honorary, but pretty good all the same. Sgt Kendrick seemed tough, but fair, had he been older I suppose I would have compared him to Jack Robertson. Fleetingly, because I felt a bit lonely, I wondered how everyone was getting on at home. Funny, I couldn't wait to get out of there, and now I was calling it home.

Sunday morning, only day three in the green machine, I really missed the RAAF meals. After four meals, I knew why Army cooks are called "fitters and turners." They fit everything into a pot or pan, and turn it into shit. After a so called breakfast, the platoon looked to me for guidance. So being the good NCO that I was, I had everyone putting their field gear together, as per regulation. When I finished putting my own gear in order, after a few screw ups and re working, so that the webbing and everything fit to near as perfect that I could get it, I walked into the main dorm area to see how everyone was progressing. I also wanted to assess the possible candidates I had in mind to get the Lance Corporal stripe. There were two frontrunners, being Merv and John. Both had completed their own work, and both were helping some of the others. As I came into the room, Merv spotted me and called "Attention!" When he called, everyone stopped what they were doing, and stood at the end of their bunks at attention. I asked "How's everyone going?" Merv replied "We're getting there, Corp." I then said "Good, after this we'll blacken our dress belts."

I let the work carry on, and after everyone had sorted out the field webbing, went to my room and returned, holding up my dress belt. I asked with a laugh "Anyone got some black shoe polish?" Everyone started laughing, and I had to duck as a couple cans of black polish that came flying my way. Laughing, I said "Okay, we don't want to shit up the floor or our beds, otherwise someone has to clean them, so let's do all this shit outside, and DON"T forget your boots." Outside we commandeered all the available rubbish bins, and as I, tongue in cheek, sang "This is the way we polish our belts," everyone laughingly took up the same chorus. Applying boot polish to our green web belts was hard going. First of all you smeared the belt in polish, then applied another coat and polished the crap out of them, wiping as much of the excess polish off from the inside of the belt. After finishing our hands were smeared with black polish. Of course, after the first couple of wears our daily greens ended up with black smears around the belt area, really requiring a trip to the laundry!

After finishing the belts, we moved on to our boots, and I said "Ok listen up. If Merv, John, or I can't see a reflection in the boots, there're not good enough!"! When we were finished, I looked at each pair, followed by John and Merv all were good so I said with a laugh "Great. Now what's the bet, it'll rain tomorrow and these'll all get dirty, and we have to do them again!" This was followed by laughter. As we all sat around smoking and talking, I asked "Has anyone got any uniform hassles?" Sure enough just about every hand went up, and I said "Yeah, mine fit like shit as well, and are as scratchy as hell. I'll make sure we all get time to go to the laundry tomorrow. Now when we head off for lunch, don't forget to grab something to clean the brass work for these frigging belts. When everyone is ready we'll head to lunch." As I was putting some stuff away in my room, Merv knocked, and informed me they were ready to head to the mess, so we marched off to the mess for lunch.

During lunch I talked a bit more with John. He was from Emerald, and had been working on a cattle station before joining. Seeing he was from up my way, we talked about locations and people we knew or had heard of. When I asked why he joined, he answered, "I know that conscription will come in, and I'd probably get picked, so instead of going onto another station, thought I may as well get it over with, so here I am." We also talked about the corps we were both interested in joining, which was transport. Then I asked him to consider taking the 2IC job on, and he said that he would consider it. I thought about it for a while, trying to decide who would be better suited, Merv or John. I would have a talk to Merv after lunch back at the barracks, and see what his thoughts were, after everyone had finished getting ready for tomorrow.

We finished getting ourselves and our gear ready for tomorrow. I had been looking into the other vacant rooms in the dorm, and one was slightly smaller than mine, mainly because it didn't have a desk in it. The other one only had a table and four chairs around the table, no bed or wardrobe; this was obviously a meeting room of sorts. I called Merv into my room, and when we were both seated at the desk, I asked "How's it all going?" He replied "Just great," and told me that he had been talking to members from the other three recruit platoons. None of them had elected a corporal, or were anyway near as ready as our platoon was for tomorrow, and said "We're so far in front of the others, it's not funny." But we were laughing and smiling all the same.

Then I broached the subject of the 2IC's job by asking "John Buchanan is thinking about the platoon 2IC's job. What about you?" He replied "No, thanks all the same, but I'd rather just stay the way I am. I want to get this basic training out of the way, and get into the corp training down at Albury. I've decided to go for cavalry, I want to try APC's (Armoured Personnel Carriers), but, I'll give you as much help as I can, Tiger." Well, that was a turn up; I had mistaken his keenness for getting the job done for wishing to be promoted. I now had some reassessment to do with my thinking, and observation of people. Mind you; I was still spot on, John had the right flair. He would probably take the job on, thereby confirming my training from Eric Petersen. After thanking Merv for his honesty, he rose and left my room. I got changed into some sports gear, went into the dorm, and called out "I think we can call it a day. If anyone wants to join me, I'm heading out to do a couple laps of the oval." John and a couple others said they'd join me, so I waited for them to get changed, and then we headed to the sports oval.

As we were jogging around the oval, John came up beside me, and after glancing around to make sure no one would hear us, asked "Corp, are you THE Tiger Davis of the 'Raiders'?" Also glancing around, I answered "Yes, why?" He replied "Well, the paper I read stated that you started playing for them when you were twelve, and that you only quit playing this year after three seasons. Wouldn't that make you only sixteen?" Before answering, I motioned for him to take a seat off the oval, and we both moved onto a bench around the perimeter of the oval fence and then I replied to his question.

"Fifteen actually, I'm not sixteen yet, so yes, I lied about my age to join." I then told him why I had done it, and then asked "But the real question is, now that you know about this, WHAT are YOU going to do about it?" Laughing, he replied "Nothing. I threw that paper away last week, and I haven't said anything to anybody about it. Besides us country boys have to stick together. I'll not be saying or, doing anything about whatever we were talking about." He held his hand out, and I shook it, and we both nodded and laughed. I then said to him "I still want you to take the 2IC job, though." He replied "Alright, I'll do it, but you owe me a beer." I corrected him by saying "We owe EACH other a beer, or three." We waited for the other guys to come round, and then did another lap before heading back to the barracks.

When I got back to the hut, I went into my room, grabbed the lance corporal stripe to give to John. In the main dorm I asked if everyone was there, and Merv said they were. I told everyone that John was now my new 2IC and presented him with the stripe, and told him to move into the room opposite mine when he was ready. I then told everyone to be showered and ready to go to dinner by seventeen thirty (half past five) and then they could do what they wished. I warned them not to have sore heads in the morning, as we would probably be in for a gruelling day.

We all went to dinner, and after that most of the platoon and me went off to the mess. As I walked in the door, I did a quick perusal of the notice board, and found a note pinned to the board addressed to me. It was from Sgt Kendrick, saying he would be at our hut at zero seven hundred, to discuss the order of the day, dress, and a few other items. I was expected to meet with him in the conference room of the hut, being the room with table and chairs. The rest of the platoon was expected to be ready for work at zero eight hundred, in fatigues (greens and boots). I did notice that even though it was addressed to me, it also had the designation of our platoon, which was 'Alpha'. That would mean the other platoons would have a designation of Bravo, Charlie, and Delta, (being one through to four). Our platoon was designated as 'Alpha' therefore number one, Bravo-two, Charlie-three, and Delta-four. Christ! You have to give the green machine 'A' for effort, with this jargon rigmarole! What a piss off! The mess also operated as the supplies canteen, so I asked Merv to grab me a can of 'Brasso' as he got the next round in. Mine was almost empty due to today's preparations, and others not having any of their own. I did show the note to John and said "I think you had better be in on this, unless Kendrick decides otherwise."

Monday morning, and right on time, Kendrick strode into the conference room where John and I were having coffee. John offered to make him a cup and was given a "Yes, thanks, standard NATO (white with two sugar)." As he received his coffee, he said "Glad to see you've picked your 2IC," and asked John for his particulars. He then commented "Got to trust the Queenslanders to stick together." We then got down to the matters in hand. These included a list of duties John and I had to perform, the fact that one platoon member had to be rostered to perform duties at the mess each day, and one for kitchen duties, as well as do their normal routine work. One member was to be responsible for the cleanliness of the hut and ablutions; otherwise we were in the shit. As NCO's, we would also need to meet each afternoon and morning to discuss the following day's activities, dress and requirements, and the timetable for each day. For example, today we would be on the parade square for an hour, followed by two lecture sessions, a half hour break to attend to laundry and uniform matters, lunch, onto our first run through the obstacle course, then knock off at sixteen hundred (four pm).

Sgt Kendrick also informed us that, due to a new procedure, we would probably be observed by two or more persons dressed in civilian attire at times during our training. He informed us they were green machine members, but would far outrank us, and to take no notice of them, unless we were addressed by them. I thought this a bit strange, but kept it to myself, and just as well that I did!

CHAPTER 15

After Kendrick had helped John and I draw up the first duty roster, he informed us that the uniform of the day would be the standard base uniform; greens, boots, and bush hats. He then said "Ok, I'll be back at zero eight hundred, have the men outside formed up ready to go." With that, he left us to get on with it. John and I finished the duty rosters over breakfast, and informed the guys of the duty rosters pinned to the barracks notice board, the dress of the day, and the day's activities. I took the first shift at the mess John took the kitchen, we rostered Merv for the barracks, then each of the other guys were given their turn.

When Kendrick returned at eight, we were outside formed up and ready to roll. He ordered the front rank to take two steps forward and the middle rank one step forward. Having me join him, he then did a quick inspection of everyone. He then had us reform the ranks, and then said "Well done, ladies, just have a glance down the road at the other platoons. Compared to that bunch of misfits and mummy's boys, you look like proper soldiers. This is Alpha Platoon, meaning number one, and I expect you to keep this standard up and better it, in your dress and in your training every day. Is that understood?" "Yes, Sergeant!" we all chorused out. He continued "Now, stand easy while your, Corporals and I inspect the barracks." John and I joined him, and we marched into the barracks.

Inside he told us to relax as we did a quick look around the barracks. After looking at the duty roster, he said "You two aren't to go on this roster, you will both have enough to do, so change it around then we'll go back outside." After redoing the roster, we went back outside and John and I re-joined the ranks. Kendrick said "Ok, girls; well done for now, but get it better! I have withdrawn both your Corporals from the duty rosters; they have enough work to do, so take note of the changes during lunch. Right attention! Left face! Quick, March!" What followed was a gruelling hour of solid marching, feet stomping as we were brought to a halt. Turns left and right, wheeling turns both right and left, and about face turns. By the end of that hour, most of us were stuffed, the temperature had already reached thirty degrees, and with the new boots wearing in, I thought I'd be lucky if I didn't end up breaking some blisters by the end of the day. All I wanted to do was get those damn boots off!

By putting both lectures together, Kendrick saved us some time, and we were dismissed until after lunch. We all returned to the barracks, grabbed the uniforms that needed attending to, and headed off to the laundry. After that I returned to my room to take those bloody boots off. After checking my feet, surprisingly enough I only had two blisters on each foot, a blister on the heel of each foot and one on the side of each foot beside my small toe. I put on a pair of issue sandshoes, and that was a relief, luckily they were to be worn for the rest of the afternoon on the obstacle course.

That afternoon we were marched down to the obstacle course, then as a group walked through it. It had looked fairly easy the other day, but after going through all of it, I was having second thoughts. Having had a break, it was then time to tackle it individually, while being timed. Shit! I was first up, and after a two second gap, followed by John and all the others. Now, I considered myself really fit, but after finishing the course in that heat I was blowing hard. While I was waiting, I guess I would have drunk close to half a gallon of water from the tap, beside the timing platform. After everyone had finished, Kendrick gave us our timings, I had come in with twenty three minutes, and was told that this was the fastest time of any recruit for their first time on the course. The rest of the platoon had all come in under thirty minutes. Again a new course record! Fan-bloody-tastic! Sgt Kendrick congratulated all of us, and then told us we could practise on the course anytime during normal hours that it wasn't in use.

After having a smoke break, we were marched back to the

barracks and dismissed for the day, except for the guys rostered to jobs at the kitchen and mess. John and I then had our afternoon briefing with Kendrick. The first order of business was the day's performance, which as far as Kendrick was concerned, was excellent for first day recruits. John and I were asked for our input, and recommendations for improvement. I said "Well, if we are allowed to continue in a set routine, and other training elements are introduced bit by bit, then there's no reason why we can't all improve." Kendrick replied, "Well said, and that's exactly the way the course is structured, but it also comes down to the leadership that you two show. I must say that you will both make good NCO's in your future careers, and I will be making those notations in your files."

The next order of business was the following day, which would be more drilling, this time with saluting practice, then into the lecture room, over to the armoury after lunch, then onto the firing range that afternoon. Therefore dress for the day would be base standard, with slouch hats in the morning for drilling, instead of the normal bush hat, and field gear for the firing range. Kendrick had one more order of business. Wednesday afternoon was reserved as sport afternoon, and he asked "Is it possible to put together a team of ten for a touch football game of rugby league, against one of the other platoons?" John just laughed and I smiled, and because of Kendrick's questioning look, John said "Tiger here used to play professionally for an 'A' grade team in his hometown." Knowing some of the background of some of the other platoon members, I said "Yep, I think we could put a good team together." "Excellent, I'll arrange it," Kendrick replied and dismissed us for the day.

After he had left, John and I made up the SOP's (Standard Operating Procedure) for the following day, and also a notice calling for an expression of interest in the footy team. Then I said to John, "I suppose we'd better get in there and inform the platoon about needing the slouchies tomorrow. Is yours bashed into shape?" "No, we'd better get onto that," he replied. So after pinning the notices up, we informed the other guys about the need to get our hats bashed. A good many of them weren't sure how to do this so John and I grabbed ours, took the bands off, and then had them follow us outside to the rain barrel. We showed them how to soak the fur felt hats, get them really saturated, and then put the shape into them. After shaping and trying them on with the chin strap in place, we hooked the left brim into place, and then tried them on again. With my hat still on, my hair, and face wet from the water dripping out of my hat said, "The trick is to wear them until they are somewhat dry. Now don't forget that if you take them off, they're going to shrink as they dry, so unless you wear them as much as possible while drying, you might end up with sore heads after a few hours once they have dried. After dinner, we put them on again until lights out, and then again first thing in the morning, just to keep them from shrinking too much. Turning to John I continued, "Make sure the other two on duty know, so they can get theirs done." "Right, Corp." was his reply. Then everyone got on with bashing their hats. I guess we looked a bit silly, walking around the barracks with our hats on, but that was my blue. I hadn't thought of doing it over the weekend.

The next morning we were outside, formed up for inspection, and as Kendrick arrived I called "Atten...Shun!" After a quick inspection, we went into the barracks for the once over, and then moved back outside. Kendrick said, "Well done, ladies, you're getting better. Are you trying to impress me?" As one we replied "Yes, Sergeant!" He replied "Good, Right face! Quick March! Left, left, left right left. Call it, Corporal!" I called it, and Kendrick would occasionally give the order to left, or right wheel, or turn, as we made our way to the drilling Quadrangle. For the next hour, we went through a series of marching and saluting manoeuvres. As we were called to a halt, Kendrick said "You're getting better, girls. Now Corporal Davis, march the platoon to the classroom, then have a smoke break, until I join you!" "Yes Sergeant!" I replied, and then continued "platoon! Atten...shun, by the right, Quick March, left. Call it, Corporal Buchanan!" As John called the feet, I steered the platoon to the classroom barracks. Once there, I called, "Platoon halt, and fall out!" Then we had a smoke while waiting for Kendrick.

Kendrick came out of the classroom barracks about ten minutes later, directed me to move the platoon inside, and to remove our hats and be seated. As we moved into the room, I noticed three weapons on the front table; a rifle, a pistol, and what looked like a sub-machine gun. Just as we took our seats, Kendrick barked "Atten...shun!" As we snapped to attention, a Captain entered and said "As you were." After we sat, he introduced himself as Captain Jacobs, the senior firing range officer. He was going to teach us about the firing range SOP's, and familiarise us with the weapons we would be using later in the day.

He started with range etiquette, which was mainly to do with safety. The main point was that if we shifted our weapons from facing the targets, or turned in any way, we'd be clobbered, and knocked off our feet, by the instructing range staff beside us! If we had a problem in any shape or form, we were to raise our hand without turning from the front. Captain Jacobs moved on to explain the workings and the cleaning of weapons. The first was the French design SLR (Self Loading Rifle). It fired a seven point six two calibre round, the standard NATO military round, and carried a magazine with a twenty round capacity. It was the main assault weapon carried by Australian soldiers. He also showed us how to adjust the gas settings, for self-reloading, and how to prevent ammunition feed jam.

When he explained this, I raised my hand to ask a question for two reasons. One, I was ambidextrous, and two, I knew a couple in the platoon were molly duikers, or south paws (left handed). After being acknowledged, my question was "Sir, if the ejected round flies out the right side, how can someone who shoots both ways, or left handed, compensate so they're not hit in the face with the ejected round?" "Good point, Corporal," he replied and then continued with his answer. "In that case, the best thing to do is experiment with the gas setting, so that the ejection is not as hard, but doesn't produce a feed jam, and it could be a very fine line.

157

Does that answer your question?" Glancing around to check if the left handers had got it, I noticed two other people dressed in civilian attire at the back of the room, and then replied "Yes, Sir."

"Good, moving on," he said and picked up the sub machine gun. "This is the M Forty, and for those of you that have seen war movies, yes, it looks like the British Sten gun. As a matter of fact, its design is based on that weapon, but as you can see, the magazine feeds from the top, and has a forty round capacity. It fires a nine milli-metre round. When firing these, they have a tendency to pull up to the right, so be aware! To fire it you need to hold it like this," and he proceeded to demonstrate. After showing us the pull down and cleaning procedure, he picked up the pistol. The Browning pistol was an automatic nine millimetres. The magazine fed through the handle, with a capacity of nine rounds and one in the breech. It was the main handgun used by officers and senior NCO's; again, its main characteristic was to pull up to the right. After running through the pull down and cleaning routine, he ended the lecture session with, "Any questions? Good I'll see you all on the range this afternoon, thank you, Sergeant!" Kendrick brought us to attention as Jacobs nodded at Kendrick as he saluted, and left the room.

After we returned to our seats, Kendrick came back to the front of the room. After having a quick conflab (conversation) with the two civilians, they left the room. He then said "Ok, soon we'll march to the armoury, where you'll be issued with a rifle, and cleaning kit. Back at your barracks, you'll fill your gun oil containers like this, (holding up a small green plastic bottle with a nozzle) and put it in your field gear, along with some cleaning cotton. At thirteen hundred we'll march to the range for live firing. Corporal Buchanan, move them outside. Corporal Davis, stay!" John got the guys out then Kendrick had me help him with the weapons. Outside, the platoon was formed up and Kendrick had John march them to the armoury. As we followed Kendrick said "When we're at the armoury, I want you to sign out a four litre container of gun oil and two rolls of gun cotton. They can be stored in the barracks. After you get the oil containers filled and give out some cotton to each man, have lunch then get them formed up ready to go at thirteen hundred." I replied "Sarge what about ammo?" He said "Don't worry about the ammo. All we'll need will already be at the range and the staff there will be issuing that." "Ok, Sarge" I replied.

Once we were all issued weapons, and the extras, we were formed up outside. Kendrick then marched us back to our barracks and dismissed us till later. After doing all the necessaries, we headed off to lunch. I was back at the barracks by quarter to one, having a smoke and looking forward to the range. I couldn't wait to see what the capabilities of the SLR were, and also looked forward to having a go at the Browning. After my smoke, I went to see if everyone was ready to go, and it seemed that I wasn't the only one raring to go. Everyone was dressed in their field gear and just waiting around. I told them to have one last smoke before we went out to form up.

When Kendrick arrived, using John and myself as the practise dummies, he taught us how to hold our rifles the correct way when at attention and at ease. How to ground weapons, how to salute with weapons, and how to march with our rifles slung on our shoulders. Because that was the last thing, John and I fell in, and we marched off to the firing range.

At the range we were ordered to stand easy, as Captain Jacobs briefed us about what would be happening. First we would move onto the firing line, and each of us would have an instructor standing beside or behind us. We would fire three rounds, make sight adjustments with the aid of instructors, fire another three rounds, make any last minute adjustments, and then fire seven rounds for a grouping. All this would take place in the prone position (lying belly down). Then, after targets were changed, fire seven while kneeling, wait for the target exchange, and then fire seven while standing. He then asked "Any questions?"

My hand went up and I asked "Sir is it possible for me to fire twice after the sighting adjustments, due to the fact I'm ambidextrous?" As he was considering my request, I noticed the two civilians were again present. Just standing off to the left of our platoon, Jacobs said "You can join the last group, and fire again from position eight, Corporal Davis." "Thank you, Sir," I replied.

The first group was up, and as we took our positions, Jacobs stepped up into the command tower, and over the PA told us to raise our hands if we were ready, which we did. He then gave the command to fire in our own time. After three shots, the first mag was empty. My sights were off to the left, the instructor showed me how make the sight adjustment, then I was ready to go again. I was handed a magazine with three rounds, then fired again. Perfect. Now the sights were zeroed in. When everyone was ready, we fired our first grouping. The instructor at my side looking through binoculars, slapped me on the back, and said "Perfect, all dead centre, and all within quarter of an inch of each other."

Then we moved on to the kneeling and standing groups. I was elated at the end of my first shoot. All three of my groupings were near perfect. The SLR, though a little cumbersome, was excellent for shooting, and I couldn't wait to see what it would feel like when I fired left handed. While the next group were going through the routine, I had my first group start to field strip and clean our weapons. When I moved into line with the last group for my second shoot, I dropped the gas setting by two, so the spent rounds wouldn't hit my right arm or face. When I went through the three groupings, mine weren't as good as my first lot, but better than the other guys, all the same. The only person who came near my score was John, and that would figure, seeing he had worked as a jackeroo on cattle stations up north near home.

Before the next shoot, we were briefed by Captain Jacobs again. It was to be with the pistols. I raised my hand with a query again, and was acknowledged by him, and asked "Sir, as the number eight position is vacant, is it possible, to save a bit of time, by giving me two positions side by side, so I can fire with both hands at the same time?" I noticed that the two civilians had moved closer to hear what was being said, and after my question, they both looked at each other. Jacobs answered "Seems like a good suggestion, Corporal. You take number one and two positions." He continued,

"You will all fire two sighting shots, and then five for a grouping."
As he finished, I then asked another question, "Sir, are they to be
aimed shots or instinctive line?" With a smile he answered "For
you, Corporal, one of each, if you feel up to the challenge." "Yes,
Sir" I replied. I then noticed that the civvies started to move, and po-
sitioned themselves behind my firing position. Sergeant Kendrick
came over to me, and said "I hope you are as good as you think
you are. The Captain has really given you a lot of leeway, and
stuck his neck out today, and he's a good officer." Looking him
straight in the eye and with a smile on my face I replied "No probs,
Sarge, I don't think, I know." With a worried smile he replied "Ok,
smartarse, go and get ready."

During the briefing and following conversations, the targets
were reset to twenty five yards. As I stepped between positions
one and two, I looked around, and everyone not on the firing line
was watching me. Shit! I thought to myself, me and my smart
mouth! I hoped I could pull this off! The instructor at my side had
put the magazine holding the two rounds into each pistol I was
to use, and as he cocked them both for me, said "Careful, they
pull down and left a little.," After thanking him, I waited for the
fire command. Captain Jacob's voice came over the PA asking if
everyone was ready, and each instructor held his arm up, and then
came the command to fire at will. I fired aimed shots with my left,
and then fired from the waist with my right. My left results were
in the heart area, about half an inch beside each other. My right
results: I had gone for a head shot and both had hit the same area,
and nearly gone through the same hole. I ejected the magazines
one handed with each gun, as the cease fire order came. As the
pistols were loaded with the five round mags, I looked around to
see the rest of the platoon, and Kendrick, silently clapping and
smiling. I moved onto the firing line, and as I did, I was congratulated by the instructor as he said, "Well done. Now do it again!"

The firing order came, and I did the same, and the result was
confirmed by clapping and cheering. My left grouping had torn
the heart out of the target, and my right had torn a one inch circle

from the head area of the right target. I still felt disappointed. One of the civvies came up and asked "Why do you look so disappointed?" "I was a little off, these pistols are too light!" I replied. He said "Don't leave the range just yet" and then he turned and went up to Jacobs. They had a bit of a conflab, and then he left the range area. As the third group made their way to the firing line, he returned, and said something to Jacobs. They both nodded, and then Jacob's ordered over the PA, "Corporal Davis report to firing position eight!" Dumbfounded and confused, I moved into line. The civvy came to my side, and showed me a pistol, and said "This is a Colt forty five. It has nine rounds in the mag, and one up the spout. The first five, fire instinctive. The second five aimed, and change your target order. Now get used to the weight, and tell me if it feels better." After holding it and feeling it, I said to him "This feels better." He replied "Just release the safety to fire, and the rest is up to you." I looked up towards Captain Jacobs with a questioning look. He had been watching me, and he smiled and nodded. I nodded back, and then waited for the firing order, it came and I let loose. Christ! What a pistol! It was marvellous, and the deep bark of sound, and recoil kick were fantastic! Oh, God, I was in heaven! The result was that all rounds went through the same respective holes, Man! Talk about accurate!

I was loath to give it back, and with a lot of regret, I handed it back, butt first into his hand. I said with awe "Thank you, that gun is beautifully balanced and fantastic." With a smile on his face, he replied "Well, thank you, and you're not too bad, either." His mate joined him, and with a nod to Jacobs they left the range deep in conversation.

We finished at the range after each firing a forty round mag off from the M forty, and Jacobs had been right. It pulled up to the right, but after his earlier warning, most of us had been able to compensate, and hold it steady while firing. But, my mind had not been able to get off the feeling of that pistol! I was still thinking about it as we marched back to the barracks, after what I considered to be an enjoyable and productive afternoon.

CHAPTER 16

Back at the barracks, Kendrick informed us that all the weapons were to cleaned and ready for the following morning, when we would drill with the weapons before returning them to the armoury. After the platoon was dismissed for the day, John and I joined Kendrick in the conference room for our daily debrief. John made the coffee, and then we relaxed with the drinks and smokes as we got down to business. Kendrick congratulated us on a job well done at the range, and told me "You must have really impressed that guy. I nearly did a double take when he gave you that pistol. What did you say to him?" "I just said, that I thought the Browning was too light" I replied. "I was dumbfounded when the Captain called me back to the firing line, but hell, I enjoyed every minute of it!"

We then moved to the next order of business. Tomorrow after returning the rifles, we would go to the Q store to pick up our dress uniforms that had come in, then sport in the afternoon. Kendrick asked "Have you got a team picked?" I replied "Yep, but we'll need about half an hour or so to work a few things out on the field." "That's ok," Kendrick replied, "You'll be playing a team from Charlie platoon, but not until two. We'll march down at one, and then have some practise till then." "Fine," I replied, and then Kendrick asked "Any questions?" John and I both shook our heads no, and he continued. "Thursday, after drill, will be more lectures and then the obstacle course that afternoon. I'll see you in the am." With that he left, and John said "I'll make sure the rifles are cleaned and racked. What do you want to do?" I replied "I'd like to have a word with our footy team volunteers, so I'll join you."

After informing the platoon that the dress for tomorrow was our slouch hats and base standard dress, I told them that drilling would be with weapons, prior to returning them to the armoury. While

John made sure all the rifles were clean and racked, I had a talk with the footy team members about play positions. We then went down to the sports field and had a quick practise, while trying out some game tactics and plays. We all knew that even though it was only supposed to be touch football, where a touch was considered to be a tackle, and the ball played, we could expect to have some rough handling mixed in. After we had practised for half an hour or so, running a few plays, I considered that we were more than ready. We were all quite confident in our positioning and what had to be done, so after a few more practise runs, we called it a day and made our way back to the barracks to relax before dinner.

That evening, while having a couple of beers in the mess, I contemplated the fact that even with the changes in my life and what I was doing, I still had ended up back on a football field! I thought this was quite ironic; here we all were training to become soldiers, probably some of us would end up in Vietnam fighting a war, and here I am, about to go onto a football field again. Had I made the right choice by joining the Army, or should I have tried a playing career for one of the city teams first? I decided that I was here now, so I may as well make the best of it. In the long run, this turned out to be the right choice.

Next day we drilled for two hours, and the summer heat was fierce. I was glad to get off the parade ground and into the shade between the buildings. After we had returned our rifles, we were able to have a smoke break before marching to the Q store. We were issued with two sets of dress uniforms and a pair of dress shoes; naturally they would have to be polished to a mirror shine. Back at our barracks building, Kendrick advised us to try on both sets of dress gear, and then go to the laundry for any alterations and to have them cleaned and pressed. He then said "Well men, you're coming along just fine, and you are impressing me. Keep it up. Now I will see you after lunch, and we'll see how good our footballers are, right! Atten...shun, Dis...Missed!"

Inside the barracks, everyone was glad to get their boots off, and then the dress uniform trying out started. Mine were a fine fit for the shirts, but the trousers needed to be shortened by an inch. The shoes were a perfect fit. When the rest of the platoon was ready, John and I marched them to the laundry, where the dress uniforms were handed over for adjustment and dry cleaning. The laundry supervisor told me he would leave a message for me when all of the platoons' gear was ready for pickup. Back at the barracks I said "Ok, the only thing on this arvo is the footy game. I would suggest that we all wear sports gear, instead of just the footy team, and don't forget to polish those dress shoes sometime, spit polish just like the boots. That's all. Back out here ready to go at thirteen hundred, dismissed!"

Either I was getting used to the meals, or the cooks were getting better. Lunch that day was very tasty; it didn't seem to be the same reheated mix of mush, even the veggies were fresh. As I left the canteen after lunch, I came face to face with the two civvies, and after acknowledging their presence, the one who had let me use the pistol asked, "So Corporal Davis, what are you up to this afternoon?" "I'm playing against one of the other platoon's football team on the oval" I replied. He then said "Well, good luck. Maybe we might get a chance to see you play." With that they carried on walking, while I continued to ponder, exactly who they were, and what they were here for.

At the sports oval that afternoon, Sgt Kendrick pointed out a couple of bins and said "Ok, the guys playing in the team; in those bins you'll find some football boots go find a decent pair before the others get here." We needed no further urging, and as we headed to the bins to find a pair of boots, I found a couple that fitted, but they were mismatched, not that it made any difference to me, as long as they fitted snugly. When we all had our boots on, we went for a warm up run passing the ball to each other, and trying a few kicks. A little later, Charlie platoon turned up with Sgt Harris, Kendrick's opposite number. Both Sergeants agreed that Charlie platoon would play with red vests on, while we would just wear our green t-shirts.

Just then, we were joined by two other Sergeants from Bravo

and Delta platoons. They would be the referees, and they called both team captains over for the coin toss. I won and elected to kick off from the southern end, and then both teams moved onto the field. Playing in my normal position, I watched the kick off, and then sprinted after the ball. Due to their only being ten men per side, I was able to get to the ball before anyone else. I scooped it up, and made it all the way to the try line to score before any of the opposition came near me. As I trotted back down the field, I noticed that the two civvies were standing on the side line and about to join Kendrick and Harris. Play got underway again with the kick off, and our centre player was touched while moving forward. The tackle was played, the ball was passed out to me, and as I was running one of the defenders grabbed me in a headlock and drove me into the ground! Ok, so much for touch football! As the game went on, there were more fists and elbows, instead of the so called touches. Obviously the rough housing had begun; well two could play at that! We went to the half time break with the score eighteen to six, in our favour.

During the break I said to my guys, "Ok, the gloves are off! From now on we give back as much as we get. They want to play rough house, let's show them how it's done." After saying this, the players were all smiles, because we had been getting some rough treatment, and now it was payback time. Kendrick was present at that time, and said "I agree with Davis. You're in front already, but don't forget you're Alpha platoon. Go and show them that!"

When we took the field again, we were raring to go, and as the ball came to us, Joe in the centre, was tackled. He smiled at the guy that had tackled him, and then smashed his elbow into the guy's face for good measure, so Joe was the first to score some payback. During the next play, the ball was passed out to me, and I made a fair bit of distance into the oppositions half before being tackled. The one that tackled me had also driven a punch into my ribs, and it was also the one that had driven me into the ground. Thinking to myself, 'this is too good to be true', I tapped the ball to play it, and then with it still in my hands, drove it into the face of the arsehole,

166

and ran over him as he went down. That was really satisfying! Their fullback was coming toward me, so I dived and curled into a ball and rolled through his legs, bringing him down. As I came out of the roll, I passed the ball to Joe, and he scored.

After that, the game became one sided. They never scored again, and we ran away with the game. The final score was forty two to six; we had well and truly won the game, and also established to all involved that we wouldn't take any shit! On the side of the field, as we were changing our shoes, congratulations were flowing from the rest of the platoon. I noticed that Kendrick and Harris had been talking to the other referee sergeants. Harris headed towards Charlie platoon, and Kendrick came over to us and said "Well done, boys. I hope you can do it again, because next week you're up against Delta platoon." All the players looked at me, and with a slight nod, I turned to Kendrick and said "Ok, Sarge, but if this is going to be a regular thing, the team deserves our own playing boots."

Kendrick seemed to think this over, and then said "Fair enough, leave it with me and I'll see what I can do." After that, we marched back to the barracks and the platoon was dismissed for the rest of the day. The afternoon briefing between Kendrick, John and I took place outside the hut while we had smokes, because it was only going to be a quick one. We already knew what was going to be taking place. After that, Kendrick left for the day.

After showering and changing into clean gear, I asked John if he wanted to join me in the mess for a couple of drinks before dinner. Over drinks I said to John, "Those civvies seem to be taking interest in us, have you been able to find out anything about them, or what they're up to?" He replied, "No, but they seem to be looking at all the platoons. I have heard that they spend as much time watching Echo as they do with us." "Okay, let's try and pick up any rumour or talk about them, as they're really starting to intrigue me, and I hate puzzles," I replied. We decided to go straight to dinner after our drinks. At the canteen we joined our opposite numbers from the other three platoons, and while we ate, tried to pick up any information the other guys had regarding the two civvies, which ended up being as much as we already knew.

I was heading back to the mess after dinner, when I came face to face with the two civvies. As we greeted each other I said "Sirs, you know me by name, but I don't know yours." The one that had given me the pistol said, "Well, Corporal Davis, I'm Mr. White and this is Mr. Brown. Can we help you with anything else?" "Yes, sir," I replied. "I guess a few of us are wondering what you're here for?" Mr Brown replied "Well, we're observing the platoons from this intake, to see how you go with handling the training sessions. It's a new innovation, and we report on any exceptional skills you may have, and in time may make recommendations to you about choice of career. We will be away after next week, and then back after Christmas, so we may see you then. Have a nice night." I wished them a goodnight, and kept heading for the mess. There I pondered over the rather evasive answer I was given, while having a smoke and drink.

I had been given no real answers, the only new piece of information I picked up was that they reported any exceptional skills. That could mean anything. What skills were considered exceptional? The bigger question was who did they report to? They did however give me something to bring up in the morning with Kendrick what we would be doing over Christmas. After a final drink and smoke, I headed back to the barracks to get some sleep.

The following morning, while doing the usual barracks inspection with John and Kendrick, I asked "Sarge, just as a matter of interest, what happens over the Christmas break which is coming up soon. Do we get leave, or do we work through the break?" He replied "I'll fill you in on that this afternoon, but no, you don't get leave, and neither do I, so let's continue."

Outside, we marched to the parade ground for the usual drill practise, before heading over to the lecture rooms. As we moved into the lecture room I noted there was a bundle of stuff on the front table covered with black cloth. Kendrick called us to attention as Captain Jacobs came into the room, without his hat on, and told us to be seated.

He said "Over the next week, you'll be learning about how to use high explosive anti-personnel devices. Both here in the classroom and practising on the range, then and only then, will we move onto a live firing exercise." "Today we will be dealing with three sorts of easily carried weapons that are in use by NATO forces. First the common hand grenade, and then a couple of grenade launchers." When he had finished speaking, he grabbed the black cloth and peeled it back to the other side of the table, revealing a number of different types of hand grenades.

He picked up the first one which resembled a short coke can, but not as wide. It had a pin and lever attached to the top. "This is a smoke grenade. They come in different colours, and the top cover colour lets you know which. In this case it's grey, which means its normal smoke colour. To use, place your finger over the lever, pull out the pin and throw as soon as the lever releases smoke starts billowing. They can be used for marking an area, or using as cover to move position." He passed it to one of the platoon members saying, "Pass it round, these are all demonstration material, and therefore rendered safe."

The next one he picked up was all green and looked like an oversize ping pong ball with a pin and lever mechanism on top. Holding it up, he said "This one is for close in operations; because it only has a two second delay once the lever flies off and arms it. It's packed with high explosive only, but still has a big punch." As he passed it on, he picked up the next one that resembled a coke can with the mechanism on top, and was white in colour. Continuing, he said "This one is a nasty little bugger. It's filled with explosive and white phosphorous. Once it explodes, the phosphorous is released and scatters everywhere and adheres to clothing and skin. In open air it burns at one thousand degrees through clothing, skin, and bone, so yes very nasty." While he passed it on, the smoke grenade had made its way back to the front, so he picked it up and replaced it on the table, then picked up the next one. It was the type you see in movies and war shows, that looks like a little pineapple, with pin and lever.

Captain Jacobs said with a smile, "This is the most common grenade in use, and has been around since before World War II. Its shape hasn't varied much over the years, it's filled with high explosive and designed to fragment the steel casing, hence its shape like a pineapple. All the indentations burst apart, filling the area around where it explodes. It has a four second delay once armed. Any questions before we move on?"

John put his hand up, and asked after being acknowledged, "Sir, what's the difference between that one and this one?" Holding up the ping pong grenade, Jacobs answered, "Well, apart from being only H.E. and the two second delay, feel the weight of both." He passed the pineapple to him, and continued "Now, which one feels heavier?" John held up the pineapple, and Jacobs continued, "Ok, the difference is because the fragmentation grenade is a heavy grade of steel. It can also be thrown further due to its weight. Does that answer your question?" John said "Thank you, sir," and Jacobs turned and picked up the last one.

It looked like an oversized bullet, and I had a good idea what it was. Sure enough as Captain Jacobs explained, I was on the money. "This is a grenade filled with H.E. and small ball bearings. It explodes on impact, but instead of being thrown, it is a round for the M79 grenade launcher." As he was saying this, he rolled back the cloth a little more, and picked up the launcher. It was about half the length of a normal shotgun, but the barrel was much rounder. Jacobs continued by saying, "As you can see, it looks much like a shotgun, and is loaded in the same way. He demonstrated. Sometimes in the movies, you'll see them snapped back into position, like this, (demonstrating) but for your own safety it's always better to close them the right way, like this" demonstrating again.

After he put the grenades that had been placed at the front again on the table, he passed the M79 around saying "Remember, it's not a toy, so be careful." He then picked up the last item saying "Most of you would have seen these in movies or news footage from Vietnam. This is the M16 Armalite rifle, the main assault weapon used by American troops. It's very lightweight due to being predominantly plastic, and it fires the NATO standard round. This one is a XM148, so called because it incorporates an M79 launcher, loaded thusly (demonstrating). Do not worry too much about these, you'll probably never use one, the newer type is the M203."

"As I said, you'll probably never see one, there are only a few of the XM148s around and are only for demonstration and edu-cational use. Later in the week, when you practise on the firing range, you'll only be instructed on the use of these two (holding up the ping pong and pineapple), as well as learning to fire the M79. Are there any questions?" After a few questions were asked and answered, captain Jacobs said "Over the next few days I'll be talking a bit further about explosives and anti-personnel devices. Thank you gentlemen." Kendrick called "Attention!"! Captain Jacobs said "Thank you, Sergeant," and left the room. Kendrick said "Right, ladies, smoke break outside, MOVE!" With that we moved outside and lit up.

While we smoked, Kendrick said "Right, listen up. This afternoon we're on the obstacle course, today you will be wearing base standard. NO changing into sneakers. Corporal Davis, march the platoon back to the barracks. Remember thirteen hundred, ladies. Corporal Davis, carry on!" "Sarge" I replied, then to the platoon, "Ok fall in, quick march!" "Corporal Buchanan, call it.," As we arrived at the hut, I had John dismiss the platoon, and we went into my room and office. With a smile I said to him "What's the difference, you bloody clown!" Laughing, he replied "Well, I had to give him something to answer," and we both continued laughing. I then said "Let's go to lunch, I got something to share with our opposite numbers," so we got up and headed to the canteen.

I checked the message board when we got there, and found a note from the laundry saying that all the dress uniforms were back and ready for pickup. I showed it to John who nodded as we made our selection from the two choice menus. I had roast silverside, while John opted for shepherd's pie. Putting our meals on a tray, we headed over to the NCO's table. The guys from Bravo were there, but not any of the others yet, and we ate while we waited for the others. When all were present, I asked "Has anyone got any dope about what's happening over Christmas?" After getting answers in the negative, I said "Well, I've got it on this arvo's agenda with our boss, so one of us will let you know what he says. Ok now, anything on Mr. Brown and White?" George from Echo asked "Who are they," and I replied "The civvies. That's the names I was given by them," and then recounted my conversation with them the previous night. That started another general conversation about the two civvies, and the answers they gave me, and about the answers not being answers at all, and nothing new from any of the others, so we were all still in the dark, regarding them.

That afternoon we were once again at the obstacle course, and being timed, and once again I was first up. Surprisingly, I found that wearing boots gave me more grip, and I was able to move a little faster. When I finished, the rest of the platoon were on the course, as I reached Kendrick, he said with enthusiasm "Well done, Davis: 21minutes 2 seconds!" "Christ! I had knocked almost two minutes off my previous time! So I replied "Thanks, Sarge, what's the record?" He answered "Seventeen minutes fifty six seconds. Keep this up, and by the time you finish training you'll be the new record holder." Our slowest person that day was Charlie Behan coming in at twenty eight minutes forty three seconds, so we had all improved our times. Kendrick gave us all our times and then said "Well done, men. You're not ladies anymore, and that was an improvement by all. I'm sure you're trying to impress me!" We all chorused "YES, Sarge!"

Back at the hut, Kendrick, John, and I had our usual conference and debrief. Kendrick was really chuffed and said "by Christ, this platoon is doing wonders, and a lot of it is down to you two. There are a lot of people starting to take note of the platoon and you guys, so keep it up, and you'll both go far."

"Now, moving to your query about Christmas, we will be working except for Christmas day and Boxing day. Every other

172

day is a working day, even New Year's day. There will be events here, and you will be taking part in them. I'll have the full schedule in the next day or so. Tomorrow the usual in the morning, and we'll be going to the explosive range in the afternoon, so field dress for that. You have any questions?" After we said "no," he continued "Ok, let's knock off, and I'll see you in the morning.," He got up and left, while John and I just looked at each other with smiles on our faces.

CHAPTER 17

After our drilling session the next day, it was back into the classroom where Captain Jacobs was waiting. On the table was an assortment of armament, some looked familiar, while others didn't. We waited for permission to be seated. Captain Jacobs said "Sit. Today I'll be continuing where we left off yesterday, so let's get on with it." He picked up what looked to be an oversized rifle and what looked like a stick with a conical end, and continued "This is a rocket propelled grenade and launcher, or RPG, and this is how it works." Passing the launcher to Kendrick, he inserted the stick into the launcher, "It's now ready to fire." Kendrick then went into an aiming stance, ready to fire, and then Jacobs took out the stick as Kendrick lowered the launcher onto the table.

With the RPG round in his hand, Jacobs went on. "This is filled with H.E. and bearings, so when it hits its target, it explodes as well as sending out a lot of shrapnel. This is a contact triggered device. It explodes the moment it hits either the ground or something else." Replacing the RPG round on the table, he picked up the next item, which was about six inches high and eight inches long with a slight bend in it and painted green. He said "This is commonly referred to as a 'claymore'. The claymore anti-personnel mine is named after its inventor, and is widely used by all NATO forces. It's an American manufactured weapon, and I suppose they consider their soldiers dumb or stupid because the instructions are cast into the mine casing!" We all had a laugh at the joke, and Jacobs went on. "It's designed to explode in a thirty degree arc, and is filled with H.E. and ball bearings. It is quite lethal, if you were inside that arc you would be cut to pieces! The claymore can be detonated in two ways, by electronic ignition, or by a built in trip wire. Any questions?"

I raised my hand, Jacobs looked around the room as he said

"Yes, Corporal Davis?" "Well sir, I have two questions. One: How are they set? And two, how good are the firing systems?" He smiled as he answered. "I was wondering if anyone would ask me about the firing, so I'll deal with that first. The inbuilt trip wire works well, but has one major drawback. It has a limited length. Usually six to eight feet and must be fully extended to apply the correct tension for detonation. Our troops have had better success with electronic detonation in an ambush situation."

"They are set in a variety of ways. For instance, you can place them on trees, against a rock, or (as he demonstrated) these little legs fold down, and can be placed into the ground. The main thing to remember is to face them the correct way as per the instructions. Being around the wrong way tends to make things awkward." Everyone laughed at his understated joke, including himself. He followed this up with another, saying laughingly "And no, you don't get to play with these either, before anyone asks."

Placing the claymore back on the table after refolding the legs, he picked up the next item. It was round, about four inches deep and about eight inches in diameter. It had what looked to be a bar across it, with a spring under the bar. He held it up and continued, "Standard anti-personnel mine, filled with the usual stuff. It gets buried in the ground in fields around emplacements, or can be placed on walking tracks. Designed to blow upward, it's triggered by stepping onto the pressure plate, and when you step off it detonates. If you are lucky it may only blow your legs off, if not…well that's you done. This can be disarmed, but it takes time. Here's what happens…." Jacobs then proceeded to demonstrate as he continued explaining, "When you step onto the pressure plate, you can actually feel the give, this light piece of wire is broken, and you can hear it break. FREEZE. DO NOT Take another step! The person helping you then clears the pressure plate, gets you to ease the pressure a little, and reinserts a piece of wire into the catch. You use your other leg to drive you into a dive away from the mine, and hopefully it won't detonate." I guess he tried to lighten the mood a little with his next comment, and with what I thought to be a forced grin, "At least that's the way it's supposed to work. I've never had to deal with that sort of situation, but I've been told that it does work. Questions?"

There were none. Most of us looked rather sombre, each thinking our own dark thoughts. Jacobs picked up the next one, the only difference being that this one had gaps in the base of the device. He said "Ok, that one isn't nice to think about, but this one is worse; it's called a 'jumping jack'. All the same as the last one, however what happens with this one is, as you step off, it jumps into the air to about waist height, then detonates. Your chances of survival are minimal, so not nice at all." He put the jumping jack down, moved to the wall, and then unrolled a diagram saying, "The only other thing to cover is this, the Carl Gustave anti-tank weapon, made in Sweden, as well as the rounds for it. In my opinion, the army could have chosen a better piece of equipment for its use."

That statement resulted in hands going up around the room. Merv had asked the question that we all wanted answered. "Sir why do you say that?" Jacobs replied with a smile "Don't any of you get me wrong, this is a damn good weapon. However, my opinion is shared by quite a few. Why? Well let me paint you a picture. The Gustave and its rounds are made in Sweden. The rounds for it are expensive therefore the Army only buys limited rounds at a time. Sweden is usually a neutral country during most conflicts, should a major war break out. As Sweden is neutral one of the first things it does is stop exporting weaponry, making the Gustave's only useful until we run out of ammo. So it would have been better for us to have bought an anti-tank weapon from a NATO member country. Do you see why my opinion is shared by many?"

There were nods of understanding all around the room, "Most of what I talked about is for your general knowledge. Some of you will gain further knowledge of some of these weapons in your corp training, dependent on which corp you choose. Remember, this is only your basic training, your corp training is much more specialised for work within those corps. Now from what I understand, you are on the range this afternoon with me, so I will see you then. Thank you." We stood and came to attention as he left the room. Kendrick then ordered "Davis, take them out for a smoke break."

Having lit up outside, there was a lot of discussion and joking going on about the mines, but it was mainly agreed, Do not get into that situation! After marching back to our hut, Kendrick addressed us. "Right, men, and remember this afternoon is just practice, but take it seriously, because our next time on the range will be for live firing. Corporal Davis, have all the dress uniforms come back from refitting?" "Yes, Sarge," I replied. Kendrick continued "Good. Be back at thirteen hundred. Platoon dis…missed."

After lunch, we were waiting outside the hut, and formed up as Kendrick joined us, then we were marched to the heavy ordinance range. It was well away from the main base areas, and it took us about thirty minutes to get there. Kendrick allowed a smoke break, and told us that we would be going back by truck, with the range staff, instead of marching back. This livened us up a bit, as the thought of trudging back on foot wasn't all that appealing!

Captain Jacobs told us in his briefing that we would be split into four groups of five, and each group would be with three range instructors. They would teach us the required techniques for both grenades. Jacobs would take one group, which included me, John, Merv, and two other platoon members, Eric and Will. Both guys were from Townsville and hoping to go into the engineers' branch or corps. The range set up was entirely different to the rifle range. There were six concreted areas that we walked into. The concrete came up to just above waist height, and looked toward the firing area. It was normal dry ground interspersed with craters and mounds that had been created by live firing. Jacobs said "As you look toward the firing area, you'll note that some forty four gallon drums have been set up. They're for you guys. Try to get your throws either in, or as close as possible to the drums." After he finished talking, I asked, "Sir isn't that just a bit dangerous?" Smiling he replied "Well, that's only for today, Corporal Davis. If we were live firing and they were there, they'd be blown to hell and back and there'd be pieces of drum going everywhere. THAT would be dangerous, but we're ok for today. They make it easier for YOU to collect all the dummies."

He then went to one of the two boxes on the ground near the edge of the concrete path, picked out a grenade, a pineapple, tossed it to one of the range staff, the same person that had been with me on the rifle range. Jacobs said, "Sergeant Taggert will show you how to use them." With that, he nodded and Taggert stepped forward. He said "First, while on all firing ranges, treat everything as live ordinance. Now, to use this, make sure your hand is around the lever like this, (demonstrating), and pull the pin. As you throw, the lever flies off and it will explode in four seconds. If you want to explode it quicker let the lever fly off as you pull the pin, like so." He demonstrated then threw the grenade. We watched as it sailed through the air, his throw had been a long one, and just as well! It landed well beyond the drums, and exploded! "Christ! Duck!" I yelled and we ducked down behind the wall just as a shower of dirt and dust flew over the wall.

In the following seconds, I noticed the other groups had stopped what they were doing and were looking toward us. As we slowly stood up we looked at Jacobs and Taggert with a mix of surprise and horror. They were standing there with grins on their faces! Jacobs looked around at the other groups and yelled, "Carry on!" Then looked back again toward us, as Kendrick raced over.

Glancing at Kendrick, then back at us, said "It's alright, Sergeant. The men have been given their first lesson in dealing with ordinance. In the reports I would like you to note that I'm also commending Davis for his very quick reactions." Turning towards Taggert, he said "Ok Sergeant Taggert, carry on." He then turned to Kendrick, and motioned for him to join him as they moved away, deep in conversation.

Taggert took us through the motions of release and throw a few times, then we practised a couple of shortened timing throws (throwing after the arming lever flew off), and then he had us work the same way with the close quarters (ping pong ball) grenades.

After all the groups had finished, we then moved onto the range to recover all the dummy grenades, and put them into the forty fours. We took them back to the emplacements, helped the range staff place them back into their boxes, and then we all got into the waiting trucks and were driven back to the main base area. Back in the base area, we marched from our drop off point (near the parade quadrangle), to our barracks hut, and after the platoon was dismissed John and I joined Kendrick for our usual debrief and briefing conference.

After coffees had been made, we sat at the table having smokes with our drinks as we got down to business. The following day we would be drawing our weapons from the armoury before our drilling session. Kendrick said "While at the armoury, you'll all draw bayonets for your rifles at the same time, then they will remain in this hut until further notice. Make sure they are locked away at all times." John and I nodded our understanding. He told us that the football game the next day would against Bravo platoon, and added "Let's hope you have another win. I really want to stick it to Sergeant Johnson over which of us has the better platoon." I replied with a smile "I don't think that'll be a problem, Sarge, we already know who's the best." He laughed and smilingly said "I like you're thinking, Davis. Oh, by the way, well done with this afternoon. Very quick thinking, you certainly surprised Jacobs, and he allowed Taggert to pull that stunt!" Seeing the stunned looks on our faces he said "Yep, it was done on purpose, to reinforce the ordinance rule. Captain Jacobs told me while you went through the training. Damn stupid, if you ask me, but no one got hurt thank Christ. Now moving on, I can tell you what will be happening after Christmas. On New Year's Day there will be a march through town. We'll be joined by the RAAF for the march, and I'll get the final timings for that in the next day or so."

"So when we start practising for that, it will be in full dress uniform, but with boots instead of shoes. It usually finishes near the RSL club where we'll be picked up and driven back here, after we've had a couple of drinks of course, so fill in the guys as to what's coming up. Unless there's anything else, that'll do for today." We both answered that there wasn't anything else, so Kendrick headed off, and John and I went into the main room, where the guys were talking, laying on their beds, or playing cards.

John called out "Ok listen up and gather round." We were both half sitting on the main table, and as the guys moved closer I started to let them know what the coming days were going to bring. As I told them about the march we would be practising for, there were understandable groans of displeasure, and I for one wasn't looking forward to all the drilling. Then John let them know about who the footy game would be against. After that, I asked "So how do you think today went??" This started a general discussion. The main topic was, of course, what had happened on the range. Letting this take its course, I then told them about finding out it was deliberate, and that really pissed them off. Now, because we had all really become experts at how the army worked, the discussion turned towards the stupidity of officers and the stupid way things were conducted. A case in point was the absurdity of buying what could become useless weapons. I think that most of us could see and agree with Captain Jacobs' point of view, but because he was an officer, and didn't know much about army life, some would disagree with his viewpoint on sheer principle.

The discussion moved on to making jokes. In the end I said, "Well guys, I'll tell you what I think. Captain Jacobs is a pretty smart man. First off, Kendrick thinks he's a good officer, which says a lot. Secondly, he knows what he's talking about, and knows how to prove a point. I was in his group, don't forget! Lastly when he says something is nasty, I'd really believe him, because he strikes me as being the master of understatement!" My last point was unanimously agreed upon by the guys. As I had been talking, John had been writing up the notice board SOP's, so I finished. "Ok, base standard tomorrow, then to the armoury. While signing out your rifle, get a bayonet as well, then we're off to our favourite parade ground, and some of us can have an easy afternoon." Joe said "That's Ok, Corp, it'll be just as easy for us footy players," and this had everyone laughing. Then I had a shower before getting ready to go to dinner.

In the canteen that night John and I joined the other NCO's and filled them in on what had taken place at the range. "Now here's an example of how and what can get distorted by rumours in what we affectionately call the Green Machine." My opposite number in Bravo, Charlie Pease (nicknamed Chick), said "Christ, we'd heard that someone had been blown up!" John, laughing, said "You wish! That's only because you're going up against Tiger tomorrow," and we all laughed. When the laughter subsided I said "By the way, Chick, it's only touch footy tomorrow. If you do try any roughhousing, we can mix it up rather hard, just ask Jim here from Echo."

Another topic of conversation later that night in the mess over a few beers was the upcoming march on New Year's Day. It would give us a chance to have a look at the town and maybe get to know something of the people that lived there. My opinion was that we'd probably not get much of an opportunity considering we were going into town with a troop of cherry berries (Military Police, so called because the colour of their Berets were cherry red). They'd probably put the lid on us doing any socialising. As things started to die down, I contemplated how much I was enjoying this part of my life. Even though all this was new, I was enjoying it and the company of others doing the same thing. I wasn't homesick or anything like that; quite the opposite. Mind you, a bit of female company wouldn't go astray either, but that would have to wait. With that last thought I drained my beer, and headed to the hut and bed.

The next day went to plan, and was quite uneventful, unless you call drilling, and marching around in thirty six degree heat for nearly three hours eventful! The game that afternoon was rather sedate, and after my warning to Chick the night before, there was only one little skirmish late in the second half, when one of my players accidently hit the player with the ball in the eye. It was sorted out amicably, and we ended up winning eighteen to six.

During the usual afternoon conference, John and I found out that the following day, we wouldn't be drilling. "Thank Christ!" We would be on the grenade range in the morning for live fire exercises, and would be going to the range by truck. That was even better! In the afternoon, back on the assault course, oh lucky us! The day after that however, the whole day drilling, and getting ready for the street march. "That statement about enjoying myself, scrub it!"

The trucks that were taking us to the grenade range were waiting for us beside the parade ground the next morning, and after boarding we were on our way. As we drove along, I made a general comment, "Now just remember guys, don't drop any of these bloody things today for Christ's sake, otherwise I'll not forgive you. You know how the machine loves its paperwork; I'd be at it for the next year!" This had everyone chuckling, even Kendrick. He leaned across to me and said "That was good, they won't be so nervous now. Well done."

Once on the range, Captain Jacobs gave us our briefing. We would be in the same groups as in practise, but this time my group would be overseen only by Taggert. Jacobs would be on the observation platform running the show. Three smoke grenades were to be let off. The first one would be red as a warning to live firing. The second green, to alert us that we could commence firing and the third, red again as the cease fire signal. He finished by saying "Now today, hopefully there won't be any surprises. I can promise you it will be noisy. Sergeants, take your group positions!"

When we were in our emplacements, Taggert tossed me one of the three smoke grenades he had already placed by the wall. After looking around at the other emplacements and the observation platform said "Ok corporal, arm and toss that as far as you can" and I did. As the smoke started rising, straight up because there was no wind, Taggert looked toward Jacobs. Receiving a nod, let the next one fly, and as the green smoke billowed, he gave us all a pineapple. He said "Ok just like in practise. Davis first, and then on down the line. When you're ready Davis, GO!"

I picked a spot on the range and threw, and I was happy to see it explode bang on target before I ducked from the inevitable shower of dirt and dust. I observed the rest of my group using my point as their target and everyone was bang on. Taggert shouted over the other explosions, "Well done, you all get two more throws before we switch." Again all throws were within two, or three yards of each other; our targeting was top notch as far as I was concerned. We then switched over to the close quarters grenade for another three throws. Taggert and all of us were pleased with our results as we got ready for the cease fire. Taggert, who had been watching Jacobs, tossed me the red again as he got the ok, and said "Go for it." After the red smoke billowed, we moved back to the observation area for Captain Jacobs' debriefing.

I could tell by the smile on Kendrick's face that we had all done well. Jacobs finished his debrief by saying "Again, well done. The other platoons now have a very high benchmark to reach, as you're the best overall platoon I've had the pleasure of seeing on this range."

The trip back to base was rather exuberant, if not a little noisy. That was due to yelling to be heard, and the continual voices rising to the bait of "Say that again, I can't hear you." We were certainly in a cheerful mood.

Thankfully, that mood carried us through the rest of the day, after lunch and onto the assault course. Everyone improved their times, even Charlie Behan dropped three minutes off his time. I was able to drop another two minutes ten seconds off mine, and I was now down to eighteen minutes fifty eight seconds. If I could knock off another minute and five seconds, I'd have the record!

CHAPTER 18

Well Christmas day came, and went. The only way we knew it was near, was that the day before (Christmas Eve), Kendrick turned up in the morning carrying a box. He started passing out those floppy red and white sock type hats, which he said was the uniform of the day. It felt quite silly marching around the parade ground with rifles and full dress uniform, with those things on our heads instead of our slouch hats, and the heat didn't help any either. Anyway New Year's Day arrived, and as we made our way to the parade ground, we were joined by the other platoons, and formed up as a company, as had been practised in the lead up to the march. After being given the order to move, we climbed abroad the waiting trucks to start the journey into town.

The journey into town took about twenty minutes, and we were taken to the actual town showgrounds. The base commander, Colonel Trickett, delivered his briefing, which consisted of the route we would take and where it would end. We would then be dismissed, and we then had two hours to make it back to the showgrounds where we would be logged back in. After that, the trucks would return to the barracks, and we were to be on our best behaviour. In other words not to get drunk, and not get into any fights, and not to be late getting back. He also added, "That it would be in our best interests to adhere to these rules, because weekend day leave could be applied for after the next week. Our behaviour that day would go a long way in determining the outcome of whether it would be granted or not. One last thing, your rifles are to NEVER leave your side!"

While he gave us this briefing, the RAAF contingent had arrived and being put through the same procedure. Shortly after, the march started forming and readied to move out. My platoon was to follow the MP's platoon, following the RAAF marching band. The remainder of the platoons followed behind us, and then came the RAAF contingent. As we prepared to move, I passed an order down the line to the guys "To remember the way back, so we don't get lost."

From what I could gather, the march was quite a success. After being dismissed, John and I made our way to the RSL. Nothing was said about our weapons. We assumed they were used to it happening. We had our hands shaken by most of the people in the room as we made our way to the far end of the bar, where we took a couple of stools, and leaned our rifles on the wall beside us.

The barmaid that served us was a cute blonde in her late teens, and she had a nametag pinned to her top, Helen. I ordered a couple of pots, and she laughed and said "I'll excuse the fact that you're from Queensland. You're in New South Wales now it's either schooners or middies." Laughing with her, I replied "Whichever has the more in it. Thanks, Helen." She laughed as she went to pour the beers. When she came back with the beers, I started to pay for them, and she said "No, it's on the house for any serving members." Turning on the charm, I said "Well, thank you, Helen. I'm Tom and this is John. We won't hold you up, but if you see us empty, can you come and fill me up please?" I let her hand go with a slight squeeze; she laughed and moved off, but kept looking back.

John and I raised our glasses to each other, and he said "You bloody smoothie, you know the beers are in schooners down here, you bastard, you were trying to charm her." With a smile and laugh I replied "Of course I do, and as for charming her, well that worked!" We both laughed, and he said "I know, you're a bloody marvel at times. You're smooth, I'll give you that. No wonder you got away with what you did, I can see how, now." I smiled and we drained our glasses. As we were about to put them onto the bar, Helen must have been keeping a close eye on us, because she arrived with two more, and a broad grin. As she was about to turn and move off, I asked "Helen, we can't stay too long, but do you work here regularly?" "Hold on" she replied, then moved off. She returned with a beer coaster, and started writing. When she had finished, she said "Yes, I'm here most of the time, Tom, but if not, that's my number," passing me the drink coaster. John was laughing as I held up the coaster, and put it into my shirt pocket, and he remarked "Now I've seen it all." I just smiled.

When Helen brought our next two beers, I said "Thank you my love, but these will be our last ones because we have to go. So come a little closer and I'll give you a kiss now." She leaned over the bar to me, and I gave her quite a passionate kiss before letting her go. She looked at me with half a smile and said "Ummm, definitely call me" and moved off dreamily, looking back every now and then. John just shook his head as he picked up his beer. I looked innocently at him and asked "What?" Then I laughed and picked up my drink. After our drinks were finished, I passed him his rifle, picked up mine, and blew Helen a kiss, who smiled. We made our way to the front door, and with our rifles slung on our shoulders, we headed up the street and made our way back to the showgrounds, laughing and joking as we window shopped along the way.

After we logged in at the showgrounds, we found that most of the platoon was already there. Only three were missing, and they turned up ten minutes later. While we waited for loading time, we smoked and discussed the post March activities. Joe, who had been at the RSL with a couple of the others, asked "Corp, how did you get that barmaid to kiss you? She didn't give us as much as a glance, she was always watching you." I replied by saying "Well, what else could you expect? She knows a perfectly handsome creature when she sees one." This elicited a lot of laughter, and some comments, and then John said "You guys have no idea how smooth he is when he's operating. He's even got her phone number." This drew some comments of "bullshit," until I smilingly took the coaster out of my pocket and waved it around. This led to some catcalls and jokes, along with congratulation and bewildered remarks. Shortly after that the truck engines started, and the drivers called us aboard. Back at camp we all agreed that it had been a good day.

Sergeant Kendrick called into the hut, after he arrived back on base, and addressed us inside the main living area. "I would like to offer to you all my congratulations on a job well done. Men, you made me proud. Tomorrow will be an easy day. No drill in the morning, instead there will be lectures on navigation and terrain. You can go shoot some targets in the afternoon, so dress will be base standard. Have a good night and I'll see you in the am." After he left, I made sure the guys had kept their bayonets and put them into their lockers, and had John make sure all the rifles were racked and locked, then got ready for dinner.

In the mess later that night, John and I were joined by a few of the other platoon NCO's and the general conversation was about what we would do when we had day leave. When I was asked I said "Well I have people to see, which reminds me, I've got a phone call to make." As I got up to make my way to the pay phone, John said "You sly bastard." I smiled and continued to move from our table; behind me I heard the others asking John what I was up to, and he started to explain. At the phone I dialled in Helen's number, and it was answered on the fourth ring. "Hello?" It sounded like her but to be sure I asked, "Is Helen there, please?" The reply was "Yes, this is Helen," so I said "Hi Helen, this is Tom Davis. We met today at the club, and you asked me to call, so here I am. How are you? You look good." This started what became a half hour conversation, with a lot of innuendo sparring, interspersed with joking and laughter.

Helen let me know her work roster, and we arranged that I would call as soon as I could when she wasn't working. After that we said good night to each other, and before re-joining the others, I grabbed a drink from the bar. When I got to the table, I was smiling, and I received comments of, "You dirty dog" and" You lucky bastard," which made me smile even more. I replied with "Suffer, boys, suffer."

The next morning, the lecture was conducted by a Lieutenant Ferris, and the first thing that we started with was the legend on maps, He passed out copies of the map for the surrounding area, showing us how to read the legend for that particular area.

Needless to say, some of his lecture was wasted on some of us, because we already had knowledge of map reading and topography. So it became a little boring. Then he moved on to working out co-ordinates, and that's when it started to get interesting. Then we had some practise sessions with questions and answers, and then came the inevitable question. Todd Monk had grown up in a city, so knew nothing about maps, unless you call a street directory a map. Anyway his question was, "Sir, how do you measure the distance to know where you are?"

His answer was the best explanation I'd heard for quite some time. "Right, each map square since 1960 has been measured to be a kilometre square. Everyone is moving to metric measurement, except our brothers from the states, and that is why they have a tendency to get lost." We all laughed at his intended joke. "So each grid we know is one thousand metres. Now, if you divide that into ten, it will bring you to one hundred metres, and so on by dividing down. They can be measured be time, for example minutes and seconds, but no one I know carries a stopwatch so it's easier to work in distance. Each map is read north to south for latitude, and east to west for longitude. If you marked the grid into ten, that would mean if you walked two hundred metres north you would be here and if you started in the centre of the grid, that would put you here, or within a metre or so." He had been marking the overhead projection to make his point, and as he lifted his head to look at Todd, I saw that Todd had got it, and was nodding his head as he said "Thank you, Sir." Lt Ferris smiled, and asked "Any other question?" When there were none, he said "Ok, let's move on to compass work. The first thing to do is to orientate your compass to the map you are using." As he was saying this, Kendrick was passing out field compasses to everyone. Ferris continued, "How this is done...," While he was droning on, I had gone to the legend on the map, got the degree of variance, sat my compass flat, found magnetic north, and adjusted the bezel of the compass to the correct degree of variance to ascertain true north. I noticed as I was looking around after doing this, that most of the guys used to maps had been doing the same thing, the rest were following Ferris's instructions.

Once everybody had finished, Ferris called to me, "Corporal, I don't know your name yet, but I noticed that you had already started using your map before anyone else. So first off, why? Second, what's the difference between what and what?" What a silly way to ask a question! Guessing his intent, I answered "Davis, sir, and I know enough about working with maps to be able to do it without instruction, sir, and the answer you want is there is eight degrees variance between true north, and magnetic north, sir!" "Good" he replied, and then continued, "Now everyone, keep your maps and compasses. Next time you will be using them out in the countryside. That's all, thank you." As he packed up his stuff and placed his cap on, we rose to attention, and Kendrick saluted as he left the room. We all filed out, Kendrick called a smoke break, and then came up to me and John as we lit up.

"Davis, that was damned stupid to get caught like that. You should know by now that the green machine isn't too keen on initiative. If you know what you're doing, go ahead by all means, but don't get caught doing it" Kendrick advised. He continued "Mind you, it was good to see you put him in his place, the damned know-it-all." At our questioning looks he said, "You didn't hear this from me, but he's one of those ninety day wonders, never been away from his mother, and thinks he knows it all. Watch out for him, he'll have you up on a charge, as soon as look at you." "Sarge," we replied as he moved away. "For explanation, a ninety day wonder is the derogatory name for an officer straight out of Duntroon Officer School, and they usually go there from university, so have no practical work experience, and think they know everything."

The rest of that day went to plan, down to the rifle range in the afternoon where Captain Jacobs briefing was "Well, if it isn't my most accurate and favourite platoon. All the usual, so go get ready, and we'll start." After we finished, with everyone attaining high scores again, during the Jacobs debriefed us. He said, "The highest scores today again go to both your Corporals. Davis first and Buchanan second; I would like to talk to you both before you go."

Kendrick had the platoon move to the preparation area to start cleaning the rifles, while John and I stayed with Jacobs. When they were out of earshot he said "Very soon your shooting training will be at an end, and that means that the base championship competition for this intake will be run. Now that means the two best shooters from each platoon go up against each other. It's not one of the mandatory qualifications, purely voluntary. Would you two be interested?" We both looked at each other; I nodded, and so did John. We both looked at Jacobs, and answered "Yes, Sir!" He replied "Good, I'll put you both down." As we moved off and joined the platoon, Kendrick looked at us enquiringly. We both nodded, he smiled, and said "Good."

Back at the hut we had our usual conference, and while this was taking place John and I both started cleaning our rifles. As Kendrick was drinking his coffee, we both completely stripped the SLRs down. As we were laying all the sections of them out on the table, Kendrick exclaimed "SHIT! You're not supposed to strip them down that far. That's an armourer's job, that's more than a field strip!" John looked at him and said "But we do this all the time, Sarge." "Shit, just don't get caught doing it, otherwise we'll all be charged. I didn't see this," we laughed and nodded. As he continued with "Tomorrow first up, we'll be meeting a truck at the quadrangle, and it'll take us to where that fucking Ferris is, for field navigational exercises," I interjected by saying "I get the feeling you don't like him, Sarge." "Damned right, I don't the stupid fool. He tried to have me charged the first day he arrived, for not saluting him as he passed. The idiot didn't even have his cap on! Just remember the warning I gave you this morning. Anyway, after lunch we'll be in the gym for unarmed combat training, so sports clothes for that. Now you'll be up against the Charlie crew this week, and you'll be playing in new boots. They'll be here tomorrow, and you'll need to collect them from the Q store. Detail a couple of guys to leave early in the afternoon to bring them back here. Ok, that's it, I'll see you in the morning, and get those rifles together."

John took both rifles, and we headed into the main room. He put them in the rack and locked it, then started writing the SOP's on the board. I called everyone together, and filled them all in about the next day, informing as well as warning them about Ferris. I finished with "Merv, I want you and Joe to leave the gym early, head over to the Q store before it shuts, and pick up all the new footy boots." The team members exclaimed as one "Yeah!" and clapped while I just smiled.

Next morning as were on the truck, I asked Kendrick, who was sitting beside me, about the weekend day leave. He said he would bring some leave applications back with him to the hut in the afternoon. I nodded, took in the scenery, and worked out that we were already past the grenade range. We were heading right up into the base back blocks, as I recalled the base layout map in my mind. We soon came to a halt beside a land rover, where Ferris was leaning against the bonnet. The driver came around and released the tailgate, and we climbed down as Ferris called "Right, gather round." After Kendrick's warning, I knew I'd have to pull my horns in with this one, and not get too riled if he had a go at me.

Ferris continued "I'll be splitting you into five groups of four, and give each group different starting points. There are markers at each part of the course. You'll collect your correct colour marker with the next set of coordinates and bring them back with you, that way I'll know that you didn't take any shortcuts. Each person will navigate one leg each, and the first one will be taken as a group. Now, this is also a timed exercise. I know how long it should take, and your times will be rated against that, so into fours, move now!" The group I was in had me, Merv, Joe, and Charlie. That was cool, as we could all map read really well. The group colours were white, blue, red, yellow, and green, mine was red. How fitting I thought, this bastard could really get me hot under the collar, treating us like school boys!

Before we started I had my group fold the maps, so that we had all the correct rectangular area ready with our present location. I had it worked out, already marked, and they'd fit into our side trouser pockets without being refolded. We were the third group to start. Ferris came over with the first group of coordinates, and pulled out a stopwatch with a green tag, and said "Ready, go!" We quickly worked out our direction to go, and left. It took us only a minute or so to reach the next post, and retrieve the marker. Merv worked out the direction of the next one, and we were on our way again. The next leg, Charlie worked out. Joe did the next. When we arrived at the last one, there was no set of coordinates written on it! Luckily I had the starting location, and as this was the last leg I assumed we were to return to the start point. I quickly worked out the direction of travel, and we headed there. When we arrived back at the vehicles, only Kendrick and Ferris were there. We were the first group to arrive back! Ferris clocked us in at five minutes forty two seconds, and said "That's impossible, you must have cheated somehow!"

"Show me your markers now!" I was already pissed off about no return coordinates. I said "Sir! This is the first one that YOU watched us work out, then each of the group kept the marker for the leg they did, and this is the last one. Someone screwed up this one! There are NO return coordinates on it, as you can see!" With that I handed it to him, he looked at it, and then said "Yes I see. So how did you get back here?" "Well sir, I like to know where I am, so I had already worked that out and marked it on my map. It's real easy when you know what you're doing!" I replied, and handed him my map. While this conversation had been going on, the red and blue groups had returned and been clocked in by Kendrick.

Lt Ferris said "Well, there's no way you could have done the course in the time it took you without cheating!" Now I was really pissed, and replied with a quiet deadly chill in my voice, "My group haven't lived in big cities, we're used to navigating around the country, quickly. Now, am I to understand that you are calling us LIARS, SIR?" Everyone present could hear what was going on between Ferris and I. Kendrick interjected by saying, "Excuse me,

192

sir, red and blue have arrived back. If there's some doubt, I could retrace Corporal Davis's route while I was timed if you like." Ferris said "Yes, that would be a good idea, it will avoid any confusion." I gave Kendrick my map, saying "The coordinates are marked at each post and the back bearing from here is already set on my compass," and I passed that to him as well. He said softly "I told you to be careful with this joker," then he raised his voice and said "Ready, sir." Ferris gave him the go and Kendrick left. As he left, the white group came in, so Ferris went across to them, collected their markers, and went to the land rover. Everyone gathered around me to find out what was going on, so by the time we had a smoke, they were all in the loop about what was happening.

Kendrick arrived back, five minutes and thirty seconds later, knocking twelve seconds off our time. John's group, yellow, still hadn't returned, and I wondered what the problem was. Ferris came over to us, and said "Corporal Davis, I owe your group an apology for my confusion." Just as I answered with a knowing smile "Thank you, sir, apology accepted," John's group came out of the scrub, and walked up to Ferris. John said "Sorry we were so long sir, but some damned fool hadn't put any coordinates on our last marker, so it took a while to work out where we were." Ferris replied, "Very well, Lance Corporal, I'll take it under advisement," and then moved away to the rover with Kendrick.

I watched him move away with a smile, thinking "you've just been given one hell of a kick up the arse, and taught a lesson by people you consider beneath you. Learn from it, you turkey!" While I had been watching and thinking, the rest of the guys filled John's group in on what had been taking place. John joined me for a smoke, and I said "You know there was a close call here earlier. You could've ended up as full Corporal, while I'd have been charged, and sent to Holsworthy for striking an officer." He clapped me on the shoulder, and said "Thank Christ you didn't, then."

Ten minutes later, as Ferris and Kendrick made their way over, I called "Platoon Atten...shun!" Ferris and I both saluted, and he said "Thank you, Corporal, men. I hope you enjoyed our little exercise, and enjoy the rest of your day. Thank you, you can now make your way back to camp." With that, Kendrick headed us to the truck where the driver was waiting, we all climbed aboard, he put the tailgate in place before hopping in, and starting the truck.

Kendrick, John and I were across and beside each other. Beckoning us to lean forward he quietly, he said "Jesus, Tiger, you were close to hitting that little prick, and I couldn't have done anything about it. As it is, you came close to being charged for insubordination. For Christ's sake, now heed my warning. Now the P.E. instructor today is Sgt Wallace, and he's just as bad as Ferris, but likes to be rough. Yes, needless to say, I don't like him. He likes to bully people, so keep your tempers in check this afternoon. Clear?" We both nodded, and then sat back up.

During lunch, we filled the other NCO's in on what had taken place with Ferris earlier. Chick, in turn, filled us in about Wallace. Bravo had been doing training with him this morning, and he said "He's a mean son of a bitch, and built like a brick shithouse; bastard almost broke my arm." Oh great, I thought to myself. It looked it was going to be one of THOSE days.

CHAPTER 19

That afternoon, as we made our way into the gym, and over to the mats that were set up, I noticed the two civvies, White and Brown, were back. They were seated three rows up on the bench seats behind the mats. Kendrick had us sit along the bottom bench. As we sat, three men entered in gym gear. I surmised that the one in the centre was Sgt Wallace; he looked to be about six foot, lean, and powerfully built. They stopped in front of us, and he said "My name is Sergeant Wallace, and these are Corporals Harrison and Rodgers. It's our job to teach you unarmed combat, but to do that we need to assess what you know, and are capable of."

As he was talking, he was striding up and down the mat in front of us, and as he continued, I got peeved with his swaggering, holier-than-thou attitude. "This platoon has a reputation for being run by someone that has, for some reason, a reputation for being tough and not to be messed with. Stand up Corporal Davis. Well, you don't look anything near the reputation you have. Do you know how to fight, Davis?" Keeping a tight rein on my mounting anger, I replied "a little, Sarge." "Probably gained brawling on a football field, from what I can gather, is that right, hard man?" He asked it with a sneer. I kept my answer short, so the fury I was feeling wasn't given away, "Possibly, Sarge." "Well, let's see how good you are tough guy! Would you like to try to take me on?" Glancing around at the platoon, some of them were making punching motions. John was nodding slowly as was Kendrick, and so I smiled at Wallace, and said "I'll give it a go, Sarge."

"Ok, I'll make it easier for you." He went across to a box on the far side of the mats, and came back holding a child's plastic bowie knife. He handed it to me, saying "Now the object of the exercise is for you to make believe kill me with that, and I'll try to stop you. Don't worry hard man, I won't get hurt!" He made the last statement made with promising menace in his voice. As we circled each other, with the knife in my left hand I was looking keenly for a weakness. I found it! He was a southpaw, so he'd lead with his left, and then I noticed something else. He didn't keep his knees bent for balance. Good, now all I had to do was think of a way to would bring him down. Coming side on to the benches, he made a feint with his right. I blocked it, and like a cat I spun around to my left, to avoid his left that was coming. Continuing my spin, I went in close and with all the power and fury I could muster, drove my right karate style punch into his solar plexus.

At the same time I stomped down on his left inner ankle with my right foot. Without waiting to see the result, I immediately spun the opposite way, collecting his right in both of mine, and drove his own fist into his head. At the same time, I lashed the side of his right knee with a sideways kick from mine, which had the desired result of bringing him down on his right. Instantly I wrapped my right arm around his head jerking it back, and said as I did with my left "Throat cut from ear to ear." I pushed hard so there'd be a line across his neck, and continued "And for good measure, a stab into the belly and rip across taking out the kidneys." I used the butt end of the knife to emphasize the stab into the belly, and drew the blade across his T shirt to his side and said "You're now fucking dead!"

I threw the knife down and stood waiting. I heard Kendrick bellow "Atten…shun! Platoon outside. Ten minute smoke break, and recess Move!" As John draped his arm around my shoulder, and moved me along, I saw Brown and White looking from me to the mat and back again, and then talking to each other. Outside, John passed me a lit smoke, and exclaimed "Christ, remind me, not to get on your bad side. Well done!" The guys were all talking in excited murmurs amongst themselves, as Kendrick came to the doorway, and said "Ok, everyone back inside." Back inside, and seated on the benches, we waited for Wallace. He came back in with the two Corporals. He was leaning on a crutch, and I noticed he had a bandage on the ankle I had racked with my foot. The

196

mark on his neck would last for a few days. He addressed us with "Today's lesson is going to be postponed, because as you can see Corporal Davis has done me some damage. Well done to him! So we'll continue this at a later stage. Dismissed." He then moved off. Kendrick came and stood in front of us saying "Ok, listen up. Buchanan will be taking you back to the barracks, while Davis and I go elsewhere. Anything you want, Davis?" "Yes Sarge. Merv, don't forget to go to the Q store and get the boots," I answered.

When the platoon had left, I asked "Where are we going, Sarge?" "We're going to the adjutant's office to see Major Ricks; we'll talk on the way." As we walked, Kendrick started talking. "First off, the Major has had problems with Wallace before. He's upfront with what he says, as well as being fair, and is a damn fine bloke. Just don't embellish anything, be straight about what took place. Secondly, we're doing this just in case Wallace tries to have you charged, and puts the blame for his injuries onto you." At that, I interjected.

"But, Sarge, I did do the damage." He cut me off there. "Are you trying to be stupid, of course you did, but Wallace is capable of lying. He could say you attacked him for no reason, and his Corporals will back whatever he tells them to. He goaded you into it, and he underestimated his target. Frankly, so did I. He does this with every class. If you had been any other person, he would have beaten the crap out of you, and I wouldn't have been able to do, or say, anything. This brings me to my point. I thought you were full of yourself when you first arrived, but even then there was something about you, so I let things take their course. You also do a bloody good job. It's as if you were born to be a leader. What beats me is why you refused officer training? One last thing, how you turned the tables on Wallace was a pure joy to watch. And quick, I haven't seen many quicker! You seemed to know what he was going to do before he did it. So for what you did, thank you, we won't get a chance talk like this too often, but please consider me a friend, even if I am your boss."

He said the last part of what he was saying with a smile and

197

continued when we were near the base offices. "When we get inside, just remember all the respect for officers. You've no hat, so no saluting, only the usual, and stay at attention, until told otherwise. Ok, let's go." Inside Kendrick led me up the hall, then stopped, directed me where to stand, then knocked on the door marked Adjutant. He went in when he was called, and shut the door behind him. After ten minutes or so, the door opened, and I heard the summons, "Come in acting Corporal Davis!" I entered, marched to the desk, and halted in front of it. I stayed at attention, and said "Acting Corporal Davis reporting, Sir."

I remembered Major Ricks from the street march. He was in his forties, about five nine but still looked lean, and then I remembered seeing him on the running oval every time I had been on it, so he was in good shape. He said "Stand easy. Now from what I hear from your platoon sergeant, you may be in a bit of bother from an incident during your first unarmed combat session. So let's hear what happened." So I started telling Major Ricks the story. At different points, he interrupted with questions that I answered, and then continued the story. When I reached the end, I stayed quiet, and waited. It wasn't long before the Major asked "Were there any witnesses to what occurred, Corporal Davis?"

"Yes Sir," I replied. Ricks said "Well, come on man, who were they?" I replied "Sorry, Sir. Sgt Kendrick's, all of my platoon, and Corporals Harrison and Rodgers, but I'm not sure if they'd give a true account of what happened, Sir." He leaned back looking at me, and said "No, I don't think they would. Were there any independent witnesses?" "Yes, Sir, the two civvies, Mr. White and Brown," I replied. This seemed to take his interest, because he leaned forward, and asked "Oh, you know them, do you?" "No, Sir," and recounted the run in with them before Christmas to him, and then asked "Sir, am I going to be in much trouble over this?" He leaned back again, seemed to be thinking, and then said "No, I don't think so, but if anything happens, you make sure that it is referred to me, understand?" "Yes Sir. Thank you, Sir." He smiled and said "Ok, that's it. Thank you both. You're dismissed." With that, Kendrick and I came to attention, and marched out.

As he shut the door, Kendrick turned to me and said "Right, head back to the hut, and I'll join you in fifteen minutes." I replied "Sure, Sarge," and headed out of the building, making my way to our hut. As I entered, I heard a lot of noise coming from the main room, so decided to investigate. Reaching the main room, I saw the footy players were trying on the new boots. John was sitting on the table beside a shoe box laughing along with everyone else. Merv spotted me, and called "Atten...shun!" Moving from the doorway, and with a smile on my face, said "Don't worry about that, as you were," but everyone had become silent, with Charlie calling out "Are you in the shit, Corp?" Merv said "Yeah, what's happening, Corp?" So I sat on the table, and filled everyone in on what I had been doing since leaving the gym. There were a lot of questions that I answered, and then talk turned to what I had done to Wallace. How he deserved everything I did to him, and then inevitable question, of how I had done it. There was only one answer I could give, "Just instinct, and my fighting reactions I guess!"

John passed the shoe box to me, and with a smile I said "Well, let's see what delights are in this box." Inside was a pair of black and green Puma brand footy boots (back in those days, puma were the best, and cost quite a deal). I flipped off my right sandshoe to try one on. They were perfect, and fitted like a glove. I couldn't wait to get on the field and try them out. As I put them back into the box I looked at my watch, and said "All right, listen up guys. The Sarge will be here any minute, so just keep an eye out for him."

I had no sooner finished speaking, and in walked Kendrick, carrying a pile of forms. "Atten...shun!" I called, and everyone stood. Kendrick smiled as he saw some of the guys with one boot on and another off, and said "Ok, let's keep this casual, rest easy." Everyone resumed their seats as he continued, "Right, you lazy lot, what was planned for tomorrow has now been changed. What you were supposed to be doing was going to be a continuation of today. As you know, it was supposed to be unarmed combat training, but because someone has incapacitated your instructor, that won't be happening." Everyone cheered and laughed, and he continued with, "All right, settle down. You don't get out of it that easy. We will be doing some physical training back in the gym. After we've all been for a run on the oval, we'll all be watching our football team and their new boots play against Charlie platoon. Sports gear all day that should make it easier for you. I know how hard it is for you find something to wear," putting on an impression of a female, which made us all laugh.

Then holding up the forms he had brought, said "These are day leave application forms. They'll be kept by Davis, in his office. Now there are strict rules that apply to them. I'll read them to you, so there's NO confusion. One, civvy gear only, In other words, you aren't to go into town in uniform. Two, anyone on day leave MUST be back on base no later than eighteen hundred. Three, be on good behaviour at all times. In other words DON'T go getting drunk, or getting into fights, and no disrepute to the ADF (Australian Defence Force) will be tolerated! I don't want some cherry berry turning up at my place, to tell me one of my soldiers has been arrested, is that understood?" We all chorused "Yes, Sarge." He went on, "Four, the platoon must remain at seventy five percent strength. In other words, only five of you can be on day leave at a time. Now, the day after tomorrow the shooting championships start. We are going to be represented by Corporals Davis and Buchanan, and the platoon will be at the rifle range. It will be over the whole day, so it looks like you'll have an easy couple of days. Then we'll be getting back into serious training. That's all for now, so consider yourselves dismissed." Kendrick then turned to John and me, and said "Right. Let's go have a bit of a chin wag."

I picked up my shoe box, and put it on my desk before going into what we called the conference room. Kendrick started by saying "I'm sorry guys, but with the day leave, one of you must be here at all times, so you'll have to work that out between the two of you.

Now, it looks like Wallace is going to be out of action for two weeks, obviously you did more damage than you thought, Tiger, so we're getting someone from Bandiana barracks down the road across the border to replace him. Be wary when he's back on deck, he may be stupid enough to look for revenge. That type always does. Back to the day leave, you'll have to sign off on the applications here under barracks leader before giving them to me. That will be during our pm briefing, and I'll give you notice whether they've been okayed or rejected the following day." Then he said "I wasn't expecting the shoot to happen so fast. Jacobs told me as I was leaving the office to come over here. Are you two going to be ready for it?" Looking at John, and receiving a nod I answered, "Sure, Sarge. We'll get our rifles prepared tomorrow afternoon before dinner." "Good, Ok. I'll see you in the morning," he said, and got up to leave. He paused and said "Davis, in case I didn't say it earlier, well done today." After I thanked him, he left.

At the canteen, when I walked in that night for dinner there were cheers and calls of "On ya Corp!" as I made my way up to the serving counter. As I sat down at the NCO's table, Greg from Charlie platoon commented "It's all over camp how you beat the crap out of Wallace, and I'm playing footy against you and your lot tomorrow, take it easy, please." Jim from Echo asked with a laugh "Hey, you bloody street slugger, did you get into much trouble?" While Chick said "some people will do anything to get out of a bit of work." So I answered all the guys' comments and questions. Before starting to eat, I said to each "I'll take it easy, if you do, Greg," told them all about my time with Major Ricks, and told Chick "You won't have to worry about a broken arm anymore, unless the new guy is just as bad." That started the questions, so John, who was nearly finished his meal, filled them in with all the latest news. After I had finished eating, I asked "Hey is there anyone taking bets on the shoot?"

Chick answered saying, "Yep I am, see me in the boozer later." "I will" I replied, and then talk turned to general matters. Later, as John and I were heading into the mess, I looked at my watch and said "I'm just going to make a quick call to Helen, to try and make a date. Can you grab me a drink please?" John nodded, and I made my way to the phone. Helen answered on the second ring, saying "Hi, Tom," so I asked "How did you know it was me?" "Apart from work, and my parents, you're the only one with my number," and I knew it wouldn't be either of them," she replied. While chatting we arranged to meet up Sunday, at the club. She knocked off at midday. Then we could spend time together.

Joining John at our usual table, I asked "Do you mind if I have Sunday leave this week?" He answered "Sure, I wasn't planning anything, so I was going to stay on base anyway." "Cool," Shortly after, we were joined by Chick and Rob, his 2IC, and then Greg, Terry from Charlie, Jim and Mark from Echo. As talk became more general, I motioned for Chick to join me away from the group. Beers in hand we moved to another table out of earshot, and I asked "Ok, what are the odds?" Chick replied "Evens on you, four to one on John, all the others ten to one." I said "Right, put me down for a grand on John." Chick stared incredulously at me, and asked "You're betting against yourself?" "Yep, I'm good, but John is more consistently accurate" I lied. I had already planned to let John win, if it came down to the two of us. Chick said "Ok done, I take it you're good for it?" In answer, I took out my wallet, showed him the stack of hundreds in it, and asked "Do you want it now?" "No, I know you're good for it now, if you lose," he replied, as we moved to re-join the others.

We won the game the next day by a margin of twelve to eight, and it was really good to run in the new Pumas. The team guys loved them, and we all thanked Kendrick after the game for getting them for us. The briefing that afternoon went pretty quickly. The only thing Kendrick needed to tell us was, "Base standard for the platoon tomorrow, but I'm afraid you two will have to have your field gear." I gave the day leave applications to Kendrick. I was the only one applying for Sunday, but four others had applied for Saturday. I had signed them off, but left it to Kendrick to sign mine off, which he did, saying "You've taken note of these; I'll put them in today." I said "Yep, John and I ruled up the white board in my office, so we can keep track." "Good, go ahead and get your rifles ready, I'll see you tomorrow."

Next Morning, as we were heading to the rifle range, I was figuring out how I would throw the competition, if it would be needed. From the odds on the betting, I had to assume that John and I were the top contenders. Arriving on site, I saw that most of the base hierarchy was there, the two civvies, and a lot of others. As we made our way to the platoon's position overlooking the range, I had a chance to get Kendrick aside, out of earshot of anyone. I said "Sarge, if you have any bets laid on the outcome, change them or double them for John to win." He stared at me for a minute or so, and then said "Right, good, thanks for that," and he headed off. I then saw him talking with Sgt Harris. Shortly after he returned and gave me a wink. Then the shooters were called to the briefing.

Captain Jacobs told us how the competition would progress. After twenty warm up rounds, we would then all fire seven grouping rounds. After that, the lowest scoring four would fire seven more, with the lowest two being eliminated. Then the highest four would fire off seven, and the lowest two would shoot against the two surviving from round one. The highest survivor would shoot off with those remaining from round two, and the highest two would shoot off against each other to determine the overall winner.

He told us that the range instructors would act as our spotters and that after our shoot, to raise one of our legs when finished or out of ammo. He then assigned our firing positions. Being Alpha platoon, I was on position one and John two. It then progressed down with Echo having seven and eight. He finished his briefing, with "Alright, move to your positions." When we were in position, the range instructors had us release the empty magazines and load the first full mag. We got into the prone position for firing, and over the P.A. I heard Jacobs voice, ask "Ready?" As each of the instructors raised their hands, the instructions "Fire at will, in your own time," came.

I pulled the cocking slide and let it go, to feed the first round into the firing chamber. I took aim, and fired three times in rapid succession. My spotter told me the results and I readjusted my aim and fired seven more, all on target. Then I moved my aim to another area on the target, letting my spotter know what I was doing, and fired three; all were on target. I fired the last seven rapidly, and looked at the target as I raised my right leg. My spotter had lifted his arm, and we waited for the cease fire order.

Hearing the cease fire order, I ejected the empty mag, waited as the targets were lowered, and my spotter handed me the next mag. After inserting it, I lay my rifle on the ground, and leaned my chin on my elbows, facing toward the target area while I waited. The new targets came up, a full standing figure, with the order "Full body shots only. Fire at will, commence!" I scooped up my rifle, pulled the cocking slide, fired all seven in rapid succession, and raised my leg. My spotter raised his arm. I then had time to look at my handiwork. They were all bang on, dead centre. After the cease fire order, we all moved off the range to await the results. Upon reaching the platoon, both John and I started cleaning or guns, as we both knew that we wouldn't be firing again until after lunch. This proved to be the case. We were the top two.

After lunch, the top four fired again. This reduced the field to me, John and a guy from Echo. Then it was down to John and I. Prior to the shootout, John cleaned his rifle, while I didn't; this would give me the excuse I wanted.

Prior to the shootout, Jacobs called us both to the bottom of the tower, and leaning over said "Three shots only, and all to be head shots. Do you want a clearing shot first?" I said "No," but John said "Yes," so nodding at John's spotter, who returned the nod, we moved back into position. When we were ready, the order came, "Clearing shot, fire!" John cleared his gun. I inserted the three shot mag, and raised my leg, saying to my spotter "Watch his shots, not mine," as we waited the order. "Three head shot rounds only, fire at will." I let John fire first, and then I was behind him. We were neck and neck, and as he fired his last, my spotter commented, "All three bang on." I took aim again, and my last shot was on target, but a quarter inch away. John had won. As we cleared our rifles, and awaited the cease fire order, I leaned across and shook his hand.

While we marching back to the hut, John said "You threw that last shot." I replied "No, mate, but next time I'll take the time to clean the rifle. Probably a speck of left over grit up the tube. One win for you. At least I'll end up with the assault course record."

CHAPTER 20

Back at the hut, while we were having our usual conference, Kendrick stated "They sound like they're in fine spirits, and so they should be. Thanks to you two, this platoon is earning high praise. Considering this is only your first few weeks here, I'm earning a lot of brownie points as well." The volume of the joking and laughter was a little higher than normal from further down the hut, where the platoon dorm was. The following day, we were going to our last session on the grenade range, so field gear, with base standard in the afternoon, and back to the assault course. This made me smile, because I wanted to see if I could break the course record, or get as close to it as I could. I had now made my mind up that I would hold the camp record before leaving our basic training behind. Before he left, Kendrick told us that all the leave had been approved.

After Kendrick left, John said "You know, the more I think about it, the more I'm sure you threw your last shot." I replied "No, definitely not, and what's worse, I lost money on a bet. Just as well I had hedged my bet, because I bet on you too, so I might have made up for what I lost." This seemed to mollify him, because he said with a smile "Well, it's my name on the camp trophy, now all you have to do is knock a minute off your time, and grab the assault course record." I replied "Yeah, I've been thinking about that, feel like joining me out there Saturday morning for some training, and then we'll see how close I come?" "No problems, but before we do anything else, let's get these rifles cleaned."

Later that night in the mess, I caught up with Chick, as he was counting out what he owed me, he said "Thanks for the heads up on John," so I answered "Yeah, well as far as he's concerned, I lost money, got it?" "Sure, ok." By now my wallet was getting hard to close, because of all the money I had travelled with, plus my pays, and now another four grand from Chick. When I got back to my room later, I emptied out my wallet, and counted what was there. It came to nine thousand, six hundred, and thirty dollars. So I put the six hundred and thirty back into my wallet, and it closed with ease now. The nine thousand I put with my bank book in an envelope with a rubber band around it, and made a mental note to find some way to deposit the money into my account.

As I was sitting at the desk, my mind wandered to the changes I had made to my life. Then another thought from school crossed my mind, and I reached for the dictionary, and found what I was looking for. 'Catalyst' in sub sections three: someone or something whose actions inspire further, usually more important events.

Reading that had put my brain into overdrive. My life had started to change at the time Jill had entered my life. Had she helped turn me into a catalyst? What important events could I inspire? Thinking deeper, I decided no, that wasn't the case. I tried to think of how I would have ended up without her being there, and came up with the scenario of me, either ending up in jail or stuck in a dead end job, in a one horse town. Then I hit the nail on the head! Jill had been my catalyst; I had started turning my life around, without even realising it, ever since we met! Well, that was a revelation, and thought I'd better get some sleep.

Kendrick had arranged the truck to be at the parade ground when we got there in the morning, and it wasn't really a nice day. It had rained during the night, and was overcast and drizzly every now and again. At the range, we were formed into our groups, had the briefing, then Jacobs made his way up to the observation platform, where the two civvies were already watching. He confirmed the red smoke, and then Taggert tossed me the green, saying "Wait till I give you the order." The order came, and I tossed the green to commence the live fire. As we each grabbed a grenade from the box, the first detonation came from over in front of number three emplacement. I had a look down range and picked a target, then pulled the pin, let the lever fly, counted to two, and then tossed my grenade, spot on target. The others used my target as their point of aim, and one by one let fly.

As we waited, Will was last up. As he pulled the pin, he slipped on the wet concrete, the grenade rolled free out of his grasp, and the lever flew! Impulsively, I was on my feet, yelling "GET OUT!" As I dived for the loose grenade, Taggert, who had been behind me, saw what I was doing and threw himself full length across everyone, while watching my progress. Coming out of my dive, I hit the concrete hard with my head as I landed. I grabbed the grenade with my outstretched hand, scooped it up, and rolled onto my back. I tossed it as far as it would go, and rolled into a ball to present a smaller target for any flying debris. Then all hell broke loose!

As the grenade exploded, whistles were sounding, and red smoke was blowing everywhere. Jacobs had seen what was taking place, and started the whistle blowing, and thrown the first red from on top of the tower!

Sergeant Taggert had thrown the second red right after the explosion, (he must have had it in his hand), as he rolled off the other guys. Meanwhile, I had rolled over onto my back again, and just lay there, looking up at the sky. I was thankful to be seeing it, but Christ my head hurt.

Kendrick came racing into the pit, looked at the other guys, saw they were ok, and then came over. He knelt by me asking "Are you all right?" Rolling my head to face him, I replied "No, half left. Shit my head hurts." As I raised myself to lean on my left elbow, I raised my right hand to my head. It came away sticky and red with blood. Kendrick said "Don't move" and yelled "Medic!" One of the other sergeants in the team came running up with a First Aid kit, and then he and Kendrick picked me up by the armpits, and dragged me over to the wall to prop me up with my back against it. He started cleaning the wound on the side of my head, saying "You're lucky, just loose skin from gravel rash." He started looking at my right arm, and after cleaning the cuts on the back of my hand and wrist, said "Yeah, this too, now this is going to hurt." He put some cleaning stuff on a gauze pad and cleaned the cuts, then put a pad and bandage on my head, and said "Just stay still here."

By this time, most of the platoon, all of the range staff, and Captain Jacobs were crowded into the emplacement. Jacobs shouted "Anyone that wasn't in this emplacement go up top, and stay there!" Then Jacobs asked if I was ok. After finding out I was fine, he told me to stay seated, and not to move. Shortly afterward Colonel Trickett and Major Ricks arrived with also a field ambulance and doctor. I was pronounced fit for duty, and they left. I could hear Col Trickett saying to Jacobs "I want all paper work and statements about this incident on my desk, by sixteen hundred today," and then he and Ricks left.

Jacobs called for Kendrick, and they stood talking five minutes or so. Jacobs came over and said "Well done, Corporal. This afternoon, you and your group, along with myself and Sgt Taggert, will be having a debriefing session at thirteen thirty today down at the admin building. Please make sure that you, and your men, have prepared written statements about what occurred, and we'll go on from there. You can join your platoon when you are ready. Would you like a hand up?" "Yes, thank you sir." Back on my feet, I came to attention and saluted, he returned the salute, and said "I'll see you this afternoon." I joined the platoon, and we returned to the truck, and back to the barracks.

Outside our hut, before being dismissed, Kendrick said "Alright, after you get your field gear off, I need Baker, Browne, and Chapman report to the conference room. The rest of you will be with me this afternoon, and until then, dismissed!" He then turned to John and I saying "Hold the fort I'm going to get a stack of incident reports, and be back in ten minutes." He moved off, and John and I headed inside to get out of our field gear. When we all gathered in the conference room, I had to send Eric to get a couple more chairs, then Kendrick got down to telling us how to fill the reports. He emphasized that we all stick to the truth, and only what each of us saw, and what happened immediately afterward. Then we all got started on writing our reports.

After everyone had finished their reports, Kendrick read them all. He had Will and Merv change a couple of words, and initial the corrections, then leaned back in his chair, and said "Good, well done, I'll give these to Captain Jacobs. This afternoon you'll be having a meeting with him, for a debriefing. No doubt, there'll probably be some interviews over the matter. Just stick to what you have put down and you won't have any problems. Don't forget, if you're asked if there were any independent witnesses, that the civvies were there, and saw everything. Stay in base standard dress, but don't wear your fatigue hats inside the building. After you're finished, you're dismissed for the rest of the day, and I'll see you later. Any questions? No, alright you can go and get ready for lunch. Dismissed."

As we entered the canteen for lunch, the place fell silent as we trooped in, and started again as we joined the others at the table. Chick said "Thanks for that. Your lot have screwed up my day, now we've got drilling this arvo, when we should be playing with the grenades. Your lot will do anything to get out of work! Looks like your all in one piece, close huh?" "Yeah, and painful," I replied pointing at my noggin. Jim said "Well, come on, tell us all about it." John and I related what happened.

Later, I marched our group down to the admin block, and as we walked in, Sgt Taggert followed us, and told us to go to the conference room at the end of the hall. As we entered the room, Jacobs, who was already sitting, directed us to sit.

Taggert then came in closing the door behind him. He took a seat, and Jacobs said "Alright we're all here, now each of you will be questioned. After you've given me your report, I'll convey my findings to you, and any disciplinary action, should it be warranted, that may or may not be taken in regard to this matter. Then I'll take everything to the Adjutant and the OC (Officer Commanding), and unless they want further clarification, that will be the end of the whole sorry incident. I have Sergeant Kendrick's report, and have already spoken to him, so we'll start with Sergeant Taggert."

One by one, we handed across our reports, and Jacobs would

write further notes on the pad he was using. As he questioned each member deeper, he would write the question he would ask first, then the answer given. After Taggert, it was Merv's turn, then John, and Eric. When it came to Will, Jacobs really fired questions about how he came to slip, and how the grenade had come loose from his hand. I was about to interject, and Jacobs seeing I was about to say something, held up his hand in a stop motion. A couple of questions later, he finished with Will, and it was my turn. After reading my report, he sat back thinking, and then he leaned forward, and started writing.

He looked at me, as he finished writing, and asked "Your report is very concise, but what I would like to know is, what went through your mind when you started moving?" His question threw me for a loop, and I thought hard before giving my answer. "In all honesty Sir, nothing. I just reacted. I can recall that as I dived over Will, I had started counting in my head. Then as I threw it, I was between second counts when it exploded. However, afterward while I was on my back, I thought, shit, only half a second between the squad's survival, and death." When he finished writing he pushed me again, "Weren't you afraid of dying?" Thinking quickly, I replied "No, Sir! I was more concerned about my men." He then stated "Admirably put, thank you."

When he finished writing my answer, he leaned back with his eyes closed, and we waited. He opened his eyes, and said "Thank you, gentlemen. The ground was wet, and those emplacements do get slippery. Private Chapman, you'll no doubt have learned, you have to keep a tighter grip in this sort of weather. If not for the actions of Corporal Davis here, none of you would have survived this accident. It wasn't preventable, and I see no cause for blame, therefore I'll be recommending that no further action be taken. Thank you. You're dismissed."

By the time we were finished, it was after three. As we headed back to the barracks, I said "Well, the day's almost over. I don't know about you guys, but I'm going to get my washing together, and head over to the laundry before they shut shop." That became the consensus, and once back there we grabbed our dirty gear, and headed to the laundry. I had put in one of my dress uniforms for dry cleaning also, just in case I wouldn't get a chance later. After being assured that everything would be ready by Monday morning, we headed back to the hut, to await the arrival of the rest of the platoon.

The platoon arrived at the hut, and Kendrick walked into the conference room and sat down. I had already made the coffee, and then we relaxed while having our drinks. As he lit a smoke, Kendrick asked "So how did it go?" I told him what had occurred, the intense questioning, and the result that Jacobs had reached, and that no further action would be taken. Kendrick said "Good, but it could have been avoided, if they'd fix the drainage in those damned emplacements." After draining his coffee, and lighting up another smoke, he continued. "Alright, well the whole platoon has been shaken by this, so keep a close eye on them. Make sure that the ones going on leave are back on time. You have a good time on Sunday, Davis, because all of Monday we'll be in the gym. We'll be going through some unarmed combat training, because we have to get back on the training schedule, so sports gear. I'll see you then, have a good weekend boys."

With that, he got up and left. John said "You know that means you're not to beat up the new guy don't you?" We both laughed at this, and then decided what we would do the next day. That night in the mess, we had a relaxed couple of games of snooker, while smoking and drinking, and then Greg and Terry from Charlie platoon joined us. As the rest of the NCO's eventually arrived, the talk turned to the week's events. We all had to agree, this week had been very eventful. Chick, ever the optimist stated "Yeah and it's not over yet. I'm just been wondering how many guys I'll have left after the weekend, they might go AWOL (absent without leave) on me!" His observation had us all laughing.

On Sunday, I rang the local taxi company from the canteen after breakfast, and booked a cab to meet me at the front gate at eleven. I figured this would give me plenty of time to get into town and have a quick look around before I went to the RSL to meet Helen. Then went back to my room, and pottered about. I had a shower, got ready to go, I told John I was off, and left.

I reached the main gate just as the cab arrived, so I hopped in and told the driver to drop me anywhere in the main drag. He pulled up at a rank in the main street, and as I paid him he confirmed that the RSL was just around the next corner. Thanking him, I went off for a wander along the street. I found the Bank of New South Wales, where my account was held, and looked at the times for their business hours. Ten till four on weekdays, and ten till twelve on Saturdays. Good, I thought if I take next Saturday, I could get the cash I had deposited.

I walked around for a bit longer killing time, and reached the RSL at ten to twelve. As I reached the bar, Helen put a beer down in front of me, and asked "What happened to you?" Spotting the band aid on the side of my head, I smiled, and replied "Long story, I'll tell over lunch." Looking dubiously at me, she said "Ok, well, I'll be ready in five minutes. Would you like to have lunch here?" "Sure, sounds good, and speaking of that, it's really good to see you," I replied. This made her smile brighten, and she was blushing as she moved toward the door at the back of the bar.

As I drained my glass, I felt a tap on my shoulder. Looking around, I saw Helen was standing there, so I asked "Ready?" She nodded, and I said "Then let's away." I stood and held my arm out, she put hers through mine, and we headed to the dining room. There were a few surprised faces, as we passed out of the room, and through the dining room door. Having picked a table, I held her chair out for her, and asked "Would you like a drink?" "A gin and tonic in a highball glass Thanks," she replied. I headed to the dining room bar, brought our drinks back to the table, and she enquired "Not having a beer?" I answered her with "No, scotch and dry is my normal drink. Now, you should know what's good to eat." She replied by saying "Actually, this is the first time I'll have eaten here, thank you." "Well, in that case we better have a look what's on offer," I replied, and we both started looking at the menu.

While we were making our minds up, a waitress came over and stood by us, with a notebook in her hand. Helen looked up as she put down the menu, and said "Hi Carol, this is Tom. Could I have the roast pork please?" I nodded to Carol and said "Make that two, but no pumpkin. Thanks." Carol said "Sure and I'll give you both staff discount. Would you like any drinks?" I replied "Not just yet, thanks," and Carol headed off toward the kitchen.

Helen picked up her glass, had a sip through the straw, and said "You were going to tell me what's happened to you," so I recounted the whole story for her. When I was finished, she said "My God, you could have been killed. Weren't you scared?" So I replied "No, only the good die young, so I'll be right for a while." She said "Humm, we'll have to see how bad you really are then." She giggled and looked at me flirtatiously, and I replied with a laugh, "Be my guest."

After a nice roast, and more flirting, we left hand in hand after I had paid the bill. She led me to her car, a Humber Sprite. Handing me her keys, I opened the driver's door for her, and getting into the passenger side, she asked "Have you seen the river yet?" Having told her I didn't know the town had a river, she said "Oh yes, the Murrumbidgee, I'll show you." As she started the car and we moved along the street, I moved into the centre, and put my arm around her shoulders. When we pulled up, I saw that at this time of year it was only like a small creek. By the size of the gully in width and depth, if full, it would probably rival the Fitzroy back home.

However romance was in the air, and we did a fair bit of kissing and cuddling, that had us both wanting more. She asked what time I had to be back. I looked at my watch, and saw it was close to two. I told her when I was due back on base, and she said "Ummm I wonder what we could do for the next few hours?" She started straightening out her clothes, then she started the car, and we headed to her place.

We were no sooner in the door of her flat, than we were in each other's arms. While we were having a very passionate tongue kiss, I started to undo the top button at the back of her dress, and then

214

slowly slid the zipper down. Still kissing me, she moved her hands so that she could unbutton the shirt I had on. I slid the arms of her dress down each shoulder, as she moved one arm then the other, before continuing to remove my shirt. Her dress slid down, as she slid my shirt off. While in locked in another kiss, I continued stroking her back with one hand, as I undid her bra with the other. She shook out of her bra, and her nipples were against my chest while I continued to stroke her, as moans of ecstasy escaped from our kiss. Coming out of our embrace, she gathered up her dress, bra, and my shirt, grabbed my hand and pulled me to the bedroom. She looked at me, saying "Cripes, you've got muscles, let's have a look at the lot," as she started undoing my strides, and slid them off, jocks and all.

As she was sliding my strides down, she took my erect penis into her mouth as I bent over and played with her firm breasts and erect nipples. After a while I pulled her up, kissed her and started kissing her neck as she groaned. Then I moved down, and slid her pants down as I moved my kisses lower, and onto her breasts. As I placed one of her nipples in my mouth, she moaned deeply. She stepped clear of her pants, pulled me onto the bed, moved herself on top of me, and put my penis into her vagina. She then came down on me to get it as far in as it would go, and released a scream saying "Oh, Yes!"

Helen orgasmed at least a dozen times before I poured into her, and she shrieked as she went over the top again. As we lay in each other's arms, with our energy spent, she dreamily said "God that was good, I've never come so much before." I just lay there facing her with a smile. After cleaning up, and showering together, we went out to a new place that had opened in town, and had a nice dinner before she drove me back to the base. On the drive out she asked "When am I going to see you again?" I replied smiling at her "As soon as I can, because, you my dear, are rather moreish!"

I checked in at the base entrance, as she headed off with a wave. Instead of going to the hut, I made my way to the boozer, ordered a drink, and sat at the usual table. I was replaying the afternoon in my mind with a smile, as I sipped my scotch.

Shortly afterward, I was joined by the rest of the NCO's, and John commented "Well, it looks like someone had a good time." I replied with the smile still on my face, "Let's just say, the pipes they are clean. Now I'm going to grab another drink." I headed to the bar followed by the jeering and cat calls.

CHAPTER 21

Monday morning, and I was still on a high from the previous day. Breakfast even tasted good, and that's saying something. Back at the hut I was enjoying a smoke with another coffee, as John came into the room. I said "We'll have to remember to get to the laundry sometime today," and he replied "Yeah, I was thinking about it, maybe after lunch would be a good time." "Yeah, sounds good," I replied. Then I looked at the time, and said "Well, it's about time to get the troops out, let's go." Just as we had formed up outside, Kendrick appeared, and he didn't look happy.

As we went through the usual inspection routine, he hadn't said a word. Back outside, he said "Corporal Davis, fallout." I took a pace forward, and he continued "You have to report to Major Ricks at zero nine hundred, base standard dress." As I gave him a questioning look, said "I can't tell you what it's about, I only just learned about this a few minutes ago. You're dismissed until then." "Sarge," I replied. He dropped his voice, and said softly "Try and let me know later," and I nodded. He then marched the platoon off in the direction of the gym.

While I stood there watching them go out of sight, my mind was whirling around, bigtime. I was wondering if I was going to be charged with some offence, or if the Major wanted something in regard to the grenade incident, and that was what I put it down to. Looking at my watch, I headed towards the laundry.

I collected, and paid for, my laundry, headed back to the barracks. I changed into a fresh set of greens, put my boots on, and with my mind still going ten to the dozen, made a coffee, and had a smoke. At a quarter to nine, I left the hut, and made my way to the admin block. I entered and made my way to the Major's office. I knocked on the door, and at the command "Come!" I entered, closed the door, marched to the desk, and said "Acting Corporal

Davis, reporting as ordered Sir!"

"Stand easy, Davis. Tom, isn't it?" I replied "Yes, Sir," and as he continued, my mind was racing and asking "what's going on? Why all of a sudden was the use of my first name?" "Well, Tom, I've been going over the reports of last week's incident. Your report as noted by Captain Jacobs is very concise, and I enjoyed reading it. You must have done well in English at school?"

"Yes sir, all 'A's Sir," I replied. "Good, good, I've also noticed that you refused officer training. Mind telling me why?" He asked. I said "No, Sir, it's just that it would seem to be jumping the queue to me, if you get what I mean, sir. Also, that if I decided the Army wasn't for me, it would make it more difficult to leave, Sir." He replied "Yes, I see what you mean. Well let's hope you decide to stay on, the army could do with men like you. Whether you do realise it or not you have natural talent. Anyway, this is getting away from why I called you in. The OC and I agree with Captain Jacobs' finding; there will be no further action taken, except one. Captain Jacobs has recommended you for, and I agree, that you be awarded a, Commendation for Distinguished Service. Well done!" He leaned across his desk and shook my hand.

"The second reason I called you in, is that those two civvies, you're Mr. Brown and White, would like to spend some time interviewing you, on and off base. As of ten hundred today, and until the end of this week, you have a permanent leave pass to come and go as needed." I was floored by both pieces of information, and all I could ask was, "Interview me, Sir, what for?" "I can't tell you, I'm afraid, because I don't know. What I can tell you is that they will be at your barracks in half an hour" he replied, looking at the clock. He continued "Once again, congratulations. That'll be all Corporal Davis. Dismissed."

As I left the admin block, my mind was numbed and going ten to the dozen, both at the same time. I was able to accept the fact that I'd been awarded a medal for what I had done on the range. But I was trying to fathom what was going on in regard to the civvies. Obviously they had some sort of clout, because the permanent leave pass like I was given would surely be near impossible to obtain without having some sort of power? Well, now, I was more determined to get to the bottom of things, and the only way to do that would soon be presenting itself.

Back at the hut, I made coffee, and was having it and a smoke in my room, as they walked in. Mr White asked "Corporal Davis could we have a word with you please?" "No problems, let's go into the conference room, there's coffee in there and milk in the fridge, if you care to make yourselves one." I placed my cuppa down and sat, and so did Mr White. Mr. Brown made them coffee, and then joined us; as he did I stubbed out my smoke, and said "Major Ricks has told me you want to interview me. Well, about what, and who are you, what's going on?"

Mr White answered "Ok, straight to the point, I like that. First, I hear that congratulations are in order, in regard to your actions the other day. So congratulations." He held his hand out, as did Brown. I shook both, and replied "Thank you, now can we get to the point?" They both looked at each other, and smiled. White said "Fair enough, we would like to interview you in regard to a position we can offer you. Before we get to that, can you tell us what Corp, you had in mind after you leave here?" As he spoke, a thought sprung into my head, and I answered "Well to tell you the truth, I'm not sure. I was thinking of transport, but haven't narrowed it down to which branch. I was thinking air, but I'm still not certain. Now, you aren't trying to find out if I'd like to become a spook are you?"

They both laughed, and White said, smiling "No, but some of what we do could be classified like that, some people do call us, ghosts." Trying to think on my feet because I needed time to work this out, I stalled for time. I said "Ok, fine, but you still haven't told me who you are, or what you really want?" White commented to Brown, "That's ten I owe you, you said he'd want it straight," Brown smiled, and White said to me "I'll give the answers you want, but not on base, where we could be interrupted. Do you have anything to do in town?" He must have been reading my mind,

and I replied "Yes, as a matter of fact, I need to go to the bank."
White replied "Fine, why don't you change into civvies, while we
get our car. We'll pick you up in ten." "Fine," I replied, and they
left the hut.

While I was changing, I was still thinking, and another thought
made itself heard in my brain. I wondered if it could be that, well
I'd know soon enough. I scribbled a note to John, saying I'd see
him later, and put it on his bed. As I grabbed the cash and bank
book, I heard the car pull up outside. The MP gate guard asked for
our names as were leaving, and mine must have been on his sheet,
because I had no trouble, and he raised the gate for us to leave. As
soon as we left the gate, from sitting in the back, I leaned forward,
told Brown which bank to head to, and said "Ok, we can't be
interrupted now, who are you?"

White turned toward me, and said "My name is Captain Mark
Ryan, and this is Sgt Bill Salter. We call him Pepper, or more often
just Pep. We are members of S.A.S. (Special Air Service), and
we've been Okayed to offer you a position." Bingo! My thoughts
had been right. I said "Sorry Sir, but I didn't know your rank, Sir."
"That's all right, now just remember, I'm plain Mark White, and
he's Pep Brown." "Yes Sir, sorry Sir, I mean, Mark," I replied.

Then Mark said "Good, you're Tom, aren't you?" I replied "Yes
s...Mark, that's right." He said "We'll leave the rest for after you've
done your banking, and we're somewhere private, ok?" "Sure,"
I replied. After I had deposited my cash, Pep drove around and
parked outside the RSL. I said "Uh, if we're going inside, this may
not be a good idea. I'm having it off with one of the barmaids here."
They both looked around at me with surprised faces, and Pep said
with a smile "Let me guess the little blonde?" I nodded, and Mark
said "Ok, we'll go into the snooker room, and grab a table there.
I don't think there'll be too many in there at this time of day." As
we walked in the main entrance, I glanced into the main bar, and
Helen was turned away from seeing us stocking the glass fridge.
In the snooker room, no one was there. We moved to a table near
the far wall, and I was asked what I'd like to drink.

Wanting to keep a clear head, I said "I'll just have coffee NATO standard, thanks." Pep went off to get the drinks, and Mark said "Alright, let me fill you in. When we spoke prior to Christmas, I told you that we were taking part in a new initiative because our regiment is short on soldiers at present. So, instead of waiting for soldiers to apply to join the regiment, the OC came up with an original idea; to actively recruit from other units. He sent out expert recruitment teams, like Pep and I, because we need more men with talent NOW. He also came up with the idea to look at the basic training intakes, and your intake is the first that Pep and I looked at, and it seems to have worked out rather well.

While he had been speaking, Pep had arrived back with the coffees, so I lit a smoke as I digested what I'd heard. So far it made sense, as I formed a question in my head. "You seemed to have concentrated on my platoon, and Echo. How did that come about?" Pep answered "When we arrived, the day before your intake, we started going through all the personnel files for your intake, and made a shortlist of possible targets to observe. You made the shortlist because of your above average scoring; also because you were offered officer training, and refused. That, and the fact your scores showed the ability for a natural talent. You went to the top of our shortlist!" Mark added "Anything you hear from now is classified, therefore not to be repeated. As of now, you are only the second person to know who we really are, and why we're here. Colonel Trickett is the only other person. In the next few days, there may be others, but not at this point in time. Clear?" I nodded my understanding.

Mark continued, "Good, first let's be clear. We're not offering you an adventure, but a career in a regiment that only has the best of the best in its ranks. Sometimes it'll be adventurous, and at other times downright dangerous, but you'll get a lot of travel to different places. You'll learn new skills, abilities, and get the chance to do things other people just dream about. The pay rate is a little bit better than what you get now, and it does have other compensations. For instance, at present you only hold an honorary rank that ends when you leave here. If you joined our regiment your full Corporal's rank would be ratified straight away, and those stripes could be sewn on to your uniforms before leaving here. I can see your question. How is that possible? The answer is that in the regiment, promotion is based on merit, not how many command courses you've done.

I sat back, not realising I had been leaning forward to hear more. Offering my smokes, we all lit up. Then he continued. "From the first time we watched you in your platoon, Pep said you were worth keeping an eye on, and this was before you ended up as a Corporal. We did review the other platoons just to make sure we hadn't over-looked anyone. After seeing you take on the assault course fairly easily, we kept a closer eye on you. Then we saw you shoot. Everyone in the regiment must be of marksman calibre with any weapon, and that's why Pep lent you his personal sidearm. We were surprised by your result in the camp challenge. You missed on purpose, I take it? Please tell me why." I smiled to let them know they were right, and then said "John is as good a shot as I am, but every now and then needs a bit of a confidence builder. I also saw a way for making some cash on the side, and besides that, I'm going to end up with the assault course record."

Then Pep took over the questioning. "That's fair enough, now tell us your story, and include why you refused officer training." I started with telling them about my family, and how I was always expected to excel by my mother, to be above everybody else as befitting my so called station in life as an aristocrat. I brought them up to date with what I'd been doing with my life to this point. The only thing I left out was my true age, and about the forgeries. Continuing, I said "Obviously you've guessed that doesn't hold water as far as I'm concerned. Not going to officer training will be a kick in the teeth to my mother when she eventually finds out what I'm doing. Taking a shortcut seems like cheating by jumping over everyone else, if you can understand that."

Mark said "Yes I see where you're coming from. It seems you've set yourself a high moral benchmark, but are you capable of killing if the need arises?" I replied "Yes, if it meant getting a job done. I've hurt people in fights, because I've wanted to win, and not cared about it. Plus I've killed enough animals while shooting for sport and food without worrying about it." Looking at each other, and then back at me, Pep said "Yes, well, we saw how you handled yourself with one of your instructors. Was that a result of anger, or cold calculation?" "Both," I replied. "Yes he was pissing me off, but I knew how I was going to handle him before I made my first move. My plan had already been formulated to teach him a lesson, before telling him what I was doing." "It was very effective and efficient, I must say," Pep commented. Mark said "Let's continue this over lunch," so we got up and went to the dining room. After ordering, Mark asked if I'd like a drink, so I ordered a scotch and dry. Mark came to the table with the drinks; two scotch and dries, and a rum and coke for Pep.

As we ate, Mark outlined more of the advantages of joining SAS. They weren't restricted to the weapons the Army supplied; each man had his personal choice, both in handguns and long arms. Also, the type of work was varied, and they operated in small groups that were answerable only to their own chain of command. Now that sounded very sensible to me. After we finished lunch we stayed in the room, and had another round of drinks that Pep bought. After lighting a smoke, I asked "Well, I've heard a lot of reasons to accept, but what are the disadvantages?"

Mark replied "There are a lot actually. The main one is continual training. Our training regime can be brutal. Each man must successfully pass all types of our training courses. For instance, if you accepted our offer, you would immediately start our training. That will be six intense months of learning to shoot any weapon, parachuting, swimming, diving, sign language, mountain climbing, rappelling from cliffs and aircraft, navigation, patrol techniques, communication, scouting and tracking, explosives, night ops, close quarter reconnaissance, air recon, ambush techniques, languages, and medical training. Each man in a patrol must learn everybody's job, so that they can do that job if the need arises. You are pushed to your limits of endurance, and only after that do you qualify to wear the regiment's insignia." Sitting back, I lit another smoke, while I was thinking. I said "That's quite a list. I can see now why I've heard that many don't make the grade. Any more for the downside, you said there was a lot?"

Pep smiled and said "Once you've done all that, you get sent to any shit-hole place the government deems necessary. You operate in all weather conditions, don't get any real recognition, or thanks, for what you do, and can't tell anyone what you do, or where you go." Mark then interrupted him. "On that last point, secrecy is the key. Your name is never released, your identity is kept secret, and your records are sealed to anyone without ultra-high security clearance." Pep continued as if he hadn't been interrupted. "You're never off duty, but it can be a lot of fun, and you get paid a few hundred a week for doing it, what could be better?"

I was really getting to like these two, especially Pep; he seemed to have the same warped sense of humour I had. I asked "Ok, what if I accept, what happens?" Mark answered "First, let me apologise. You won't have the time to break the camp assault course record. As of earlier you are on leave, so you won't be participating in any more recruit training. This is a big decision and you will have to think long and hard about it. You have till Friday night to think it over, and contact us with your decision. If you accept, we will talk with you at your hut Saturday morning, and be prepared to move to a new location. We will leave the base at zero eight hundred, and our plane will have wheels up by zero nine hundred. We'll arrive at our base by sixteen hundred, where your training will immediately commence with Pep. There will be no leave until you finish your training. If you accept, you will need to have all personal and issued gear packed and ready to go. Keep your backpack with you to pack a spare field uniform, and last minute toiletries, and we'll travel in dress uniform. Have you anything further you would like to ask?"

Thinking quickly if there was anything more I needed to know, I leaned forward and quietly replied "No, Sir." Mark replied

"Good. If you're the man I think you are, you'll be heading for the Q store and drawing enough sets of stripes to be sewn on your uniforms. Colonel Trickett has already been informed of who we are looking at, so if you have trouble at the Q store, have them contact him. Please don't forget you have a leave pass for the entire week, so use it to your advantage. Anything else?" With a mischievous smile I asked "I don't suppose you'd let me know who else is getting this offer?" "No," Mark replied. I then asked "Before we leave, can I have five minutes to sort something out?" With that being granted, I went to see Helen and asked what time she'd be home. After telling her I'd call her then, I joined Mark and Pep for the trip back.

We arrived back on base at sixteen twenty (4:20pm), and Pep parked outside the admin building. We went our separate ways after I was informed how to contact them in the future.

As I entered the hut, Kendrick was about to leave. I said "Don't go just yet, I need to talk to you, and John. Also in the next day or so, I might need some advice." He nodded, turned, and went back into the conference room. John had heard me talking to Kendrick, put a coffee in front of my place at the table, and was seated waiting. Kendrick and I pulled up a pew, and I said "I was going to fill you in on my visit to the Adjutant's office, and the rest of the day, but first I'd like to see what you two know first, and I'll fill in the blanks." Kendrick started, saying "All I've found out was that you weren't in trouble, that you've been recommended for a gong, and that you have been removed from the duty roster. We were discussing that, just before I was about to leave. Now you're back. Congratulations by the way."

I replied, "Ok, here's the full story. After telling me about the gong, the Major told me that I was going to be interviewed by White and Brown, the two civvies. They aren't civvies at all. Only two people on base know who, and what they are; the OC, and now me. I'll tell you who they are in a minute. The Major also put me on permanent leave until the end of the week, at their insistence, because I would need a lot of think time, without training distractions. I've been with them the whole day, and we only just got back. Sarge, you may have an idea why I'm going to need that time, when I tell you who they are, and what they are doing here. Now this really top secret, if it gets out, they'll know where it came from, so it can't be repeated to anyone."

As I was saying this, I had got up, and shut the door, so we couldn't be overheard or interrupted. I continued "I can't tell you what was said today, or why I'm not training, at least until next week." Kendrick said "Alright, that's understood, so who are they?" I replied "This is going to blow your minds. Mr. White is a Captain, Mr Brown is a Sergeant, and they are serving members of the S.A.S." Kendrick leaned back and whistled, and John sat there with his mouth hanging open. Then Kendrick came forward and said "And you can't, or won't tell us what it's all about?" I replied, "That's right, Sarge, as per the agreement I made with them."

Kendrick asked "Ok, is that all?" "I'll still need your advice in the next day or so, if you don't mind. I will leave it until an end of day thing, so we'll have time to talk, if that's ok?" I asked. He replied "Yeah sure, that'll be alright, but for now I'd better get going." He then got up to leave for the day.

I turned to John, and he said "Well, you've definitely had an interesting day. A week off and winning a medal to boot. Cripes, you're full of surprises!" I just sat there with a smile, nodding. I got up again, closed the door, and he looked at me inquiringly. I said "Get ready for this, but nothing more can be said about it. Now, I'll tell you the whole story…" When I had finished, he said "Shit! What are you going to do?" "Exactly what I said, I'm going to think about it."

At dinner that night, I got the usual ribbing from the other NCO's about being awarded a gong, and Jim from Echo was even more jovial after I told them about my week off. He probably thought that without me playing this week, they'd have a chance at winning a game.

Later in the boozer, at seven thirty I rang Helen. She was full of questions about how come I'd been in town, and in the club without going to see her. I told her that I had been taking care of some business, and then told her about my week off, and asked her what she was up to. After she told me that she wasn't working until six the next night, we arranged that she'd pick me up at the base entrance the following morning at nine thirty. After talking to her I had a couple more scotches while I thought over the day's events, and what I would do. I must admit my first thought had been, yeah go for it, but I really needed to stew over this one. Did I really want to go and see what happened, or would it be wiser just to finish my recruit training and go into the transport corp, or was this one of those opportunities that was too good to miss?

CHAPTER 22

The following morning, Kendrick had a quick word with me as he made the usual inspection. I was at my desk when he came and sat down, saying "Tiger, I've been thinking, that if you need to talk, we could do it at the footy game tomorrow, how's that sound?" Answering, I said "That'll be great. I can at least watch the game, even if I'm not playing. Oh, by the way, Sarge, I'll be off base for the rest of the day; I just thought I should let you know." He nodded his head, and got up to continue the inspection.

I was at the base entrance having a smoke, as Helen's Humber came up the drive. Crushing the smoke out, I climbed in the passenger side, leaned over, gave Helen a kiss, and then she headed the car towards town. She asked while driving, "Anything special you'd like to do today?" When she looked at me, I said with a smile on my face and a leer in my voice "Yep, you." This made her giggle and say "I thought you'd never ask."

Inside her flat, she made us each a coffee, and we sat side by side while I told her why I had been at the club. I only said "That I was there with a couple of people who had offered me a place in their regiment, and they'd arranged my week off, so that I could think it over." She stated "But you'll still be here for another couple of months to finish your training." "No," I replied. "That's the point. If I accept, I'll finish my training in their unit, and I'd have to fly out Sunday morning." She sat with her cup in hand slowly sipping her drink, as she pondered over what I had said. Then asked "Is it what you want to do?" My reply was "This sort of offer is quite rare, and at this stage, I'm considering accepting. Is it what I want to do for the next 'x' number of years? I'm not sure, that's what I've got to work out."

She thought it over, and then said "We really haven't had a chance to get to know each other, and if you go, we won't, which is a shame. I don't want you to hold back on my account, you have to do what you think is right. We won't get a chance to be together for the rest of the week because of work, except for Sunday afternoon, but you may be gone by then. So let's enjoy ourselves, in case it is the last time." So we started making love on the couch, losing some clothing as we went. After we had moved into the bedroom, and satisfied our lust, we lay on the bed in each other's arms, before showering together. Then she drove me back to the base, before going to work. That was the last I saw of Helen.

After dinner that night I headed for the boozer, and decided to sit by myself over in one of the corner tables, so I could wrestle with the dilemma I faced. Did I play it safe and continue here? If I did that, I'd still have to face the choice of which branch of transport to move onto at a later stage. Would that be enough to satisfy me? Whereas with the offer I'd been given, I already knew what I would be facing; heaps of training, and preparation for what I imagined would be tough jobs, because easy jobs wouldn't be given to the supremely elite troops of SAS. Being the best of the best doesn't mean getting to do it easy. It would be challenging, but I knew enough of their reputation to know that they did travel worldwide on assignments. Sure mainly to hotspots and do jobs, that the general public never heard, or knew anything about.

I think I was really contemplating whether I could do the job without failing. Would I be able to pass into their ranks or fail the training? Would I become one of the soldiers that fail, or would I be the one of a hundred? Would I be able to live with myself if I failed? I hadn't failed in anything I'd attempted yet, no matter how hard it was to do, I'd always found a way to win. What would happen to me, if I gave my all, and failed? Then it dawned on me that was my problem! I was afraid of failing, because I never had! As I came to realise this, I was also able to see the solution, if you give something your best shot, and it doesn't come off, you don't fail. Giving up before you try is how you fail!

I'm the type of person that likes to finish something I start, however if I decided to accept the offer, that would mean I'd be leaving my recruit training unfinished, which went against my grain. After a lot of soul searching, I rationalized that I really wouldn't be giving up on my training, because I'd still be doing it, albeit in a more specialised manner. My training would now become my corps training that would take place after leaving the recruit training anyway, no matter which corps I had picked. However, there was one thing that I did need to finish if I could, and I would take steps the next day to see if it could be achieved. Having decided all this, I had another drink and smoke, and searched my mind further to start making a to-do list of things that would need to be completed. After all that, having a last smoke, I headed to the hut and bed.

Next morning during inspection, I asked Kendrick "Sarge, are the guys doing the obstacle course anytime this week?" "Yep, it's slotted for first up in the morning," he replied. I nodded and said, "Fine, I'll see you after lunch, Sarge." Thinking that things were falling into place, at nine I headed to the Q store, and requested six sets of stripes for my greens, and two sets for my dress uniforms. Then headed to the laundry, and after finding out they could sew them on, I asked "How long it would take for them to be finished?" The guy in charge said, "If they went in today, I can have them for you by lunch time tomorrow." "Fine, I'll be back in fifteen," and headed back to the hut. I changed the shirt I had on to a green T shirt, gathered up all my uniform shirts, and headed back to the laundry. I gave him all my shirts, and the sets of stripes, and told him I'd see him just before lunch the next day.

Back at the hut, I unlocked the gun rack, took out my rifle and bayonet, and then locked it again. My next sojourn was to the armoury; after having my rifle signed in, I still had my rifle sling and bayonet, and was told that I keep hold of them. As I was about to leave, I noticed a lot of stacked rifle crates. I asked "Are you expecting a war?" "No, there're for the next two intakes. We'll have six platoons each intake, and all of them conscripts. The platoon sergeants are going to have a hard time for the rest of the year, until the next intake for proper regular soldiers" he replied.

After getting back to my room, I thought over why the guys that had been conscripted were looked down on. Surely they deserved recognition for the fact that they'd all be going into infantry units, which would boost the numbers of the frontline troops. Most of the guys in my platoon were all set on going into more specialised fields. There were only four that I knew of, that were going for the infantry. So one would think that more numbers in the infantry would be a blessing. But regular soldiers, for some reason, didn't see it that way. I decided that if I had a chance, I'd bring it up as a topic of conversation with Kendrick later, and the other NCO's over lunch or dinner.

I made a coffee, and moved on to the next item of my mental list, which was sorting out and packing my footlocker properly. The easiest way of doing this was to empty it all out, and start repacking it properly. As I did, I came across an item I'd forgotten about; a dark blue beret that was worn with either greens or dress uniform.

Knowing I'd be travelling in dress uniform, I decided that wearing it would be easier than my slouch hat, so kept it out. Then I started repacking the footlocker with the lesser used items of kit first. By the time it was packed, I had plenty of room for my uniforms. Boots to go in on top, my duffle bag would sit on top of my uniforms, and I would put my boots in last. The only thing I had left out was my field pack I would use as carry gear; a set of greens, boots, and toiletries.

As I put the finishing touches to the footlocker, I heard the platoon arrive back for the lunch break. A few minutes later, John knocked on the door, and entered saying, "Well, we've just had an interesting morning, doing navigation with that dropkick Ferris again." He didn't seem happy when I started laughing, and said "Oh what I pity I missed it." He informed me that it wasn't as bad as the previous exercise, but close, and then we headed to lunch.

When I joined the other NCOs, Jim had a pained look on his face, and said "Damn you're here, that means you'll be playing, and here I thought we had a chance." I replied "No, don't forget I'm on down time, which means I'm not officially here. I'll be watching though." That put the smile back on his face, and talk turned to general matters. I didn't get the chance to bring up what I'd been thinking in regard to Nashos. This was the term used for conscripts those days, in short for National Servicemen.

After lunch I went to the playing oval with the rest of the platoon, and gave the team a quick pep talk before they started their warm up. "Now, even though I'm not playing, I'll still be watching. So far Alpha has a record for being unbeaten, so let's carry that through all the time we're here. Now, get out there and have fun!" As our team moved onto the field, Kendrick and I moved further down the field, to where we could talk without interruption, and not be overheard.

I started the conversation with, "Sarge, the other day I couldn't tell you the whole thing. The upshot is that they offered me the chance to join SAS, and I'm supposed to be thinking about it." Kendrick replied "I thought that may be the case, when you told us who they were. I take it that anything you tell me is off the record, but can you tell me if this has something to do with the advice you wanted?" "Yep," I replied. "If I'm going to join, I will have to leave with them on Sunday. What I'm asking your advice on, is whether you think I should join, and following that I have a request to make."

"I see," Kendrick said. "Well, you should consider it an honour, and I think you're worthy of it. You've got the makings of being a first class soldier, and you're the best I've seen come through here. I think you've already made your decision, and all I can say is good luck, you'll do well." "The fact that I might fail the training is what worries me," I replied. "In that case, the best I can advise is don't quit, keep going, do the best you can, and you won't fail. Just remember, they came to you, because they think you're good enough, not the other way round," he replied.

"Thanks, Sarge," I replied. "And, Yes I'd all but decided to give it a go. Now let's move on to my request, Sarge. I'd like a final crack at the assault course record. Could you turn a blind eye in the morning, so I join the platoon?" With a laugh he said, "Now what did I say about quitting on something? Ok, but no matter if you do it or not, I'll not be able to record it, due to you officially being on leave." "Fine, Sarge. I hate leaving something unfinished. While we're here though, I'd like to get your opinion on Nashos. Are they worth it or not?"

"Well, that opens a whole can of worms. This is only my opinion. As far as National Service is concerned, in peace times I think it would be great, for two reasons. One, it bolsters the ranks in the services, and some guys may opt to enlist full time. Second, it would cut the unemployment rate, and keep some kids out of trouble, or jail. However, in wartime, it's not a good idea, for a number of reasons. Would you like to be TOLD that you're going into the Army, whether you like it or not? Of course not, so you'd try to get out of it anyway you could, even if it meant going to jail. Now mothers and fathers get told the same, so that starts the ball rolling on civil unrest. This present liberal government have not taken any bloody notice of the past during World Wars I and II. It didn't work then, and it won't work now. When there's a war on, people will enlist, out of duty to the country, wanting some adventure, or just for recognition and glory."

However, this time it's different, Vietnam is not our war. We've been suckered into it, by President Johnson and the US. Because they don't have enough ready combat soldiers, and we're tied up with them through the defence alliance we have with them. It's not a popular war, here or in the States. All you have to do is listen to the news, to see the riots going on over there, because of this war. It's seen as just America flexing its influence, both here, and there. Now, due to our bloody government's commitment, we have to have conscription."

"I do feel sorry for the guys that get picked, because it's not what they want, and it's my job to try and teach them to stay alive, so we really have to crack down harder on them, as opposed to regular voluntary intakes. It's easier to teach willing personnel who want to be here. If you ask any regular soldier if we should be in Vietnam, nine out of ten will answer "No." I hope that answers your question." I nodded that it did, and it answered a few questions, except one.

So I asked "I understand all that, but why are the Nashos frowned upon?" Giving his answer some thought, said "To tell you the truth, I don't know, unless it's because others think that anyone forced into a war will cut and run if it gets tough, which does happen in some cases. But Aussies aren't like that, ninety nine percent of the time, if push comes to shove, we'll get stuck in, and do the job, whether we've forced to be there, or not." Thinking about that, I asked "Then they're frowned on because of a misconception in thinking?" He replied "Yes exactly, unfortunately for them."

After watching the game on the field for a while, Kendrick asked "I know you've been doing a lot of thinking over the last couple of days. Have you had any time to think about who's going to replace you?" I had a quick think, and said "No I haven't, but it's a real easy choice. My recommendation would be that John moves up to full Corporal, and Merv gets made up to Lance Jack. Even though he didn't want to take it on in the first place, he might now, and I think he'd do a good job. Now I haven't said anything to the rest of the guys yet, I was going to do it this arvo. I could see if Merv will take John's position before that." He replied "That would be a good idea. I'd rather that the choice was made within the platoon, than me ordering the change. If you can make the change today all well and good, but you'll get to keep your room until you make the move. Let me know how it pans out in the morning." I nodded, and he asked "So, what do you still have to do?" I replied "After lunch tomorrow, I'll be going down to HQ, to see the OC, and let him know my decision, so he can pass it on. Then they'll be coming to see me Saturday morning, and then I'll probably be flying out Sunday."

Then Kendrick said, "I'll let them know at HQ this afternoon that you'll be there tomorrow." He reached across and shook my hand, saying "We probably won't get a better chance to do this, so good luck. It's been a pleasure getting to know you, and I know the platoon will miss you also. Take care of yourself, but we'll see each other before you go."

The guys were just coming off the field, and we joined the rest of the platoon. They had won by a margin of twelve points. After we had been marched back to the barracks, Kendrick addressed us. "Tomorrow morning we're back at the assault course so usual dress. In the afternoon, sports gear again for more unarmed training." Turning to me he asked, "Do you have anything to add. Corporal Davis?" I replied "Yes, Sarge. I want to see everyone inside after we're dismissed, but I also want five minutes with Corporal Buchanan before that. So those going off for the routine duties, hang in until I've finished with you. Thanks, Sarge." Then Kendrick dismissed us for the day.

John and I talked outside while having a smoke, and I said "As of today you'll be taking over my job. I'll make Merv your 2IC, unless you'd rather have someone else. You won't be able to move into my room until Sunday though. When we get inside I'll give you my stripes, and you can give me yours to pass on." John replied "So you're going to take it on. I thought you'd made up your mind when I saw your rifle gone. Merv is a good choice, I would have asked for him anyway. So you leave on Sunday, I'll be here to see you off then." Then we went inside, and after swapping rank armbands, we headed into the main room.

As we reached the room, Merv called attention, and I told everyone to rest easy before I spoke. "This will come as a shock to some of you, but I've made sure that everyone is here to hear this from me. On Sunday morning I'll be leaving here to take up training at my new unit. Yes, I know it's a bit unorthodox, leaving before finishing recruit training, but it can't wait. I have to go, sorry. So here's what's going to happen: John will take over from me, and your new Lance Corporal will be Merv. Are there any questions, apart from what I'll be doing?" There was one from Will, asking about the assault course record, and I answered. "Tomorrow I will be coming with you to the course, and I'm going to have a go at cracking it. Because technically I'm on leave, if I do crack it, it won't be recorded, so tomorrow is just for my satisfaction alone.

Sarge is turning a blind eye to me doing it, because of the circumstances, so yes, I'm going to try for it before leaving. Now unless there's anything else, Merv, I need you to join John and I, and the rest of you are dismissed. Thank you." John, Merv and I adjourned to the conference room. Once inside, John started making the coffee, and we all lit up as we sat. I gave Merv the rank armband, saying "Sorry about this Merv, last time you didn't want the job. This time you've got no choice, I'm afraid. I thought it would be better coming from me, than Kendrick."

Looking at John, I said "You two will have to arrange the duty roster again, and I'll leave you to fill Merv in on what you do. Now Merv, John won't be moving into my room until Sunday, then after that you can swap into his room. Tonight, we'll take you into the canteen with us for dinner and introduce you to the other NCOs. Now, onto business. I didn't see Mark Hyland on the field today, and com to think of it, I haven't seen him for a day or two. Have either of you have any clue where he is?"

Merv said "One of the guys on his team said that he'd been given leave, also Charlie Mann, but he doesn't play in their line up." John said "Yeah, that gels with a couple of comments I've heard. Jim was saying that he was two men down." I looked at them both, and said "Merv, you're not aware of what's going on yet, and it's probably better that way. The reason I'm leaving is to join SAS, but John can fill you in later, and it's not to be repeated to anyone." Then I said to John, "Now it looks like I know who'll be coming with me." He smiled and nodded, and then I continued. "Now Merv, from now on there's things you'll hear in your new job, that can't be told to anyone. Get used to it, and if there's a problem, you talk to John first. John, Quiz Jim a bit tonight, and see what you can find out. Is there anything else before we call it a day?" I left the two of them talking, and headed to my room.

That night we introduced Merv to the other NCOs at dinner, and I also informed them that Merv was taking over from John, and John was moving into my place because I was leaving on Sunday. This started a conversation based on a lot of questions, but my answers were short, and didn't give much away.

Later in the mess, before we were joined by the others, John said "It looks you were right. Mark and Mann where put on leave, after having appointments with your two mates." "Well, at least I'm not the only one," I commented with a smile. Then I asked "And Merv, how do you think he'll shape up?" He replied "He'll do fine." "Good," I said. Soon after we were joined by the others, and Merv was made welcome. We played the newest NCO buys, game on him, and he fitted quite well to my way of thinking. Eventually each person drifted off, and I was left alone to have my usual mental debrief with myself, before heading off to catch a few 'z's prior to the morning.

After breakfast, Kendrick and the platoon made its way to the assault course; I was going in my usual first place, as Kendrick got the stopwatch ready.

I loosened up a bit with stretching and warm up exercises, and then waited for the go ahead. Kendrick then moved up to the observation platform, and then after a slight pause, yelled "GO!" I took off, and unbeknown to me, Kendrick hadn't sent anyone off after me. This meant the whole platoon was watching my progress through the course. Meanwhile, down on the course, I was not really thinking about the time. I was concentrating on what obstacle came next, and I was mentally prepping for it, that way there was no hesitation as I approached the next obstacle.

As I approached the finish, I could hear the yells of encouragement from the platoon, but didn't let my concentration lapse for the last obstacle. After that, I made for the finish line. I was sweating profusely and breathing hard. As I went over the line, John tossed me a towel that he had brought in his field kit. While I was recovering from the exertion, I glanced up at Kendrick, and he was looking disappointed. "Shit! I hadn't made it," I thought. After a short moment while silence descended, everyone waited for Kendrick to speak and announce the time. He came up to me and said so everyone could hear, "Seventeen minutes, twenty two seconds. Unofficially, you've broken the record by thirty four seconds. Congratulations, Corporal Davis." He offered his hand, and smiled. The platoon members were all cheering as well.

When the noise died down, I said "Thank you all, but you're here to do some training, so get yourselves ready!" Sergeant Kendrick and I moved off to sit down, and watch the guys as they tackled the course.

CHAPTER 23

Well I'd done it! Pity it wasn't official, I thought to myself as I watched the platoon go off one after the other. When the platoon finished, and Kendrick announced the timings, again everyone had improved, and I was satisfied with the results. Soon after we marched back to the hut, and after being dismissed, I went to the laundry to pick up my shirts before changing and going to lunch. Having my rank sewn onto my shirts caused a bit of ribbing to come my way from the other NCOs. I just answered the jokes calmly with a smile. I got my own back by saying "Well boys, I can't help it if my promotion has been ratified and made official, where as some are just trainees."

When the platoon left for the gym that afternoon, I made my way to the HQ admin building, and asked to see the OC. Lieutenant Ferris came to usher me into the Colonel's office. As we walked up the hallway, he said "I'm sorry we got off on the wrong foot, Davis. I'd like to add my congratulations on your gong, and I hope we can work better together in the weeks ahead." I replied "Thank you, and it's very unlikely we'll work together again, as I'm leaving." As I finished saying this, we reached the Colonel's office. I was marched in, halted at attention, and said "Corporal Davis requesting a few minutes of your time, sir!"

With Ferris standing in the back of the office Trickett said, "Ah Davis, stand easy. First off son, let me tell you that you're the first person to be awarded a commendation while still in training. You should consider that an honour. Unfortunately, it seems that I won't be the person presenting it to you, as I take it that you've accepted your promotion, which means you'll be leaving us early?" "Yes, sir, I have," I replied. Trickett continued "Well done. Good. I'll pass your acceptance on to the other two and they'll be in touch. Well done on your award, your new OC will no doubt present it to you when it arrives. Is there anything else I can help you with?" I replied "No. Sir and thank you Sir." "Well, in that case, all I can say is take care. You'll do well with all your endeavours I think. Dismissed," Trickett said. I replied "Thank you, Sir," and Ferris marched me out of his office.

Walking down the hall, Ferris said "You've gained a good reputation and caused some havoc while you've been here, Corporal. Do you mind if we talk outside for a bit? I've nothing on right now." I replied "That would be fine Sir, as long as I can have a smoke."

Outside, I lit up a smoke and offered one to him, which he accepted, and as he lit up also, he asked "So where are you off to?" "Swanbourne Barracks, Sir," I replied. He said "But, that's where…" I cut him off with "Yes, sir," and he continued while looking shrewdly at me. "There's obviously more to you than meets the eye, Davis! I would also like to offer my sincere apologies for what happened at our first meeting." Taking pity on him a little, I said "If I can talk frankly Sir? (He nodded) Don't always take what's written down as gospel, not everyone is a dummy, there will always be someone who knows what their talking about through experience, and never make assumptions about people. To do that you make an ass out of yourself and them, here endeth the lesson."

I think I rocked him a little with my pearls of wisdom, but maybe he would take some of the advice on board. He replied "Well, thanks for that Corporal. I wish you well with whatever you do," and he offered me his hand. I shook it, and then said "If that's all Sir, I'd better get going." He nodded, so I saluted, he returned the salute, and then I headed towards the hut.

That night in the mess, I had arranged to meet up with Mark from Echo, who was back on base. While we were waiting for the rest to arrive, Merv checked the message board, and came back with one for me. It was from Mark Ryan (Mr White), stating they'd got the message, and would see me at zero nine hundred Saturday morning. The others arrived, so as they all settled down with drinks, and the conversations started, Mark and I moved to where we couldn't be overheard. I asked "Well, are you coming with me or not?" Taken back a bit he said "So you're one of the others! Yeah, I'm still thinking it over, but I think I'll be going as well. Do you know who else?" I answered "I think so, Charlie Mann. It's only you me and him that have talked to White and Brown." "So that's why I haven't seen Charlie, did they offer you the full rank? Is that why you've got them sewn on?" I replied "Yep, how about you?" He answered "No, I'll just be going in as a private I think. They didn't say anything about whether I'd keep the Lance Jack stripe, but it should be fun all the same."

Having re-joined the others, we settled into a couple hours of drinking, and the usual bull shit that men talk about in the boozer. One of the subjects covered was what had been on the news. About happenings in the states, and the new election slogan that Johnson was sprouting 'All the way with LBJ', to victory in Vietnam. We all considered that complete crap, as Australia was in there too!

Later that night during my mental debrief, I considered that point over in my head, and wondered if good old LBJ was playing with himself, as he certainly wasn't a student of history. No one had ever had a victory in Indo China. Genghis Khan had bypassed it on his way to China, the Japs had problems there in World War II, and the French had been in there for thirty years before pulling out. I guessed that if you were to throw enough troops in, it could possibly be done.

The next day, I was at a bit of a loose end, so went down to the oval, and ran a few laps, then made my way up to the gym, for a hard work out. As I entered, Sgt Wallace came limping out of his office, and asked "What are you doing here, Davis?" I replied "I was going to have a bit of a workout, Sarge. Sorry about the knee, I hadn't planned to strike that hard." He answered "That's ok, it's on the mend, and at least I'm not on crutches now. I won't underestimate you next time." I said "Well, there's not going to be a round two, Sarge. I'm leaving for my unit on the weekend." He looked a little perplexed, but didn't push it, and said "Well, good luck then. Go right ahead, there's no training scheduled today."

"Thanks, Sarge," I replied and moved over to the climbing ropes.

After a solid hour's workout, I finished, and headed back to the hut as the platoon arrived. While we were in the canteen for lunch, Mark asked if I could spare him some time that afternoon, and I told him to drop by whenever he wanted. Then I went back and was doing some last minute packing when Mark knocked on the door. After he was seated, he said "I informed the OC this morning that I was going, and he is passing it on. Also I found out that Charlie isn't going, he knocked it back! Surprising really, considering I thought he was the gung-ho type." I replied by saying "Well, sometimes you never know. I've been informed that they'll be here to see us in the morning. I've been told nine, how about you? How's your packing going?" He answered "I was told probably nine thirty. Yeah, most of mines done, just the last minute stuff, but the waiting around with nothing to do is a killer." I answered "Yeah, I know how you feel. It was getting to me earlier, so I ended up having a run, and then worked out in the gym for an hour. I'm just pottering about with last minute things now. You know we're supposed to be travelling in dress uniform, but I'm going to wear my beret instead of my slouch hat. I take it you've been told that?" He replied "Yeah, they told me that. Thanks for the tip about the beret though, I'll do that too. Anyway, thanks, Corp. I just needed to talk to someone, kind of edgy you know? I'll get going. Thanks again." "Anytime" I replied, and he left.

That night in the boozer, there was a lot of joking around, as well as the usual conversations backwards and forwards. Jim had introduced his new 2IC, to replace Mark, so there was another game of the newest NCO buys. Naturally that went across well, plus it was Friday, which meant we all let our hair down a bit. Even though I'd had quite a few scotches, which would normally give me a good sleep, that night my sleep was fitful. I kept tossing and turning, and waking up, so I wasn't in my best shape come morning. After breakfast and half a dozen coffees I started to come good, and by the time Mark and Pep arrived, I was back to ninety percent on my game.

John showed them into the conference room, and then informed me that they were here. I joined them, closed the door, and stood at attention. Captain Ryan said to relax and sit down, so I made a coffee, and joined them at the table. Mark said "I just wanted a quick word with you, then Pep will go and get someone else, and then brief you both as to what will happen. There was to be another couple of candidates, but one has pulled out." I stopped him at this point, and informed him that I knew all about Mark Hyland and Charlie Mann, and that is was Charlie that pulled out. So Mark laughed, and asked "How did you find out?" I replied "It wasn't hard when I found out they were both on leave. After seeing you two, it was easy to figure out, but I probably knew that Charlie had pulled out before you did!" With a smile he said to Pep, "They'll have to work it better, if there's a next time. Better make a note of that. Alright, you'd best go get Hyland." Pep nodded and headed for the door.

When Pep was out of the room, Mark said "You're good at observation, and working things out. That's good. I think I'll make a brew while we wait." Then he got up and helped himself to coffee, as I lit a smoke. Sitting back down he said "Tom, just between you and I, the training you're in for is not going to be easy. The best advice I can offer is to rest as often as you can, and keep trying to recoup your energy." As he finished saying this, Pep and Mark Hyland entered the room. After they were seated, Mark asked "How much luggage does each of you have?" After being told, he continued "Good, bare minimum. At fourteen hundred, Pep will be driving a van to each of your barracks to pick up everything except your field packs. Your field packs will have all your last minute gear, and a set of fatigues and boots. Tomorrow for the flight, we'll all be in dress uniform and wearing berets. Pep has a regimental beret for each of you, which you'll get shortly. Any questions?"

We didn't have any, so Mark continued "Hopefully we'll be in the air by zero eight thirty. Now it's a long flight, and we should arrive around fourteen hundred. We'll be driven to the barracks, and then Pep will get you settled into quarters. First thing Monday, you'll be tied up with getting gear from the Q store, and having security passes made. After that, you'll be taken to the weapons range where you'll test and fire both long arms and short arms, to find something that you find suitable. The ones you choose will become yours, and your responsibility, and then the following day your training will really start. Questions?"

I asked "So we'll have our weapons from then on, Mark?" He answered "No, the weapons you choose will be noted, and we'll obtain new ones for you. Now, be warned. There is a standing order that recruits will at all times carry arms wherever they go on base. Those arms are in the shape of six foot lengths of telephone poles. They are to be carried at all times, even into the toilets and showers, and when in full field gear. You don't go anywhere without your pole, is that understood?" He looked at both of us and we nodded slowly. He smiled and continued "It's really not as bad as it sounds. We can usually procure your weapon choices within a week. Once you have obtained marksman status with your preferred choices, you can be relieved of your pole. Unfortunately for you Tom, because I've sent the report of your ambidextrous skill, you have to qualify with both hands before you can be relieved of yours." Oh, just great, I thought.

Continuing, Mark said "There's one important matter. Due to our strict policy of equality within the ranks, unless you are within the HQ building, there is no saluting or "Sirs." Everyone is known by their first, or nickname. For instance, Tom, your nickname is Tiger, so that's what you'll be called. I haven't been given a nickname yet, except arsehole, so I'm still Mark." We laughed at the joke he was trying to make. Although we laughed just to keep him happy, he did have a valid point. "One of the first things you'll be learning is probably the hardest for you at this time. That is sign language, because everything is done in silence. To give you an idea of what you face, I've been on an active patrol for a ten day stint, where not one word is spoken, from start to finish, everything was by sign."

Now that was food for thought! I could imagine how hard that would be. I was used to thinking, and doing things alone already, but not one word? Shit, that could be difficult, but at least we were getting some prior warning.

Mark's briefing went on for another hour or so covering some of the things we could expect. At the end of it, I was amazed at how complex this would all be. Unlike Hyland, I took it on face value, and was prepping myself to hack it. Mark Hyland however, started to look as if he was getting jittery, without seeing what it was like. I wondered if this briefing was, or had been designed this way on purpose.

After the briefing, it was Pep's turn, as he handed us the regiment's sand coloured berets. He said "You'll get three more of these from the Q store when we're there. Each man has four as regular kit. Yours don't and won't feature the regiment's insignia, until such time as you pass your training, and are qualified to wear it. Now, I'll be responsible for your training, and I can promise I won't be mollycoddling you. Because there are only you two, you won't get away with anything, not like a large group. So when I say 'jump', you're only response should be, 'how high?' At times we'll join with bigger groups in training. Remember, I'm your boss, no one else. I can be fair, and allow for initiative and certain personal acts of flair, but I'm not an easy man to please. If you get that, you'll do well. That's all I have to say. Thank you and both of you be ready at fourteen hundred with your gear." Once Pep had finished, our briefing was over. Both He and Mark got up, as Mark said "Thank you, gentlemen. I'll see you just prior to wheels up in the morning. Don't get too drunk tonight."

Once they had left, I turned to Mark Hyland, and asked "Well, what did you make, of that?" He replied "To tell you the truth, it was starting to put the wind up me, Christ! What have we let ourselves in for??" Answering, I said "Yeah, but it sounds as if it could be fun, though I'm not sure if I like the idea of lugging a pole around. By the way what is your nickname? Mine's 'Tiger' as you know." I laughed when he told me, and so did he. "Kilt as in highland kilt." "Oh, good one," I stated.

John and Merv came in, and asked "How'd it go?" As they made coffee, and sat down, I said "Kilt, these guys are aware of what's going on, so you can talk freely, at least I think Merv is now fully aware of our situation (he nodded). And to answer the question, apart from putting the wind up us a bit.

In brief, our stuff gets picked up at fourteen hundred, and then we have to be at HQ at zero seven hundred tomorrow. I guess we'll have to get up early, and then head to HQ after breakfast, so you two can start moving your stuff tomorrow."

John said "Well, it looks like its farewell drinks in the mess tonight, so how did they put the wind up you?" Kilt answered that, and after he'd finished, Merv asked "You're kidding, aren't you?" I replied "Well I certainly hope so, but they definitely didn't look, or act as if they were. I guess we'll be finding out by Monday." Then we were making jokes about carting around poles every-where, and questions were flying about if you had to sleep with them, and along that sort of vein. The joking and conversation lightened the mood, and Kilt looked almost back to his cheery self. Christ! What a nickname, it took a bit of getting used to.

After an hour or so of general horsing around, I said "Well I don't know about you guys, but I've got a bit of work to do. After that, I'd like to talk to the troops, if you don't mind John." John nodded, Kilt said he'd head back to his hut, and see us all at lunch. Then we went our separate ways.

When I got into my room, I sat at the desk, and started to mentally note all the last minute stuff to be taken care of. Apart from just the last minute packing that I would do later that night, I had to ring Kendrick, and let him know what was happening; talk to the guys about my farewells, and of course the piss up after dinner in the mess. I did, however, let my mind drift to as many real, and imaginary, scenarios that could occur due to the choice I had made. Some of what I thought about made me smile, but there were a few thoughts that had me frowning. I knew that, with my decision made, if I passed the training, there was no doubt that I would end up in Vietnam. Training is one thing, but reality is quite something else. The thought that I could die never entered my mind, because in those days, like most others, I considered myself invulnerable. Let's face it I thought only the good die young. With the life I had led up until now I'd done some pretty shitty things, as far as other people were concerned. Therefore, I thought, I'd be good for at least a hundred, if not more. The thought that if I died due to my own fuck up, that was reasonable. If others died because I'd screwed up, well, I didn't like that thought at all.

It's amazing what you think of as you face your own mortality. I was so young then that I figured what the hell, it's my choice, and no one could take that away from me. Coming out of my reverie, I started to address what I was going to say to the platoon, and let that run riot in my head. After a little while I'd sorted it out, and I was ready. Now all I had to do was deliver.

As I left my room, John came out of his, and asked "Are you ready?" I replied "As ready as I'll ever be, I guess." He replied "Ok give me a minute, to get them sorted." "Go for it," I replied, as he headed for the main room. There were two out on leave that day, so I figured that they'd be filled in by the rest of the crew later.

When I entered the main room, John called "Atten...shun," and everyone came to their feet. I said "Rest easy guys. Now, you already know that I'm making tracks soon, so here's the gen. I've finally received my timing orders, and as you know I'll be leaving tomorrow. What you don't know is that it'll be early; I have to leave at seven, so I'll be up and having breakfast early. I would like to thank you all for giving me your best. Because of that, Alpha has gained the reputation of being the best platoon on the course. It's because you've given me your best, and I hope that you'll continue giving it to John and Merv. Hopefully you'll all be fine in whatever corps you finally decide on. Once again thank you for your efforts and the first round in the boozer tonight will be on me." After I had finished, there were comments of "Onya, Corp," "Thanks, Corp," and "Way to go!" Will called for a round of cheers for me, and when the cheering died down, I thanked them again. I told them to carry on with whatever they were doing, and with a smile, not to forget to shine their boots. They all laughed, and I left them to it.

In the canteen, before grabbing my lunch, I made a phone call to Kendrick. After he picked up, I said "Tom Davis, Sarge. Thought I'd fill you in on the latest while I had a chance. My gear goes this afternoon at two, and I and one other from Echo will be leaving base at zero seven hundred. I just wanted to say thanks for all your help while I've been here." He replied "It's really me that should be thanking you. All I can do is say is that I wish you well. Just remember what you've learned, and you'll do fine. Take care, Tiger, and thank you for the call."

Over lunch, the other NCOs were already making plans for our send-off party that night, and as usual there was a lot of joking, and clowning around. After lunch I went over to the mess, saw the Corporal in charge, and gave him a hundred dollars. I said "That's for anyone in Alpha tonight. It's for the first round for each man, and then let them drink out the rest." He replied "Sure, Tiger, I'll take care of it," and with a nod of thanks, I headed to the hut.

Bang on fourteen hundred, Pep arrived. I had been sitting on one of the steps having a smoke while I waited, with my footlocker, suitcase, and carry all stacked on top of each other. As we loaded them into the van, he said "I'll be taking these on board the plane today, and I'll see you at HQ in the am, Tiger." I replied "Thanks Pep." Then he drove down the road towards Echo's hut.

That night in the boozer, it was party time. There were a lot of drinks, loud music, well wishes, and a lot of general fun and horse play. The next morning, I was up, showered, and dressed by five forty. I had taken my time doing all this due to the hangover I had. The shower and a couple of coffees helped. I put my beret in my pocket, and left my room. As I was about to leave the hut, John and Merv joined me, looking a little the worse for wear. John said "We thought we'd have breakfast with you." I smiled and nodded, and we headed to the canteen. After eating, Mark and I said our farewells and shook hands with the NCOs that had made it to breakfast.

As we left the canteen, we both put on our berets as we marched down to the HQ building. Once there, we both decided to have a smoke while waiting. Pep wasn't due for another five minutes, but he turned up as we were half way through our smokes, and he told us to finish our smokes. When we got in the car, he drove to the RAAF base, and to a hangar past the main buildings. We boarded what looked like a converted seven two seven jet. Mark was already aboard, and he shook our hands, saying "Good morning, take a seat, and I'll see how long before we're airborne." Pep came aboard just as Mark came back from the cockpit, and said "Good, looks like we'll get away earlier. We'll be on the move in five minutes, and you can spread out if you want to. We've got the whole plane. Toilets are down the back, and that's where gear is if you want anything, and feel free to smoke." As he finished speaking, the plane started moving, and we were in the air ten minutes later.

I never saw John or Merv again. I did hear a year later Merv had been killed in Vietnam, while driving a fourth cavalry FSV (fire support vehicle), after it had been hit with multiple RPG rounds.

CHAPTER 24

Well, with a long flight in front of me, I wondered about what to do. I looked down on the countryside passing beneath us from the window. After a while I moved seats, and sat beside Mark Ryan. He was doing some paperwork, but put it aside and asked "Something on your mind, Tiger?" I replied "Yes, s... Mark. I know about some of the history of Indo China, but can you tell me exactly, why Australian troops are in Vietnam?" He answered "Well, I can tell you what I know. How about that?" I nodded in reply.

Then he told me what he knew about our reason for being there. "Before the Korean War started, the French ruled Vietnam as one of their colonies. The northern part of the country wanted to rule themselves as a communist regime, but the southern part wished to remain a democracy. Now the French decided to split the country into north and south, this is very similar to what happened in Korea. Because the French decided to halt the advance of communism to its colonies, the people of the Northern provinces were denied access to the south, which started rioting and unrest. The French authorities cracked down hard, and the north asked the Chinese government for help. So China provided weapons, ammunition, and covertly trained the North Vietnam army. By this time the Korean War was almost over, and now Korea had been divided into two by the thirty eighth parallel."

Pausing for a drink, Mark then continued. "What happened then was that the north, full of communistic rhetoric, decided to invade the south, so the whole country could be ruled as a communist regime. The French sent in battalions of the Foreign Legion. France had too much going on in its other colonies, so it eventually pulled out of Vietnam, deciding to let them sort it out for themselves. The South then appealed to the US, John Kennedy was the president then, and he sent in military advisers to the South. You have to remember that all this came about at the same time as Russia was flexing its muscles. The Yanks had a policy of fighting the spread of Communism wherever it reared its ugly head. Anyway, Kennedy's advisers decided that the South would need seasoned troops, or they wouldn't be able to contain the North. Kennedy sent in about seventy thousand soldiers to help the South, but then he got himself shot, and Johnson took over. He's a Texan, and very anti-communist. So he sent in more troops, and more again, but they still need more."

"So many more that he can't produce. So he's pulled a rabbit out of the hat, by asking our government to honour the ally's agreement, and send troops also. Mind you Holt, McMahon, and Gorton are as much anti-communist as Johnson is, so there was no problem in complying with his request. Now the full time army is only thirty thousand strong, and we'd be lucky to have ten thousand in the infantry, and they'd have to be rotated to have fresh troops. So the idiots have introduced conscription, and I think there'll be hell to pay over that decision. Does that make it any clearer for you?"

Answering, I said "Yep, but what I'm also trying to do is work out how it all came about. The countries in that region didn't really exist, prior to the later part of the last century, due to the English and French colonising different parts of the area. Those countries weren't really heard of before the Japs occupied them in the last war, and from what can be gathered from the history books, the Japs had a hell of a time fighting there before their occupation. So they could be fairly tough opponents."

Mark answered, "Well, I'm not sure of what the history books say, but I've already done one tour there, so my knowledge is first hand. Our main job is reconnaissance, and that means that we try to avoid open fighting because we work in small groups. The irregulars, the Viet Cong, aren't all that tough. The regular NVA troops aren't either, but where they do present a problem is in the sheer weight of numbers. They keep coming and coming, much like the

251

Japs did in World War II. The best advice I can give you is learn everything we teach you. The training will help keep you alive, I'm sure of that. After your training, you'll probably be assigned to the next squadron in the rotation. If not this year, most probably the next, you'll get a chance to see for yourself." After I finished talking with Mark, as I was heading back to my seat, I noticed that Pep was staring out the window. I sat beside him, and asked "Pep, can I ask you a few questions?" I never forgot the answer he gave me, "Well, son, you don't learn unless you ask questions."

So I asked, "Have you done any tours?" "Aye, I've got two tours of 'Nam under my belt, and possibly another soon." He replied in a more pronounced Scottish brogue than I'd heard him use before. "I've three slope scalps up, with a few other possible." I had to ask, "Slope?" He replied "Yeah, there's two main ways we refer to the natives; slopes or Charlie. Me, I just call them nogs."

I questioned "nogs?" He replied "Yeah, slopes, and Charlie, are used usually. Charlie mainly for the VC, but due to my heritage I just call 'em nogs. Short for 'nignogs', which any brit uses for foreigners. Here, I'll show you the sign for Charlie we use." After he demonstrated, I asked, "So that's the sign used for the Viet Cong?" "Yep," he replied, so I pushed a little further. "So how come you're in this outfit?"

He replied "well, that's a long story. Suffice to say, I was once in the Brit Army Commandoes. After moving here, and working as a brickie, my marriage went tits up, so I decided to re-join. After that, I ended up here, and have been doing this since. I love it, it keeps me on the edge, and to tell you the truth, I've never talked to someone, about me, for so long. What's your secret?" So I replied, "Just easy to talk to, I guess." Our conversation drifted a little towards me, so I fobbed it off, and asked "Can you start teaching me some of the sign language we're expected to learn?" "Sure," he replied, and then we settled down for a few hours, with the intricacies of sign language. It was easy for me to pick up, and by the end of the flight I was getting quite adept at it.

We landed at Pearce RAAF base at about thirteen forty in

the afternoon. As we circled Perth to line up with the east-west runway, Pep pointed out where the barracks were. I saw that the base was roughly just to the northwest of the city. As we landed, we taxied to a hangar near some parked C130 Hercules transport planes, at the furthest end of the runway, and actually rolled inside the hangar before stopping. There was a truck and Land Rover parked inside the hangar. The drivers waiting for us, and we transferred our gear from the plane to the truck, and then hopped into the Rover for the ride to Swanbourne. Twenty minutes later, we rolled onto base, and pulled up at a barracks hut, with a T one painted on the side. The truck stayed with us as the rover with Mark drove elsewhere. Pep said "Right, get your gear stowed. Tiger room one, Kilt two, and be back outside in twenty dressed in your fatigues." Twenty minutes later we were outside smoking as Pep came around the corner. He stood in front of us and said, "Right. We'll be taking a little stroll to show you around, but first come with me." We all walked together to a fenced off area that had a whole heap of telephone poles lying on the ground. Pep said "Ok, boys, go pick yourselves one, that's your armament to be carried everywhere from now on." I thought to myself, shit! They weren't kidding at all, Christ! This was going to be downright embarrassing, and I picked one that seemed to have good balance.

Christ, it was heavy. After placing it on my shoulder, I realised that it wasn't as bad as it seemed, and it was definitely going to build some more muscle. After Kilt had picked his, we set off on our orientation tour, and as we went along, Pep kept up a running commentary. Showing us the ORs combined mess and canteen, Pep told us the daily meal times, and the mess hours. Because the mess and canteen were combined, there was no alcohol served until after dinner, and they didn't finish serving dinner until eighteen thirty, bugger!

Continuing our tour of the main base area, Pep showed us the Q store, armoury, rattled of the functions of the main headquarter, buildings, and the locations of the lecture and planning building. After the tour, we returned to our hut, and Pep said "Secure your arms in your rooms then join me in the main room." I placed my pole in the corner nearest the door, and then made my way down to the main room Pep had placed some pre-drawn maps on the table. They showed all the main area buildings, all numbered, and corresponding to the legend box with the building names, and a sort of flowchart. He said "Ok, sit and I'll go through this quickly. I've given you the building maps so you can't get lost, and now I'm going to explain this flowchart."

"At present, SAS is made up of four squadrons. The HQ Squadron and three sabre or fighting squadrons. Each squadron is made up of six troops, each troop is made up of x number of patrols, dependent on the size of the patrol. Number two sabre squadron is deployed in Vietnam and due for rotation soon. Number three squadron is in preparation to deploy, and number one squadron is in training. Also we have engineers, medical and signals corps attached to us for our training and preparation. Now that's enough for today. Tomorrow at zero even thirty, we'll get your kit from the Q store, get your dog tags and security passes organised in the security building, then we're off to the armoury and firing range. Don't be self-conscious about your poles in the mess. Everyone's used to seeing new recruits carrying them. Do you have any questions?" I asked "Pep, do we unpack our gear today, and what's the dress for tomorrow?"

Pep answered, "Yeah, get unpacked, and this will be your quarters for the time being. Tomorrow's dress is fatigues, boots, and beret. Actually, that's what you'll be wearing most of the time, if there's any change I'll let you know. Is there anything else?" We both answered "No," and he said "Okay, that's it. I'll see you in the morning." And he left, so we did our unpacking, and then headed off to the mess for dinner.

Arriving at the mess with our trusty poles, we were met by a smiling Corporal who said "Just leave them propped up against the wall. My name's 'Red'." He held his hand out, which we shook, and introduced ourselves by our nicknames. He said "Well come on, and I'll introduce you around, we're pretty informal around here.

254

So when did you two arrive?" Kilt told him that we'd arrived earlier today from Kapooka, and Red asked "Let me get this straight, you both came from basic training to here?" We both nodded, and Red said "Wow. You're special, then" and started, introducing us to others in the mess. After a while, he said "Let's grab something to eat, and you can join us at our table if you like."

After sitting down at a table with Red and a few others, we started eating, and one of them, Jake, I think asked "So when do you start the silent routine?" With a frown on my face and a questioning look, I asked "What?" He replied "Sorry, forgot you're newbies. When you start your signing training, you're only allowed to communicate in sign language." I replied "Well, we're going to the Q store and security tomorrow, and then to the range, so we've no idea." Red said "You'll probably start after that. It's pretty routine, and nothing to worry about, but it's a bastard trying to order a round of drinks!" Every one of us laughed at his last comment. With the announcement that the bar was open, I said "Well, I'm going to get a round in while I can still speak. What's everyone having?" Over the drinks and smokes, I started to relax and took delight in getting to know these guys. One thing I did notice though was that no matter what the subject of conversation was on, it always came back to work. Most of them were in one squadron, which meant they had already done a tour in Vietnam. They'd be handy to have around in the coming weeks, because they had been there and done it.

Later in the night while doing my mental debrief, I made the decision to play the cards as they fell. In other words, I was going to take each thing as it came along, and not worry about incidental things that I had no control over. Then I started making up sentences in the sign language Pep had taught me, without trying to say them aloud. At first it was hard, because I could speak faster than make up the signs, but the more I practised the easier it became, because my fingers started to cooperate with what my mind was making up. It became faster, and with fewer mistakes, mind you that was only to my way of thinking. It would be interesting to check with someone who could sign. After an hour or so at this, I decided to call it a night. Roll on tomorrow.

In the morning, we were having a smoke as we waited for Pep to arrive. We had only just finished our smokes, when he came around the corner of the hut. Without breaking stride, said "Right. Fall in and let's go." So we hefted our poles and fell in beside him, as we headed to the Q store. The Staff Sergeant in charge issued us with three more berets, six corp badges, four dress uniform epaulette corp bars, and two corp coloured lanyards. We also got three more pairs of boots and socks, a helmet, a roll of mottle coloured light cheese cloth like material, and a box containing a dozen tubes of different coloured grease paint.

Pep had procured a wheel barrow. We put what we couldn't carry into it, and left to return to the hut. Pep pushed the wheel barrow. Back at the hut, we unloaded the barrow, and Pep said "Take your gear inside, and then wait till I return." He headed back the way we had come with the wheel barrow. We took our gear into our rooms, and then went back outside to wait for Pep and have a smoke. Next we went off to the security hut; we handed in our previously issued dog tags, and received the newer ones now being issued. Next we had photographs taken, and were fingerprinted for our ID cards, then we were issued a pager each, and instructed to carry them at all times whenever we were off base, and not to get them wet. They were for readiness recall purposes only.

Leaving the security building, with our ID's, new tags, and pagers, the next stop was the armoury. A truck was waiting to take us and the armoury guys to the firing range. Once the truck was loaded, and we were all aboard, the truck headed off. Along the way to the range, Pep pointed out different places to us. As we passed what was starting to look like a building, Pep informed us "That's something the new boss has had built, and none of us are sure of what for yet." Just after that we stopped at the range, and as the truck was being unloaded, and the armoury guys were setting up, we went over to what looked like an observation area. While we were having a smoke, Pep briefed us on what was going to take place.

He said "First, it'll be handguns. Just get the feel of them, and pick one or two. Then they'll be loaded, and you can feel how they fire. Then we'll move on to the machine pistols, then the long arms, and finally the scoped selection. Tiger you first. Oh, also we're not going back to the barracks for lunch. A vehicle will be bringing it out to us, so there's no interruption to your selections."

I moved to the table that had a wide selection of pistols laid out, all autos, and the standard issue Browning at the top. I bypassed it, and looked at the Colts. There were two models; a Government and a Commander. Pep's gun that I used at Kapooka was a Government model. I picked up the Commander model, and got the feel of it, and picked up the Government in my left hand, and compared the weight and feel of both. The Commander was just a tad lighter, and not as long in the barrel length. I elected to try both, and while I was choosing, Kilt had settled on a Berretta Parabellum and the Browning.

Both guns were loaded with full mags. I approached the firing line, and fired from both hips, three rounds from each weapon. I then switched the Government to my right hand, and the Commander to the left, then fired another three. After surveying the results, I put the safety on both, and handed the Government to the armourer to hold. I then fired three more as aimed shots from the Commander, exchanged guns, and did the same with the Government. After looking at the results, I fired off the remaining rounds, and switched back to the Commander to do the same. As I took them back to the table, the Sergeant who was standing beside Pep, asked "Very impressive form, what do you think?" I replied "Well I hate to say this, Pep, but the Commander is a bit shorter in barrel length, a tad lighter, and gives me more control. If I opt for a Commander, do they come with combat handgrips?" Mick, the Sergeant, replied "Yes, and we can also do any fine tuning of the action here by our own armorers." I replied "Ok, make it a Colt Commander for me, then." Mick nodded and made notes on the clip board he was holding.

Kilt had done his firing, and when asked, took the Parabellum as his pick. After Mick had made his notes, he said "Good. Ok, let's move to the machine pistols. I'm afraid that there's only a very small selection, and even though they can be fired without suppressors (silencers), in our line of work, we always use the suppressors." He finished talking as we reached the table with only two choices. One was the Sterling machine pistol, which we had seen at Kapooka. The other, I learned was an Ingram. Both fired at the same cyclic capacity, so really there wasn't much difference. Both weighed the same, and had the same length. However, I noticed as I got a feel for it, that the business end of the Ingram didn't drag down as much as the Sterling. After the test firing, we both opted for the Ingram. Mick said with a smile "How come it's always the short guys that pick the Ingram? It's my pick also, and I'm the armourer, so well chosen."

As we headed along the table line to the next selection, Mick said "Ah, here comes lunch, so we'll get to these after," and we started moving up towards the truck that had brought lunch. Lunch consisted of an assortment of sandwiches on white bread. The bread was fresh, and if you didn't like ham, cheese, and tomato, the other choices were ham, cheese, and tomato. There was an urn full of hot coffee but there was no sugar or milk. I think that started my preference for black coffee way back then, because it tastes better and stronger without the additives, and goes better with a smoke.

After we had eaten, we all sat around talking, and chatting about the merits of one firearm against another, and about weapons in general for about half an hour. Then we got back to the matter in hand. On the rifle table, there was an assortment of different rifles, along with the standard SLR. One caught my eye; picking it up, I asked "Mick, is this the newM203?" He replied with a smile, "Yep, you know your weapons, Tiger. Want to give it a whirl?" I replied with enthusiasm "Yes, please!" He showed me how to adjust, zero the sights, and then I made my way to the firing line. I took three sighting shots, made the necessary adjustments, and banged off another three. One more tweak, then three more- bingo the sights were working well now. I reloaded to a full mag, and fired seven for a grouping. All shots were bang on target. I switched to my left hand, and again all on target. I shot off the remaining rounds, switched to a full mag, turned the safety switch to full auto, and shot off the mag in short bursts. Excellent, I thought to myself, and asked Mick "Can I try the grenade tube?" Passing me a round, he replied "Go right ahead," and then yelled "Fire in the hole!" Everyone stopped as I loaded the grenade, picked a target, and popped off the grenade. Yes! Bang on! I thought it over; the M203 was as accurate as the SLR, lighter, could fire on full auto, could be fitted with a silencer, and had the grenade capacity as well.

I turned to Mick, and as I replaced the rifle on the table said with a smile "You can put me down for one of those." Kilt preferred to stick with the SLR after trying a couple others. Then we moved to the last table, where Mick said "Snipers usually have their own preference rifles, but these are good for up to a thousand yards." On the table was a SLR fitted with a telescope. The other was a scoped thirty-thirty Remington. It was bolt load only, so could only fire one round at a time, not magazine fed. After firing both rifles Kilt and I preferred the scoped SLR.

After he had finished making all his notes, Mick and the armourers started packing up all the weapons and accessories. When everything was loaded onto the truck, Mick said to us, "Ok, all of the weapons you've chosen will be here in a week. I'll let Pep know when, and we can come out again to test them out. Any necessary adjustments can be made before you start your qualifying tests." Then we all climbed aboard and made our way back to the main barracks area.

At the armoury, all the gear was unloaded from the truck. Once we had retrieved our poles, Pep said "Righto. Make your way to the hut, and I'll join you shortly." Hefting our poles, we set off to the hut, and after putting our poles in place, we went to the main room. Pep joined us carrying a couple of books as Kilt was making coffee, so we sat around with our drinks and smokes, while Pep gave us a debrief. He said "Well, for your first day that went fairly well, not that any of it was hard work yet. Now, from now until I say otherwise you aren't to say anything. You're starting your silence training, so you best start learning your sign language pretty quick." He handed us a book each, and continued. "You'll need to keep these with you until you become fluent. Now, everyone on base has gone through this, and has standing orders to report any breaches, so beware! Accidents do happen though, and are taken into account. Understood?" We both nodded, and he went on. "All day tomorrow, you'll be in class with one of the signs people, learning more about sign, and some variations. You know your way to the lecture room, so I'll meet you there at zero eight hundred, any questions?"

We both shook our heads, and Pep said "Ok I'll see you in the am," and left the hut. We looked at each other, and I smiled, shrugged my shoulders, and signed to Kilt that I was going to my room. Then got up, taking my book from the table.

CHAPTER 25

Well, Red had been right about it being a bastard to order something. That night as I ordered dinner, the guy serving said with a smile, "Sorry, Corp, but we don't have any pink seas." I held my arms out palm up, and looked upward in exasperation, then pointed to the steak. The guy said, still smiling, "Oh, why didn't you say so?" Annoying prick, I thought to myself. Kilt, the smartarse, didn't even try, he wrote his order down. As I turned to him, he smiled. "Arsehole"! Was my immediate thought to his smile.

The rest of the guys gave us as much help as they could that night. At one point, I ripped the notebook out of Kilt's hand, then took everyone's order, and passed the note across to the smiling barman. When I got back to the table, I signed 'More than one way to skin a cut', and Red corrected me, by telling us the subtle difference between "a" and "u." So my first night of using sign wasn't as bad as I thought it would be, and I thought that after another couple of day's I should be quite good at it.

Now I'm about to digress a little, so please bear with me. I've asked a lot of guys how do you know when you've spotted the girl you're going to marry? The answers I've got have been "It's like a sledge hammer blow," "You just get a feeling," or it's like "Love at first sight." Well, the first time I saw my future wife, I thought "I wonder what she's like in the sack?" I looked her up and down; about five-five, nice roundish face, hazel and green eyes, nice short brunette hair, nice figure, really nice moderate breasts. To tell you the truth, though was sort of, more in lust than anything else."

The next morning, we met Pep in the lecture room, and as we were sitting down, in strolled a signals Corp, female Private in dress uniform. As she took her beret off and placed it on the table, I turned sideways and signed to Pep, 'She's cute'. He smiled. She laughed and said "Well, thank you Corporal. My name's Sharon Dawsett. Now, I want each of you to sign me your name, and we'll go from there." The rest of the day went fairly quickly from then on. By the end of the day, I was flying ahead with the sign, and Kilt was getting better and better. She told us we'd be with her the following day, and then probably we would continue the following week after our field exercise. Now there was a piece of news! What field exercise? Obviously Pep had been holding something back, or hadn't got around to telling us.

Back in the hut that afternoon, Pep informed us of the upcoming exercise we were going to embark on. I don't think he was too pleased that Sharon had let the cat out of the bag, and after hearing what we would be up to, I didn't blame him. The upshot being, that the day after tomorrow, we would be getting our kit together for a forty mile run. By getting our kit together, I mean that we were going to be wearing full battle field gear, and our field packs were going to weight forty kilos. If they didn't come to that weight with our gear, rocks were going to be added to round out the weight. The morning we were to leave, we would be drawing out a handgun and combat hunting knife each, from the armoury prior to departure. After hearing this, I already could start to feel my aching back. Oh Lovely! I thought.

During the following day, I found another disadvantage of sign language. It's very hard to try to flirt with someone, when everyone can see what you're saying! In the end, I waited until we were finished for the day, hung back a little, and asked Sharon for a date. She signed back "Ask me when you're finished your training and we'll see." Well, that was better than I had hoped; she hadn't said "No," but then again she hadn't said "Yes" either. Pep was laughing aloud as we walked away from the lecture room, saying "Jesus, Tiger, you've got balls. Trying to flirt with someone in sign, what next?" I signed "Well it was worth a shot", and he said, "Forget trying to get your end in, and concentrate on the training. Your training is going to require you're full concentration. Remember: one slip up and you're out."

Thinking about his comment that night, I decided he was right, and that Sharon was one of those incidentals that I wasn't going to worry about. The next morning after breakfast, Pep joined us at the hut carrying a set of scales. He then told us to get our gear. I had removed the shoulder harness from my field belt and added two more water bottles. As he saw what I had done, Pep gave a nod of approval, and said "Belt and Pack, on the scales." Total weight came to thirty kilos, and he asked what I had in the field pack. I signed "Spare boots, fatigues, bayonet, ground sheet, and sleeping bag." He nodded approval again, and then said "Go outside and get some of the garden rocks." When I came back, the total was up to forty two kilos, and he said "Yep, that'll do. You should be able to handle the extra." When it was Kilt's turn, he ended up with thirty nine!

At the armoury, we were given the handguns that we had chosen, a webbing thigh holster that clipped around the leg, and a combat hunting knife that we were to keep. I asked for another leg strap, fixed the knife onto my left thigh, and tied the bottom of the sheath around the bottom part of my thigh with some thin cord. Meanwhile Pep had been given two rounds of ammunition, which he placed in his shirt pocket.

After leaving the armoury carrying our poles, Pep showed us the path to the beach. He said "Go down to the beach, turn north, then start running. Ten miles up the beach you'll come to a wide creek mouth, and that's where I'll meet you. I'll be able to see you from the road, and I want to see you running all the way, under-stood?" We nodded our confirmation, and he said "Right. Off you go." We started running down the beach path, five minutes later we were on the sand, and headed north. Now it's not too easy to run in sand, but trust me it's no picnic in boots either!

For the first fifteen minutes, it was hard slog. Running with all the weight, and trying to balance the pole from thumping down on my shoulder. Then I decided to move down closer to the water's edge where the sand was firmer, and the going became easier. I beckoned Kilt down, he joined me, and I slowed a little to keep pace with him. After every half hour I would change the pole to my other shoulder, and that eased the thumping on my shoulders. After the second hour I stopped concentrating and let my mind drift to think of other things. It helped matters immensely, but I found that I had reverted to my normal pace. As I twirled around, I found that Kilt was nearly two hundred yards behind me, so I slowed again until he had caught up.

Up in the distance I saw the creek mouth, so I gave Kilt a quick nudge and pointed ahead. Up until this time he had been running with his head down, and was flagging, and I think that he thought the end was in sight. However, I ran over what we had been issued, and I had a sneaky suspicion that this was only the start! As we drew nearer to the creek outflow, I saw someone standing off toward the right of our direction up beyond the beach. Sure enough as we drew nearer, I made out that the figure was indeed Pep, and he beckoned in a wave for us to come in his direction. Three minutes later, I reached his position, with Kilt close behind. I stood my pole on the ground, and grabbing a water bottle, took a long mouthful, letting the water trickle down my throat slowly.

Kilt however, had just let his pole drop to the ground. I noticed the quick disappointed frown on Pep's face, and he said "Ok boys, take ten, and relax." He looked in my direction, and indicated that I accompany him out of earshot of Kilt. He said "If you hadn't been pushing him, he wouldn't have made it this far. Now I know that ingrained thought, to look after your workmates. In this situation, it's survival of the fittest; you don't let someone else pull you down. Now think about this, truthfully do you think he will make the grade, considering this is only the start of what's to come? You've got to sort that out for yourself. It's not my job to mollycoddle. Remember, think about that. Now move back over, and I'll fill you in on the next phase."

As I sat on my pole beside Kilt, Pep brought over some sandwiches for lunch and a thermos of black coffee. As we ate, he filled us in on the next part of the day. "The next stroll is to cross the creek here then up a little further you'll pass a couple of shacks.

That's called Lancelin. You'll continue on after that to the second sort of township, it's called Jurien. Away from the township you will stop. You should reach there by sixteen hundred, find an LUP (laying up area), and there is where you spend the night. Your food for the night is what you kill, and eat. DO NOT fire toward the town." As he said this, he passed us each one round for our pistols, saying "That's all you get, so I suggest you don't miss. I'm also going to split you up. Tiger the beach, Kilt the high ground. I will find you both, and call in on you tonight, and in the am. Questions?" We had none.

The creek crossing was a bitch, as the water reached up as far as my shoulders. I thanked Christ that I had made sure the weather proofing in my pack was done up right, which meant that none of my gear would get wet. After the crossing I was sopping wet, but after running for a half hour in the hot air, my clothes were dry again. Not so my boots and socks, so I took time out to exchange them with the dry ones I had in my field pack. When I got on the move again, I had tied my boots together with the laces, and hung them round my neck. This had the annoying result of them banging against my body as I ran, so making another stop I secured them to the back of my field pack. Feeling relieved, I wondered why I hadn't thought of doing that in the first place.

A couple hours later, I was on the southern side of Jurien, so looked for a likely LUP. I found one amongst the dunes, like a cove with an outcropping of dune either side. Settling myself down, I made the cove liveable.

After establishing camp, my watch told me it was fifteen forty five, so I was in place within the allotted time frame. Ok, what next? I asked myself, and got a very intelligent answer. Look for some fire wood. So, scouting around the area, I found enough to last the night. I also came across a fairly straight piece of wood that gave me some thoughts about dinner. Looking toward the clear water, I started sharpening one end of the wood with the bayonet I had carried. After I had a fair imitation of a spear, I stripped off, and made my way slowly into the water. Within five minutes I had speared a couple of decent sized fish, a parrot, and a coral trout. Oh, I was going to eat well tonight, I thought to myself, and thinking of that put me in mind of how I was going to cook them.

Rummaging in my pack, I found what I thought I had put in there weeks ago. I found I had about a metre of tinfoil. You beauty! I thought. I grabbed a fairly flat piece of timber, and made my way to the water's edge, and proceeded to clean and fillet the fish using my hunting knife. I had enough for dinner and breakfast, and some foil left over. Back at the fire, I sat and lit a smoke as I waited for the firewood to reduce to a good bed of coals. I sipped some water, then stripped the pistol down, and dried the working parts as much as I could.

As the sun was low in the sky, I was dressed and laying out my groundsheet. Before eating, as I heard a noise. I quickly retrieved the pistol round from my pocket, fed it into the gun, then whirled and cocked the gun as I pointed it toward the top of the dune behind me. Pep came into view at the top, and as he saw my preparedness, said "Whoa, laddie," and started making his way down to me. While he did this, I uncocked the gun and ejected the round. As he joined me, he asked "Nervous?" I signed "No, just on unfamiliar territory, would you like something to eat?" He replied "Sure, if you've got enough." In answer I just smiled and started uncovering the coals from the fish. Using the slab I started uncovering dinner, and sat it between us, as we ate with our fingers. After finishing, he said "Ummm that was good. Where'd you learn to look after yourself?" "Back home in Queensland" I signed, and he just nodded his head. I asked '"Do you want to know what time I got here?" He replied, "No, I know. I've been watching you from the town. Your mate's over there, about three hundred yards away, and he's not in good shape. If he doesn't improve, I'll be taking him back tomorrow in the rover." Knowing what that meant, I just nodded my head. He asked "Are you ready for tomorrow?"

I nodded, and he continued, "After you've caught yourself some breakfast…," I stopped him at that point and pointed to the fire. Seeing a bit of alfoil poking out of the coals, he laughed and continued. "Ok when you've finished eating, break camp and head back to base. I'll meet you there when you arrive." I nodded, and handed him the bullet round, and he said "Keep it, in case you need it, and give it to me when you get back. Clear?" I nodded, and he said "Ok. Have a good night, and I'll see you tomorrow afternoon." He headed towards the beach then rounded the dune and was gone. I got out my sleeping bag, took my boots off, threw a cover over them, put the round back in my gun, grabbed my field pack as a pillow, and settled down for the night.

The next morning, I was awake at dawn, and stirring the embers of the fire that was still warm. I pulled out the other pieces of fish I'd left overnight, and had breakfast with swigs of water, and wished I'd have thought to pack some coffee. Then I set about packing up, and scattered and buried the remnants of the fire. I put my gear on, lifted the damn pole, and set off on the return to base. A few hours later at the creek crossing I took the time to remove my boots and socks for the crossing, and replaced them afterward. I arrived back in the base area at thirteen hundred, and sure enough Pep was waiting on the beach. He said "You're earlier than I expected. Come on up to your quarters. You've missed lunch, so I grabbed you some sandwiches, and you can eat as I tell you what happens for the rest of the day." At the pained expression on my face, he commented "You're not getting away with only a half-day's work."

After placing my pole in the room with my other gear, I sat at the main table with a cup of coffee and eating. Pep said "I don't think this will surprise you, but your mate failed and is being sent back to Kapooka. The rest of the day will be on sign, and first up tomorrow you'll be examined. Your weapons of choice have arrived, so if you don't fail your sign exam, we'll go to the range in the afternoon." By this time I'd finished eating, drinking my coffee, and having a smoke, so Pep asked "Ready?" I nodded, and we left the hut, to go to the lecture room.

Sharon was already there and waiting as we walked in, and signed "I'm impressed, I didn't expect to see you until tomorrow,

I only got the call fifteen minutes ago." Pep smiled and signed "This one's full of surprises." Sharon signed to me. "You look exhausted, are you sure you're ready to continue?" I nodded.

She continued to sign "Well, ok. Tomorrow you're taking your exam. Now the pass rate is ninety five percent, and it's a timed exercise for accuracy, so we'll practise the exam scenario. For example, tell me if you know this word, and have I spelt it correctly?" She signed the word "exasperated", but with two, 't's, so I corrected her. So we did that for a while, and then it was my turn to make up words with correct spelling. Then I had to sign a list of words she gave me and spelt correctly while being timed. After an hour, she signed "If that had been your exam, you would've passed with a hundred percent rating." Then Pep interrupted by signing, "So you think he's ready?" She replied "He's amazing, and yes, he's more than ready."'. Pep replied "Good, who's taking the exam?" Sharon replied "Sgt Wilson," and then Pep signed "Good. Let's call it a day. Thanks for your help." She replied "My pleasure, and good luck tomorrow, Tiger." Her wishing me luck really surprised me, and I smiled at her as I looked at Pep, getting up to leave.

The following morning, the sign exam took only an hour. I aced it, and then Pep and I headed to the armoury. Mick, the armoury Sgt, greeted us. He said "Well, your guns are here, Tiger; would you like to see them before we head to the range?" Now that the sign exam was over, I could speak, and replied "Yes please." Mick reached under the counter, and brought up the handguns first, then the holsters. The M203 was next, and then the scoped SLR. He also placed an ammo box on the counter and said "In there's four spare mags for each weapon, all the cleaning gear, plus oil and gun cotton. When you two are ready, we'll take the rover, and head down." Pep said "No time like the present." Mick grabbed another ammo box and picked up four boxes each of seven point six two rounds, nine millimetres, and forty five calibre rounds. He put them into the ammo box, and said "Right, let's go."

Pep picked up the two rifles and the holsters while I grabbed the two pistols. After placing the guns on the seat, I lay my pole in the bed of the rover, and then hopped aboard. As we drove to the range, I strapped the holsters on to each thigh. I placed the pistols into them, and withdrew them, doing this a few times to shape the holsters, and get used to them myself. After that I locked them into place, making sure to secure the butt straps. At the range, after taking my trusty telephone pole out, Pep gave me a hand to fully load all the magazines I had. From the supply Mick had brought with us, after all the loading there were still a few boxes of ammo remaining.

Mick said "When you're ready, start with the colt. Let me know everything that you think may need work, even the slightest thing. Ok. "Stepping to the firing line, I started. After five rounds from each hand, I ceased firing. Mick was soon beside me, and we went into a conversation about how it felt, and fired. I had a few concerns, and after I had finished, he said "I think to solve the recoil problem I could take out a couple twists of the spring. Then I'll give the workings a polish. Go ahead with the others, and I'll return in thirty." After ejecting the mag, he took the pistol, and headed to the rover. While he was gone, Pep watched as I sighted and made adjustments to the rest of my weapons. As I fired the last grouping shot from the SLR, Mick returned, and walked up holding the gun out to me saying "Try that now."

After the first shot, I could feel and tell that the changes he had made were perfect. I proceeded to go through all the magazines, in different ways of shooting, and the gun just felt like an extension of my arm. I was rapt! Whilst I'd been firing, Pep had been reloading the magazines from the boxes left over. I joined him to reload all the mags for the forty-five, and he casually asked "Well, do you think you'll be right for qualifying now?" By this time Mick had joined us, and I replied "Yep, when can I do it?" Pep looked at Mick, and he said "I'd have to arrange the team, and a couple of verifying officers. I've got targets back at the store, how about after lunch at thirteen hundred, at the armoury?" I looked at Pep, he nodded, and I replied "Done." We loaded the rover, and headed back. Mick dropped Pep and I back at my hut, and after

269

saying "Thirteen hundred," drove off.

We went into my room and Pep, after laying the rifles on the bed, reached into his pocket and gave me a slip of paper. He said, "That's the safe combination," indicating the safe beside the four piece rifle rack. He pulled a lock and key from his pocket, and said "And this is for the gun rack. Your side arms and spare mags are to be kept in the safe, and the rifles in the rack. If you're moving around the base with weapons, they have to be fully loaded, with the safeties on. Right, sort them out, give them a clean, and I'll meet you at the armoury after lunch."

I was able to catch up with Red at lunch, and he told me the latest news. "Our troop's off to parachute training soon, which means we'll get a few day's leave while we're over there. I can't wait- we'll be training for HALO jumps, and that should be a hoot." I just smiled, not knowing what the hell he was talking about.

As I approached the armoury that afternoon, I saw two officers. One was Mark Ryan, and after marching up to the armoury, I was introduced to the other by Mark, and he was Major Teague. He said "This is for qualifying, Tiger, so you can rest your arms by placing it against the wall." With his directive, I placed my pole up against the building. Pep joined us Mick came out of the building carrying a box of ammunition for each weapon, and passed them to me with a wink. Then, getting into the rover, we headed for the range. Mick said "The crew have already left, and should be close to set up when we get there." After arriving at the range, Mick gave us a briefing and the shooting order. He and the two officers went to the observation platform, as Pep and I went to the firing line, and waited for instruction.

"Target one, right hand instinctive, seven body shots, commence!" I fired all my weapons, both left and right handed, as ordered. I thought I'd done bloody well, but I wouldn't learn the result until later. Trader Teague called from the observation deck, "Tiger, you're using an M203. Can you take out targets one, two, and three with the tube?" Mick dropped three grenade rounds to Pep, I replied "Yes, Sir," took the rounds from Pep and obliterated the targets that he requested.

Back at the armoury, Mick, Mark, and Trader went inside to look at the targets I'd fired at; and each had been written on with the order of shot. After ten minutes, they came out, and Trader said "Corporal Davis, you'd best pick up your pole." He paused, my heart sank. Shit! I'd blown it. As Trader continued "And place it back where it was issued to you. Excellent result, way above average, Congratulations." I shook his outstretched hand, and said "Thank you, Sir."

After Mark and Trader left, Mick said with a smile "Get that bloody log off my building, and then come back." "Sure thing, Sarge," I replied. After taking the telephone pole back where it came from, I returned and retrieved my weapons. Mick gave me a belt full of grenade rounds, saying "It's easier to wear them like a bandolier, across your shoulder, than as a belt. Now piss off, Tiger." With a smile I thanked him, and Pep and I headed for my hut.

CHAPTER 26

The following morning, I was woken by Pep turning on the hut lights, and saying "Come on, get up!" I looked at the clock it was only three in the morning. Shit! Pep had made a brew, and poked his head around my door. He said "Full battle dress, and enough changes for a week. We depart at dawn. MOVE IT!" The first thing that went through my mind was "Fuck, the shit's hit the fan, something's wrong." I threw the covers off, and started doing half dozen things at once. I unlocked the safe, got dressed, pulled out my field gear to pack, unlocked my rifle, and slurped my coffee down as I went. Within fifteen minutes, I was dressed in full battle gear and ready to go. I made my way to the main room with my coffee mug, and rifle. As I made another coffee and lit up a smoke, Pep rattled off items, and I called "Check" as he listed them.

After the preparation list was confirmed, he smiled and said "Well, that was bloody good, but it wasn't an exercise. We WILL be leaving at dawn, joining a troop from one squadron, heading to Pearce, and then onto parachute training." I replied "But they're doing HALO jumping, whatever that is." He answered with a smile, "Yes, and we'll be doing your qualification jumps, and then your HALO qualifications as well. HALO stands for "high altitude, low oxygen," which means jumping from heights above thirty thousand feet! Don't worry, you'll love it. After you do your first jump, you'll be hooked!" Not feeling all that sure or enthused as he was, I just nodded, and asked "Does that mean we'll be getting leave?" He answered with a laugh, and smile. "They will when we get there, but you and I; no. You'll be learning and going through the qualification course I mentioned." My first thought was, "bugger, it would have been nice to have some leave," and then I started thinking about what I was facing, and started to feel enthusiastic about it. Then he said "Ok, let's go get some breakfast." We picked up our rifles and gear, and set off to the OR's mess, which was feeding all ranks for breakfast. Pep moved to a table where his opposite numbers were sitting, while I made my way over to join Red and the others.

Red asked "So you're coming along. Does that mean you're going on leave as well?" I answered "No, I'll be doing the qualification course, but if I pass that, I'll probably be doing the HALO course as well." "Way to go," "Good on ya," "Alright," is some of the sentiments expressed.

After breakfast, I trooped out with the others to have a couple of smokes while waiting to depart. Everyone was in full battle gear, and carried an assortment of rifles, but all the rifles fired the standard seven point six two NATO round. The day grew progressively light, and as I stubbed out my third smoke of the day, three trucks rolled into base HQ area. The Officers and Sergeants started us moving toward the trucks. Once everyone was aboard, we started off towards the Air Force Base. At the RAAF base, we drove past all of the main buildings and pulled up beside a Hercules transport plane that had the engines, and propellers turning over in warm up. As we disembarked from the trucks, the guys were formed up and Pep put his hand on my shoulder to hold me back. As they were marched onto the plane through the rear ramp, Pep and I went last, and we were seated near the rear of the plane near the ramp.

The first class seating hadn't changed since my last flight in a Herc, and as I stowed my gear under the webbed seating I wondered what sort of entertainment would fill this trip. Soon after loading, one of the plane crew came down the back to raise the loading ramp. As he made his way forward, he stopped in front of Pep and I saying "There's coffee brewing up forward, and the shitters are up near the front. There are two on each side of the plane, port and starboard." He followed this procedure a few times as he made his way to the forward crew area. Then the Herc started moving, and we were in the air five minutes later.

During the flight, Pep tried to prepare me for what lay ahead, explaining the order of the training, and what I had to achieve for my qualification. After the initial learning how to land and roll, I had to learn it again after releasing my own harness off the ground. I next had to do three static line jumps, the last two in full battle gear, and one of them at night. So I asked what he meant by static line, and he explained, "Well, you've probably seen in old war movies where they hook a catch on a line before jumping out." I nodded. "Well, that means that you don't have control over when your chute opens, because it opens automatically after a set distance." I nodded my understanding, and he went on. "Now, after your three static jumps, you'll do three free line jumps in the same order. With free line, you'll be given a wrist altimeter because you have to keep a close eye on your height. At a set height, you pull your chute open. If you're late in pulling it, you will get injured, or worse! You'd become a training statistic."

Ohhkay. That was a sobering thought. Pep went on. "The beauty of free line is that you get the time to enjoy the sensation of flying, even if for only a short time. We've only got four days to get you qualified before the HALO course, so it's going to be bit of a rush. Usually qualifying takes place as a two week course, but I think you can handle the pressure." I thanked him for his confidence in me, and then asked "So what sort of height are we talking about?" "Static line is between ten and eleven thousand feet, free line is up to fifteen thousand and the HALO over thirty thousand," he replied. "Shhhit," I thought to myself. Then I smiled and made a flippant remark, "I suppose there wouldn't be much left, if you screwed up on a HALO jump then??" He laughed and replied in the same vein, "You'd be past caring by then anyway."

Not long after, Red came up to us and asked, "Anyone up for a game of five hundred?" Pep declined, but I told him to count me in. He went to find other players, and he came back with two others, Stretch and Mo, and was carrying a box that we used as a table. Red sat opposite me, as my partner, Mo and Stretch sat on their packs in the walkway, and we got a game under way. It wasn't too long before I decided that Red was a crappy partner, as he would make some dumb calls. If we got stuck on one of those calls, it was virtually up to me to try and salvage the hand, but it was amusing and helped pass the time. So what the hell, we weren't playing for cattle stations.

The game broke up, and we had lunch. At least with the RAAF doing the catering, the sandwiches were an assortment, not just ham, cheese and tomato, and I washed these down with a mug of coffee. The five hundred game didn't resume, but Pep pulled out a magnetic chess set, so we settled down to a couple of games. As we were about to set up for the third game, Pep said "Don't bother setting up. We're starting to lose altitude, so we'll be landing soon." Half an hour later we were on the ground, and disembarking the plane at Richmond. RAAF trucks were pulled up at the rear of the plane while ground crew were putting wheel chocks into place, and one by one the engines were shutting down. We placed our gear in one truck, and climbed aboard the other. As we were pulling away from the plane, I noticed a fuel truck parked beneath the portside wing of the Herc, with a hose being handed to staff on the wing. As we drove through the base, I took note of the signage, and we pulled up at a building designated Parachute Barracks. The Officers and men from one squadron were being quartered on the ground level.

However, Pep and I were assigned rooms on the floor above. The rooms were quite large, and there was even a desk with two chairs in the room. There was also a jug and coffee bottle, tea and sugar, and a small fridge containing a bottle of milk. As I was sorting my gear into the wardrobe and rifle in the rack provided, I put my side arms into the set of drawers beside the bed. My ammo was in the pouches of my field belt, so I put this on the bottom shelf of the wardrobe. Pep came in and said "I know my way around this place, so when you're ready we'll go for a walk and I'll show you around." I answered "Ready to go," and after locking my door, we went for the ten cent tour.

We walked past the combined mess and canteen, which was for all ranks attending parachute training, and made our way past a couple of buildings. We came out onto another runway that had an old DC3 sitting on the tarmac outside of a couple of hangars. Pep told me the functions of each of the hangars, and then we moved along the road to where there were a couple, of purpose built open towers, with a lot of ropes strung between and down to the ground. The ground in the whole area was sand, and I was told that this is where I'd start my training and learning how to land, hang, and all the ground side of the course. We moved back towards the main course building complex, and went into the mess. Over a couple of drinks, Pep told me more of what to expect, and as he did, I realised that I was really starting to like him. He was a couple inches taller than me with darkish hair, and an angular sort of face with brown eyes. I'd say that we'd have both been close in the body shape department, and he had that weird dry Scottish sense of humour that was very much like my own. Also like me, if nothing needed to be said, he'd remain silent.

After our drinks, we moved into the canteen area for dinner. While we were eating, he said "We probably won't see any of our guys in here for at least a couple of days, as most of them would have left on leave by now. We may as well enjoy the peace while we can. Christ, this roast is good."

The following day was full on, and by the end of the day I had completed two of the three static jumps, with the third scheduled for that night. It seemed that I was no sooner on the ground, than I was climbing back into the rattling DC3 again. Pep had to wake me for dinner otherwise I'd have gone hungry, and after dinner I had to force myself to keep going. The jump had been slotted for take-off at twenty thirty.

The cool wind blowing in my face, while I stood in the doorway of the plane that night, woke me up a bit, and I waited for the tap on the shoulder which would green light the jump. The jumps during the day had gone perfectly, and I had landed smoothly in the middle of the x target spot both times. I was mentally reviewing what I needed to know, the altimeter on my wrist was showing a height of eleven thousand, and I knew that when I got within ten feet of the ground I had to pull down hard on the braking rope. If I didn't, I'd likely over shoot, and I didn't want that to happen. I wouldn't be satisfied now unless I had gained three prefect landing scores.

The tap on my shoulder came, and I pushed myself out the door. As I waited for the upward jerk of the chute opening, I replayed everything Pep had advised me about the night jump. Wait for the jerk; check. Grab the control lines; check. Look around below for the four red marker lights and the centre white strobe light; yeah, got them. Swing your approach, so you come into the wind; check. Use the strobe as your target and correct the approach if you need to; check. Keep an eye on your altimeter; check. Ten feet brake! Done! My landing was spot on over the strobe, and on my feet, yeah! As I started hauling in the parachute lines, one of the ground crew helped me out of the harness, and I unslung my rifle from my body and slung it on my shoulder. The Jump Master came walking across with Pep, who was smiling, and the Jump Master said "Well done Corporal, another perfect landing. I couldn't have done better myself. Now go and get some rest, you've had a very big day. First jump tomorrow is wheels up at zero ten thirty. Goodnight; I'll see you two in the morning."

I think that I was asleep before my head hit the pillow that night. When I woke at six, I saw my clothes were in a heap on the floor with my gun belts. My boots were in front of the chair lying on their side, and my rifle was still propped against the wall. So I got up and headed to the showers. After that, I was feeling refreshed. I got dressed in the same gear, made a cuppa as I made the bed, then had a smoke with my coffee. I had left the door open, and Pep strolled in. After looking at me said "I'm about ready for breakfast. Don't forget you won't need battle gear for the first jump." Smiling, I answered "Yeah, well, it's becoming second nature," as I started taking off and putting away my field gear and guns. "Ok I'm ready let's go," and we headed out to the canteen for what was a fabulous breakfast.

When we made our way to the tarmac, there was a Caribou sitting in the place of the DC3. The Jump Master came out of it, and said "This one's much better suited to free line jumps. Now, if you'll go get your chutes, we'll get ready, and have the briefing when you get back." As we headed to the chute hangar, I asked Pep "Are you jumping as well?" He answered "Too bloody right, I love free fall jumps. The only thing better is the HALO jumps," and we both laughed as we walked. At the hangar, we grabbed chutes and altimeters. After checking the servicing tags of the altimeters, stepped into the chute harnesses, strapped them into place, and then headed back for the briefing prior to take off.

While the Jump Master was giving the briefing, the air crew were checking our chutes and harnesses. They checked that nothing would snag the primary and reserve ripcords, and our knives were free of obstruction, and our altimeters were tightened on our wrists. That adrenalin charged excitement was gripping us both as we listened to the rest of the briefing. We were moving, shuffling our feet, springing on our toes, and rocking on our heels. With the briefing over, we started to move into the plane, and before long were airborne. Once leaving the ground, the plane banked to the left and lifted nose upward as it climbed for height.

After a while it levelled out. Five minutes later one of the air crew came to the back, indicated we put on our eye protectors, and pushed a button that lowered the loading ramp. We stood up, gave each other a quick check over, and then a thumbs up, and shuffled to the ramp watching for the green jump light. After a minute it came. I ran, launched myself out, and it felt great! As I flew I was able to turn myself and do a couple of rolls. Then I flipped over and spread myself out, with my arms and legs wide. Oh, this was fun! Keeping an eye on my altimeter, I saw Pep out beside me. I banked myself over his way; he grabbed my hand, and swung so we were face on to each over. We both had wide grins on our faces, gave each other another thumbs up with our right hands, and let go. It was close to pull time. All too soon it was over! I pulled the ripcord at eight thousand, as I'd been instructed, and after the upward jerk of the chute opening, started to look for the drop zone marker I spotted it, and the control lines to change direction, and came in against the wind for another perfect landing. I then grabbed the chute lines and moved out of the way for Pep's landing, which was on target, and perfect.

The Jump Master came over from beside the vehicles after Pep landed, and said "Well, you two looked like you were enjoying yourselves up there. Another perfect landing, Corporal, and Sgt I wouldn't have expected any less from you." I asked enthusiastically "When do we go again, Sergeant Major?" He laughed and said to Pep and I, "Looks like I've got another convert. Umm let's see, I could probably do your night jump at twenty one hundred tonight, and your last at eleven hundred tomorrow. Do I put you down for tonight?" "Yes, please Sarg Major", I replied.

As we helped gather up our chutes, we moved toward the vehicles for the ride back to the field. When we got there, the Jump Master said "Briefing at twenty thirty, see you then," and we marched off towards our quarters. As we went, I kept talking and talking to Pep about the jump, laughing all the while He asked "Didn't I tell you, that you'd love it?" I replied "Yep and you were right! What a buzz"…... and continued on again about another part of the jump! Christ, I was stoked. I couldn't wait for the night to arrive.

Late in the afternoon, Pep came in, and with a quick glance around, said "ok, you'd better come with me." I noted everything was ready, so closed the door, and went with Pep to the mess. Inside he said "Take a pew; I'll be back in a sec." As he came and sat, he was carrying two tumblers, both half full, and with a piece of ice in each. He placed them on the table, one in front of each of us, and said "Strictly speaking we shouldn't be having these. I'm doing this because you're wired tighter than a cable drum. Nothing to worry about, it's just nervous tension, you'll get used to it. The main thing to do is relax, so sit back with the malt, sip it slowly, and let the tension release." We both sat back, and savoured our drinks; he was right! After a couple sips of the single malt whiskey, I could feel the tenseness starting to dissipate, and was able to relax. I hadn't been aware of how tense I had been until I felt my body relaxing.

Half way through my drink, Pep asked "Feel a bit less wired up now?" "Yeah, thanks. I hadn't noticed how wound up I was," I replied. He smiled and said "Like I said you'll get used to it. Tomorrow I'll show you some ways to counteract the tension build up. It gets easier as you go along, but for now just relax in the moment." I asked "So how did you know?" He laughed and replied "Well, apart from myself, I've seen nervous tension, in a few guys." He paused to take a sip of the scotch, before continuing.

You had all your gear laid out, ready to put on and go. That's not a bad thing, but four or five hours before time, that's a sure sign of nervous tension. You couldn't keep still. You were sitting down, yes, but your legs were going ten to the dozen. I'll bet that you felt as if you were in a cage, and you didn't know what to do next to be ready." "Well, he certainly knows how it felt, so he's probably right," I thought. I said with a laugh "Spot on, so you'd better teach me those tricks, it wouldn't do to get a skinful every time it happened, would it?" He laughed and replied "no it wouldn't."

We had a late dinner that night, then went back to our quarters, put on our battle gear, then made our way to the tarmac. After collecting our chutes, we headed for the loading ramp of the Caribou that was warming up. The Jump Master gave us the briefing, which was pretty direct. "You both know what to do, so go do it, and I'll see you at the DZ (drop zone). Away you go." As the plane took off, I started to feel the nervous tension starting to rise again, and mentioned it to Pep. He said "it's ok to have it now, it'll go soon. Now, remember this is no different than jumping during the day you've done it all before. Ready?" I nodded, and just then the crewmen came by. As we put our face protectors in place, as ramp was lowered, and with the green light, I ran and jumped out yelling "Yeehaa!" Oh, the freefall was brilliant, and I really had fun. With the chute opening jerk, I got down to business. My feet were over the top of the white strobe as I landed perfectly again, then got out of the way for Pep.

After Pep landed, the Jump Master came over and said

"Corporal, another perfect score. You're becoming my best trainee, well done." I asked "Sarge Major is it this good all the time?" He laughed and replied "Every jump, son, every jump." On the way back, he informed us that we'd be doing the final jump at thirteen hundred, instead of eleven, so the briefing was at twelve thirty.

The next morning Pep and I went to the gym, and Pep stated "You've had martial arts training, so you would have been taught meditation. I'm going to teach you another form of that meditation." Wondering how he knew, I asked "How'd you know that?" He replied "I've watched the way you move, your quick reactions, your speed, even how you move when you shoot, and the way you took down your instructor. All of that is learned, and you're probably unaware of the way you move, and act. To you, its second nature, part of you, always there."

Well, I'll be buggered, I'd never even thought about it. I guessed he was right, I wasn't, or hadn't been, aware of it until now. Pep continued "Now using that same meditation, or mind focusing, we're going to sit. I want you to focus on using your mind to blot out everything else, and concentrate on my voice only." He had me open my eyes and watch my legs and feet, as he described the lead up, putting on a chute, the briefing, the lowering of the ramp, and the jump itself. Then he said "Now look at yourself, how do you feel?" I looked at my legs and feet, they weren't moving, and I felt calm. I told him so, and he said "There you go. That's all there is to it, now hop up." Damned if he wasn't right; no tension, just calmness, and ready for the job, and it's worked ever since!

I really let myself go, and experimented with different ways of changing direction, speeding up and slowing down during my last jump that afternoon. I even went below the eight thousand mark, by three hundred feet, before pulling the ripcord. This time I waited for Pep to land first, before I swooped in for another perfect landing. While getting out of our gear, the Jump Master approached us, and said "This is getting boring, but well done, another perfect jump, and landing. See me in the office when we get back."

Back at the field, we returned our chutes, and went to the Sergeant Major's office. When he called us in, he put his signature to some paperwork, stood up, came around to the front of his desk, leaned against it facing us, and said "Corporal Davis." I came to attention, and he waved his arm toward the desk, saying "That was your paperwork that I just signed, passing you with high honours on the course. Congratulations." He then held out his hand which I shook, and gave me a flip up jewellery box. There were also quite a few cloth badges to be sewn onto my uniforms. He said "These are your wings. Welcome to the paratroopers. As a top student, you get this also." It was a brand new altimeter in a gift box! I thanked him, and after I did, he said "I understand you'll be staying for the HALO course, so I'll see you at zero eight hundred tomorrow. Once again, Congratulations and well done. That's all, gentlemen."

CHAPTER 27

After leaving the field, we walked, and I looked at the cloth badges. Pep said "Top of left sleeve on all uniforms, even your dress ones. Your wing bar, above the left pocket above your medal and service ribbons." The timbre of hardness in his voice was enough to warn me, so I asked "Have I done something wrong?" "Yes, and if I'd have said anything, you'd have got a right bollicking, and maybe you'd have failed the course," he replied. Surprised, I asked "What?" He stopped walking, and said "You didn't pull at the designated red line. Luckily it was set at well above the minimum height." I was a bit confused, and asked "How did you know I was below eight thousand? Why was it set higher, as you say, than minimum?"

He said that he would answer once we were back in our quarters, and so we continued walking, a little faster now, towards the barracks. Once there, we went into my room, and we both got out of our field gear and put our rifles on the bed. Then I made us coffees and as I placed them on the table, I said "Right. Let's have it!" He replied harshly "I pulled spot on eight, and you went past me before you pulled, a fair bit past me, so that's how I know. If he'd seen that you'd have failed! The minimum height set for these chutes is six and a half thousand, after that you don't have any time to correct chute problems, or deploy the reserve if the main doesn't open, and YOU DIE! Here the red line is set well above minimum for safety. These canopy chutes take a while to open. Things may change in the future, with the new wing cell chutes that are being experimented with, but for the time being, this is all we've got, so don't get cocky, stick to the rules, understand?"

Feeling thoroughly and rightfully chastised, I replied quietly, "Yeah, sure Pep. Sorry." After that, he lightened up and said laughing "Well, consider yourself told. Now tell me, did you have fun on the jump, and why did you go below the red line?" And so we ended up talking about the jump, and what I'd experimented with. Then I said "As to the pull after red line, I guess I was being cocky, wanting to see if I'd get away with it. Sorry. It won't happen again." Then he said "Good, but don't sweat it, we've all done it. Now, we've got nothing on til the morning. Is there anything you'd like to do before dinner?" I replied "Yeah, I wouldn't mind getting some exercise. How about we go over to the gym and do some fight training and some sparring?" He thought about it for a minute, and said "Ok, I'll teach you some stick fighting. Let's get changed and head over."

That night at dinner, most of our guys were back from leave, so the talking volume was louder than the last few days. Pep joined the rest of the Officers and Sergeants, and I sat with the other NCOs, so it ended up being a rowdy night in the mess. The following morning after breakfast we all trooped into the lecture room for the start of the HALO course. Those that had already done the course stayed toward the back, except for being called on for help during the course. Pep was amongst those five. The course was going to take ten days, and we did the first jump on the fourth day. I had a laugh every now and again to myself, thinking how relaxed this course was compared to my hectic first one.

That first HALO was stupendous and exciting! We jumped from thirty two thousand feet, and the freefall was incredible! I was in seventh heaven the rest of the day! Talk about an adrenaline rush! The worst part was that I had to wait for another couple of days before the next jump. The reason for the wait was that they were going to be done as tactical exercises, and our "enemy" and terrain had to be organised. The next day's jump was to take, establish, and hold an area capable of landing airborne troops. The "enemy" was to be two commando companies in both exercises, so they were Special Forces trained. The day jump was held over the Holsworthy training area, and everything went well and according to plan. The troop had been split into five patrols; the fifth patrol only had three men, so Pep and I were to make up the numbers.

How cool was that! Only a trainee, and taking an active part in a full on exercise as a fully-fledged combat ready team member. I do think however, Pep had a bit to do with that. He'd had some words with Trader, who was the troop leader of the course.

Our last qualifying jump was to be the night jump. It would take place in a couple of nights, but we started the planning in the lecture room the next day. It was at this time that we were all told what the surprise was going to be. Not only was the jump to be at night, but we were going to be jumping into water! Not only just water, but into the ocean!

So we then had lectures for the rest of the day, concerning techniques and safety measures for this type of jump from the Jump Master, and his staff. Then that night after dinner, the patrols exercised at night in different areas of the base. Pep was the patrol leader for our group, we were Five Patrol. We practised different scenarios all night and only went to bed for much needed sleep after breakfast.

At sixteen hundred, we all gathered in the common room downstairs from Pep's and my quarters, and then we were briefed on the following night's weapons. There was going to be a type of paint gun that was a cross between our machine pistols and our rifles in length. They could be strapped to our thighs, but they only had a range of fifty yards. After being shown how they operated, we were issued one each, and fifty paint bullets to practise with that night. After that, we all went across to have dinner, and then grouped up into our patrols for the night's exercises and practise.

In the morning at breakfast, I gathered that I wasn't the only one who used quite a few trees for target practise during the night. The operational briefing was scheduled for seventeen hundred. After that, we'd have dinner before being taken to the main runway for wheels up at twenty hundred, so we all went off to bed for some sleep. I woke and had a shower at fifteen hundred, and then started getting ready. As I was putting my boots on, Pep strolled in and sat, saying "Tonight you're really going to have to focus. Try to stay in a calm state, we've practised it all, so you know what we'll be doing. Keep the tension buried and use it when it's needed. Let's go get the job done."

The briefing was in the main lecture room, and started with the Jump Master saying "My staff and I will be observing the jump from the ground. Remember to release your harness at ten feet and drop out of it into the water. Otherwise you'll get tangled in the lines, and that won't do you any good. Remember ten feet. This is very dangerous, and you don't want to drown. None of the parachutes will be picked up until the morning. We'll have boats to retrieve them, so don't be surprised to see them. Good luck." Trader then gave the full operational briefing suppling the target's coordinates and bearings to each patrol. Only when a patrol's target had been taken out would radio silence be broken. This would be done by pressing the transmit button the number of times for the patrol. The radios would be monitored by each patrol and Operations. We were to stay in place with the "dead" and "prisoners" until operational staff relieved each patrol. After being debriefed, we'd be transported back to base, have lunch, then reconvene at fourteen hundred.

In the mess while having dinner, there was enough tension in the air that you could cut it with a knife. I thought to myself that if not for Pep showing me the way to focus the tension deep, and remain calm, I would be like some of the others; jittery, and unable to keep still. I was able to remain calm by playing it all over in my mind; move and countermove, check for variables and counter them. While doing this in one mental compartment, I still had the full function of the rest of my mind and body, and was quite cheerful.

The Herc was warming up as we trooped up the cargo ramp. We were each carrying a mask and set of fins, and dressed in black overall rubber suits with our chutes harnessed on the outside. Inside the waterproof suits we were wearing our uniforms, boots, and our paint guns strapped to our legs. As I sat down, I started to tape the fins to my lower right leg, as the others were doing. I strapped my waterproof compass, already set on our bearing, on my right wrist, and the altimeter on my left. I was passed a half-used tube of black camouflage paint. I squeezed some out and passed it on, then applied the cream to my face and neck. The aircrew lifted the cargo ramp and we were in the air five minutes later.

Fifteen minutes later, the aircrew gave us the signals for us to go on oxygen. We put our masks on as the chief crew member spoke into the intercom. He then put on an oxygen mask, and the body of the plane depressurized. The ramp was then lowered. Patrol Five was to be the first out, so we were all standing, waiting for the green. As it came, we ran and launched off the ramp. The freefall was, as usual, marvellous, and as I focused on the job, I had time to admire the view below. Even in the night, I could see where each patrol member was in relation to me. We were all in line, and about one hundred feet from each other. "Good" I thought, plenty of room for the chutes to open. I pulled at eight thousand, and then because we had no marker, I made sure I was close to the others. I started watching the altimeter, and as soon as it hit ten, I hit the quick release buckle of the harness. I held my fins in place with one hand, my mask in place with the other, and had my knees bent. Even with the suspension of bent knees, the ocean was still hard as I hit and entered the water. Quickly ripping the tape on my fins off, I strapped them to my feet. As I was about to swim off on the bearing, I was joined by two others, and as we swam we came upon the other two, Pep being one of them. He halted us, and as we tread water, said "Ok, we're two hundred from shore; we'll glide in slowly, and crawl to the dunes."

The sea was cooperating that night, and there wasn't much swell, so we made it to the beach easily. Removing our fins, we started the crawl up the beach towards the dunes. Moving slowly, I was about to move again, when I froze. A figure appeared on the skyline, and another, about a hundred yards further to the right. As I watched both figures, I noticed a quick flash of light in between them, and they both moved toward it at a stroll. When they were gone I moved to join the others by the dunes. They were getting out of the rubber suits, and loosening the guns. Pep looked at me and I signed what I had seen, and as I got ready, we had a signing conference. Pep asked "How many I'd seen?", and I told him two, and where.

Pep made the quick decision, and signed "Tiger, you take out the sentry this side; Slick, you the other. Harry, you go with him. Sparks and I will trail Tiger, and then we move to the dugout. Right, go?" I moved slowly up towards my target, with Pep. Sparks was below me, as I inched forward. Bugger me if the sentry didn't nearly step on me! I swept my arm around and knocked him off his feet, and then smacked him in the side of the head with my elbow. I quickly secured some left over tape across his mouth, and with the paint gun barrel across his throat whispered "How many in the trench?" He held up two fingers. I put a zip tie around his wrists, took a black marker from his pocket and wrote on his arms "throat cut," and told him to stay there until I came back. As I was about to move I heard a twig snap, and whirled with the gun ready to fire. I saw a person standing with a reflective vest and his arms up. The vest had "observer" on it, so I put my finger to my lips to gesture silence, and he nodded.

Moving, I signalled Pep to join me, and when he and Sparks came over, filled them in. Pep nodded and was about to move off. I held him back, signed an idea I had, and he agreed. We moved to my "dead man." I took his hat and, with the observer following me, strolled slowly toward the dugout. Pep and Sparks were on the ground beside me as we reached it. Pep got up, and we went in and shot both of the soldiers inside. Soon, Slick and Harry joined us, and as we all stood outside with the observer. Slick said he had a prisoner; Pep turned to the observer, and said "Do you think we've taken this position?" He answered "Yes, and very efficiently. Well done." Pep then turned to Sparks and nodded. Sparks sent the signal, saying "We're number two, Sarge," Pep said with a smile "Well, let's get our dead and prisoners together, and they can brew up for us." Well done, Tiger, and now you have your first kill." We all laughed.

An hour after hitting the water, we were having coffee, with our "dead and prisoners", and the observer. All were laughing and joking, with no hard feelings. When it started getting light, I had Pep's map out, and was quietly sitting above the dugout having a smoke, while the rest were either sleeping or lazing around. Pep came and sat beside me and asked "Still keyed up?" After thinking for a moment, I replied "No, that subsided after we'd done the job. I was trying to figure out where we were, and guess what? A couple hundred years ago if we'd been here we'd have seen Captain Cook sail in, this is Botany Bay." He replied "Well, bugger me. Mind you if that were the case, we'd both be a bit long in the tooth by now," and we both laughed.

Around nine, two trucks and a rover arrived. The observer went to the rover, and talked to our operations people, one of them was Trader, of course. We were all outside the dugout milling around, and waiting for instructions, when Trader started walking away from the vehicles toward the beach. He called for Pep and I to join him. As we approached he turned and said "Well done Pep. Corporal Davis, to you also, well done. It seems that your observer thinks that you should have been in charge, and wondered why not. By the way, he's Captain Richards from intelligence at GCHQ here in Sydney. The poor bastard nearly had a heart attack when I told him of your status. It is going to change because of his report, and that of the Jump Master. From what I've observed personally, I'm going to be recommending that you be accepted into the regiment as soon as we return to base, even though you still have more training to undertake. Also, by the way, the Jump Master is going to be awarding you the "Best Student" award for this course. That's two, in two weeks, bloody good show, congratulations." He held his hand out, and I shook it blurting out a "Thank you, Sir" at the same time. After that, we boarded the trucks, and after shaking the hands of the commando company's men, headed back to Richmond for lunch and a rest before the debriefing.

Back at Richmond, we were deposited back at the parachute barracks. After getting rid of the battle gear, we went and had a shower before going to lunch. The general topic was the previous night's work, the jump, and some were plotting about how to

289

kidnap the RAAF cooks, so we could take them home with us. Prior to the debriefing, we all gathered up our paint guns and remaining rounds to hand back in. There was staff collecting them before the debriefing got under way.

The Jump Master called for order at fourteen hundred, on the dot, and the debriefing began with Major Teague (Trader) letting us know the result of the mission we took part in. Overall it had been a huge success because we had found ways to circumvent early detection, and establish a dummy beach head. It was now up to the planners to implement strategies to prevent what we had accomplished. All patrols had taken their respective targets within two hours of take-off. Trader said "I'm proud of you guys, and congratulations on a job very well done. You all deserve to applaud your own efforts, so go ahead and thank you."

After the applause died down, the Jump Master stepped up, saying "Well, I must say that this has been a very interesting course to run and organise, considering it turned into a tactical exercise as well. I'd like to thank my team for the help they gave beyond their normal duties. To all my staff: Thank you!" We all applauded again, and he continued. "To all of you that took part in this course, well done. You all passed, so as you are called, please step forward and receive your new wings." The first couple called out were sitting beside me, and showed me the difference in the wings. The canopy of the chute had a circled red H in the middle of it, and as a higher achievement, replaced the normal wings on uniforms. I received mine along with a heap more cloth patches, then when everybody had received their wings the Jump Master had more to say.

"On every course, there is always a standout student that receives the best student award, and this course is no different. This course's best student award goes to someone who came here with you. While you were off on leave, I had him working his ring off, so much so that he was the best student on that course too. That wasn't too hard considering he was the only student," he paused for the laughter and applause. "He came here as a new trainee vying for a place in your regiment, and from what I've been told," he looked around to Trader and got a nod of affirmation, "he will be going back with you as a new member of your regiment! Corporal Tiger Davis!" There was applause and back slaps as I made my way to the front, to receive what turned out to be a waterproof watch and altimeter combined in the one. After shaking hands with him, Trader and the other officers, and thanking them for their congratulations, I made my way back to my seat, just up from Pep, and signed to him "This is partly yours as well."

Trader came back to the front, and said as the noise died down, "Ok men, we leave after breakfast tomorrow to return to base. Wheels up at zero nine hundred, our transport will outside the barracks at zero eight thirty. Dismissed!"

Back in our rooms, I looked at the watch/altimeter box. It had a tin plate on the lid which read in three lines: "Best Student Award, Halo Course No 2 1970." I took it out of the box with the instruction book, read the book, then set the correct time. The watch dial was in twenty four hour format, and the altimeter was in digital format, and emitted an alarm at redline as well. Cool. I took off my army issue watch, and strapped it on. I wore that from then on, until it was broken years later. Then I started packing my gear, to save time in the morning. The old watch I put into the first "Best Student" presentation box, and switched the altimeter into the empty second one. They both went into my field pack, along with both sets of wings and the cloth badges. I left out a fresh set of greens for the trip home, and continued wearing the ones I had on. I'd pack them last thing in the morning. Pep popped his head in the door, and said I'm going for a drink then dinner. Want to join me?" "Let's go," I replied. Outside I was about to put my beret on, when Pep said as he fished in his shirt pocket "Stick this on your beret." It was the regimental insignia badge. As I looked at him, he said "Don't worry about replacing it, I've got heaps of them. Congrats," and we shook hands. With the insignia on my beret, I had an extra spring in my step, and smile on my face, as we made our way to the mess.

It was a little rowdy as we entered the mess, and this was only the beginning of the night. At the bar I ordered two double single malt whiskeys with a block of ice in each, and sat a table that Pep had grabbed. He stood as I handed him one. He looked at it with a smile, looked at me and we clinked tumblers. Both sat, nothing needed to be said, we both knew what the other was thinking. He knew I was thanking him, and I knew he thought I'd done well in his eyes. After a couple of sips, he leaned forward to have a look at the watch. He pursed his lips, nodded his head with upraised eyebrows, and raised his glass to me. I reciprocated, and we both took sips of our drinks at the same time. Once our drinks were done, we headed in to eat before the crowd hit. As we ate, I asked "So what's next on the agenda, when we get back?" "It'll either be radios and communication, swimming and scuba training, or explosives," he replied.

"I'll have to find out what's available, when we get back. One way or another you'll end up doing everything anyway. No shortcuts I'm afraid." I laughed and said "Oh, of course not!" That comment made him laugh. After dinner we went back into the mess, and naturally everyone was having a few drinks before dinner and letting off a little steam, now that the course was over. They were also celebrating their coming deployment, as One Squadron would be starting another tour in the next few weeks. As I was at the bar getting a round of drinks, my pager started beeping. As I reached for it, everyone near me fell silent and, watched me as I read the message. I put it back in my pocket, while looking around and shaking my head, to let everyone know it wasn't a recall. Grabbing the drinks, I took them back to the table, and then showed Pep my pager. As his started beeping, everyone close by fell silent again, and Pep called "Carry on." He showed me his message, which was the same as mine, "CO's office Mon nine am. Dress uniform."

As we sat down, he said "Don't even bother trying to think what it's about, we'll find out on Monday." He was right of course, so we continued to enjoy the end of course celebrations that night.

There were a lot of sore heads and groaning at breakfast the next morning. The trucks arrived to take us to the field on time, and we were all ready, dressed in battle gear. The routine was the same as we arrived, all the field packs in one truck and us in the next one, as we made our way to the plane. It was warming up, with propellers spinning. After sorting and collecting our gear, we each made our way onto the Herc via the loading ramp, while trays of food and drink were loaded into the galley area through the side door. Most of us slept on the trip back. We arrived at Pearce at nineteen thirty, and had dinner at the RAAF base before being transported home to Swanbourne. Once on base, Pep and I had a quick chat, and decided he'd meet me at the hut in the morning before we faced the CO. Then I went to my quarters to unpack and get some sleep. I'd worry about the morning in the morning.

CHAPTER 28

I was up early the next morning. I sorted out the washing, counted out how many of the parachute wing badges I had, and put the number I needed to go with the washing. Then I pulled out one of my dress uniforms, put the wings pin on the shirt, and left them hanging to change into later. I then put all the regiment insignias on all of my berets and slouch hat, and went to breakfast early so I could get up to the laundry just after seven when they opened.

The laundry chief had one of the girls; sew the wings patch onto both of my dress shirts while I was there. The rest would be put on my greens after they'd been cleaned. I told Mal, the Chief, that I had four more shirts that required the patches sewn on. He told me to bring them up and they'd be done while I waited, so I shot off to get them while the dress shirts were being done. I returned just as the last dress shirt was finished. Next, they did the shirt I was wearing, which I was putting back on five minutes later. After fifteen minutes all the sewing was done and my laundry would be ready that afternoon. Mal said to pay him for the lot later when I picked the others up.

Pep joined me at eight, and we both relaxed with a coffee and smokes. Pep said "After we see the boss, I'll be taking you down to the sigs squadron, for an orientation to the radios we use on operations. Do you know Morse code by any chance?" "Only a little," I replied. He said "That's ok; you're going to learn it anyway. We'll stay in dress until later. We might have time to change after lunch; we'll see how we go."

At ten to nine, Pep said "Well, we better get going," and we left the building as we were putting our berets on. We took our berets off as we entered the HQ offices, and Pep told the staff why we were there. We were marched into the Commanding Officer's office, and we both came to a halt in front of Lieutenant-Colonel

Larry Clarke. Pep said "Sergeant Salter and Corporal Davis reporting as ordered, Sir." The Colonel looked up from what he had been reading and said "Ah yes, Corporal Davis, you've been making a bit of a name for yourself. I've just been reading a letter from a Captain Richards at GCHQ, about you and Salter's tactical op during your night jump. Damn fine job, both of you." We both replied at the same time with "Sir!"

"Now, further to that, I've also been looking at the reports from your Jump Master at Richmond. He was surprised at the ease with which you handled your initial Parachute course. Then to take best student on both courses is absolutely outstanding. Now I can see why one of my sabre squadron commanders requested that you be accepted into this regiment. Even though you haven't completed selection or passed all the requirements, as you know, I did go along with his request. But what do I do with you now? I can't put you into a sabre squadron yet, as you still have to be trained. What I'm going to do is assign you into the HQ squadron, so you can finish your training with Sgt Salter here, and then I may have a job for both of you. By the way, there'll be a medic's course opening soon, are you interested?" "Yes, Sir," I replied.

"Good man. Now, the main reason you're both here. Oh, stand easy-both of you. You're making me nervous standing there rigidly at attention. The reason you're here... Excuse me for a moment." He got up and went to the door, and yelled "Captain Ryan!" Then he came back and sat at his desk. Mark Ryan came into the room, saying "Sir!" Clarke looked up and said, "Good, you're here. I've just told Davis that he's being assigned to HQ until his training is completed. You're his commanding officer, so fix it, will you?" Mark replied "Yes Sir," and Clarke continued. "Now, the reason you're all here. In your previous life, Davis, you did something that was witnessed by these two men. For your actions you were accorded a Commendation for Distinguished Service. It has arrived, and because you missed out on the proper ceremony that is usually accorded to receiving this medal, I thought that it was only fitting, that these two men be present to witness it being presented to you. So Salter, Davis, one step backward." Both Pep and I came to attention and stepped back. The Colonel came around his desk, stood in front of me, and read out the reasons I was being presented with the Commendation for Distinguished Service. He said "For those actions, it gives me great pleasure to present you with this Medal," and pinned it to my shirt. "Congratulations, well done," and he shook my hand, as did Mark and Pep. The Colonel gave me the written Commendation and the flat case that was the presentation box, which also had the miniature bar in it.

After that, the Colonel said, "Well gentlemen, thank you. I'm sure we've all got work to do. Dismissed." With that, we all said "Thank you, Sir," and walked out of his office. Once we got down the hallway, Mark said "I'll see if I can get you some quarters in the HQ squadron barracks. Until then just carry on as normal." "Sir," I replied.

As we left the building, Pep was smiling and said "We'll go down to the sigs company after we stop by your quarters, and you can put that stuff away," referring to the paperwork and presentation case I was carrying. When we got into my room, I put the paper scroll and medal into the case. I pulled out the miniature bar and pinned it to my shirt, then placed the case away in my desk drawer. Pep said "Of course, you know that the boss has done you, me, and Mark a favour by assigning you to HQ squadron."

"How so?" I asked. He answered, "Well first off, both Mark and I are assigned to HQ, and knowing Mark, he'll find you a room in HQ barracks pretty quickly. That means we'll both be in the same barracks, so it'll be quicker getting to you. That job the boss talked about? From what I can gather, it's something special, and Mark will be heading it. So guess who'll be picked? Now since you're assigned to a squadron, you're able to leave the base. If nothing's on, that should give you food for thought." What an understatement, as I was already thinking of things that I could do. Way to go, boss!

When we got to the sigs company, Pep told them we were expected. After a phone call was made, we were directed to another hut, where their lecture room was. Going inside, we were met by Sharon. Taking in our dress uniforms, she said "Looks like you two have been a bit busy. What would you like me to start with sergeant?" Pep replied "If we start with the radios, it'll go quicker. Tiger will have to learn Morse, but let's leave that to last, as he'll probably need a few days at it." Smiling, Sharon said "I've already got them in place in the lecture room, would you like to have a smoke before we start?" I said "That sounds like a good plan," so we all went outside and lit up. Being a gentleman, I lit Sharon's smoke for her. She said "Thank you, it seems you've been busy." She was looking at my shirt, which was now sporting the medal bar, my wings, and my beret sticking out of my trousers pocket with the regiment badge. I just laughed and replied, "Yeah, a little bit." She asked what the ribbon bar was, and I told her. Her eyebrows raised and she said "You'll have to tell me about it sometime soon."

After our smokes were finished, we moved back inside, and as we did Pep whispered in my ear "Focus," and I looked at him with a grin. In the lecture room was an array of radios, from small hand-held up to big desk sized units, and we started going through them one by one. Sharon told me the name of each one, and described their use and operating range, and good and bad features.

I was most interested in the ones used on patrol more than anything else; as these would probably be the ones I'd need to know about, and it helped to know what shortcomings to expect. Pep also contributed to the discussion, as a seasoned veteran of patrol work, and was able to supply Sharon with some input in that regard.

Then we started going through the use of code books, and how to send and receive a coded message. This led into Morse code and why we still used it. Each member was required to be proficient with its use. For testing purposes, I'd be required to send and receive ten coded words a minute. She gave me a book with the Morse alphabet, a code book, and then explained we'd first be learning Morse, and then using it in conjunction with the code books. She said "It's going to be long and is considered boring by your lot, and easier if you spend your time down here in our lecture room, because we'll have access to the devices used. This will take time, so don't expect to breeze through it."

Before we broke for lunch, she had me tapping out each letter to get used to it. After lunch, we were going to tackle full words, and possibly sentences, depending on my progress. Then Pep and I made our way back for lunch, as we walked he said "You make your own way back after lunch, I've got a few other things to do. You don't need a nurse maid, and you'll be at this at least until the end of the week. I don't need to be there, and if there's any change, I'll send you a message on your pager."

After I'd finished lunch, I headed to the laundry to see if Mal had my gear ready. It was, so I paid for the work and took my clean gear back to my quarters. After looking at the time, I decided I had enough time to get out of dress uniform and into a set of fatigues, and then headed back to the sigs lecture room. I was looking forward to some one-on-one time with Sharon, and now I had the opportunity.

During the afternoon, I was making up full words with Morse, and she asked me to try making up a full message. She would write out what I tapped, and would reply the same way. I thought of something, smiled and tapped out "I still think you're beautiful", and she replied "Thank you, and I like you, too." I looked over to her, and she was blushing. It seemed as if I was making headway with her, so I got daring, and decided to try and take it to another level.

Smiling as I went, I tapped out "Would you like to join me for a drink after work, so we can talk?" Her reply was, "I'd like that. Where will we go?" I tapped "How about the mess?" Her reply was tapped out really fast, and I was hard pressed concentrating and writing what she sent. Her reply was "Yes, ok, but it would have to be the mess here, because we're not allowed to be in your mess." I frowned as I read her reply, then smiled and replied "That's fine with me, but if you're not allowed in my mess, am I allowed in yours?" "Yes" she tapped back, "But I can only have a couple of drinks, because I have to drive home." Unconsciously I tapped the query "What?" Her answer came so fast and unexpectedly that I missed her first words, and asked her to repeat. "I live off base now because I found a nice flat down the road, and it looks out over the beach. It's much nicer than living in quarters."

Right, now I got really daring. I tapped "It also has a lot of advantages than being on base. It's a lot more private, if we decide that we don't want others watching us. For instance, if I decide I wanted to take you in my arms and kiss you, there would be no around to catch us." Her reply was quick "There isn't any one here anyway." I got up pulled her into my arms and kissed her passionately on the lips. She responded by melting against me, and our kiss became more passionate. After our kiss, I released her from my embrace, and she said "Umm, I could do with a lot more of that. I think we could go for that drink now, it's close to knock off anyway."

We walked over to the sigs mess, and as I removed my beret, I asked "What would you like to drink?" She replied "A glass of Chardonnay, thanks. I'll find us a quiet table." After I returned with the drinks, she said "Would you like to tell me your story, and I'll tell you mine?" I smiled and said "Oh, a bit like 'you show me yours, and I'll show you mine'?" "Well maybe at another time," she replied with a laugh. I replied "I'll hold you to that," and she replied "Promise?" "You bet!" I said smiling. I then told her about myself, and how I ended up here, but left out my age and how I got in.

Then it was her turn. She was from Brisbane, and had joined the Army last year when she turned eighteen, after doing grade twelve at high school. She had always wanted to join the Army, and after ending a romance with her boyfriend, decided that was the time. This was her first posting, and she was hoping Brisbane would be next. She'd find out after three years.

The time we spent together that afternoon went too quickly, and both of us didn't want it to end. In spite of the attraction we were starting to feel for each other, she had to go home. I made the tough choice and said "I would like to spend a lot more time with you, but we both have things to do. Let's get together out of hours soon. You never know- you may wish me to visit you on the weekend maybe? I'll leave that up to you, but we'll see each other tomorrow. It's time we made a move, even though I'd rather stay with you." As I held her car door open for her, I was sorely tempted to kiss her, but we might be seen and fraternisation was a no-go on base.

The next morning, after making sure no one was around and we couldn't be seen, I pulled her into my arms for a tight embrace and kiss. As I released her from my grip, I gave her hand a gentle squeeze said "I've been waiting to do that since yesterday afternoon." "Me too," she replied. Then I asked "So how do you think I'm going? Am I getting better?" "Yes, and today we'll concentrate on coded transmissions. The idea is to get as fast as you can, so messages are short and precise. We'll recap on yesterday, and then move on," she replied. By the end of the day, I was becoming very proficient. As we were putting the books away, she leaned against me. I was getting used to the way she would try to touch me at odd times through the day. It seemed that she wanted to hold or touch me whenever she could, as if she didn't want to let me go. She said "I think you might be ready to take your exam in another day or so. We might run through an exam scenario tomorrow, and see how you go. Right now it's my turn to buy you a drink." Giving her hand a squeeze, I said with a smile "I thought you'd never ask," and we made our way to the mess.

As we arrived at the mess, she went to get the drinks while I grabbed a table. She leaned over to put my drink down, and after a quick glance around I kissed her on the cheek. She sat down, blushing. She asked "So how did you become accepted into a squadron when you haven't finished your training? That usually doesn't happen." So I told her the factors that brought it about, and the advantage of being able to leave base when not on duty. I finished with saying, "Sometimes, I think that someone up there is looking after me. I know I'm good, but not to the extent of all the luck I've had so far. That or I'm better than I think. I've gained a good reputation somehow." She replied while laughing, "Don't forget your humble modesty, either." I laughed along with her, saying "Yeah, that too." Ever so casually our hands would touch.

After I had collected another round, she asked "So what do you do next?" I replied "Well, I'm not sure. I'm leaving that up to Pep. Even though things are done at a hectic pace, it's as though I could be doing a number of things. I do know that the boss has me slatted for the next medic course in Adelaide, but not when. Next, according to Pep, could be swimming and diving, working with explosives, or learning patrol techniques. I'd really like to spend more time with you." She replied "I'd like that too, if you're not doing anything on the weekend, how about I pick you up, and I'll cook you dinner?" I replied smiling "I'd like that, but it could become habit-forming," I warned. She smiled and said "Let me worry about that." Again, it was hard for us to part, but we both had a lot to do, and there was always tomorrow.

I made my way to sigs the following morning after breakfast, and as Sharon and I were alone, I scooped her into my arms for a morning embrace, before we got down to work. Still a little flustered, and blushing from the passion that we'd shown each other with our kiss, her hands were shaking as she gave me a sheet. It was an actual patrol report account of an incident to HQ Vietnam, sent during last year's tour by One Patrol from Two Squadron. On the table where I usually sat, she had set up an actual Morse key. She said "You have ten minutes to disseminate that report, and send what's required using Bravo code. Your time starts now!" I did what was required, and sent the twenty word message under one minute, awaited the reply, and acknowledged it. As she was telling me what had been wrong, and what had been right, Pep walked into the room. He said "I need to take Tiger for an hour or so. Can this be picked up after lunch?" "By all means Sgt I'm also recommending that he sits his exam tomorrow morning, if that's alright?" Pep said "As right as rain, lassie."

As we exited the building, Pep said "Take a minute to light up, and I'll let you know what's going on," so I lit a smoke, and he continued. "I told you Mark wouldn't take long to find you decent quarters, now we're going to move your stuff into your new quarters in the HQ accommodation block. Once you've moved, I'll fill you in on the rest of what's happening." As he had a rover, we took all of my gear to my new quarters, which were only two buildings over and across the road from the mess. I was on the second floor, and the room was great; it had a desk, bar fridge, kettle, toaster, gun rack and safe, plenty of room, and best of all, it had a walk in wardrobe, and its own toilet and shower.

As we brought my weapons and gear up to sort out, Pep said "The safe in this one is unlocked, and you can set your own combination, preferably to something you won't forget." After Pep showed me how it was done, I set the new combination, and then placed the spare magazines, ammo, and my pistols into it before locking it. I placed both rifles into the rack, and as I sorted out the rest of my stuff, Pep, sitting on one of the chairs near the desk, started to fill me in on the latest.

Once I was finished with the radios and Morse course, on Monday he would be taking me to the engineers. There, I would learn about explosives and bomb making in detail, and that would be a two week course. Following that, I'd be going to Adelaide with three others for the medic course which would take a month. Seeing I would be doing my Morse exam tomorrow, if I finished by lunch, I would have the rest of that day and the next to learn diving at the pool. That left me a free weekend, and I knew how I could spend it.

Pep explained what he would be doing while I was away on courses. He started by saying "I think Colonel Clarke has a fair bit of foresight, and is ahead of his time. He's given Mark the task of putting a team of people together that'll operate independently of a squadron. I've been given the job of putting that team of eight or ten together, and, yes, I've saved you a spot, if you measure up of course. That is if you want it?" I replied "You bet I'm in." Smiling at each other, he said "Good, all of this is on the QT. Nothing gets said to anyone, its top secret." I nodded that I understood. Pep continued "if you've any mates in One Squadron, you best say any goodbyes at lunch. They fly out tomorrow, and Three Squadron will be on leave after they fly in over the weekend. Hopefully, when you're back from Adelaide, I'll have the team picked, and we'll be able to commence patrol training." As he had been talking I'd sorted everything out and found homes for them. Some of my personal gear I left in my locked suitcase. Seeing I was finished, he said "Don't forget to put your name on the door. Come and find me at HQ when you're finished tomorrow. Now it's time for lunch."

That afternoon I was back in the lecture room with Sharon. After we had a very long kiss, and she still had her arms around my neck, I told her that I'd be free from Friday afternoon, til Monday morning. Monday was when I was due to start an explosives course with the engineers.

After deciding to make some plans for that afternoon in the mess, we got down to getting me ready for the exam the next morning; it was going to start at eight with Sgt Wilson being my examiner again. So, really getting into it, by the end of the day, I was quick and extremely proficient. I could send and receive up to forty words a minute.

In the mess at the end of the day, Sharon and I made plans for the weekend. When I finished on Friday, she'd wait for me at the mess, and then she'd take me home with her. We could spend the weekend with each other, and she said "If you're lucky, I might even cook you dinner." I replied laughing "If you're lucky, I might even eat it. What I'll do, honey, pack some clothes tonight, and give you my bag in the morning. That'll save some time on Friday afternoon, but I'm going to miss not having you within touching distance over the next day or so." She said "Me too, also not being able to kiss you each day."

Next morning, I gave her my bag while we were waiting for Sgt Wilson to arrive. She'd put it her car after the exam got underway. Sgt Wilson came in carrying some books and writing pads, and said "Well, Corporal, we meet again. Are you going to impress me the same way you did last time?" "I hope so, Sarge" I replied. Wilson looked at Sharon and said "I hope my best teacher has been looking after you." Both she and I smiled, and I replied "Sure has, Sarge." He continued "Good. That'll be all Sharon. Thank you." She left the room, glancing at me with a smile, as Wilson said "Right, let's get on with it."

I was finished the exam by eleven, and I had impressed Sgt Wilson again with perfect scoring. This brought to an end my sigs training. I left sigs and headed to HQ to find Pep. After letting him know I was finished, he went to make a call. He came back saying "Right, after lunch meet me at the pool, wear sports gear, and bring your swimmers."

CHAPTER 29

When I met Pep at the pool, I let him know that I'd made plans for the weekend, and would probably be off base from the following afternoon. He said "That's fine, be sure you have your pager with you." We were then joined by someone else, and Pep introduced us. "Tiger, this Sergeant Tindall, he's going to start your dive training. Hopefully, you'll get all your pool training done, and we'll leave the ocean dives until later. Ok, Pat, he's all yours."

Tindall said "Alright, Tiger go do some hard laps while I talk to Pep for a minute or two." I started to swim some laps; the water was cold to start with but I got used to it quickly as I swam the first lap. I started to pick up my speed, and by the time he halted me I'd swum thirty laps and was feeling good. He said "Pep told me you're fast, but I didn't expect that fast. Have you swum in competitions before?" I answered his question by saying "No, Sarge, only when I was in high school." He said "Humm, he also said you're quick at learning, so hop out and let's see." On the side of the pool was a couple of air tanks, and what I assumed to be some breathing hoses. He explained how everything operated, how they all went together, and then told me to put them together. I did, and after examining my handy work he said "Well done. Now turn the air on, and take a breath." Taking the breath, I thought that it wasn't oxygen, and said as much to Tindall. He explained that only normal compressed air was used for diving, not oxygen. Then I got into the pool with the gear on, and we went through a buoyancy exercise to determine the correct the number of weights on a belt that would allow me to sink with the scuba gear on.

After that, he let me swim around to get used to the gear. I noticed that even though the gear was heavy out of the water, it didn't seem to weigh as much, or be as bulky, in the water. Not having to surface for a breath was great. Soon he got into the water with the other set of gear, and indicated to me to come up to the shallow end and surface. Damn, I thought, just when I'm having fun, work has to get in the way. We went through some exercises, like how to clear water out of the mask, and how to don and doff the gear, all underwater. Near the end of the day, we both got ourselves and our gear out of the water, and he took me to a shed near the deep end of the pool. There, he showed me how the air compressor worked and how to fill the tanks. Once they were filled, he said "Pep was right, you're a natural."

The day finished with Tindall telling me that we'd meet in the lecture room at eight, and be at the pool by eleven. After a couple hours at the pool, I'd be finished the pool part of my diving course. Then I headed to my quarters pulled out my personal pager, and it seemed funny to be pulling this out again for use. I plugged in two new batteries, got into a set of greens, and headed to the sigs mess, hoping to catch Sharon. She must have seen me coming, because she had a drink waiting for me. I said "I didn't think I was that predictable," as I gave her a kiss on the cheek in front of everyone.

She was smiling with surprise and joy, and as I sat down said "You aren't, especially now. I was about to leave and I saw you coming this way, so I came in and got us drinks. Now word is going to get around about after that little display, not that I mind of course." "Good, at least your lot will know that you're my girl, and if mine find out, which they will eventually, so what!" I replied. She asked "Am I your girl?" I replied "You are if you want to be," and she replied "I'd like that, and I want to be, but we haven't even been out together yet!" "Well, that's going to change tomorrow, isn't it?" I replied. Her answer was "Oh yes, most definitely," then she took my hand in hers, and we continued holding hands. I gave her my personal pager number, which she wrote down. I told her, "I'm going to look like a right idiot carrying two pagers around, just as well they don't have the same sound," and she laughed. Then curiosity got the better of some of her female counterparts. A couple came over and one of them said "Sharon, aren't you going to introduce your boyfriend?" So she did, we each had another drink then we got up to leave. As she got into her car, she gave me a kiss while I held the door for her, and as she drove off, I headed to my room.

Later that night in the mess, I was doing my usual daily mental debrief, when my personal pager sounded. It was from a number I didn't know, and guessed that it was Sharon's, considering she was the only person I'd given the number to. I stored the number before reading the message, which was "Good night my love, tomorrow night you'll be sleeping with me." That put a smile on my dial, and soon after I went up to my room, had a shower, and went to bed.

Next morning, Sgt Tindall and I went through the theory and scientific facts regarding scuba diving. I did the theory exams, and then we headed to the pool for some more practical exercises we were done by thirteen hundred.

After being in the pool I was hungry, and went to the mess for a late lunch before they finished serving. After eating, I went to the phone found the number for the sigs company and dialled. When it was answered, I asked "Could I speak to Private Sharon Dawsett please?" Five minutes later, Sharon came on the line. I said "Hi honey, it's me. Just ringing to let you know I'm finished for the day, so if you want to go early, we can." She replied "That's great I've only got to do a couple more things. How about I pick you up in thirty minutes?" "Great. I'm in the HQ accommodation wing across from the mess, I'll be waiting for you outside," I replied.

Twenty minutes later I was downstairs having a smoke as I waited for Sharon. Pep came walking by, and said "In civvies, going off for the weekend huh. Got your pager?" I replied "Yeah Pep, I might not get back before Monday morning. I'll be here by eight at the latest, how about I meet you at the engineer's HQ? I can probably get dropped there if you like." "Yeah, that'll be ok, I'll see you then." Before he went upstairs to his quarters, I asked "Pep, do you want my personal pager number in case I'm needed?" "No, I'll get it at another time. Enjoy your time off, I take it you are going to be spending your time with that girl from sigs?"" he replied. The smile on my face was enough of an answer, so he continued "Ok fine, just be careful. I'll see on Monday," and went into the barracks building. As I watched his silhouette climb the stairs, Sharon's car drove up. I got in; we headed for the main gate, and left the base.

As Sharon drove to her place, she kept my hand tucked into her lap. While she drove, I was mentally taking in the way to her place. After about five minutes of driving, she turned into a driveway that led to four garages in front of a double story brick house. It had been divided into four flats, two upstairs, and two below. When we got and locked the car, she came and took my hand as she bouncingly led me up the stairs towards the top left hand flat. She unlocked the door, led me inside, and gave me the ten cent tour. There was a laundry near front the door on the left then a spare bedroom, then a toilet and bathroom side by side. The main bedroom had an ensuite that had a bath and shower combined, plus the toilet and the usual bench and sink with cupboards underneath. The bedroom had full glass doors that led to the outside balcony, and faced the ocean. The other side of the flat had a dining room at the front door end, then the kitchen, and then the lounge, with the same sort of glass doors as the bedroom that led to the same balcony.

Her flat was brilliant, roomy, and the ocean view was superb. No wonder she liked living here, instead of on base. She asked "What do you think?" "I think it's marvellous, just like the person that lives here," I replied. She started blushing, and still holding my hand she turned to me. I wrapped her into my arms and we had a very long passionate kiss. She was breathless after our kiss, as I said "Now there's something we can't do on base." Laughing and nodding her head in agreement, she asked if I'd like a drink, and I answered by saying "is the Pope a Catholic?" She laughed again and said "I got some scotch and some dry ginger yesterday, but you'll have to pour your measure." As she took a tumbler and wine glass from the cupboard, I poured a scotch while she poured herself a wine. She said "Ice is in the freezer. I would like you to treat this place like your own. Who knows? You may get used to it."

With drinks in hand, we went out on to the balcony, and as we stared at the view I lit a smoke for her, and then myself. She put an ashtray on the balcony rail top board, and then she placed her arm over my left shoulder. She gave me a kiss on the cheek, and then leaned her head on my right shoulder, as we stared at the view, sipping our drinks and smoking. She said "Umm, this is nice." I nodded with her comment in agreement. After we finished our drinks, we moved inside, and while I was pouring us another round, she said "I'm going to change out of this work uniform, into something more comfortable. Your bag's in the bedroom if you want to get changed. Would you like to bring the drinks in?"

She started to take her shirt off, as I sat on the bed. She was getting out of her skirt and as she straightened, I noticed her skin. She was tanned but not too much, and what I saw of her body I appreciated. While she was still in her bra and pants, she turned and came to stand in front of me as I passed her the glass of wine. I pulled her closer to me; she leant over and kissed me, and straightened again. My arms were still around her waist, so I pulled her closer and kissed her tummy lightly. She moaned with pleasure, and I pulled her down on top of me as I leaned backwards on the bed. I kissed her as she lay on top of me, at the same time I was stoking all of her back. She moaned and kissed me hard. Then I undid her bra, and lightly scratched her back and shoulders where her bra had been. She responded by grinding her lower body against mine as she became more excited. After recovering her breath she raised herself off me, and knelt over my by body. With a leg on each side of me, she started undoing my shirt buttons. As she rose, her bra fell away, and I saw her breasts for the first time.

They were perfectly rounded, and her nipples were swollen with desire. I pulled her down and took each nipple into my mouth and kissed each in turn. Then I pulled the back of her head down toward me so I could kiss her full on the lips again. As our lips met, I slipped my tongue into her mouth, and that drove her into a frenzy of sexual energy. Our lips were locked, and her hands were trying to undo my trousers. When her hands didn't cooperate, she moaned in frustration, and passion. I halted our kiss, rolled her off me, and got up. I urgently took the rest of my clothes off as she lay on her back and watched. Then I leant over and kissed her stomach again, and at the same time slipped my fingers into each side of her pants. I slid them down slowly, kissing her body and legs until they were off. She slid further back on the bed, and I joined her. As I did, she rolled over me, knelt above me, grabbed my swollen penis with her hand and guided it into her, and came down slowly. As I entered deep inside her vagina, when it was as far as it could go, she gave a convulsion and moan, as she had her first orgasm.

As it subsided, I began to move, and as I did she groaned with pleasure, and matched my movements. She convulsed with another orgasm. Moans of pleasure escaped her lips, and tears fell from her shut eyes. I brought her to another couple of orgasms, each more intense than the last. As she recovered from the last one I had brought her to, I rolled her over onto her back, and started moving in and out of her again. Very soon she was climaxing again and again. As she was in the middle of a climax, I came, and poured all of my seed into her. As I did, it evoked a scream of pleasure and ecstasy; tears were streaming from her eyes. I collapsed on top of her, and rolled so that she had her head on my shoulder. Our arms wrapped around each other tightly, and we fell asleep together in our embrace.

I awoke after about half an hour, gently extricated myself from her arms as she still dozed, and gently covered her with the sheets and blanket. Taking our drinks and my pants, I moved slowly out into the lounge. After putting the glasses down, I shrugged into my trousers, took my unfinished drink with me out onto the balcony, and lit a smoke. As I sipped my drink, I watched the sun low on the water. I thought to myself about how I felt toward Sharon. I hadn't made love to a woman like that in years, the last person to elicit responses from me like that was Jill. That seemed a long time ago now. Was I falling in love with Sharon, or was it just lust?

While I was making another drink inside, Sharon came out of the bedroom wrapped in a short dressing gown. She sleepily moved into my body with her head against my chest. As I folded my arms around her, she snuggled in as close as she could get, and murmured "Umm thank you. I feel like I've gone to heaven." She then pulled my head down to give me a kiss on the lips.

After we came out of our cuddle, she grabbed her wine, and said "Can we sit over on the lounge and talk for a while?" I replied "Sure, I'll just get the smokes and ashtray," I pulled one from the pack as I sat down, and offered her one. I lit it hers, then mine, and placed the ashtray on the arm of the lounge. As I sat back, she cuddled in against me, and we enjoyed the moment for a while. Then she stubbed out her smoke, and asked "Tom, where did you learn to make love like that?" I replied "From a very good teacher. Why?" She replied "Well, that's the first time I've ever come so much during sex. Once, maybe twice, but never that many times, and the intensity, Wow! I thought I was going to burst! It must be true." "What?" I asked. She replied "Well in the magazines, they say that having sex with someone you love makes it more intense and mind blowing and very special. Believe me, I feel really special and loved. I think I started falling in love with you the first time I saw you! Does that make sense to you?" I replied "yeah, I guess so, but how do you know it's not just lust?"

She thought for a while and then said, "No, it's not just lust, though I'll take as much of that as you give me, especially if the result is the same as it was a while ago. But I know how I feel about you, and the way you make me feel, when I'm with you. What about you??"

I lit a smoke while I thought for a little. I said "Well, I was trying to work that out when I got up. I haven't had sex like that in ages, and that was with the person who taught me how to make love. I think I was in love with her, because it was like I was gutted when she left, so that wasn't just lust either." Sharon said "She must have loved you a lot to teach you something that special.

311

I'm glad she did." Then I said "I do like you one hell of a lot, but I really don't know just yet if I'm in love with you. All I know is I enjoy being around you, and I miss you when you're not near me. We do make love together really well, and yes I do lust after you, so I guess that's a form of love. Is that enough for you at the moment?" "Yes it is," she replied.

After staying cuddled up like that together for a while, she got up and closed the curtains. I turned the light on, and she went into the bathroom in the bedroom. She came out after a couple of minutes, and came over to me. She held her hand out for mine, and gently pulled saying "Come with me, and we'll have a nice bath and soak together."

As we relaxed in the bath, she leaned back on me. As I lay against the back of the bath, we talked about what I had coming up, and what she did in the sigs company. She wasn't too happy with the fact that I'd be off to Adelaide for four weeks, and said "Well, I suppose I'd better get used to you being away at times. It comes with being married, or the girlfriend to, a SAS trooper I guess." I replied "Sure does. But are you going to be able to handle it?" She said "Of course I can, we're both in the system. I work with your regiment, so I know what I'm in for." She didn't realize that her answer would come back to haunt her one day and replied "Good, just as long as you do honey." Then we washed each other off, before getting out of the tub. She said "I'd better find us something for dinner. The way to win a man is through his stomach, or so I've heard." She said this laughing, and I carried the joke. I gave her a flick with my towel, and laughed while saying "Not the only way, as you've found out," and flicked her again. She ran out of the bathroom, giggling with laughter.

When I had dried off and put on a pair of shorts, I wrapped my arms around her back as she was standing in the kitchen thinking. I gave her a kiss on the back of the neck that made her shiver and gave her goose bumps. I dropped my arms, and started to make another drink, asking "Problem, Sweetie?" She replied, "I'm not sure what to cook." I said "Well, we can always go out to a restaurant if you like." She replied "No, I'd rather stay at home with you; I want you all to myself tonight." Note to the reader: In 1970, you have to remember that there was no such thing as dial in an order for delivery of pizza, or a meal.

I asked "Are you hungry?" She replied with laughter and a smile "For you yes. Food wise, not very. Why?" I replied, "Well if you keep me supplied with booze, and give me a hand, I'll cook us a light dinner. How's an omelette sound?" "Yummy, if I don't have to make it," she replied. I said "Ok, let's see what we've got. Eggs, milk, cheese, ham, do you have any cans of peas, onion, and where are your spices?" As I asked, she showed me the pantry and her spice rack. I said "You finely chop an onion, while I get the rest of this going."

And so we cooked our first meal together. She was amazed when I took the frypan with the omelette, and placed it into the griller. Even more so, when we finally sat down to eat at the table. She tasted my concoction, and smilingly said "Umm that's it. From now on you can do the cooking." "Oh, no not all the time. You were supposed to be cooking me dinner, if you remember," I replied with a smile. After we ate, and did the washing up together, we adjourned to the couch. After she put the radio on softly, she cuddled into me on the couch, and said "You never did tell me how you got your medal." I proceeded to tell her about the incident, and we just talked for an hour or so before making our way to the bedroom. Once in bed, we made love to each other again before drifting off to sleep in each other's arms.

In the morning we woke, made love again, and as we lay there in each other's arms, recovering from our exertions, decided what we would do for the rest of the day. Sharon hadn't been in Perth all that long, so as yet hadn't done any of the touristy things. After having a shower together, and making love in the shower, we got dressed into some smart casual clothes, and went off to do some sightseeing together. She asked "Do you want to drive?" Her car was a red Holden HT Monaro two door, with a six cylinder motor and a column shift two speed Power glide auto. With a smile I said "Pity it's not the V8, but yeah, if you don't mind," so she gave me the keys. I unlocked the driver's door she slid over so I could get in, and we drove into Perth with her sitting up against my side.

We went to have a look at Kings Park, and the lookout, then went down into the city and parked the car. We walked around the city buildings, down to the bell tower, and ferry terminal, went to the zoo, and came back to the city on a ferry. We picked up a brochure about Rottnest Island, and decided we'd go over one weekend. We went back to the car, and made our way down to Fremantle. After parking the car, we walked around the streets, had a look at the Naval Base, and around the port foreshore, and then went to one of the pubs for a drink. While we had a drink, we decided to visit one of the restaurants for dinner, considering that it was getting quite late in the evening. We had a lovely seafood dinner, before making the drive back to her place. Back home we curled up on the lounge and watched a movie on the television before going to bed. In bed, wrapped up in each other's arms we discussed what we thought of Perth, and some of the places we had gone during the day.

The following morning we didn't get out of bed until after eleven. This was due to some intense love making, and lazing about in each other's arms. We read the brochure on Rottnest Island, and planned to go there for a weekend together. We decided where to stay and what we'd do while we were there, after showering together. Over breakfast we decided that we could afford to have a lazy day together, after going down to the beach for a swim.

Over dinner that night we chatted about being back at work the next day, and got our uniforms out for the next morning. As we were doing this, I said "I may as well leave my other stuff here, because we'd be spending the next weekend together, and any other time I could." We also arranged to meet up each afternoon in her mess, after each day's work I was on the explosives course with the engineers.

After an early start the next morning, Sharon dropped me off at the Engineers Company HQ, She gave me a kiss saying "I'll see you later my darling," and headed up the road towards the Signals Company. As I watched her leave, Pep came into sight. Once he had joined me, we went into the HQ building.

CHAPTER 30

After asking for Sergeant Teasdale, Pep turned to me and said "Hope you had a good weekend, with young Sharon I take it?" I smiled and nodded, and he said "Good for you. I take it you'll be seeing more of her, which means you'll be spending a lot more time off base?" I replied "Well, I'll be seeing her as much as I can, but that's not going to interfere with my training. I'll still be focused on work when I'm here or elsewhere. The job comes first." He said "Glad to hear it and I hope it goes well for you. Now, you'll be spending the next two weeks with these guys, so learn all you can. They'll be sending their report about how you go, and it'll go to Mark, so you'll get a heads up if anything's not right. Once I leave you with them, I'll probably not see you until later next week, so take it easy, and remember to learn all you can."

I was introduced to Sgt Teasdale, and we went over to the lecture room, where I met the rest of his team, sapper's Jones, Lonigan, and Baird. Teasdale said "We've all worked on missions with your guys, so we have an idea of the things we can teach you. From what I'm told, you'll also need to know more than the usual stuff we teach, so you're in for a crash course of specialist demolition. We'll be working in here for theory work. Out in the field, you'll be handling live explosives, and learning what we know. We don't stand on ceremony here, I'm Te, Jonesy, Loni, and Box and you're Tiger, so any questions?" I replied "Yeah, just one. Te, when do we start?" He laughed, and said "Right now, boyo." All of that day was spent in lectures about the characteristics of chemical elements, what could be mixed with what to result in an explosion, and due to my knowledge of science, at times I was answering their questions, before they became questions. This surprised me as well as them, because I thought I'd only learnt the stuff I needed to know for exams, but obviously I'd learned a lot more. Thank God for Smithies science classes!

That afternoon I met Sharon, and after a drink together, we drove over to my quarters. I picked up some fatigues, and some more of my civvy gear, and we took them to her place, so I'd always have some at her place. She gave me a spare set of keys to the flat, in case we weren't there together. This started a discussion about me having to get my car across to W.A. sometime when I had a couple of weeks leave. Over dinner, we talked about our weekend at Rottnest, and I said "If you can, make a call and book a place, so we can go Saturday."

The next day was spent learning about the different types of fuses, and what would work with which explosive. In the field, I learned how to shape plastic explosive to produce different results; for instance how to shape it so the explosive charge could be shaped to blow downwards or sideways instead of upward. By the end of that first week, I became a very accomplished bomb maker, and good at demolition jobs, using all sorts of fuses, timers, and electrical detonators.

Sharon and I went home on Friday night. We cooked dinner, and after watching a bit of television, got our gear ready for our weekend that was booked at Rottnest Island Lodge. We decided to leave the car at home, and ring a cab in the morning to take us to the ferry terminal. We arrived at the island at around eleven, asked for some directions from one of the locals, and ten minutes later we were checking in at the lodge. Our room wasn't ready, but the staff offered to look after our luggage, and gave us an island map. While we went out to do some sightseeing, Sharon mentioned she could ride a bike. I was directed to a hire shop on the corner, and hired a couple of pushbikes for the weekend.

We headed towards what was called Oliver's Hill, and along the way came across quite a few of the island's animal population. They're called quokkas, something like a smaller version of a rock wallaby they only lived on this island. Not surprising really, it was a long swim to the mainland. They were really tame, and of course Sharon fell in love with them, and wanted me to take a picture

317

of them crowding around her as she patted and stroked them. Smilingly I did, and then opened the pack of biscuits that Sharon had brought along. They loved the peanut biscuits we fed them. After that pleasant little break to our ride we continued on our way. On the hill we explored the gun emplacements and tunnels that had been built during World War II for coastal defence. We joked about it being an interesting spot to make love, and we should come up here with a blanket next time.

We arrived back at the lodge at fourteen thirty, and after unpacking, changed into swimmers and rode down to the beach. We went swimming in the crystal clear water, and as we swam I thought this would be really cool if I had some of the regiment's dive gear with me. As it was, we were able to see turtles and rays gliding through the water, and heaps of different types of fish.

After our swim, we lay on our towels to let the sun dry us, while we held hands and chatted. Around sixteen hundred, all dried off, we rode back to the lodge for a shower, then made our way to the bar and restaurant. We ordered a couple of drinks, found a lounge chair to cuddle up in on the veranda as we had our drinks and a couple of smokes, after a few more drinks we looked at the menu. We decided what we'd have for dinner, and then had another smoke before moving into the restaurant, and taking a table that had a brilliant view of the street and boat lights around the bay.

To say we had an enjoyable weekend would be an understatement. We both decided to come back every now and again, because it was a quiet, laid back sort of place and not all that far from work. We arrived home about seventeen hundred, had dinner, and then watched a bit of television. We both got bored with what was on, and decided that going to bed was a better proposition.

I drove us to work the next morning, and then walked over to the engineer's lecture room. Te and his gang came in, Jonesy and Box, and they took some stuff out of a case that they carried and started putting the contents on the table. Te said "Today we'll work on improvisation. Tiger have a close look at this stuff on the table. Could you make a workable device with what you see?" On the table were two fifty calibre machine gun rounds, a block of C4 explosive, a piece of primer cord, bits of metal shrapnel, a tube of grease, some electrical tape, and a piece of pipe two inches long. I replied "Yes, an anti-armoured vehicle or personnel bomb. There's one thing missing, that's easily obtained." Te said "If you can make a bomb that can crack open an armoured vehicle with what's there, go ahead, even I can't do that. First, tell me what's easily obtained, and Jonesy will get it." I replied "An old sock," and they all laughed. Te said "A sock? Why, an old sock?" "Well, considering this is a demo only, I'm not going to use one of mine," I replied. Laughing Te said "Well, this I've got to see. Jonesy go get Tiger a sock. Ok Tiger, make a believer out of me."

First, I taped up one end of the pipe, placed the metal fragments into it, and taped up the other end. I moulded the C4 around the pipe, leaving enough excess to shape into a bowl shape, then prised the bullet out of the fifty calibre rounds. I poured the gunpowder into the little bowl in the C4, placed the primer cord into the gunpowder, and closed the C4 around it. By this time Jonesy had come back with an old sock, and some rag.

Before I placed the device into the sock, I passed it around for inspection. Te was the last to inspect it, and said "Ok, that primer fuse only burns for a minute, how are you going to attach it?" I replied "Well, that's what the sock is for.

I'll have to show you the rest near the target, so where are we going?" "Follow us" he replied, Carrying my bomb, I picked up the rag, sock, and tube of grease from the table as I passed it, and put them in my pocket. Box lit me a smoke when we were away from the buildings, and passed it to me, and then lit one for himself. We walked to an open area that had an old APC body sitting on the ground without wheels. We halted about one hundred yards away, and Te said "That armour is half an inch thick. The only thing that can crack it open is an RPG. If you can I'll kiss your feet, and call you 'God'." I nodded and said "Alright, can I run the ground first?" Te replied "Go ahead."

I asked Box to time me, and yell when a minute was up. Box

yelled "Go," and I ran toward the APC, skirted it and got back to them as Box said "Now." I nodded my thanks, and then started putting the bomb into the sock, making sure not to dislodge the primer cord as I closed the sock around it. Then I took out the tube of grease and poured it all over the sock, and then smeared the grease all over. I said with a smile "Anyone want to inspect it?" Knowing my offer would be declined, I continued "When this fuse is lit, I'm going to go at this in a combat scenario. Be prepared to hit the deck when I yell. So who's going to light the fuse?" Te said he would.

As I got ready, Te said "You're going to have to be quick." I smiled and nodded. As he lit the fuse, I took off running. I thought to myself "Tiger, you're being a smartarse again. You better hope the theory is right and this works, or you're going to look like a right idiot." I turned away from the APC twenty yards away, and hurled the bomb. With a quick glance, I saw that it had stuck to the side of the APC. When I was a few feet from the group, I yelled "Fire in the hole!" Then I launched into a dive and flipped and twisted my body one hundred and eighty degrees to land on my belly. I was facing the APC, and as I watched there was a flash of light milliseconds before the sound of the explosion. After a minute we got up to go and inspect the damage, if there was any. As I got closer, I saw that my bomb had blown a hole two feet in diameter in the side of the APC. As we circled it, we saw that the other side was bulging from the concussion force and the side door had been blown off. We then moved into a group near the front where we were able to see both sides of what was the vehicle.

After a couple of minutes of admiring my handiwork, Te said "I'm a man of my word." As he said this, he knelt down before me and kissed my boots. He said "Oh my God, everybody in there would have been killed. Well done, Tiger. You've taught me something." Then he got up, and shook my hand, saying "I wouldn't have believed it, if I hadn't seen it. How do you know about that sort of device, and what do you call it?"

I laughed as I cleaned my hands with the rag. I lit a smoke, and said "Well, the grease and the sock will make it stick. I could have used just the C4 and the gunpowder with the primer cord, but having the pipe and shrapnel gave it a bit of extra punch. It's called a 'Sticky Bomb'. The Yanks used to make them in World War II, as a way of stopping tanks." He said "Well, you've certainly earned not only my respect, but with that little demonstration, you've passed your course. We still have a few things to show you, and I want you to write down your Sticky Bomb recipe. Let's get back to the lecture room."

We walked back to the buildings and the lecture room. Te gave me the whiteboard marker, and said "We're the class, and we're all yours, so show us." I proceeded to tell them how to construct a Sticky Bomb. Jonesy asked "Why gunpowder?" So I replied "Well, as you know, C4 will not detonate without an electric charge, or a miniature explosion as a catalyst. I only used the gunpowder and primer cord, because there wasn't a pencil detonator here to use."

After I had finished, I gave the marker back to Te, who started talking about other improvisations that can be explosive, such as water and caustic soda, or ammonium nitrate and diesel. As he mentioned that combination, I raised my hand and asked "Which way of improvisation are you talking about? I knew two." He replied "What are the two you know? We only use one." I said "You're probably talking about where the combined mix is dried, but requires a detonator." He nodded, and asked "And the second?" I replied with a laugh "Well, if you really don't like someone, here's what you do. A guy I used to know did mixed a little together, and actually painted it onto the door handle of a house belonging to this person he didn't like."

"Once it dried, just the friction of putting his hand on the door handle and turning it set if off. It blew the guys hand off, and a hole in the door, and that was only a little." Te laughed with the others, and said "Well, yeah, that would work as well. Remind me not to get on your bad side." Then he continued the improvisation lecture. After lunch, we were outside making makeshift bombs, exploding them, and then analysing the results. Later in the day,

I met Sharon at her mess. After having a drink, we headed home.

The following day, we were going through how to disarm different explosive devices, and most timing mechanisms. We were covering a bit of revision work when Pep joined us. After talking to Te for a while, he came over to me, and said "Got a minute?" We moved away from the group, and Pep said "Teasdale rang Mark this morning, and said that you've learnt everything that they can teach you. Once again, you've passed another course with praise and full credit. Are you staying on base tonight?" I answered "I can, if you want." Pep said "That would be good it'd be easier if you can stay on base for the next two nights. What I want you to do is finish off the day with these guys. Tomorrow, we'll see about finishing your scuba diving course." After we re-joined the group, Pep and Teasdale spoke for a bit, and then Pep headed off towards our area. Te came over to us, and said "Well, boys, Tiger will be leaving us today. It's been fun with you here, and you've taught us a thing or two. Thanks for that. Now, let's spend the rest of the day sending Tiger off with a few bangs. Let's go blow something up."

At the end of the day, as usual, I met Sharon at the mess. She wasn't at all happy when I told her I'd have to stay on base that night and for the next couple after that. She said "I'll miss you, not having you near me, especially in bed. This is the direct line to my desk, and you know the home number. Will you keep in contact each night, Honey, just to let me know you're ok?" I said I would when I could. After we finished our drinks, we walked out to the car and I kissed her goodbye. I held her door open, as she drove off; I headed to my quarters, had a shower, and then went to the mess.

After dinner and a couple of drinks, I went back upstairs to my room. About twenty minutes later Pep popped his head in, so we had a cuppa and a smoke. He told me that Pat Tindall could finish my dive course, and that we'd be going down to the Fremantle Navy base, and using one of their boats.

Pat was going to meet us at HQ, and then Pep would drive down to Fremantle and come with us for the dives. We'd doing this for the next two days, so I needed to be at HQ both mornings at zero eight hundred. Then on Saturday, I was booked to go to Adelaide. We were flying commercial, not service, this time, and we'd be coming back the same way. I had to be at Perth airport at thirteen hundred, so I said to Pep "I could get Sharon to take me to the airport, after spending the night with her. Would that be ok?" He laughed and said "Yeah that should be ok, seeing you're going to be gone for a month; I won't deprive her of your company for that night. Pack civvy gear, and you fly in dress uniform. That's the only time you wear your uniform. They all know you're coming, and you'll be picked up at the airport."

I nodded, and said "No probs. Oh, what're we wearing tomorrow?" After being told the usual fatigues, I asked "While I've got you, where can I make a phone call without going over to the mess?" He looked around, and said "I'll get one organised while you're in Adelaide. In the meantime, there should be one near the common room." I said "Thanks, yeah, there's a phone jack. As you can see no handset. If you can get one, that'd be great. I've got to make a call soon, so I'll go down the hall in a while." After he left, I went down the hall, and thankfully there was a phone beside the common room. I called Sharon to let her know what was going on, and she was happy that we'd have the night together before I flew out. After we said goodnight to each other, I started organising some clothes to go with me to Adelaide, and put them in my kit bag, before turning in for the night.

It felt strange to be lying in a single bed again, and without having Sharon beside me. I thought how quickly one can get used to something, and take it for granted, until it's not there.

The next morning Pep, myself, and Sgt Tindall made our way to the naval base, and there was a sixteen foot tinnie with a centre control, that was set up for diving waiting for us. On the wharf were six air tanks, weight belts, harnesses, and regulator sets and three wetsuits. All three of us went to the ablution block across from the wharf, and changed into swimmers and the wetsuits. The wetsuits were one piece with a heavy duty plastic zip from crotch to neck.

After zipping them half way up, and leaving the rest dangle, we put on our green T shirts, made our way to the boat, and loaded the gear.

Sgt Tindall told us to wait for a bit, and he walked off. He came back fifteen minutes later carrying two thermoses and a container that was full with sandwiches. He passed them to us to stow in the boat, saying "Don't know about you but I'm always hungry after a dive. Let's crack one of those thermoses, and have a coffee before we go." After we all had finished our coffees, Pat fired up the boat, and we headed out of the harbour and towards Rottnest Island. Twenty minutes later, we were anchored towards the north end of the Island about two hundred yards from shore. After Pat told me to put on a weight belt, I was in the water, and checking my buoyancy. With that done, Pat put his gear on and rolled over the side into the water. He came up beside me and said "Now, Pep is going to put your gear into the water. Your job is to swim down and put it all on, while you're down on the bottom. I'll follow you down. We've done this in the pool, only here it's a little deeper, so when you're ready, let's go."

Pep had turned the air on, and passed the harness and the tank with the regulator attached into the water to me. As I put the regulator in my mouth I let myself sink down, until I was on the bottom. There, I put the tank into the harness and strapped it onto my back, and Pat signed for me to do a couple of exercises. Pep had joined us, and we went for a swim round, looking at the fish life and coral. After thirty minutes we surfaced, boarded the boat, got out of the gear, and let the sun dry us. After coffee, smokes, and a couple of sandwiches each, Pat told me that I was a natural. He said that he couldn't see me having any trouble in the water, and that we'd be doing another dive in half an hour, before heading back. Tomorrow, we'd be diving at a spot off the base area about a mile out from shore, and after I'd completed those dives, he'd certify me for diving.

That night I spent in camp, phoned Sharon after having dinner, and then had a few drinks in the mess. The next morning we went through the same ritual, and headed out to the dive site. When we anchored, Tindall said "The first dive is going to be deep. We'll be down at a hundred and twenty feet, so our bottom time will only be twenty minutes. We'll do a decompression stop on the way up, and while we're down there you'll be doing a math problem, much like this one. I'll time you while you're doing it. This is mainly to see how you react at depth." He passed me the problem and timed my solution, as this gave him an idea of how quick at solving problems I was. He then wrote another on his slate for later.

Once we were on the bottom, he passed me his slate. While watching me and his watch nodded his head. After I passed back his slate he wrote a time on it. We then had a quick swim around, and headed to the surface, stopping at the ten foot mark for ten minutes. As we hung off the anchor line, I watched the assorted fish life going by as I waited to continue to the surface. Back on the boat, Tindall debriefed me on the dive, and he remarked "Well, your problem solving was good, and only a little slower than up here on the surface, so I would say that you'd be spot on to work at depth, if required. After we've eaten, we'll move to another spot for your last dive."

During that last dive we played around with an inquisitive pair of dolphins that circled us in a playful manner, and then swam off. After surfacing, we got the boat ready to return. Before turning over the motor, Pat held his hand out and said "Congratulations, you're now dive rated." I shook his hand, he started the motor, and we got back to the Naval Base an hour later, and were at the barracks by sixteen hundred. Pep told me we both had to front Mark at nine the next morning, so I elected to stay on base that night. Pep and I headed to our quarters, but not before he followed me into mine. I noticed the new phone straight away, and turned to Pep. He said "I was able to get it installed earlier than I thought it would take. It's a direct line number, so now you don't have to worry with pay phones. I've already got the number; it's written on the dial, should you want to pass it on to anyone." He smiled, and I thanked him, then he headed upstairs to his quarters.

CHAPTER 31

Well, I just stared at the phone in wonder for a minute or two. I decided to have a shower, and get into clean clothes before giving Sharon a bell to tell her what had been going on. When she answered her phone, I said "Hi, Honey. Hope you're feeling ok. I thought I'd give you a call before going to the mess. If you've got a pen, I'll give you this number. It's to the new phone that's been installed in my quarters, courtesy of Pep, and the green machine." I gave her the number and brought her up to speed with what was going on. She told me she'd be knocking off early the next day, so I said "Well, if I'm finished with the squadron CO early, I'll give you a ring on your direct line. I'll just have to see how things go." She told me that she missed me, and I told her ditto, and I'd most likely ring after I'd had dinner.

Later that night I had a couple of drinks after dinner, and then rang Sharon. I talked with her, and gave her a detailed account of what I had skimmed over earlier. Then I went through my usual mental debrief, and went to sleep. The following morning, Pep knocked on the door as I was finishing a coffee, I said "You're lucky, I was just about to go have breakfast." He replied "Good. I'll walk down with you," As we went down the stairs, he said he'd meet me back at my room at eight, then we both headed to our respective messes for breakfast. At eight, we were both sitting at my desk with coffees and smokes, and he said "The meeting with Mark shouldn't be long, and you could take off after that. I'll see you at the airport at thirteen hundred tomorrow." I nodded, and he went on to tell me that the team numbers he was putting together had finally been agreed on. It would be a team of eight men, and he'd be choosing them from Three Squadron while they were on leave. He also said he'd leave a place for me on the team, due to my expertise with weapons and explosives. That really made my day, and then we got ready to head to HQ and see Mark.

At the HQ building, we went straight to Mark's office. Informal as usual, had us take seats in front of his desk. He handed me my plane tickets, for the trip to Adelaide, and the return flight. As he passed them across to me, he said "Pep will be taking all of you to the airport, but I'm afraid that we won't be able to have anyone pick you up when you return. You'll have to make your own arrangements, and as you can see you'll be coming in on a Saturday again, so you'll be free until zero eight hundred that following Monday."

He paused, and one of the staff knocked, came in, and put some papers into his in tray. He continued "As I was saying, you'll report back to me here that following Monday, because I'll have a few things to discuss with you." As Mark said this, he was looking at Pep, who gave him a nod. Mark went on saying "Now, you'll be going with three other members; Tag Wilson, Doc Martin, and Buzz Tyrell. They're privates, which means, you'll be the ranking member, and they'll be looking to you to lead. Now, apparently you'll all be billeted in the nurse's quarters. Please try to keep a lid on any hanky-panky, or at least be careful. Any questions?" I replied "No, Mark." He said "Good. Take care, and I'll see you when you return. Oh I almost forgot forget about standing orders for this one. No weapons go, just your pager." He stood up and shook my hand, and that ended my session with him.

Soon after leaving HQ I was in my quarters packing last minute items. I rang Sharon's direct line, and she must have been waiting for the call, because she picked up on the first ring. Without me speaking asked "Are you ready to go, Darling, because I've done my work for the day?" So I told her I was ready, and she said she'd pick me up in ten. Pep was coming up the stairs as I was going down, and said "Have fun, and be there at thirteen hundred, no later." I replied "Sure Pep, no probs, See ya."

At the airport the next day, Sharon was dressed in civvies and I dressed in full dress uniform. We were there before Pep arrived, and when the others got there, introductions were made. We stood around talking, Sharon with her arm around me, as they announced the flight boarding. With a handshake from Pep, and a kiss from Sharon, I made my way through the boarding gate. When all four of us crossed into the plane we were directed to the business class section-great! Way to go, green machine. That was a surprise for all of us, and I remarked "Now this is the way to travel, sure beats service air." We all laughed as we made our way to our seats; we were seated opposite two each side of the plane.

Once we were in the air, we were the only passengers in business class. This was handy, because I was able to move around. I stood in the aisle and had a quick briefing, telling them were we were billeted, and this brought smiles to every face. I said "I know there'll be hot and cold running women, but try to keep the focus on work, and keep the playing around to a minimum."

That caused some laughter, so I continued, "I know it's going to be difficult, because from my experience with nurses, they'll all be trying to get their jollies with each of us. Just use a bit of decorum and don't get caught. Don't forget anything that goes on there is reported back to HQ. Also remember what happens on tour stays on tour, so no sprouting off after we're back, is that clear?" Tag asked with a cheeky grin, "What about you, Corp?" I replied with a smile, "Put it this way, Tag. My girlfriend would have my balls in a wringer, if she had any idea of me playing up. So I'm not going to be any fun for any of the nurses, but what you do is up to you. I also know that you and Buzz have had to forgo your leave for this course, and after being in 'Nam with your squadron, a bit of blowing off steam would be par for the course, but please, just don't get sprung."

When we arrived in Adelaide, we were met by Dr Michael Cord, who was to be our liaison person with the hospital, and also our main teacher. He was ex-military and was used to Army personnel doing the medic course here. On the drive to the hospital, he gave us an idea of what we were in for. We had the rest of the weekend to settle in, and then we'd be starting at eight each morning of that next week having lectures all day until sixteen hundred. If we passed the theory exams, for the following three weeks we'd be doing twelve hour shifts in the emergency department, under the guidance of the on call Shift doctors. I asked about drinking facilities, and where we'd be eating, and was told there wasn't any drinking areas in the hospital grounds. Most of the staff went to the pub down around the corner, and as for meals we'd be eating in the staff canteen. He told us we'd be using a voucher system, which meant signing for a voucher daily, before leaving our quarters. He would introduce us to the matron in charge of the nurses' quarters, from whom we had to get the vouchers. Seemed like a silly system, but when in Rome...

After being shown our rooms by the matron, we were told the showers and toilets we were to use were at our end of the wing. She also informed us that there was to be no fraternising. Yeah, well. As if. After the matron left, a couple of nurses came down from the floor above and introduced themselves. They said they'd be happy to show us the local boozer, and we all agreed to meet them out front in ten minutes, because we were all hanging out for a drink. When we got outside there were four girls waiting for us. Introductions were made all round, we headed off to the pub, and as we went the girls told us some of the house rules.

The pub was a pleasant little place much in the style of British pubs. I discovered from the owner, who I had engaged in conversation with, that the patronage was mainly medical workers. That meant that they catered for afterhours drinking via a side door, and that was handy to know. After asking him about the cops, he said they left him alone due to the fact some of them drank at his pub, making use of the after hour's facility. With a laugh and a smile I thought that there was always one pub somewhere that fulfilled that particular need.

The other guys seemed to be having fun with the nurses, so after a while I left them to it, and headed back to the quarters. I got two vouchers off the matron when I got back; one for dinner that night, and the other for tomorrow. I had a shower and got my gear sorted, thankful we had another day before we started. Considering it was

329

a rest day, I'd probably go and do some sightseeing. Just before dinner, the other guys and the nurses came back, and we all went to dinner together. All through dinner, a cute red head was trying her best to get me into a conversation. Knowing that wasn't all that she was trying, I decided to forestall any further advances. I politely told her I was in a relationship with someone and that I was the faithful kind, so I wasn't interested in any flirting or jumping into bed with anyone. I also asked her to pass that along to any other interested party. I finished with "I don't mind being a friend or helper, but as for anything else I was off limits."

The next morning after breakfast, I headed into town for some sightseeing. I found that the parkland, near the weir on the Torrens River, was quite nice. I did the obligatory paddle on the river in one of the hire boats, and after a few hours of wandering around I headed back. I ended up in the pub, where I saw Tag with another nurse. I smiled and thought that I could have had a field day on this course, with a different bird every night. Oh well, the joys of being one of those rare monogamous types.

Next morning, we started the course, Christ! The textbook we were to refer to during the lectures would have taken a year to get through. Even though we had five monotonous days of that stuff, and then tests on each subject, I thought that the week was pure hell. I tried to imagine it for a full time nurse or doctor. They deserved all the credit they got. I only had one week of it, and that was bad enough. I soon learned that week was the easy part.

What followed that was three weeks of solid work in the emergency department, working twelve hours at a time. It seemed that you'd no sooner gone to sleep, when you were due back for the next shift. No wonder nurses and doctors partied hard it was to take their minds off what they did at work. We got to see it all, in most cases doing the fix up and stabilising work ourselves, under the direction of the duty doctors. They'd jump in and help us if required, and the nurses were of great support to us. As I said, we got to see it all; road accident victims, pregnant women, fist fights, and once or twice, drug overdoses. One of the most memorable cases I had was, one night a cop came in with a knife still stuck in his chest. He was dragging a guy he was handcuffed to that was unconscious and bleeding from the head. The cop had lost the key to the cuffs during his fight to arrest the other guy.

While waiting for some other cops to arrive with keys, both were placed on beds side by side, and worked on at the same time. I got the cop who was still conscious, and after administering a local anaesthetic, took the knife out. I was hoping it hadn't pierced anything vital, and luckily it had missed vital organs. After cleaning the wound, I sewed him up. After both had been treated, then the other cops put in appearances, and unlocked the cuffs. Anyway, finally the course came to a close. Dr Cord gave us the final results the Friday before we were to leave; we'd all passed with flying colours, and Tag had ended up as best student.

On the flight home the next day, we all agreed that it had been a gruelling four weeks, but worth it. We were all damn glad it was over, though. When we landed, it was fourteen hundred, local time. Perth was two hours behind the Eastern states, but only half an hour behind Adelaide. Tag, Buzz, and Doc were going to grab a cab to the base, and I assumed that they were going to be on leave for a while since they were due. I was going to ring Sharon to pick me up. It only took Sharon twenty minutes to pick me up, and after flying into my arms and kissing me, we headed for home. She was asking questions the whole time as she drove, the main one being of course, how I got on with the nurses. When I told her that we were actually living in the nurse's quarters, she almost ran a red light. I thought to myself, just as well I hadn't told her before I left that we were going to stay there. She'd have had a fit, and I'd have been in for a hard time.

She was more than mollified after I stated that I'd made it known that I wasn't in interested in any playing around. She relaxed even more after reaching home and having a shower. I undressed her and took her to bed, where we whiled away the rest of the afternoon, before she got up to make dinner for both of us. The next day, I did the washing I'd accumulated after breakfast, and we more or less had a lazy day.

Next day I was back on base, after taking my clean clothes to my quarters, and having another quick coffee. I was seated opposite Mark at his desk, after he had me close the door. I handed him the paperwork, that Dr Cord had given to me pass on in a sealed A4 envelope. I gathered these were our course reports, and he opened it, had a quick glance, and then put it into his in tray. He looked at me, and said "Well, Tiger, you've come a long way from when Pep and I saw you in action at Kapooka. At times I've reserved my judgement. Pep has seen more in you than I thought. You still look fresh faced and too young, but you've handled everything we've thrown at you, and with ease I might add. Your passing scores are a credit to you, and your dedication, and now I have to ask you to make the hardest choice you'll probably have to make. Unlike the time we gave you at Kapooka to think it over, I'm going to need an answer by the end of the day."

I looked at him, trying to read what was on his mind. I had no luck in that direction, and so I said, going out on a limb "Go ahead, Boss. Let's hear it." He seemed to have something shift in his thinking, as he replied "Alright, what you hear from now on is ultra-top secret; it can't go further than this room." I sat back, ready for whatever he was about to divulge. He began by saying "I know Pep has given you an idea of what may be happening, but until a couple of days ago, even he didn't know the full scope of what is being proposed. When the new CO took over, he had been thinking about what is likely to happen after the war in 'Nam is over. He seems to think that not only will we have to deal with the country's defence, but we could also be involved with small brushfire wars, and possibly terrorism. With that in sight, he's decided to form a special force that will operate on its own, away from the mainstream sabre squadrons. It will be commanded by HQ squadron here, regardless of where they are. At present it will only consist of an eight man specialist patrol that Pep is getting together now. The only reason it's going to be one at present is because of budget constraints, and as yet hasn't been authorized."

He leaned forward on his desk, and interlocked his fingers, and looking me in the eye continued. "Pep, as the leader of this special patrol, is being given his pick of every member of the regiment. If they accept, of course, one of the people Pep has requested is you. As the patrol comes under my responsibility, it's my job to ask those picked. I don't want you to answer straight away, because I've yet to mention the drawbacks, and the possible advantages. Once you have a clear picture of what you're being asked to do, the decision will then rest with you."

As I waited for him to continue, I was re-running what he'd already said around in my head. "Before I give you the pros and cons, I'd like to explain a couple of other things. First, you were chosen for a number of reasons; you are an above average marksman, more or less a pro with explosives and that comes from men of very high standing in their field. You learn quickly, and you can adapt to any given situation. You think, and would make an excellent planner. Finally, you haven't been assigned to a sabre squadron yet, so you have no bad habits to unlearn. Secondly, Pep has also asked that you be second in command and because of what I know of you, I've granted that request, if you join the team, of course."

Now my mind was really working overtime, Pep had said he'd save me a spot, but I had no idea it would be as his 2IC. The praise from the engineer's, I must have really impressed Sgt Teasdale. Mark sat back in his chair as he continued, "Now for the possible advantages. A lot of travel, each job would be unlike any you've faced before, learning on the hop, an infinite number of new situations and experiences, no peacetime restrictions on activities." He leaned forward and continued, "Now, I'm going to let you know the downside, and there's a lot. This is the most important though. Everything is top secret you can't tell anybody what you do. As far as the rest of the regiment and outsiders are concerned, you'd always be away on training. Your records would be sealed and classified ultra-top secret. Request only. That's probably the worst. The rest includes; being on duty twenty-four-seven, letting us know where you are when not on a mission, no fixed duty area, constant training, elevated alert levels, and no recognition of what you've achieved. You remain in the team. No quitting without damn good reason. As I said there's a lot of reasons not to accept, and I think I can foresee a time when the team may be shunned by other members of the regiment. It will be hard work, but you may find it could be rewarding on a personal level, Tiger. I think you'd enjoy this opportunity, but that's for you to make up your mind about. We'll leave it now and reconvene at fifteen hundred."

After I left Mark's office, my head was in a whirl, thinking over what he'd said. I needed some alone time to sort things out, so I headed for my quarters. Once there, I closed the door, made a coffee, and sat at my desk. With the coffee and smokes, I ran everything over and over again in my head. After about an hour of ruminating, I decided that I needed someone to talk to, and dialled Sharon's direct line. She was able to fit me in for an hour's signing rehash, if I could be there in ten minutes. After telling her I'd be there, I hung up, did a quick tidy up of my room, and headed to the Sig's company lecture room.

Once we'd had a kiss and cuddle, I said "I've got a problem, Sweetheart, and I sort of need to talk it over with you." She asked "Well, if you think I can help. What's it all about?" I replied "Well all this is classified top secret. I've been offered a job that means I could be away a lot, and I wouldn't be able to tell you where I was going, or what I was doing. I'd be on twenty four hour call, and have to let base know where was at all times. It could happen in war or peace times, and you would only know that I've gone, or that I was back, or that you'd get notification that I was dead or wounded. I'm trying to think whether you could handle that, or not." She said "I live with that every day I know what being in love with a SAS member is like. I know that you guys are the dirty tricks department of the Army, and I know you can't tell me a lot of things. I accept that, and as far as secrecy is concerned, well, I've got that as well. There's things I can't tell you either, so yes, I can handle it! Plus my darling, I know you enough by now to know that you've already made your mind up to accept. We'll be able to work it out. We love each other. I'm not going to hold you back from your job, the same as I know you wouldn't do it for me." After that was cleared up, I felt a little better, and after telling her I'd meet her in her mess later, I made my way to my mess for lunch.

Dead on fifteen hundred, I was again seated opposite Mark at his desk, and said "Ok boss, I'm in, can you tell me more?" Mark smiled, and replied "I had rather thought you'd accept. Welcome to the SRT (Special Response Team). Each team member is a specialist, with two of each specialist. As usual, each member is required to be able to do the job of any other. SRT one is comprised of two medics, two marksmen, two explosive experts, and two signallers. Some of the team has yet to be asked and respond, due to being on leave. They'll all be privates, except for you and Pep, and that's why he wanted you as 2IC."

He then went on to tell me that some had already agreed to join, and that he was organising their quarters in our accommodation building. I asked "Who's already accepted, boss?" He replied with a smile, "You know some of them. The medics will be Tag Wilson and Buzz Tyrell. You're one of the marksmen, Snagger Brown is the other. Pep is one of the bang boy's, and Dumper Marsh is the other. We're hoping to get Sparks Reilly and Wires Ellis as the coms men." He handed me a bunch of personnel folders, saying "These are their records, study them overnight, and return them in the morning. After that, it may be an idea to go to the gym, and do some combat training with sergeant Swifty Lewis. If Pep gets back early, I'll let him know where to find you." I replied "Thanks boss, I'll get these back to you after breakfast," holding up the files.

As I was about to get up and leave, he said "Tiger, Pep tells me you're spending time with one of the sigs girls. That's fine, you can come and go on base as you need, but there'll be times that you have to stay on base. I'll need to know if it develops into something serious, considering your job now." I looked at him before answering, because mentally I was saying that my love life had nothing to do with the system, then realised that it could be construed as a distraction. I said "Mark, Sharon is the one I'm seeing, and it's possible that sometime in the future we may get married. As I've told Pep, the job comes first, and our love life won't be a distraction in any way."

Mark looked at me and said "Fair enough, and I know you mean what you say, so good luck with your relationship. I hope it stands the test." As I rose and took the personnel records, I thought to myself, so do I.

CHAPTER 32

Well, as soon as I left Mark's office, I took the folders to my room and put them on my desk for reading later. After locking my room, I headed for my rendezvous with Sharon at the Sigs mess. Over a drink and smoke, I told her I'd accepted the offer and that I'd not be coming home tonight. I explained I had to do some paperwork, but if she missed me too much, she had my direct line number. We had a couple more drinks, and as we were about to leave the mess, I bought a bottle of Johnny Walker Black and a large bottle of dry ginger from the bar. I carried the bag outside to the car, and Sharon drove me over to the barracks, where we kissed good night. I took my bag of drinks upstairs, put the dry into the fridge, the JW on top, and walked to the mess for an early dinner.

After dinner I returned to my quarters, settled down at my desk, and started reading the files of the other SRT members. I read the easy ones first.

Ernest 'Tag' Wilson. Medic. Born in Victoria, five eight, joined the regiment one year ago at age nineteen. Active duty ten month tour of Vietnam on multiple patrols; under fire on twelve occasions; confirmed kills two; possibles one. Earned his nickname, Tag, by pinning a tag of paper with notes to medical staff on every wounded soldier he came across.

David 'Buzz' Tyrell – Medic. Born New South Wales, five seven. Joined the regiment sixteen months ago at eighteen; active duty ten month tour of Vietnam on multiple patrols; under fire on seventeen occasions; confirmed kills three, possibles one. Earned the nickname Buzzard because he hovered over any patient he had, later shortened to Buzz.

Phillip 'Snagger' Brown – Sniper. Born in Victoria, five ten. Joined the regiment two years ago at nineteen; active duty two ten month tours of Vietnam with multiple patrols; under fire on forty-one occasions; confirmed kills thirteen, two possibles. Earned his nickname due to his over use of the term "snagged it."

John 'Dumper' Marsh – Demolitions. Born in Victoria, five seven. Joined the regiment one year ago at eighteen; active duty ten month tour of Vietnam on multiple patrols; under fire on twenty-two occasions; confirmed kills twenty-nine; fourteen possibles. Earned his nickname due to dumping an explosive down the shitters at Nui Dat to get rid of some rats. Consequently, it blew the whole building to bits.

James 'Sparks' Reilly – Signalman. Born in Queensland, five nine. Joined the regiment a year ago aged nineteen; active duty ten month tour of Vietnam on multiple patrols; under fire on twelve occasions; confirmed kills two; three possibles. Nicknamed Sparks due to being a radioman.

Rick 'Wires' Ellis – Signalman. Born in Queensland, five seven. Joined the regiment a year ago at age eighteen; active duty ten month tour of Vietnam on multiple patrols; under fire on eleven occasions; confirmed kills four; possibles three. Earned his nickname because of always having spare electrical wires hanging out of his pockets.

The files gave me insight into the men I would be spending a lot of time with. There were two more files to go through. The first one I was really waiting to look at; the other one I was sure wouldn't have too much inside but would be interesting to read all the same.

Michael 'Pepper' Salter – Marksman, Demolition, Signalman, and Paratrooper (H), born Scotland, five nine. Previous experience: two years British Commandos; active duty two six month tours of Belfast; joined the regiment in 1965; aged twenty two; active duty one six month tour (advisor) and two ten month tours of Vietnam on multiple patrols; under fire on sixty-eight occasions, confirmed kills forty seven; possibles seventeen. Decorations: Medal for Gallantry (British), Military Star (British), active service Medal (Vietnam), Medal for Distinguished Service. Promoted to Sergeant 1967. Earned the nickname Pepper due to surname, later shortened to Pep.

Pep had been downplaying his true service record, I mused. Not surprising, really, considering we were in a regiment where recognition was kept low key. I looked at the last file, knowing it would not measure up to any of the files I had read previously.

Tom 'Tiger' Davis – Marksman, Demolition and Paratrooper (H), born England, five seven. Joined regiment 1970; active duty nil; confirmed kills nil; possibles nil. Decorations: Commendation for Distinguished Service, promoted to Corporal 1969 during basic training. Earned nickname Tiger from previous usage. Notes: refused recommendation as officer candidate. High recommendations: classified above average explosives expert, cleared for deep underwater demolition, passed medical criteria, signal criteria, extremely competent above average soldier and selected as 2IC SRT one.

It was interesting reading, at any rate, but it looked really pathetic considering what I'd read previously.

I freshened my drink and lit a smoke just as the phone rang. I answered by saying "Davis," and Sharon replied, "Hello darling. I just wanted to hear your voice and tell you I love you before going to bed."

I hadn't realized the time and said "Shit." I was quick to apologize. "Sorry, sweetheart. I didn't realize the time until you rang. I've been doing a lot of reading, and I guess time got away from me. I'm not sure what I'll be doing for the next few days, but I'll try to be at your mess just after knock off if I can. Hopefully I'll be able to come home a couple of nights. You go to sleep, and hopefully I'll see you tomorrow. Love you, good night."

She replied, "Kiss, kiss, love you, darling," and hung up.

I finished my drink and smoke and started my usual mental debrief as I had a shower, and then went to bed.

After breakfast the next morning, I took the files back to Mark, who asked for my comments.

"Everyone seems to have good character references and the capabilities for what could be a very elite fighting force. However,

I'm not sure if I measure up to any of these guys, and I'm starting to doubt Pep's thinking in choosing me. I wonder if it's just because he likes me."

Mark laughed and replied, "I had the same misgivings and was starting to doubt Pep as well, until I heard your comments. You talk like an intelligence officer giving a situation appraisal, and again I find myself wondering why you refused the officer training option. You'd have made a damn fine one. And yes I've heard your thoughts about why, and I can only think that you're wasting your potential. However, all these men started from scratch just like you. In a year's time, I'd bet my last dollar that you will far exceed their exploits, especially now as SRT you'll have a lot more opportunity to shine in your own right. What are you going to be doing for the rest of the day?"

"I was going to try and spend the next few days with Sgt. Lewis Boss. My last unarmed combat session was interrupted, so I'd like to bring my skills up to scratch," I replied.

He laughed as I said this. "Yes it was, but done well as I remember. I don't think you'll have any trouble with Swifty, and you can learn a lot from him. Concentrate on that until Pep's back, and we'll see what happens then."

For the next three days I learned and honed my unarmed combat skills with Swifty. When I first encountered him, he reckoned I was a boxer, a martial artist, and street fighter all rolled into one, without using any to the right advantage. After the second day, I was becoming lethal in the hands and feet department, and he showed me how to combine all three of my styles into a completely effective fighting and killing style. By day three, he was hard pressed when sparring with me and decided he needed some help. At the end of that day, I was sparring against five experts at once and winning.

Just before knock off time, Swifty asked who my CO was and I told him and asked why he wanted to know.

"Because I would like to tell him what an efficient unarmed killer he has available, and now that I find out you're with HQ,

I'm going to recommend he place you in a sabre squadron. You're damned excellent and shouldn't be wasted shuffling papers. As a matter of fact, I'll go see him right now." Without a further word, he stormed out.

As I was heading to meet Sharon, I laughed out loud thinking about what Swifty was going to say to Mark and the response he might get.

I had been meeting with Sharon every afternoon, but this time, when we were half way through our drinks, my pager went off. I looked at the message which read "HQCO NOW!"

I showed Sharon and said, "Wait for me, honey, this won't take long."

I ran to Mark's office. He looked darkly at me and said, "I've just been chewed out by a sergeant for being incompetent in my choice of personnel. It seems I have a paper shuffler here that should be leading a sabre squadron patrol because he's a natural. What the hell have you done to him?"

I couldn't keep a straight face and burst out laughing, and Mark joined in. I replied, "Well, we've been working on my style and speed, and today I was sparring with five of them. If it had been the real thing and I wasn't pulling my punches, they'd have all been dead. Swifty asked where I worked, and being unable to say exactly, I said here."

He burst out laughing again and said, "You did the right thing, and you are about to get another recommendation added to your file. See, told you how easy it was. Now get out of here."

I was laughing all the way back to the Sigs mess, where I decided after a couple more drinks to go home with Sharon that night.

The next morning I was back in the gym with Swifty, and after a warmup session with the body bag, Swifty and I went through some fight scenarios slowly so he could assess any errors or weaknesses. I did have one weakness: when striking with a hand sword punch, I was pulling it, not focusing full power, so we moved over to the body bag and kept going through it. In the end, he was yelling at me to unleash, and I got so pissed off my next punch went right through both sides of the bag. Dumbfounded, I stood there, my arm out, my legs balanced and ready for the next strike, sand pouring out of the broken bag.

Swifty looked at the pouring sand and commented, "Come over here away from that mess, Tiger. You're damn good. If you focus and do that every time, you won't lose. There's nothing more I can teach you. Good luck, son."

After helping clean up the mess I'd created, and replacing the bag with a new one, I went through some more moves with Swifty. We were gently sparring without connecting. Most of my punches were fast enough to get through his defences, and the only thing stopping him from being hit and injured was that I'd pull my strikes an inch away from his face, neck, or body. As we were practicing, I noticed Pep come in out of the corner of my eye, and when we stopped the next time, I turned away and dropped my arms.

"Hey Pep, you're back."

Swifty stopped turned and said, "I might have known he was one of yours. How are you Pep?"

Pep answered his question, turned to me, and said, "I need to talk to you. Let's go to your quarters."

I nodded, turned to go, and stopped as Swifty said, "You're alright Tiger. Pep, can I have a quick word before you go?"

Pep turned to me and said, "You go ahead; I'll catch up."

Outside the gym, I lit up before heading to my quarters. I finished my smoke as I walked and was almost at the door of the building before Pep caught up. We walked into my room. Inside he put the jug on and made two coffees as I sat and watched. After passing mine across to me, he sat and pulled out his smokes, offered one to me, which I accepted, lit up, and took a sip of the coffee and relaxed.

"The whole team will be together in the lecture room at eight sharp on Monday, and we'll all be going on exercise for at least ten days. It's our job to have them working together as a team by the end of that, yours and mine. You already know that you're going to be my 2IC, and Mark told me about your misgivings. I think you're up to the job; otherwise I wouldn't have picked you. Any questions?"

"Yes," I replied. "Is it everyone you wanted? In other words, the same blokes I had the files for?"

He raised his eyebrows and smiled as he answered. "Yep. In the meantime we've got until Monday to get you up to scratch with them. The one thing you haven't learned yet is what these guys have been doing for the last ten months, so after lunch, we're going to be working on your helicopter skills, getting in and out, rappelling, and climbing, and how to ride the skids. Meet me at HQ after lunch in full combat gear, and we'll head out to Pearce. We've got a chopper and crew for unlimited time."

"So, in other words, this is going to be a crash course, so to speak."

He laughed and replied, "Yep, and it's going to be tough. We'll be at it until I think you're good enough, and we've only got a short time to get you good enough."

When he finished, I asked the question I was dying to ask. "What did Swifty want with you?"

He laughed and answered, "He told me about the dust up he had with Mark over you and asked me the same thing, so I told him you were still training and that HQ was the best place for you at present. He also wanted to tell me how good you are. I've seen him kill four VC barehanded at the same time. If he says you're good, that means you're bloody excellent."

At thirteen hundred, I was outside HQ dressed in full combat gear. Pep came out dressed the same, and after hoisting my backpack a few times, he said, "Good. Into the staff car," and pointed to the green Ford in one of the parking bays.

The next three days were a blur and seemed to be all rolled into one. In the chopper, out of the chopper, standing on skids, jumping off skids, touch and go landings to load, touch and go landings to unload, rappelling out, climbing up and in, dust off (medical evac) techniques, emergency evacuation procedures, hot LZ's (dangerous and under fire landing zones), hover loading and unloading, and we practiced these over and over and over again. By the end of day three, I swear I could do them all in my sleep, and I think with a couple, I did. It got to the stage that we were eating most of our meals at the RAAF base because we were either leaving too early or getting back too late for meals at our base.

At one point I said to Pep, "Leave me here I'll sleep in the chopper. Wake me in the morning."

After doing the whole routine once Saturday morning, Pep called a halt to any further exercise by saying, "Ok you're ready. That's it. We'll call it a day."

We thanked the chopper crew for their hard work and finally headed back to Swanbourne. Pep was pleased with what I'd accomplished, but, quite frankly, I was too tired and worn out to give a shit. When we got back to my quarters, he said, "Ok get out of your shit. What's your girl's number?"

He rang Sharon, told her who was calling, and asked her to come and pick me up. "Sharon will be here in ten. Go home, get some rest. See you at eight on Monday, bright eyed and bushy-tailed."

Sharon arrived as I was stubbing out a smoke, and after I got in the car and gave her a kiss, we headed home. While I was in the shower, she sorted out my washing and put a load on as soon as I was out of the shower. I had a drink with a towel wrapped around me, and she joined me in bed.

I must have zonked out as soon as my head hit the pillow and my arm went around her, because the next thing I knew she was bringing me coffee at around ten the next morning. She told me that my washing was drying and brunch would be ready in ten. After a nice breakfast of bacon, sausages, scrambled egg, toast, and another two hits of caffeine, I started to come alive.

About half an hour later we went down to the beach for a swim and enjoyed some lovemaking in the water. Back at the flat, we showered together. While she did the ironing that afternoon, we watched the afternoon movie Rio Bravo with John Wayne and Dean Martin. We decided to go down to Freo (Fremantle) for dinner that night.

Over dinner I warned her that I would be away on exercises for the next couple of weeks and would probably be leaving the next day. After dinner, we headed home and went to bed early, not that sleep was on the agenda until later. She had an early start the next day, so we drove into base at zero six hundred. She dropped me at the barracks, and after a good bye kiss, I took my clean gear to my room and went to the mess for breakfast.

At zero eight hundred, all the SRT team members were in the lecture room. Some were wearing camouflage fatigues that had been procured from some of the yanks in 'Nam, while some of us were in normal greens. I thought to myself that I'd have to get some of the cam gear if the opportunity arose; it looked good, and from what the guys wearing them had to say, was really comfortable to wear.

We introduced ourselves to each other. Mark and Pep walked in, and as I called attention, we all rose.

"Be seated." Pep closed the door and moved towards the back, and Mark continued. "I'd like to welcome you all to what will hopefully be the first of a few special teams that will operate outside of the normal sabre squadron criteria. Let me stress that you are the first, and if you succeed at fulfilling the requirements and missions we've assembled you for, there will be other teams. You're the ground breakers, and that alone is an accomplishment. Shortly, you'll be called on briefly to introduce yourselves to each other, paying special mention to your specialties, strengths and weaknesses. Please be honest. Each of your teammates' lives could depend on it." Mark looked at each man in turn before continuing. "But first, the command structure. Pep Salter is the team leader, and his 2IC is Tiger Davis. For those of you who don't know them, you will, but overall command is me and me only.

You answer to no one else, even if they outrank me, understood?"

"Yes Sir."

"I answer to the Base Commanding Officer, so I have the weight of a colonel behind me. Each one of you has been hand-picked from every member in the regiment, no mean feat, I might add. You're all here for that reason. Your numbers include long serving members and the latest addition to the regiment. Your first two missions have already been selected, and you'll be briefed on them at a later stage. First off, you need to get to know each other and learn to start working as a team. Remember, if one thing goes wrong, the whole of it can go wrong. We'll start with your team leader."

Pep moved up to the front and introduced himself with rank, experience, specialties, and a brief resume of his time in the regiment. He finished with, "This team is an experiment, and I'll do my damnedest to pull it off, but we will be using regiment SOP's where each man needs to know the job of everyone else, the same as Tiger will be learning from me, you'll be learning from him and each other. Speaking of, Tiger's next."

I stood and moved to the front. "Pep talked about this being an experiment, and in many cases, I'm a big one. I was asked to try out for the regiment while still in basic training. By then I was already a corporal, and I left Kapooka before finishing basic after being decorated for distinguished service. Unlike most of you, I was accepted into the regiment before even two-thirds of my training was completed, and since then I've been doing a crash course. I've been asked to join this team, and as 2IC. Christ, if that's not an experiment, I don't know what is. However, I believe in the merits of what is trying to be achieved by forming this team. I know I have still a lot to learn, and a lot of expectations to live up to in your eyes, but if I didn't think I was up to the challenge, I wouldn't be here now. Thank you for the chance to prove myself to you. Snagger, you're next."

As I walked back to my seat, the guys applauded, and I got a couple pats on the back as well. I looked over at Mark and Pep.

Pep was smiling, and Mark was nodding his approval. They both knew I had won the team over and earned their respect at the same time.

Each team member took their turn up front, and we learned a bit more about each other. Sometimes there were laughs and jokes thrown in, but that was to cover the nervousness of public speaking.

After we had all introduced ourselves in front of the group, Mark returned to the front and said, "Well, that seemed to have broken the ice a bit, and I'm rather glad that I have such a good bunch of public speakers under my command." We all laughed at that comment because we knew he was talking bullshit, and so did he. As the laughter died down, he continued, "Before I said you come under my direct command, but that doesn't mean me personally. It falls under the HQ Commanding Officer, so if I'm posted elsewhere, whoever takes my place becomes your boss.

"Now, we're going to move on to what you'll be doing next. Tomorrow morning you'll leave for Pearce and take a chopper ride to the Kimberley's, with a refuelling stop at Karratha. You'll be set down here," he pointed to a spot on the map on the wall, "and you'll establish an LUP to be used as a base. Three Commando company will meet you there the day after tomorrow with your supplies for the exercise, which will require rock climbing and abseiling. They will bring you that gear amongst your supplies. Rations will consist of five boxes of ten-man ration packs. You'll also take from here five one-man ration packs per person, and if that's not enough food, live off the land." More laughter. "Full combat dress for the duration. Sparks, Wires, you'll need to draw your equipment from sigs, radio sked (schedule) sixteen hundred each day. Ok, gentlemen. Good luck and have fun."

CHAPTER 33

After that briefing, we all had an idea of what we were in for. The rest of the day was our own, so after some general chit chat, we made our way to the mess for lunch. While there, I became the focus of the team, so we sat at the same table. Some of the guys wanted to know how I received my decoration and how come I'd been picked straight out of basic, and most importantly, how did I get accepted into the regiment before even finishing my qualifying period? My answers had them a little amazed at times, but they gave respect where it was due, and as far as they were concerned, the respect was there. They considered me one of their own. So there was a fair bit of ribbing over my answers.

After lunch I went and checked all my field gear and went to the Q store to get the five one-man rat (ration) packs. I took them back to my room, put them in my field gear, filled my water bottles, unlocked the safe, and grabbed my ammo and pistols. The pistols needed to be cleaned and oiled, and I stored the ammo mags in the ammo pouches of my field gear. I cleaned and oiled my rifle and made sure I had a full bandolier of grenades. I spread it all out on the bed, ready to grab when it was time to go.

I headed over to the sigs mess to meet Sharon for a couple of drinks. I told her that I would be leaving the next morning and I would let her know when I'd be back. She was aware that something was in the wind due to Sparks and Wires having been there to draw their comm's (communication) gear, but she didn't comment or ask questions.

After our drinks, we headed home, had dinner, and went to bed for an intense session of lovemaking.

The next morning, Sharon dropped me at my quarters and I went upstairs, put on my pistols and the rest of my field gear, grabbed my rifle, and headed to the HQ building. Outside there was a truck waiting, and after throwing my back pack into the rear of the truck, I joined the guys who were already there and lit a smoke as we talked amongst ourselves. By eight everyone had arrived, and we loaded ourselves into the truck, which took us to the Chopper pads at Pearce. When we boarded the chopper, I saw the sense of keeping the team at an eight man patrol, as opposed to the original ten. A 'Huey' (Bell UH-1 Helicopter) could only carry ten men with their gear, and then it was crowded, so sticking to eight made perfect sense once we were in the chopper took off.

Once airborne, the pilot did a circuit of the base then headed north to our refuel point. The side doors were closed for the flight so there was less wind drag, and it made it a little quieter inside. Three hours later we landed, and while the Huey was being refueled, we took the time to stretch our legs and have a couple of smokes. After refueling and another half an hour in the air, we reached the designated LZ (landing zone), where we would then move on foot to our LUP. We reached it fifteen minutes later and proceeded to set up our base camp, dig some slit trenches for defence of the perimeter, and where we would sleep, dug another pit in the centre of the LUP. We got a fire going and brewed up some coffee. We got out a rat pack each and warmed up one of the tinned food cans for dinner. We sat around the fire, eating, drinking our coffees, smoking, and talking as the sun slowly disappeared.

Because we were treating the exercise as a war time operation, we were all awake at four and standing to. In other words, we were in our perimeter trenches, scanning the terrain for possible enemy attack as the sky lightened and dawn broke. The only exception to the rule was the LUP; it was our base camp where we could be found by other units if they knew our location. In a real situation, the LUP was a place to hole up and sleep without giving any indication we were there. For instance, no fire pit or supply stack, and we'd be constantly on alert for movement near our location.

After it was full light, we made breakfast and ate as Pep gave us a briefing as to the day's events. We'd be practicing patrol techniques, which meant complete silence and going to ground at times, so to an observer we wouldn't be seen or heard.

After his briefing, he said "However, if we find a decent animal we can eat, we'll take it. I'm already sick of this rat pack shit, but sometimes you got to go with the flow."

While we were patrolling near a river close to lunch time, Dumper, who was the forward scout, halted and moved back to us to report what he'd seen. He'd spotted a salt water crocodile sunning on the bank, which gave me an idea. I signed to Pep what I had in mind, and he nodded agreement.

Snagger and I crept forward. When we spotted the croc, which was approximately nine feet in length, I asked Snagger if he'd be able to shoot it with his .308. He nodded that he could, so I gave him the go ahead. Snagger took it with a clean head shot, and the rest of the guys joined us as we moved closer to look at what was to become meals for the next day or so.

After skinning it and taking what fresh meat that could be collected, we left the rest of the carcass for the birds and wildlife. Pep decided we'd head back to camp and take care of any preparation work for cooking the croc. For some of the men, it would be the first time they'd eaten croc meat. Pep was one of them, so I volunteered to take care of cooking of the meat. After preparing a makeshift stretcher, we placed the fresh meat and skin on it and headed back to camp.

The fire pit would be working overtime with all the cooking, and on the way back, I kept a lookout for some ingredients I could add to make the croc tasty. When we were back at camp, I had everyone turn out the leftover parts of their rat pack, selected everything I needed, and showed Dumper and Buzz some of the things I'd collected on the way back. I asked them to scout around and find me some more.

While I took care of the cooking, Wires, who'd been brought up in the far north of Queensland, took care of treating the skin, which we'd take back with us. Luckily, we had plenty of tinfoils, so we had steaks that night for dinner. I'd also put a roast with scrub veggies in the coals for tomorrow, as well as precooked the rest of the meat. Some we'd have for breakfast the next day. We had a plentiful supply of cooked meat, and the best way to keep it fresh was by burying it, unearthing it as required. I think my cooking skills were responsible for my estimates going up in everyone's eyes that night.

After stand to the next day, we had some of the croc steaks I'd precooked and warmed up. During his briefing, Pep told us that the group from three Commando company were due around ten. We were to take positions on each side of the track and conceal ourselves. He would move around our positions, to see how well we were concealed and showed us where he would be waiting in plain sight. We weren't to move until he'd whistled an all clear. All of us were able to see his position as we prepared and moved into place.

Readers Note: If you think staying in one position without movement is easy, try it. If you move as much as a finger, or twitch your toes, you fail. The average person can only stay completely still for no longer than ten minutes, so in my line of work, being still and quiet for up to ten hours at a time was quite difficult, but there are tricks of the trade that help in those situations.

In the forty plus degree heat, it was hard to stay still, but eventually I got some added stimulus to be still, because a king brown snake decided to lay beside me in the shade my body created.

Four hours later, the snake decided to move away, and shortly after it had gone, I felt a vibration in the ground. I figured out what it was as I saw two land rovers in the distance heading our way, and fifteen minutes later the second one was parked on the track not more than six feet from my position. The people inside climbed out and looked toward the front to see what was taking place. The next thing I heard was Pep whistling. I stood up opposite of Sparks, and the men that were standing in front of us looked startled as they turned and saw us.

The unit was part of the long range desert surveillance company that patrolled near the northern coastline. Most people weren't even aware that this happened, but it does, and it has been in operation since before the Vietnam War started. The work is done by all the Commando regiments and SAS Reservist units in rotation.

Once our supplies had been unloaded, they spent lunch with us before continuing on their patrol, leaving two of their number with us as instructors for rock climbing. They would return after four days to pick them up.

We got busy sorting out the gear and being briefed on how to put the gear together and how it was used. We spent the next few days learning the art of rock climbing and abseiling down and off cliffs. It was hard considering we had to practice wearing full combat gear, so we learned the hard way how not to get tangled up and how and where to secure our long guns and equipment. Once we all got the hang of it (pun intended), we found the whole experience quite enjoyable, especially the abseiling and launching off cliffs face forward. There is a certain kind of exhilaration running down a vertical cliff face; not as good as freefall, of course, but good all the same.

By the end of our time in the Kimberley's, we'd gotten used to being in close quarters with each other. We respected each other and learned how each other thought. We had become a very tight knit group, a fighting force to be reckoned with. It wasn't always plain sailing; for instance, Sparks and Wires had almost come to blows over a disagreement on which model radio was better, but the worked it out. In my case, I was one of them; I was trusted by them and they would follow my lead whenever directed. The funniest thing was that even Pep would, but only at certain times, like with the croc, for instance.

At the usual radio sked time on our twelfth day, Pep requested transport back to base for ten the next morning. On day thirteen away from base, we were airlifted for the journey home, our training and exercise a complete success.

We arrived at Swanbourne just before dinner time, and a message had been left for us by Mark: the debriefing would take place in the lecture room at zero eight hundred the next morning. We were dismissed until then. We headed for our quarters to drop our combat gear before going to the mess for dinner, and after that I had a couple of drinks with some of the team members, I went back to my room for a shower and to sort my gear out before giving Sharon a call to let her know I was back.

The next morning at eight we were assembled in the lecture room as Mark entered and began the debriefing. This took most of the morning.

When Mark had finished the debriefing, he said, "Well, it sounds like you all had a bit fun, and you're all probably champing at the bit to get into some action. Until Friday morning at zero eight hundred, you're all on leave. You'll be briefed on your first mission. Pep, Tiger, both of you need to be here after lunch Thursday. Ok men, that's all."

After the rest of the team trooped out, Pep and I stayed behind with Mark. He said, "I'll give you all of the details on Thursday, but you'll be going to Vietnam via New Guinea for this first one. You'll have two major demolition jobs that need doing, and I thought it'd be ideal for a first job. Now get out of here and enjoy your leave." Pep and I nodded and left the building, going our separate ways.

I headed to the mess for lunch and then over to my room. After gathering my dirty gear for washing and folding a dress uniform, I started packing my kit bag with clean sets of gear. I put in a spare beret and pair of boots, and I had plenty of room left for my washing. When I brought it back, I put my washing into a spare bag. I rang Sharon's line, and she answered on the second ring. I told her that I would grab a cab to the flat and see her when she got home. We could talk over a few drinks.

After starting my laundry, I went down to the beach for a swim. After swimming for an hour or so, I headed back and by that time the machine had finished. I hung out the laundry before going up for a shower.

Sharon was home by sixteen fifteen, and I had her drink waiting for her and dinner cooking. As we sat out on the balcony watching the sun go down, I told her where I'd been and what I'd been doing. I was on leave until Thursday, so we could spend time together.

She was happy with that news, but a suspicious look came into her eyes and she asked, "So how come you're on leave until then?"

This was going to be hard for me to answer, so I bought some time to think about what I was going to say. I replied, "How about I tell you over dinner? Let's move to the table."

"Ok, but I still want to know what's going on," she replied.

"Sure honey, just let me get dinner dished up." While preparing our plates, I thought about how to break the news.

As soon as I sat down after I'd served dinner, she asked, "Did you bring any washing home?"

"Sure did, but I've already done it. It's dried and in the spare room," I replied. "You know how we've been on exercise? Well, on Thursday, Pep and I have to report for a briefing. It's going to be an interesting one because we'll be operational after that. We'll probably be leaving over the weekend."

"Shit, I knew it! Where to?" she asked.

"Well, first into New Guinea, and then onto Vietnam, but it's not going to be for a full tour. Just a few months, maybe, but I can't tell you any more than that."

She got up from the table muttering, "Shit, shit, shit," over and over again. She walked to the bedroom. I thought to myself, well that didn't go too well.

I followed her into the bedroom; she was sitting on the edge of the bed rocking backwards and forwards, crying. I sat beside her and put my arm around her.

"Hey babe, you knew this was bound to happen, and it's not as bad as being away for nearly a year, which most of the other guys have to do. Besides you told me you could handle it," I comforted. That last comment I made was what really brought her around.

She looked at me and said, "I can handle it. It's just that I don't want you leaving so soon. I thought we'd have longer together, and I don't want you getting hurt either."

"Nothing's going to happen to me. I'll be back before you know it."

She nodded and, with tears in her eyes, said, "Promise me you won't go and get killed."

"What a silly thing to say. I promise I'll try not to get hurt. Is that ok?" She nodded, and I continued. "Come on, honey, your dinner's getting cold. Let's go finish eating." She nodded again and I pulled her up.

She was more composed and nearly back to her old self when we sat down to finish eating. After dinner, we put some music on. The first album was her favourite, The Lemon Pipers, and we talked, enjoying quite a few more drinks and cuddling on the couch.

I'm glad I didn't have to go to work the next day because I was about three sheets to the wind by the time we went to bed. I was thinking that I'd probably have to call Sharon in sick as well because she was fairly blitzed and she'd likely have a massive hangover in the morning.

The alarm went off the next morning, and she was up and getting ready without so much as a sore head, let alone a hangover. I was a little seedy but that was all. After she went to work, I lazed around for the day.

Sharon came home early that day, and while I made dinner, she did my ironing. After she finished, I asked "Do you want a drink, sweetie?"

"No, I don't think so. I had more than my fair share last night, but I'll make you one if you like."

"Is the pope Catholic?"

She made my drink and brought it out to the balcony. I was having a smoke, so she sat outside with me. We chatted about her day and inconsequential things. After dinner, we decided on making it an early night, with a lot of lovemaking before drifting off to sleep.

The next morning Sharon dropped me off, and after a kiss goodbye, I told her that I'd ring her that night. I went and had breakfast in the mess after leaving my clean gear in my room. I wasn't under any time constraints, so I lingered over breakfast before going back to my room and packing my gear. All the stuff going with me was out and in the corner of the room ready to go by the time I left for the briefing.

After lunch, I had a smoke before heading to the lecture room. As I entered, I saw a map of Vietnam, a larger one of South Vietnam, and a map of the eastern side of New Guinea. On the South Vietnam map was an area around Xuyen Moc in the Phuoc Tuy Province circled in red. Nui Dat was also marked, along with Vung Tau, Nui Dat 2, Long Tan, and Nui May Tao in Long Khanh Province. As I was perusing the map, Mark and Pep entered the room.

"Ok, let's get down to business," Mark said. He continued to give us an overall briefing of what we would be doing and why. "Your objective is going to be destroying two bunker setups discovered by a two squadron patrol last year, just near Xuyen Moc. They weren't able to destroy them because they were occupied by a major VC force.

"Both of the complexes are large. One has six major bunkers, and the other has five, so as you can see, this is going to be a major demolition job. It's going to require a fair bit of explosives. A rough estimate by the patrol leader who found them is around eight hundred to a thousand pounds, which isn't going to be carried easily. We've been keeping tabs on these complexes, and for the last few months they haven't been occupied, and that is the window we've been waiting for.

"What's been proposed is that insertion is made by two choppers, one carrying the explosives that will have to be unloaded quickly. Establish two LUP's for the explosives near to each complex. They are only about a thousand yards from each other. Your alpha target is the biggest one first, then the secondary. Observe both for at least a day before deciding to your plans. Once the job is done, you'll stay with one squadron operating on normal patrols until I recall you.

"Our HQ squadron at the Dat (Nui Dat) have been informed to expect your arrival. The Q store staff is trying to procure some sets of camouflage fatigues from the yanks for you and your men to use in the field. They're better than our fatigues for concealment. Training for this will take place in the old Jap bunker emplacements at Salamoa Peninsula near Lae in PNG. You'll be met at the military airfield in Lae by an officer of the Lands department of the PNG government, who'll give you access to the bunker systems on Salamoa. You'll have two weeks to acclimatize and train before going in to Vietnam, landing at Vung Tau, and transferring to a chopper from nine squadron RAAF that'll take you to the Dat. Any questions?"

Pep asked, "What about communication?"

Before answering Mark passed us two code books each, one red, one blue, and replied, "The red one is used in country, but you'll need to get the secondary one when you're there. The blue one is for direct communication to here. It's been arranged that we will get a copy of any communication sent from your team whilst in country and anything you need passed to us will be from the blue one."

Pep and I nodded our understanding, and Mark pulled two pieces of A4 paper from the folder he'd brought with him. He leaned forward and continued, "These are a mud maps of the complexes drawn at the time of their discovery. They're marked A and B. B is the alpha site, and I've got copies for both of you." He passed across the copies to us, and I crossed out the B and renamed it Alpha site and crossed out the A on the second one and renamed it Beta.

Pep and Mark watched me, and as Pep started doing the same to his set, I said, "This way there's no confusion."

Mark laughed. "Why hadn't I thought of that?" He did the same with the originals.

After the renaming had been done, Mark continued, "You'll be leaving here at midday Saturday to go to Pearce, and from there you'll fly to Tindal in the Territory. Overnight there and fly on the next day to Lae. Unless there's anything further, we can wrap this up. Any other details can be taken care of tomorrow at the full briefing."

Outside the building, I had a smoke before heading to the Sigs mess to have a couple of drinks with Sharon before she went home. Over drinks, I let her know we were leaving on Saturday and that tomorrow was to be the full mission briefing and preparation. I also told her what would be happening after the mission was successful and that I didn't expect to be in country for long before being recalled here.

Once we'd finished our drinks, I walked her to the car, gave her a goodbye kiss, and opened the door for her. As she drove off, I headed back to my mess for a couple more drinks before dinner.

CHAPTER 34

Everything went as planned over the next two days: the full briefing was about four hours long, getting target coordinates, radio frequencies, the latest intelligence concerning the targets, and discussion on how to distribute the weight of explosives for the move to each LUP. The radios and explosives we would get in country, but the detonators, charge cables, and timers would have to be taken with us, so after the briefing, Dumper and I would head down to the engineers to get what we'd need.

While we were with Sgt. Teasdale, he gave us as much advice as he could, and we left with two fairly heavy, hard plastic cases full of the supplies we'd need. We left for Pearce on time, and landed at Tindal for our overnight stay. The next morning, we boarded the Herc for the Flight to Lae, taking off at eight.

During the flight, Pep unpacked the charge cases and inspected each device. After nodding his approval, he repacked them, making sure each case had the same amount of devices and detonators so we could use either case.

Considering we were the only cargo, we were able to use the whole cargo bay to relax during the flight. I was stretched out, lying full length and dozing, as were most of the guys, when one of the flight crew came down and said "The boss wanted me to let you know that because it's a minimal length runway, he'll be under full brakes the minute we hit the ground. Be ready for the abrupt application of brakes and reverse thrust. We'll be there in ten."

We got ourselves ready and into the sitting upright position and held onto our rifles. The landing was smooth, but just as well we'd been given some warning; without it some of us would have gone tumbling.

As the cargo ramp was lowered, we sorted our gear and kit

bags and disembarked the plane. We headed to the main hangar, and a person walked forward to meet us. He was close to six feet with dark hair and dressed in a white shirt with dark trousers. He shook our hands and introduced himself as Tim Leah from the lands ministry.

After we moved into the shade of the hangar, he told us we'd be on our way to Salamoa soon. He was waiting for the arrival of two helicopters from a private company that did contract work for the government called Pacific Helicopters; they'd ferry us all across to Salamoa.

The two choppers arrived five minutes later with float bags on instead of the usual skids. After we loaded our gear and ourselves into them, we took off for what turned out to be a ten minute trip.

I noticed that the airport we'd landed in was near the main town, and the end of it faced the sea beside what looked to be a boat marina. When we landed, I understood why the float bags were needed; each chopper landed and pulled up at the end of a sub-stantial wooden jetty. We got out and unloaded our gear, and the following chopper moved toward the jetty. After moving to the end of the jetty, we faced a large two story beach house that Tim opened for us.

"This place belongs to another of us old colonials, Jack Pearce, and we'll be using this for our stay. I've had the fridges and freezers stocked, so there's plenty of food. I didn't know what you guys drank so there's only the local brewed beer in the drinks fridge, I'm afraid. I've arranged for a couple of house Mary's to do the cooking and cleaning up. They'll arrive from the village shortly," Tim explained.

Tim showed us the rooms; there were enough for each of us to have a room to ourselves, so we picked one and stored our gear before reassembling in the main lounge area. A nice breeze was coming in from the open doors to the balcony.

Over a cold beer, Tim told us, "If it's ok with you, we won't bother going up to the caves until the morning, and as you're probably aware, I'll be staying with you while you're here."

Standing on the balcony, Tim pointed out where the caves were located and told me that nearer to the caves, about two hundred feet from the shore, the water was four hundred feet deep. A Jap battleship, the Yokahama, had sunk there during the war. He pointed out to me other diving reefs in the close vicinity.

The following morning, we set off for the caves. Tim explained that the tunnel complex started about five hundred yards from the end of the village. It didn't take us long to get to the entrance, which was close to the sea and roughly close to the wreck Tim had told me about. Probably a hundred feet straight up from the water was an easy way down, but it would be a bugger to try and climb it.

We came to a set of green doors that had been set into the rock with cement, and Tim unlocked the padlock that chained the doors together. Off to the right inside the doors was a clear area with a big generator sitting on a concrete pad, and my eyes followed the track of the power cables running into the tunnels. After checking the generator fuel, we cranked it up; at first it sputtered and then came to life.

"We try to keep it tanked up because your lot do a bit of training here. That's why we have the jerries here; when it's full it lasts for roughly eight hours," Tim explained.

I looked toward the tunnels, and sure enough, after the first bend, I could discern a glow in the distance.

Tim continued, "Australian troops placed the generator here and ran the lighting, and since then it's been under our control. If we didn't keep it padlocked, we'd probably have some of the Nationals living in here trying to claim it as their own."

We spent the next eight days exploring the underground complex, and after we concluding it was just packed earth without any shoring up timbers, Pep, Dumper, and I looked at possible ways to demolish it, and we figured out the best way to collapse the network. We trained the team towards that aim, training constantly over the following days and nights.

On day twelve in PNG, we were ready to pack up the next day and return to Lae. The last night in Lae we spent at the Lae

International Resort, courtesy of Tim and the PNG government. The next morning we returned to the air base, said good bye, and thanked Tim. We shook hands and headed onto the Herc for our flight to Vietnam via a refueling stop at the RAAF base, Butterworth in Malaysia.

We landed at Vung Tau on July 21, 1970, at zero eleven forty Golf local time. I was a month into my sixteenth year, and everything I'd endured and trained for, for the last eight months had finally brought me to Vietnam. As we trooped out of the Herc, I had a self-satisfied smile on my face. We were all geared up, carrying our kitbags. Pep and Dumper were carrying the charge cases as we made our way to the flight office at the main hangar. An hour after the Herc landed, we were standing at the chopper pads at Nui Dat, a truck waiting to take us to the SAS squadron HQ. The guys unloaded the gear, and Pep and I went into HQ to meet Major Trader Teague.

After introducing himself, Trader said, "Glad to see you got here in one piece, Pep. Tiger, good to see you again. I've made arrangements for your team to be billeted in a tent of your own. It's directly behind this building four down on the right, across from the Q tent. I think they have stuff waiting for you, but for now go and settle in. I'll have a message sent informing base you've arrived. I'll call you both back here later for a briefing." He started to turn away and let us handle our business, but he turned back and said with a wink, "Oh, the boozers not far from your tent either."

We gathered the men and headed to our tent. After a quick settle in, we trooped across the road to the Q tent, where we were given eight sets of camouflage fatigues each. They were impressive; the real acid test would be when we put them on.

The SSM told us that if we needed more or needed to change them to see him at any time. Sparks and Wires were issued a set each of the radio gear we'd need, and we were all given an SR10 set as personal low range radios. I also asked for a bushmaster combat knife, and the SSM told me he needed two days and he should be able to get one. I thanked him, and we headed back to our own tent.

Back in our tent, we were trying on the new cam gear, which fitted to a T and were lightweight and durable. After trying a set on, I decided to keep them on, as did all the others. Until I left the army, I wore cam fatigues, which begged the question: How come the yanks always have the best field gear?

Later, Pep stopped and asked me, "Why did you ask for a knife? You've already got one?"

I smiled and replied, "Of course, but I figure this would be the best place to get a bushmaster. They're exceptional, so if he gets me one, I'll take it with a smile."

"You cunning bastard," Pep replied, laughing.

Later on, as we were cleaning our weapons amid jokes and laughter, a private dressed in pressed fatigues walked into the tent and asked Pep and me to report to Trader. We looked at each other and nodded, left our rifles on our bunks, and headed to HQ.

Trader called us into his office immediately and closed the door. We sat opposite his desk and waited.

After sitting down, he said, "Ok, I've gotten word from base. Your mission window will be in three weeks, so you need to train until then. I could use you to do a couple of patrols if you wish."

We sat upright in our chairs and nodded. Trader continued. "I need a clearing patrol around Nui Dat Two, and all of my guys are out in the dark green at present. I've only got you guys available, and it needs doing in the coming week. Are you up for it?"

Pep answered for us. "Sure are, boss. We could do with some field work. What've you got in mind?"

"It's coming up on the anniversary of Long Tan, and command needs a clearing patrol around Nui Dat Two. It was established as a fire base after the battle, and every year since the VC like to probe our outer defences there; hence the clearing patrol. Since you've agreed to take it on, let's reconvene at nine tomorrow for a complete briefing."

Pep replied, "Sure thing, boss."

363

"Ok, go have some dinner and drinks, and I'll see you both here at nine,"

While we were having what some would loosely call dinner, we informed the men as we ate that it was possible we'd be doing the clearing mission that Trader required, so everything needed to be battle ready. After dinner, we went to the wet mess for after dinner drinks and talk at our table was low key and centred on the possible upcoming mission. At about twenty one hundred, I called it a night and headed back to our tent.

The next morning, Pep and I joined Trader for a full briefing. What would be required was a full three hundred and sixty degree sweep around Nui Dat Two about a thousand yards out, which would bring us close to the Long Tan village. It had been cleared of VC on numerous occasions, but they still considered it to be of strategic value, so taking a look was a secondary objective.

Trader showed us on the exploded view map of the area some of the LZ's that had been used in the past. He said, "I know that as patrol leader you'll want to do an air recce, so I've got one scheduled for nine tomorrow. You'll both be going?"

After we nodded in agreement, Trader went on to tell us that the latest Intel reports stated the area was clear, but we were to take that with a grain of salt. We discussed where the sweep would start, but it had to be confirmed with our choice of LZ.

The following morning, we were driven to the landing pads and met our pilot for the mission, a man Pep knew. He introduced us. "Tiger this is Tex Randall, the chopper pilot in the RAAF's nine squadron. Tex this is Tiger Davis."

We shook hands and said our hellos, and Tex turned to Pep. "So they still haven't retired you, you old war horse." They both laughed as I looked enquiringly at them both.

"It's a long story. We go back a ways together," Pep explained.

Tex told us there'd be three choppers going, his and two gunships behind and on either side of us. We climbed aboard, clipped our seat belts into place, and put on a set of internal com helmets each. As he warmed up the chopper to full rotation, Tex checked the coms. We each responded to his question of could we hear him, and he nodded his head and concentrated on getting us into the air.

As we flew towards our objective, I scanned the countryside we passed over. We were only flying at about a thousand feet, and something on the ground caught my eye.

Beside a couple of trees, I saw two figures in black with the round conical hats the VC wore and then a flash. I instinctively knew what it was and yelled through the com mic, "Fuck! RPG port, pull up!"

Tex pulled back so hard on the stick that the chopper flew vertically, and just as we did, the RPG flashed straight through the cabin. As I think about it, I still feel the heat of the rocket as it passed through the chopper, but Tex hadn't finished his evasion tactic yet. The chopper turned around in a full three hundred and sixty degree loop. My brain was yelling at me that this was impossible; this can't be done without falling from the sky. But as we came out of the loop and returned to horizontal, I imagined my face was as white as Pep's.

During all of this, my brain registered that the gunships had attacked the area and were hosing it with M sixty rounds. Once everything returned to normal, if that's what you'd call it, I said into the comm's, "Fuck, how did you do that? It's not supposed to be possible."

Tex replied, laughter in his voice, "Shit, Tiger, we're Aussie's mate. We can do anything! After that interruption, let's get back to what we were supposed to be doing. Thanks for the warning, though. It came at the right time; otherwise it could have been another kettle of fish."

"I'm just glad it didn't hit anything on the way through," I replied.

Pep chimed in and said, "Can we just get on with this, please?" I looked at him with a smile on my face, while he was frowning deeply.

Tex's voice came through the comm's. "What's the matter, old man? Too much excitement for you?" Pep replied with a string of four letter words, while Tex's laughter roared through the comm's.

After deciding which LZ would be the best, we continued the circuit of Nui Dat Two in the hopes that any prying eyes might think that ours was just a patrol flight. We returned to base.

Back on the pads, as the rotors were slowing down, we all hopped out. I walked over to Tex and shook his hand.

"Man that was something else. Thanks," I said to him.

"Anytime you care to learn how to fly one of these babies, come and see me," he replied with a big grin.

"I might just take you up on that one day," I answered him, and we both laughed.

"Anytime," he said and patted me on the back with his big hand.

Back at HQ, we debriefed with Trader: how we'd settled in, how the sweep would take place now that we'd decided on the LZ. We would use that same LZ, which would also be our extraction point after the sweep.

After deciding the full sweep would probably take at least four days, without the secondary observation of Long Tan, it was decided we'd complete a six to seven day patrol. Our radio sked time was set for seventeen hundred each day, and we would start the patrol in two days just after first light. We'd need a chopper at four in the morning that day. Trader would make those arrangements, and we would get what rations and ammo needed from the Q store.

As we left HQ, Pep said, "Well, how did you like your first taste of combat? You seemed pretty calm and collected as far as I could tell."

I thought about it before answering. "Apart from the heightened rush as I saw that RPG coming towards us. It sort of seemed as if things were going in slow motion for a bit, if you know what I mean."

He smiled and said, "Yeah, I know exactly what you mean. Get used to it, because you're going to see and feel it a lot during active service, but you keep cool and think fast. That's what will help you from now on. It's what I like to call survival instinct. Some of us have it, and some don't, and those who don't tend to be a liability. In time you'll be able to tell the difference. Above all else, trust your instincts. You did well, and that's why I picked you for this job," he concluded. Then with a slap on the back, he said, "Enough of this psych bullshit. Let's get a drink after we round up the lads."

The team were in the tent, lounging around or cleaning weapons, and they all looked up as we entered.

Pep said, "Ok everyone, check your ammo. We are a go in two days. I want everyone with a full measure of ammo, and some to spare. Also we'll be taking seven one-day rats. Sparks, Wires, check out those radios. From now on we all leave our pagers turned off and in our kitbags. Make sure all the SR tens are checked by Sparks and Wires. Anything you need, let Tiger or me know, but you can take care of all that after we have some lunch. Tiger and I definitely need a couple of drinks after what happened." That started the questions; they all wanted to know what had gone down, so I answered. "We'll tell you about it at lunch. Let's go."

Over lunch the boys got the whole story, and the comments we got were varied. Some of them couldn't believe what Tex had done with the chopper, and others were sure we were pulling their legs about the RPG passing right through the cabin.

Pep piped up and said, "You think this redness on my face is sunburn?" He reached over to my chin and turned my head to the right. "And do you think that's sunburn? Bloody good sun to affect us in only one spot each, you bloody stupid Sassenachs." I laughed; the angrier Pep got, the deeper he slipped into his native Scottish brogue.

The next day, we went over to the Q tent with a list of supplies that were required for the following day's mission. As I walked in, the SSM spotted me and walked over. He was carrying a knife and showed it to me. "Just the man I wanted to see. How's this meet with your approval?"

He passed the knife and scabbard that had a sharpening stone clipped into it to me, and I undid the hilt fastening and drew it out. It was eight inches long and two wide, then tapered down to a clip point. It had wire cutting teeth on the top of the blade, and I whistled as I ran my fingers down the side of the edge. I figured it was razor sharp and said, "Sarge Major, you've made my day. Fantastic. Thank you."

He smiled and said, "Is there anything else I can get you, Tiger?"

I asked for six more cam sets, which he grabbed out of the back for me. I gave him the shopping list; he looked at it, and said, "Smoke, grenades, ammo, rations, and radio batteries. Looks like your team's going out to stretch your legs. I'll put this all in a box for you and have it ready in fifteen, if you'd like to come back."

"I'll send a couple of the men over soon," I replied. I lifted the knife and gestured at him with it. "And thanks again."

When I got back to the tent, I tossed my knife to Pep and said, "Now tell me that the knife I've already got would do the job better than that one." I raised my voice. "Tag, you and Dumper go over to the Q store in ten, please. Do you and Buzz have enough medical gear?"

"Yes Corp," they replied in unison.

Pep had been looking at the knife. "It is a thing of beauty, lad. I might have to get one as well, I'll mention it the next time I see him."

We were all awake, armed, and geared to the teeth, putting on the finishing touches of cam cream to our faces by four the next morning. We were at the chopper pad five minutes later. Our pilot was at the controls, warming up the chopper, and when we were all in seated, he turned with a smile and gave us the thumbs up. Pep returned it and the Huey started to lift.

We neared the LZ just as it was becoming light. When we were a little out from it, the pilot turned so we came in with the sunrise behind us. The insertion was easy, and the chopper was back in the air two minutes later. We moved into the trees away from the LZ and adopted a stand to in a circle until full light. Everything was done by hand signal now, as this was a patrol in enemy territory.

Silence and observation was now the key to our survival. We moved slowly and carefully with fingers never too far from the trigger. We had moved approximately a mile from the LZ and were looking for a spot for an LUP. Pep decided we had enough personnel to allow us to take turns at sentry duty throughout the night, so after making contact with base, we went into stand to mode until it was full dark. Over tinned food warmed up on hexamine tablet stoves and water for coffee heated, it was decided we'd take turns of an hour at sentry duty while others slept. I decided to take the zero three hundred to four hundred.

We repeated this procedure each day we were out. The patrol was a quiet one, and we came under no fire. After observing Long Tan village for two days, we continued with the patrol. By day six we were within five hundred yards of our extraction LZ and would be in place for our extraction by thirteen hundred the next day. After relaying this to base during the radio sked, we were told to use blue smoke when the chopper could be heard.

Our pilot for the extraction was Tex, and as we climbed aboard, he yelled with a smile on his face over the rotors, "Come on, ladies, this ain't a walk in the park, you know, and I've got whores to visit."

CHAPTER 35

Well after arriving at HQ, we had to face the debriefing with the intelligence officers. Trader sat in on the session as well. When we talked about our survey of Long Tan, we were asked why we had stayed so long. Our answer was simple. We did it for two reasons: one, to gather as much Intel about what was going on in the village as we could, with regard to whether there was any extraordinary activity. Secondly, we reflected on what had happened there almost four years previously. In August, 1966, one hundred and eight men of D company 6RAR were in a fire fight that lasted three days with a VC 275 regiment that numbered two and a half thousand men. When help finally arrived, they were almost out of ammunition. Eighteen Australians were dead, twenty four wounded. The VC lost 247. It inflicted a huge defeat to the VC in what was considered one of their own stronghold areas.

During the debriefing, I had time to reflect on how lucky Pep and I had been a couple of days earlier in the chopper. If not for Tex's quick reflexes, or if the chopper had moved an inch either way, instead of the missile going through the cabin, it could just as easily have hit either side. It would have been all over red rover. Was it just sheer good luck, or were our guardian angels really looking after us that day? Whichever it was, I started to feel like a cat with one of its nine lives gone, so I was either exceptionally lucky, or if you think the other way, I still had something to do before shuffling off my mortal coil. Whichever it was, I generously accepted it.

After the debriefing session that lasted almost three hours because we were spoken to individually, we were dismissed and went for showers, food, sleep, and drinks, in that order.

When we arrived at the tent the next morning after breakfast, we spent a few hours stripping and cleaning our weapons. Just before lunch, the Staff Sergeant Major of the Q store sent a member of his staff to inform us that our explosive ordinance had arrived. Pep told him to convey to the SSM that we'd come over after lunch to check it. Over lunch, it was decided that the team would practice some field craft out near the perimeter fences during the afternoon, while Pep, Dumper, and I would be at the Q store to check the explosives. Pep left it up to me to place Tag in charge of the team's afternoon practice.

As we walked to the Q store, Pep said, "You made the right choice with Tag. We really should think about having him made up to Lance Jack."

At the Q tent, SSM Jock McDonald was waiting for us. "I've got it all out back, gents, but before we go out, I'll get you to have a look at these."

He placed a pile of cam-coloured sheets on the counter. He continued, "These are yank poncho liners, but they make light-weight, easily stored blankets, much better than our sleeping bags. Wrap one around you, they're warm as well. I can give you one for each man if you like."

"Sure Jock, we'll take 'em. Now about the bang stuff?" I inquired.

He smiled and said, "Follow me please."

We followed him out the back of the tent where a pallet stood with a tarpaulin cover over it. He grabbed the edge of the tarpaulin and whisked it off; boxes and boxes of semtex and C4. Pep pulled a list out of his pocket, and we proceeded to unload the pallet box by box, marking it off the list. Sometimes we would open one of the boxes so we could inspect the condition of the contents. We put three bricks of C4 and semtex aside and reloaded the pallet. I asked Jock how much notice he'd need to have it shifted and loaded aboard a chopper.

"Oh, I think an hour's notice would be fine. Just let me know when, what chopper number, and I'll be able to fix it."

We nodded our thanks and turned to leave with our bundle of

cam blankets. We went into our tent to get six pencil fuses, three from each case. I dumped the blankets on my bed and left with the explosives in hand.

We made our way to an unoccupied area near the far boundary with a block of semtex each. We dug a hole each, and after placing the fuses in each block, covered them with earth and moved a safe distance away and waited for the explosions. We repeated the procedure with the C4, except we shaped the charges to explode downwards before setting the fuses in. We moved away to wait again. After the charges had gone off, we were also able to note the timer accuracy. We'd brought ten minute fuses, and they all went off within five seconds of the allocated time, which was brilliant.

When we got back to the tent, there was a note pinned to the door flap asking Pep and me to report to the CO. Pep and I walked up to the HQ. Trader called us into his office as soon as he knew we were there.

"From what I can gather, you and your men have started some training for a task. That's good because your window of opportunity opens next week. I assume you'd like to take a couple of reconnaissance flights to scout for an LZ?" We both nodded in affirmation. "I know roughly where you're going, but that's all, and I'll need to give the RAAF a proposed flight area."

He left his question hanging, so Pep answered. "We're after the bunkers at Xuyen Moc boss."

Trader responded, "Oh damn good. It's about time they were taken care of. Right now, I can give some of the LZ's we've used there in the past if you'd like. There's a couple that might fit the bill for two choppers. Are you thinking of going in at dawn again?"

"We're not sure yet, boss, but we're going to need up to the minute Intel before we even try a recce," Pep replied.

"Ok, leave it with me and I'll see what I can get for you. How can I get hold of you immediately if required?"

"We've got SR10 sets, Trader," I explained.

"Good. Set one to channel sixteen. I'll call you on that if I need you, and meanwhile you go ahead with whatever practice you need. You did the right thing keeping it toward the perimeter."

When we left the HQ, I pulled my SR10 out and set it to sixteen as we walked back. In the tent the rest of the team had returned, so we filled them in on the updated window for the mission go ahead. I passed out the cam blankets for them to try, and the group consensus was to take them instead of sleeping bags.

We decided to work on fire and movement after enemy contact drills the following day, along with breaking contact during a fire fight. We ate dinner shortly after, and in the mess I spotted some of the guys that had been on the HALO course. After eating, I joined a couple of them for drinks and learned that two patrols had come in from the bush and another was due in the next day. Naturally they tried to find out what Pep and I were doing there, but I told them we were there at the request of base HQ getting some in country training. After that I wasn't asked any more questions.

That night, during my usual mental debrief before sleep, I realized how tense I was getting waiting for the go order, so I started the meditation technique that Pep had taught me. After a while, the tension left me, and I felt a lot more relaxed.

In the morning I wasn't as wound up, and over breakfast Pep said with a smile, "Works doesn't it?" I smiled and nodded in return.

After breakfast we started our practice near the perimeter; each person on the team had to take a turn doing the scouting as lead man. At different times Pep would call out, "Contact front, right, rear, or left," and we'd respond as if attacked. Pep called a halt near lunch time and we marched back to the main camp area.

As we were walking back, the radio in my pocket started squawking. When I pulled it out of my pocket, I spoke into the radio. "Go for Tiger."

Trader's voice came back, "Tiger, you and Pep, my office after lunch."

"Roger that."

I looked at Pep, and he nodded his head, looked over at Tag, and said, "Tag, you're up again this afternoon."

Tag replied "Sure thing, Pep, no worries."

Pep and I walked over to HQ after lunch, and as we entered Trader's office and closed the door, we propped our rifles against the wall.

Trader got straight to business. "All current Intel has the target listed as quiet. I've also got one of my patrols doing a recce for you, with orders to not be seen or engage any enemy. I'll have their report by tomorrow night. These are the LZ coordinates I was telling you about, and I've arranged for the two of you to go to the RAAF operations office tomorrow at ten. I'll have a driver pick you up at your tent at zero nine thirty, and he can wait to bring you back. You'll have to liaise with them as to when to do the LZ inspections, so I'll leave that in your hands. Also, I've requested to have constant Intel updates for the area so we don't get any surprises. See me when you get back tomorrow," he dismissed us abruptly.

Pep said, "Thanks, boss, we will." We left his office and headed for the tent.

Deciding that we needed a map of our target locations, I went across to the Q to find Jock. He showed me three: one of the whole country, one of the whole province, and one that showed from the Dat to the Binh Tuy province border. I elected to take all three, and while I was there, I got two of each colour smoke grenades because, honestly, you can never have too many.

When I got back to the tent, Pep and I went over the regional map from the Dat to Binh Tuy because of the larger detail. First we looked at the target coordinates for both targets. The Alpha target looked easy enough, but to get from the Alpha site to the Beta site, we'd have to go down one hillside, cross a creek, and go up another hillside. Even though the sites were only a thousand yards apart, taking into account the topographical gradient of the hillsides, we figured it would take nearly a day's travel between targets.

Next we looked for possible LUP sites near both targets. We also looked at the LZ coordinates Trader had given us and marked them. One looked to be right in the middle of both targets. This one we'd have to have a look at; if it turned out to be suitable, it would be ideal for the job. If not, we'd have to have a rethink and come up with another option.

The next morning, after we'd had breakfast, Pep and I were waiting for our driver. Tag had already taken the boys off for more practice. I'd made a change to their field packs; they were only carrying one spare set of clothes and had packed in as much weight as possible. Each man would be carrying over a hundred pounds, and Tag was to give Pep and I a report on how things went when we got back from the RAAF operations office.

At the RAAF operations office, we met Flight Lieutenant Cory Maxwell. He took us into his office, and we explained what we needed, and where, and wondered if he had another suggestions. After we showed him the sites we already had, he said, "Give me a minute." He left the office. He came back carrying a more detailed map than we had, and it was marked with different LZ's used in the area.

After we looked it over thoroughly, he said, "I think that your first choice would be ideal, depends on what it's like now. When were you thinking of doing a recce?"

"As soon as possible, and if it's suitable we'd probably go for a dawn insertion. It would be good if we could have Tex fly the recce for us," Pep answered.

I added, "And if possible have him fly the explosives for the insertion as well."

Maxwell sat back in his chair, a frown on his face, deep in thought. "Just give me a few minutes again, guys." He rose and left the room again.

He came back carrying the daily flight schedule and spread it out on his desk. He was looking at it, turned a page, then another, left it open on that page, and said, "I can give you the day after tomorrow for the recce with Tex at zero nine hundred." He looked at us, and we both nodded after exchanging a look, so he grabbed a pencil and marked it into the schedule.

"Now for the insertion. You need two, with a gunship for cover, and with a dawn insertion. I can't do it for at least a week, but we'll need to pencil it in now. How about we do that, and if there's any change, you can contact me here."

We both nodded the affirmative. I said "That's good, but I'll need to know what chopper number to have the explosive loaded into the day before."

"That won't be a problem. I can notify your HQ which one to load it into marked for your attention the morning before the lift, and I'll make sure it doesn't go anywhere that day until after your insertion the next morning."

"Brilliant, thanks," I replied.

After some general chatting, Pep and I got up, shook hands with Maxwell, and left the building. As we left the building, our driver started the rover, and we headed back to our HQ to inform Trader what had taken place.

After listening to the plan, Trader said, "Ok, so the recce day after tomorrow, and then you insert at dawn a week later. Sounds good. It's not right on but a little after your go window, which should be perfect. Still no flags coming up on any of the Intel reports. I'll pass it on to base HQ, and my patrol came in and your AO (operations area) is clear as far as they could make out. In theory, two weeks from now it won't be a thorn in our side. I love that. Ok, boys go get some lunch and rest up."

Back at the tent after lunch, we went over everything with a fine tooth comb to see if we could find any flaws. We went over the equipment list as well. It was going to be hard on all of us carrying the excess weight, but at least we'd only have it from the LZ to the LUP. We decided that instead of separating the explosives into two, we'd use the same LUP after the alpha target had been blown to see if anything unforeseen eventuated. If not, we'd stay there overnight and move on to beta target the following day. The only thing we had left to get in the way of equipment would be rat packs for the time out in the bush and any ammo that might need replenishing.

The guys returned just after sixteen hundred. They looked a little worn out, and Tag told Pep and I, "We practiced the entire day with the extra weight. It was hard going for the first hour, but after that we were able to move a little closer to our average speed, including during contact drills."

Pep answered by calling for everyone's attention. "Ok, Tag's told me you all did well out there today. No doubt Tiger's not your favourite person after what he made you carry today, but there was a reason for it. Tomorrow is going to be a rest day, because we're going to be doing a full briefing to bring everyone up to speed. Between now and tomorrow, check all your ammo and gear and see if you need anything. If so, give Tiger a list. However considering we haven't had any real incidents, everyone should have all the ammo left over from that last little stroll we took. The briefing will start at zero nine hundred."

The following morning after breakfast, Pep and I put the two maps onto the table, and after everyone had gathered, I said "Ok, I haven't any gear requests, so I'm going to assume that you've all got everything you need."

Dumper piped up. "Apart from food, Tiger." Laughter and chuckles echoed across the room.

Smiling, I replied, "Yeah, well, I'll be taking care of that detail later. I promise I won't let you starve, Dumper." More laughter.

After it died down, Pep said, "All right, let's get down to business."

The briefing took up most of the morning, and afterward I went across to the Q. Jock gave me two cartons of rat packs, each containing fifty, so we'd have a few spares. After that I went up to HQ and asked if I could ring the RAAF operations office. I spoke to Maxwell and everything was a go for the recce the next day. After hanging up, I went to see Trader in his office.

"Tiger, what can I do for you?" he asked when I was admitted into his office.

I replied, "Well, boss, Pep and I keep meaning to see someone about getting one of our men promoted to Lance Corporal. He's been running things when Pep and I aren't around and doing a damn fine job."

"Hum, who is it?"

"Tag Wilson, boss," I replied.

"If I remember correctly, he's one of your medics?" At my nod, Trader continued. "He should have been made up when he qualified."

"Yes sir. I was on the course he was on in Adelaide, and he passed with top marks," I commended Tag.

Trader nodded and said, "Ok, leave it with me. I take it you're in camp today due to your briefing?"

"Yes boss."

"Ok. I might drop by later."

"Sure boss," I replied.

We were seated at the table with coffees and smokes, chatting generally about the upcoming mission, and Pep was saying that we'd probably be able to have it all wrapped up in ten days. Trader walked in, and I spotted him enter and called "Attention." Everyone jumped up at attention.

Trader told us to sit and carry on. "I need Tag to sign this. He handed Tag a piece of paper.

Tag took it and read it. He looked up and asked, "Does this mean what I think it means, sir?"

"Yes. It does. The minute you sign that acceptance, you'll be Lance Corporal Wilson. Now sign it." Tag sign the acceptance as we all watched. Trader shook his hand and said, "Congratulations, Lance Corporal. I'll leave you to carry on. Thank you, gentlemen." With a wink to Pep and me, he left.

I smiled, shook Tag's hand, and said, "Of course you know that the newest NCO buys drinks tonight."

Tag laughed and yelled, "First drinks are on me tonight!" Everyone cheered and congratulated him with much patting on his back.

Pep pulled me aside and asked, "You had something to do with this, I take it?"

I smiled and nodded. "Well, you know, we were always going to do it. While I was at HQ I had a word with Trader about it, so now it's done."

He smiled and said, "Well done."

The next morning we met Tex and his crew at the chopper pad. After he looked at our map, he nodded his head. "Hop in and let's go have a look, see what we can stir up."

Thinking about our last recce, my eyes looked skyward for any sign of an enemy but could see nothing. As we took off, the adrenaline kicked in and I sat back to enjoy the ride. I've always liked the thrill of take-off, and in an open Huey it doesn't get much better. It took about twenty minutes of flying time to get near our intended goal, and like the rest of the crew, I kept scanning the terrain.

Tex's voice came over the intercom. "Ok, we're coming up to it. What would you like to do? Just a flyover or a good scout round?"

Pep answered loudly, "Let's go for a flyover, and if we don't draw any attention, we'll swing around for good look."

"Roger that."

After a flyover at height, Tex swung around and came in lower. Pep and I were looking at the clear LZ area and at the terrain. We were able to see both targets, and there didn't seem to be any sign of occupation. While we scouted the area, Pep and Tex were talking to each other through the intercom, discussing the merits of the LZ, if it was large enough to land both the choppers at once, which would save on time on the ground. If the explosives chopper landed a minute after we did, we'd be ready to do a quick off load as it landed, so that was the course of action we agreed upon.

Once we'd sorted that out, I asked Tex to do a flyover of the targets at treetop height. I had spotted something that didn't seem right, and I wanted to check it out. As we went over alpha, I pointed out what had drawn my attention to Pep. We stared as Tex came in low over the target, and sure enough, we spotted it: a wisp of smoke coming from one of the bunker entrances.

After the flyover, Tex moved toward our second target; this one seemed completely unoccupied, and we looked hard after what we'd found at the alpha site.

Once we had our low level flyover of both targets, Tex flew on a little while before banking into a turn that would take us back to base. During the flight back, Pep's voice crackled over the intercom. "That was a good pick up back there, well spotted. At least we know now to expect some opposition."

The rest of the trip back we talked with Tex and the crew about their thoughts in regards to the best time to insert. The general consensus was we had picked the best time to make the insertion, and again Tex offered, "The best approach would be swing away from the Dat and come in with the sunrise at our backs. Don't fly in that direction to start off with. Do a complete loop, well away from the target LZ."

Pep and I agreed this would be the best way to do it.

Back on the ground at the chopper pads, Tex said, "I'll arrange the flight so we come in on the vectors we worked out. I'll clear it with our mob. I'll see you a week from today at zero four hundred."

We shook hands, and Pep and I headed to our HQ to tell Trader the plan.

CHAPTER 36

For the next few days, we practiced our close quarter's observation techniques and ran through the techniques we would use during the operation itself. This involved having Snagger up high and covering us while we were inside the complexes. Sparks would stay on the outer perimeter with Snagger at the OP (observation point). The main assault and demolition team consisted of me as forward scout, Tag, Dumper, Pep, Buzz, and Wires, in that order.

During the first day of practice, I took Pep aside to point out something we hadn't considered. "Pep, there's something we haven't considered that we're going to need. Lighting!"

Pep replied, "Christ, of course. We'll have torches, but it wouldn't do to have a whole lot of them flashing about. Tell you what, I'll send you to have a word with Jock at the Q. Maybe we could use chemical glow sticks. You'll have to see what he has. If you can get white ones, that would be good, but if not, you know we'll be running wiring and connections. Get the best ones he can give us."

Nodding my head, I said, "I'll get on it after we break for lunch."

After lunch, while the team headed back to practice, I went to the Q and asked Jock what he could get us

"Let me see what we've got." He disappeared into the back, and came back after ten minutes carrying a box. "I can give you about a hundred that are off-white. Other than that, all I've got are green or blue."

I thought it over and replied, "I'll take eighty of the off-white. That should be more than enough."

He smiled and passed the box to me. "I thought you'd say that. Here are eighty in the box ready to go."

"You're a cunning old shit, or I'm getting too predictable," I commented.

With a laugh, he replied, "Less of the 'old' stuff, thank you. As for being predictable, no, I just know underground demo work. I wasn't always a stores walla, you know." We shared a good chuckle, and with a wave and thanks, I took the box to our tent.

I divided up the sticks, twelve for each member of the assault team, and put the surplus in with the leftover rat packs. I stored my twelve in the ammo pouches of my field gear. After that, I went up to HQ and arranged our radio sked times with the communication guys for each day we would be out in the bush.

The night before our insertion, we had a quick, last-minute briefing over coffee and smokes. Earlier in the day, an orderly from HQ had come to the tent carrying a message from F/LT Maxwell stating the number of the chopper being used to carry the explosives and confirming the zero four hundred take-off. I took the chopper number over to Jock, along with the two charge cases, and he had his team start loading the explosives to go to the chopper pad.

We were up at three getting dressed. Prior to putting our combat gear on, we passed around a tube of cam cream while finishing our coffee. After applying the face paint, we tore a strip off the cam sweat cloth roll, placed it around our necks, and tucked the excess inside our shirts. We donned our combat gear.

Looking around at the guys, I received nods of readiness, and we left the tent and walked through the camp and up to the chopper pads in silence. Tex met us on the pad and introduced the other pilot as Tom Webber and the gunship pilot as Ben Krieg. After checking the load in Tex's chopper to make sure everything was there and secure, the pilots started warming up as we climbed into our seats. We lifted off and headed towards Xuyen Moc.

The pilots veered south, and closer to target, banked to turn left towards the west so the rising sun would be behind us. As we dropped to tree height for the approach to the LZ, the gunship circled at height. Tom dropped onto the deck and we scrambled out. As he lifted off, Tex landed and we ran forward to unload. He was on the ground for two minutes before lifting off, calling out to us, "Good hunting."

Snagger and Dumper were inside the tree line guarding the LZ. I placed as much of the explosives into each pack as I could fit, and they knelt with their backs to me to load the field packs. Tag was first, and as I gave him two light thumps on the shoulder, he moved to join Snagger and Dumper. I started loading Pep's and saw Dumper making his way to the rest of us.

When I tapped Pep, he grabbed one of the charge cases and headed into the bush so Snagger could return for his load. As each man was loaded down, they headed into the jungle to join the others. Dumper and I were the last ones. I loaded him and then we switched positions. He grabbed the other charge case as we moved to join the others.

We left the LZ area without any explosives left behind within fifteen minutes of landing. Once we were together, I took the scout position as we cautiously made our way to the LUP position five hundred yards away. As we moved toward it, I was about to move across a small clearing and spotted a trip wire. I held up a fist to halt the advance and pointed it out.

Pep and Snagger followed the wire to a branch that had been strung back, and three sharpened stakes had been lashed to it. If released, it would smack into someone at chest height; a nice little rib tickler. What cheeky little bastards. Pep cut away the stakes and re-covered it with foliage, but we didn't cut the wire so it would look as if it hadn't been disturbed. We carried on moving cautiously even more than before, keeping an extra eye out for booby traps.

When we arrived at the LUP, we decided it would be perfect for what we wanted, and while Snagger went into a tree to keep a lookout after leaving his field pack, the rest of us sorted out the explosives. The stuff we would use at alpha was redistributed into mine, Pep's, Dumper's, Tag's, and Buzz's; the rest would stay at the LUP and be sorted into loads after alpha was destroyed.

Sparks laid out the aerial for the 64 set, and Pep coded out the message for him to send to HQ. The message read "Insertion complete success. LUP fine. Moving to Est OP alpha." He handed it to Sparks and nodded, and Sparks started sending it in the Morse key. After receiving a reply, which was "Roger last, usual sked," Sparks repacked the aerial and Morse key.

After having a brew up and something to eat, we left Sparks behind to look after things and the rest of us moved toward the target three hundred yards away. When we were within twenty yards and could see the complex easily, we looked for a suitable tree in which to establish the OP. We found a suitable one, and after passing up some dead branches, we had a suitable platform twelve feet up amongst the foliage of the tree that couldn't be seen from the ground below. Snagger climbed higher and reported back he'd found a perfect location to cover the assault team and keep an eye on things while we were inside.

Pep established a roster system which would have two of us watching from now to when we decided to go. The rest would stay at the LUP before moving up for their time on the OP. The roster would stay the same through the night as well. If the stand to overlapped the roster, the OP crew would wait until relieved.

A climbing line was put into place, and after that, Snagger and I elected to take the first watch. We settled down to observation and silence as the rest withdrew to the LUP.

While we watched, I saw the same wisp of smoke again, nudged Snagger, and he had a look through the scope on his rifle. We both gave the complex a complete once over with binoculars and telescope, conversing via sign language as we visually swept the complex again and again. We saw no movement of any kind, nor could we hear any noise, but every now and again we definitely saw a wisp of smoke.

When we were relieved by Tag and Dumper a couple hours later, I let them know about the smoke and to keep an eye on it. Snagger and I made our way back to the LUP. Pep was on the perimeter as we neared the LUP, and I went over and signed my report about the smoke. He nodded and signed for me to get some rest.

When I awoke about four hours later, Tag and Dumper were back and Buzz and Wires were gone. Everyone else was awake. A coffee was passed to me when I joined the others, and we had a signing conversation. Pep decided we'd all do the stand to at the OP and split up into two teams after that. Each team would watch the ways into the complex. Sparks would take one of the 64 sets with him to keep the radio sked with HQ while we were on stand to, and after two hours of observation, each team would head back to the LUP for grub up and sleep.

After the radio sked and stand to, I walked with my team, which included Tag, Wires, and Snagger, to the western entrance of the complex and watched. I had chosen this one because this was the entrance most of the smoke wisps had originated, but after two hours, nothing untoward was seen, so we moved back to the LUP.

Over dinner, it was decided that we'd have stand to at the OP again, and after eating breakfast in the morning, Wires would leave his 64 set at the LUP, the assault team would move up to the OP, and we'd make the assault from there. Wires would take my pack since I would be the forward scout during the assault. I would leave my rifle and grenade bandolier at the OP, which meant I my side arms and knife were my only weapons.

We settled down to get some sleep; I was awakened by Pep and helped him wake the others. We took only our field gear and silently made our way to the OP, where we stood to. Nothing happened as the sun rose, except Snagger saw the unexplained wisp of smoke again. At full light, we went back to the LUP to brew up for breakfast.

Once we'd eaten, Snagger and Sparks prepared to head for the OP, and the rest of us cleaned up the area and buried any rubbish. Wires took my backpack as the rest of us prepared to move to the OP. I went ahead as forward scout, and the others followed about twenty yards behind. When we reached the OP, Pep spoke to Snagger and Sparks both, with the result of NTR (nothing to report). He informed them we were going in and walked back to us. He looked at me and nodded, so I left my rifle and bandolier and proceeded into the complex.

As I moved into the tunnel entrance, I halted and waited for the others; this gave my eyes time to adjust to the dim lighting.

Pots of oil burners with wicks were producing the light. After pointing out the oil lamps, Pep nodded, and I took out my Ingram and fitted the silencer to it. Tag did the same, and I moved off with him close behind me. We checked each doorway and tunnel that branched off from the main tunnel; they were empty, and no oil pots were lit in any of them. We would throw in a chemical stick, and if there was no movement or response, we kept moving forward down the main tunnel.

I looked back; in the glow I saw the team slowly moving forward, checking the empty rooms and passages we'd thrown the glow sticks into. After Tag cleared a room on his side, he motioned to me in a gesture meaning he saw a brighter light further around the bend in the tunnel. His side of the tunnel gave him a better view of the room we were approaching; he pulled back and signed that there were two occupants. I peered around the entrance and saw one with his back toward me, but I couldn't see the other. I surmised he was on the right hand side of the room. The only course open to me was to step into the room.

Silently I moved into the room; I saw a movement to my right and fired two rounds in that direction. I shot the one in front of me in the head as he started to turn. I sensed movement behind me and whirled, ready to shoot, but it was Tag holding another slope around the neck as he brought his pistol to his side and shot. He held onto the slope until he went limp and then dragged him into the room. All three were VC.

We waited until the whole team had come into the room and getting the go ahead from Pep. We kept scouting; the three we'd killed were the only inhabitants. Pep went through their pockets, passing what he found to Wires.

After checking the room, we found only three sets of gear and some eating utensils. We assumed they had been the only occupants. After piling the bodies into a corner, it was decided to make use of the fire to brew up some coffee before we laid our charges.

As I drank my coffee, I thought how easily I'd been able to kill, without hesitation, and I wondered just how much of that was training and how much of it was in me. I was barely sixteen, and I'd killed two people without feeling anything. Pep must have seen the frown on my face because he signed the question, "Are you all right?"

I replied the same way, telling him what I'd been thinking. I left my age out, though. He signed back, "I felt the same way my first time, but you get used to it. After a while it doesn't bother you anymore. Look at it this way, if you hadn't done it, someone else would've had to. The first kill is always the worst, and you took out two in under a second. It's good work. They would just as easily have killed you." I looked at him and nodded my acceptance about what I'd done.

Once everyone had finished their smokes and coffee, we split into teams of two and started laying our charges. Tag and I started at the far entrance and worked back towards the kill room; Pep and Dumper had taken Buzz and Wires with them. Pep and Wires headed for the entrance, while Dumper and Buzz started from the kill room. When we all were back in the kill room, Pep and Dumper started from my end and checked every connection, and as we left the kill room, they checked all the connections on the way out.

Dumper pulled the wiring loop from the case and connected the cable. We were able to move a lot easier now that the explosives had been removed from our packs. After the connection was made, Dumper tied the cable around a log near the entrance and moved toward the OP, playing out the cable. We followed him, scanning the direction in which we were heading. Just short of the OP but inside the scrub line, the cable ran out, and Dumper proceeded to connect the firing switch.

I signed the question, "Are we far enough away, considering the amount of charges we placed?"

Dumper signed with a smile. "Sure we are; the charges were shaped to explode down and sideways. We probably won't hear much either, maybe the outer charges at each entrance, but that would be all."

With the firing switch connected, Dumper waited for Pep to give the signal. Pep decided to check with Snagger and Sparks, so I went over to the OP. After being told things had been quiet, I let them know we'd be blowing it shortly. I retrieved my rifle and bandolier as I headed back to Pep, nodding when I got there. Pep looked around at everyone with a smile, and nodded to Dumper. Dumper smiled and turned the switch. He had been right; we barely heard it. The ground seemed to heave and collapse while we watched. Every one of us were smiling as we made our way back to the OP. Snagger and Sparks came down with smiles as well, and we headed silently back to the LUP.

Back at the LUP, we slapped Dumper on the back in congratulations. After we'd eaten, Pep decided we still had plenty of daylight left, so we'd move to the LUP we'd use for the beta target. After distributing the remaining explosives, we set out for the next port of call.

As we moved quietly towards the LUP, we were close to a small track that ran close to the direction we were taking. Out of nowhere, three VC came onto the track. Snagger, who was tail end Charlie, was about to yell a warning when he was shot and went down. I turned at the shot. Pep was racing toward the slopes firing his pistol. He took out one of them out, and then went down. I fired an aimed shot and hit one in the head. As the third turned to run, I nailed him square in the middle of his shoulders, and he went down.

The skirmish had only lasted four to five seconds, but it had been deadly. Tag was already with Snagger, Buzz moved toward Sparks, and I went over to Pep.

I turned him over and noticed he'd been hit three times in the chest but was still alive. He tried to undo his shirt pocket, so I helped. He took out his code books, handed them to me, and said while coughing up blood, "Finish the job. It's been a joy to know you, Tiger. They're all yours now,"

He smiled and coughed once more, then died. I was close to tears. I released the clips on his backpack, shut his eyes, and folded his arms on his chest. I got up to find out what other damage had been done. Tag told me that Snagger had been shot in the shoulder blade and was out of action, and Sparks had been shot in the hip; again out of action. I decided because we were closer to the LZ than the two LUP's we would move everyone towards it and find an LUP near the LZ.

Tag took my pack and Pep's as I lifted his body across my shoulders. We set off towards the LZ. Dumper led while Wires helped Sparks and Buzz helped Snagger. Dumper found a suitable LUP within twenty yards of the LZ, and as we moved into it, I had Tag redistribute the explosives into his, mine, Dumper's, Wires', and Buzz's backpacks.

I coded a message to HQ, and another coded from the blue into the same message, knowing it would be passed on to the WA HQ.

"Alpha blown but have one KIA and two wounded badly due to enemy contact. Calling for dust-off to insertion LZ ASAP. Once dust-off completed, continuing with mission. No sked until in new area. Tiger."

The blue code to base HQ read: "Alpha gone, Pep killed, two wounded, continuing with mission, Tiger."

I had Wires prepare to break radio silence so he could send the message and wait for a reply. I helped Tag put Pep into a body bag, and gave Tag Pep's code books. I told him about the two codes and that we'd leave the radio and explosives in the LUP. We'd move closer to the LZ when we heard the chopper and cover the dust-off, but I would take Pep's body to the chopper.

Wires handed me the reply and waited for my reply. The message read: "Dust-off arranged and on way, red smoke if hot, blue otherwise, proceed if able."

I signed for Wires to send "Roger that" and then shut down. I then signed to Buzz, "Can you handle both Sparks and Snagger?" He nodded.

I then signed to them all, telling Tag to take Snagger's rifle ammo and keep it with us. We'd move to the LZ; Dumper, Tag, and Wires would cover the landing chopper and us. Once I was sure everyone understood I gave the order to move.

When we got to the LZ, I pulled a blue from my field gear, hoping I wouldn't have to change to red, as we heard the chopper. We scanned the scrub; seeing no sign of resistance anywhere, I lobbed the blue smoke. Within minutes the chopper was on the ground, and Buzz and I moved to it. The crew helped Snagger and Sparks into the chopper, and I lay Pep's body on the floor. I placed my hand on his body for a second or two, reflecting how we had become friends. With a sigh, I gave the thumbs up to the pilot; he nodded and the rotors sped up to take off.

Buzz and I ran hunched over back into the scrub and headed to the LUP. Soon the other three joined us, and I told them I'd decided to stay the night here and move to the beta LUP after breakfast in the morning.

In the morning we stood to at zero four hundred, and after full light, we had breakfast and prepared to move to the next LUP. With three men missing, the move to the LUP took nearly four hours due to the full loads we had to carry. Once there, however, it didn't take long to find an OP spot to observe the target. The OP was only ten yards away from one of the entrances; we'd each take watch for two hours at a time. I had a word with Tag, telling him he'd be taking Snagger's spot when I decided to do the assault so he better get the ammo sorted out when he got back to the LUP.

I decided to do the same as Pep had done and have the stand to at the OP. After sending the others back to the LUP, I took the first watch. I saw no sign of occupancy during my watch, and when the others joined me for the stand to, we moved back to the LUP for some dinner and sleep.

CHAPTER 37

Needless to say, I wasn't in a very good mood during dinner, and trying to sleep was impossible. I lay awake for quite some time, going over the events of the past twelve hours, wondering if I could have done anything to prevent what had happened and just how much the surviving team members trusted me. Would they follow my directions now that Pep wasn't with us? I grew angry at the thought that I hadn't been able to take my friend home; I had let him be taken away by chopper. Was I wrong in making the decision to continue with the mission?

One of Pep's rules had been to finish the job, so was I right to continue. But would it be perceived that I was just granting a dying wish? I thought, no, it's because the job has to be done; otherwise someone else would be stuck doing it. If we couldn't pull it off, it would be deemed as a failure, and I was not going to let Pep's last mission fail. If we pulled this off, his death wouldn't be meaningless. I wanted him to be remembered as being killed during a successful mission, not a failure so he wouldn't have died in vain.

After the soul searching, I realized I needed to get some sleep and used the meditation techniques to relax and finally drift off. My internal clock woke me at three. I roused the others, and we headed to the OP for stand to. When it was full light, Tag signed to me that he'd take the first watch and have a cold breakfast in the OP. I thanked him and took the rest back to the LUP, where we brewed up and had coffee with breakfast.

Dumper was on the next watch, so instead of going back to sleep or resting, he started gathering the explosives and checking the contents of the charge case. I helped him, and when we were finished, we divided the explosives into five backpacks, one of which would be carried because this time only four of us would be going in. I intended to have Buzz stay at the OP as lookout and cover us with Snagger's sniper rifle.

He left soon after, and as I waited for Tag to get back, I had another coffee, brewing one for Tag as well. Just as I finished, Tag arrived. He signed his thanks and reported that the target could just as well have been a grave site. No movement in or around the target. I nodded and told him what I was thinking about doing. After I'd finished, he signed back that it seemed like a good plan.

I thought for a minute and signed to him, "The only thing that worries me is will the guys accept me as the leader now that Pep's gone, and will they follow my commands?"

He smiled and lit us each a smoke and signed, "Tiger, we accepted you as the boss even without Pep being around, so why would we change now? Of course we'll follow your orders. We trust you, and we know it wasn't you're fault that the thing went pear shaped, so stop blaming yourself. You lost a good friend, but we only knew Pep a little while, and I think we all hope that the powers that be will let you keep leading us. Now I'm going to get some kip time."

I smiled and watched him roll himself in his cam blanket and shut his eyes.

What Tag had said put my mind at ease. Only time would tell. Meanwhile, I had a job to do, and I was going to do it come hell or high water. While I was waiting to wake Wires, I drafted up and coded the message for the radio sked at eighteen hundred, hoping I wouldn't have to change it.

"LUP at beta loc, NTR from OP after eighteen hours, assault tomorrow am, Tiger."

After coding the message, I cleaned my Ingram and added three more rounds to the magazine so it was fully loaded again. I cleaned my rifle, again replacing the missing two rounds from the magazine. I woke Wires for his OP watch, and when Dumper returned, I asked if he could stay awake long enough to wake Buzz for his shift because I needed some shut eye. He said he was planning to brew up and have some lunch before nodding off anyway and told me to hit the hay.

I was wakened by Tag at sixteen hundred for my watch at the OP. After rolling out of my cam blanket and collecting my gear, I was ready to go up to the OP. Before going, I told Tag to bring the boys up for stand to and to make sure that Wires brought the 64 set for the sked. I moved off to the OP.

While I was at the OP, I pulled a leftover can of bully beef and beans from the rat pack in my ammo pouch and ate it cold. I finished it off with a teeth-breaking chocolate bar. When the team joined me for the stand to, I passed the message to go out on the sked to Wires, who had finished laying out the aerial and was getting ready to fire up when the time for our sked was close. I had decided during my watch that we were wasting time.

I spoke aloud to the team. "I don't know about you guys, but I'm sick of this silence bullshit. After being here for the eighteen hours without spotting or hearing anyone in the neighbourhood, let's see if this draws any attention. If not, if we keep it down to a dull roar, we can get some work done faster. Wires send now. We'll keep watch."

There were smiles all around as we faced outward, scanning for any opposition. Wires had received a reply; after decoding it, he read it to us.

"Acknowledged, assume acting SGT position, your call on op, will await extraction call, Trader."

I then coded the reply message: "Roger, understood" and passed it to Wires.

As full dark descended without any mishap, I said, "Ok that's it. Let's get back and have some dinner and I'll tell you what I've figured out."

Back at the LUP, as we brewed coffee and warmed rat pack tins, I said, "Ok, listen up guys. First up, the word from HQ is I'm now acting SGT." Murmurs of congrats and good went around. I continued, "Buzz, apart from me, you're the highest qualified marksman, so tomorrow you'll have Snagger's rifle and ammo and remain at the OP as lookout and sniper to cover us. Because I'm an explosives expert, I have to be on the assault team. I'll also act as scout. Everyone else will be on the assault team positions: me, Tag, Wires, and Dumper as tail end Charlie. Now, how we worked last time won't work here, so we'll move in as a group and lay charges as we go. When we get to the end, we'll make all the connections as we retreat. As before, I'll give the final word on the go, and after waiting for any reaction, we'll pull back to here, clean up, and make our way to the LZ for extraction. With a bit of luck, we'll be back in the Dat by this time tomorrow. Any questions?"

Dumper put his hand up, and after my acknowledgment, asked, "Does that mean you're buying tomorrow night, Sarge?"

We all chuckled, and I replied, "Yeah, I guess it does. Now, when we move from here at stand to, it's the same as before. We take only the explosives. Leave the radio, Wires. After the blow, as I said, we move back here. Everyone clear?" There were nods of agreement all around, and we settled back to eat and sleep.

During my nightly mental debrief, I thought about the plan for the next day, and even though it was off the cuff, so to speak, that's why the SRT had been formed in the first place. It gave a lot more control to those on the ground so we could adjust and adapt to changing situations as they arose. What I had proposed to the remnants of the team seemed like the best choice to bring about a successful outcome, and I think I had inadvertently come across a new style of leadership.

Where I had proposed an idea and given the team a chance to voice any concerns or give a better alternative, I suppose that when push came to shove it would be interesting to see if they would follow my lead if they disagreed with my proposal. I went through the mental exercise of preparing for the next day before drifting into sleep.

My internal clock woke me at three, and I slowly began preparing for the day prior to waking the others. As the coffee brewed, I woke them one by one. By the time everyone had finished a hot cuppa, it was time to head to the OP and stand to.

Buzz whispered in my ear after stand to, "I'll stay at the OP and have a cold breakfast while I keep watch over the target and the gear."

I thanked him and led the others off to have breakfast and prepare. After we'd all had breakfast, coffee, and smokes, it was time to move. We made our way to the OP, and Buzz signaled NTR as we got the gear. I gave Buzz the thumbs up, and we started into the complex.

I left my rifle at the OP, like last time, and had my Ingram in my right hand, still set on single shot. I approached the tunnel entrance; it was different from last time. There were no oil lamps glowing, so it was possible we were the only one's there. I grabbed a glow stick, snapped it, and shook it into life. I threw it as far down the tunnel as I could.

In the soft glow I was able to make out a couple of branches off the main tunnel, and as the others joined me, I signed for two on each side. I snapped another glow stick into life, holding it out to my left. As we came to a branch off or doorway, we'd throw in a stick and move into it; usually it was only rooms, so we started laying the explosive charges and moved on.

Eventually we reached the other entrance and started connecting the wiring to the charges we'd set. As we came to the last connection at the exit, I told Dumper, "Take everything you need out of the case because I'm going to put this case into one of the rooms and rig it to destroy everything."

He nodded and grabbed the firing switch and the roll of firing cable out of the case. "All yours."

I put a small amount of C4 into and stuck a half hour pencil fuse into the C4, closed the case, and took it into the first room and left it there. As we left, Dumper made sure the firing cable wouldn't come apart and unrolled it all the way to the OP.

After connecting the firing switch, he looked at me and said, "This one is yours; do you want to be the one to blow it?" I nodded. He then stood up and moved out of the way. "It's ready."

I looked around and asked, "Everyone ready?" I received nods of agreement from them all. "Fire in the hole."

I turned the switch; again there was no real noise of an explosion, just the same upheaval and collapsing movement. Say goodbye to another bunker complex, Charlie!

We cleaned the OP area so there were no signs of usage. We moved back to the LUP, and after doing the same with it, I led the team back to the alpha LUP. Once we got there, everyone checked the area and found it clear of any enemy.

"Ok, someone make me a coffee while I code up the extraction call. We'll be here overnight, but hopefully we can be lifted out early," I whispered to the group, who smiled at the idea of extraction.

While camp was being established, I coded the message for Wires to put out at the sked time. "Beta gone, returned to alpha LUP, will wait for extraction tomorrow am, Tiger."

The message for base HQ read, "Mission completed, both targets blown, returning to Dat HQ after extraction, request all team members be risen one rank, Tiger."

I had Wires send the message at our sked time while the rest of us were standing to. He passed the reply to me, and I quickly decoded it. "Same LZ zero eight thirty, blue smoke, all report HQ on arrival, congratulations on job well done, Trader."

I nodded to Wires to send "Roger that."

At full dark we returned to the LUP proper to brew up and have dinner. As we were having dinner, I let the guys know we were returning to the Dat in the morning. I told them the extraction time and what smoke, and I told them we have to report to HQ when we returned.

After stand to and breakfast the next morning, we moved to the LUP we'd found closer to the LZ. We moved towards the LZ as our extraction time neared. We were just inside the tree line as I heard the chopper. I threw the blue smoke, and the Huey flew overhead and dropped into the middle of the LZ. We ran to it and boarded.

Tex yelled from the pilot's seat, "Tiger! Should have known it would be your mob that got me up before breakfast!"

Everyone had smiles on their faces as we lifted off, and Tex banked in the direction of the Dat. We arrived on the pads twenty minutes later.

Once the rotors had wound down, we disembarked, and as I left the chopper, I gripped Tex on the shoulder and shook his hand.

"Too bad about Pep," he said. I could feel the pained look on my face. Tex continued, attempting to give some comfort. "But the old bugger would have liked to go out that way."

I nodded and left the chopper. The men and I marched to HQ in single file, me in front and Tag bringing up the rear. When we reached HQ, Trader was waiting for us with three other officers.

"We'll use the end office for the debriefing, but we want to speak to you one at a time. The rest of you sit and relax. I'll have coffee brought out for you. Smoke if you wish." He looked at Dumper. "Dumper, we'll start with you."

We lazed around and smoked as we waited our turn. As each member finished, they returned to the group. Buzz was called after Dumper came out.

Dumper told us, "Those other three are intelligence and quizzed me on terrain and any enemy we saw. Watch out, Sarge. They were asking about your leadership."

I replied "Christ. Well, I hope you didn't say anything about us breaking SOP's."

"Shit no, boss. I'm not stupid. I want to stay with this team, especially if you're the boss," Dumper answered, and I smiled in thanks.

As Tag went in, it became obvious I was going to be last, so I said to the guys, "You lot may as well head to the tent and have showers. I can smell you from here."

They all laughed, and Wires' commented, "Yeah, you smell pretty good, too, boss."

We laughed loudly and I replied, "Yeah yeah. Go get yourselves cleaned up and relax. It looks as if I'll be here awhile. I'll send Tag down when he comes out." They trooped off in the direction of the tent, laughing, relaxing with every step.

When Tag came out, I told him to head back to the tent and get cleaned up. He replied out of the corner of his mouth softly, "Stay cool. They'll hit you with why we didn't pull out." I nodded my thanks and walked into the office.

Inside the office, I took off my backpack and reached into it. I passed across all the documents we'd collected. "These are the documents we took off the three slopes in the alpha site, and these were collected off the three we came into contact with that resulted in SGT Salter being killed."

Leaving the papers where I'd placed them, they asked for a mission report that concerned terrain and enemy sighted. I gave them a blow by blow account of the whole mission. When I finished, one of them said, "Very accurate account of your movements. Well done. Now tell me how you are able recall every detail?"

"That's an easy one, sir. I have an eye for detail and a near photographic memory. Elephants love me."

They all laughed at my reply, but one of them was frowning. "That's not possible, sergeant."

Trader interjected, "Perhaps I can prove Sergeant Davis' claim, gentlemen." He wrote something on three pieces of paper out of his notebook, passing each to the other officers present. He faced me and asked, "What colour shirt was I wearing when I returned from leave on the HALO course, Tiger?"

Without hesitation, I replied, "You weren't wearing a shirt, sir. It was a blue Malibu T-shirt with a picture of a surfer on a wave on the front."

The officers looked at the pieces of paper he had written on, and the doubting Thomas said, "Well, you're definitely a find. Correct. Well done."

The other two were impressed as well, if the looks on their faces were anything to go on.

The doubting Thomas continued, "I only have one other question. Why didn't you call off the mission when one of the team members was killed and two others severely wounded?"

I looked at him coldly and lowered my voice to what others who knew me would recognize as my deadly tone. Menacingly, I replied, "To answer that, sir, the team had been assigned a mission and all the parameters thereof. Half a mission is NOT a successful outcome. I considered my options and had enough personnel to complete the mission assigned to our team. As far as I'm concerned, sir, I made the mistake of calling in a dust-off. That cost us a day, but I decided the two wounded men needed to be airlifted so they had a chance of survival. Secondly, SGT Salter was my friend, but he was gone and the decisions were then mine to make. Did I hate what happened? Yes. I would have preferred no one get hurt, but that only happens in fairy tales. We operate in the real world. So to go back to what you asked, I fulfilled the mission the team was given. Do I regret that decision? No. Did I like making that decision? Again, no. Would I make that decision again? Yes."

I think at one point during my answer, Trader was thinking that I was likely to reach across the table and choke the shit out of the smug bastard because he physically relaxed when I stopped talking.

One of the others said, "Yes, well, thank you for your candour in answering our questions, Sergeant Davis. I trust all of this will be in your mission report when you submit it."

That was a dismissal if I'd heard one, so I glanced at Trader, who nodded. I stood, came to attention, turned, and marched from the room. Outside, I gripped the railing so hard I thought it might crumble under my grip.

As I lit a smoke to calm the fury that had built up, Trader came out of the office. "Go get cleaned up, Tiger, and come up when you're ready. I'll find you a space to write up the mission report. It can wait until tomorrow if you wish, but it's better to get it down while it's fresh. I'll leave it for you to decide. Go. I'll see you later."

I nodded and headed down to the tent. The boys were waiting for me to see what happened, so I held out both arms and said with a smile, "Well, I'm still here." They laughed and cheered. "But because of some comments I've been getting, I'm going to get a shower and clean up. See you in a bit, you bunch of misfits."

A half an hour later I returned to the tent to put on fresh fatigues. The men were still there, and Tag asked, "You ready for lunch, Sarge?" I smiled and nodded, and we all trooped off to get some food.

During lunch, I told them I had to go up to HQ and write up the mission report, but they had the rest of the day off to spend how they wanted. I gave them a hint that getting the weapons and gear cleaned would be a good idea if they had some loose time. "If any of you come across a base laundry, let me know so I can have some fatigues washed. Some of you have been here before, so you know if there is one." I looked at the remnants of my dinner and pushed it aside. "All this good stuff after our healthy rat packs is bad for you. I'll see you later."

They were full of laughs and good advice as I left them to it. I went back and left my dirty fatigues at the end of my bed, knowing my washing would be taken care of, and headed to HQ to write up my report. When I returned four hours later, my washing was on my bed all washed and pressed.

I said as Tag passed a coffee, "Ok, who do I owe and how much?"

Dumper piped up. "That'd be me, Sarge, and it was bloody expensive. It cost a bloody dollar. The local slopes are ripping us off big time."

I laughed. "Well, I'll do better than that. I'll pay for your first drink in the mess tonight. Deal?"

"You're on, boss," he replied with a smile.

It hadn't taken long for word to get around that we were back and what we'd been up to. In the mess that night, all the SAS members in camp had put tables together, taking up a fair bit of room and insisted we join them, which we did. As usual, they wanted details, which the guys provided.

After a couple beers, it was my turn to share a round. I came back with the drinks and handed them out. I remained standing and put two glasses of single malt scotch, each with a single cube of ice, on the table.

"Gentlemen, a toast. To a man who was my friend and colleague to all that are here and a damn fine soldier. To SGT Pep Salter."

Everyone stood and raised their drinks. "To Pep Salter."

I emptied my scotch and upturned Pep's, and as the liquid seeped onto the table, we bowed our heads for a minute in remembrance.

The next morning, Trader came into the tent carrying a whole lot of paperwork. Tag was the first see him and called, "Attention."

"As you were. Everyone come to the table, please."

Some of us had been stripping and cleaning weapons, so we left the pieces on our beds and walked to the table.

"Ah good, getting ready for your next one. Good, good." Trader laughed and we joined him. "My congratulations on a job well done, guys. Now, acting Sergeant Davis, your promotion has been ratified by HQ, so you're now Sergeant Davis. Please sign your acceptance." He passed me a sheet, which I signed.

"Congratulations. Now then, due to a certain team leader's insistence, everyone in SRT One has been promoted one rank. Tag, you're now a full corporal and Tiger's 2IC. The rest of you are now lance corporals. Congratulations all. Please sign your acceptances."

Cheering and laughter broke out, and above the din I said, "Well Tag, looks like you and I might get pretty pissed tonight with all these new NCO's buying drinks." Trader joined in the laughter.

CHAPTER 38

Over the next few days we rested. As I was going through our leftover supplies we still had stored in the tent just to see what we had left, instead of returning any, I decided to keep the left over rat packs and glow sticks. The ammo was distributed to the boys, except for a couple boxes of 308 rounds for Snagger's rifle and a box of forty five rounds that Pep had put aside. Considering my colt was the same calibre, I kept them. Snagger's rifle and ammo I put aside to return to the Q. Then I started the job I really didn't want to face but knew had to be done.

Tag saw what I was up to and asked, "Do you need a hand clearing Pep's gear?"

Looking at Pep's bed, I nodded, and we started by taking everything out of his kit bag. Apart from uniforms, shaving gear, and gym gear, there was a white singlet with a rising sun on it. In Japanese characters down the left side, barely legible unless you looked closely were the words, "Fuck Off."

I smiled as I recalled seeing him in it several times, and if he was annoyed with someone, he would say, "Read the words."

Tag held it up and said, "What does this say?"

I laughed and replied, "Look at it closely." He did and chuckled.

I put the singlet aside and took out his pager and altimeter. The rest we repacked into his kit bag. I kept the singlet, and I still have it, the pager, and altimeter. I would return these to Mark when we got back home. We did the same with Sparks' and Snaggers gear. I kept the pagers and altimeters and put them in a separate bag to go back with us to give to Mark.

After it was done, Tag, Dumper, and I took the kitbags, rifle and ammo, and SR10 sets back to the Q tent across the road. Jock saw us and came over.

"These all need to be shipped back to base. What you do with the SR10 sets and the rifle and ammo is up to you. These guys will not be coming back," I said to him.

Jock replied, "Yeah, Tiger, sorry about Pep. You two were close."

I sighed and nodded. "Yeah, so am I."

"Is there anything else I can do for you while you're here?"

Tag answered him. "Yes, Sarge Major. Have you got any more of those cam blankets?"

Jock replied with a grin. "Sure, heaps, and I've also got half a dozen of the wet weather ponchos they tie into, if there any good to you?"

"Christ, you're a good salesman, Jock. We'll take the lot," I replied.

"I'll get them for you. Hang five."

He came back with the ponchos and an armload of the cam blankets. Tag and Dumper grabbed them and took them back to our tent. I needed a further word with Jock.

"What happens to Pep's stuff, when it gets back?"

He replied, "Well, what usually happens is that all his issue gear goes back to the store, but any personal items go to his next of kin. I would assume that his quarters back in Aus have already been cleared, and the same thing happens to that stuff. They'll wait til his gear from here arrives before shipping it. It'll go to the people he named in his will, if he made one; otherwise it'll go to his immediate family."

Nodding, I said, "Good, thanks for the info. No doubt I'll catch you later."

After I returned to the tent, Tag informed me that an orderly from HQ had been down; I was to report to the CO. After thanking him, I headed up to HQ, and asked to see Trader. I was ushered into his office almost immediately.

"Ah Tiger, just the man I want to see. I've had word from Base HQ. At present they'd like you to stay under my command until next month when the first two troops of mine return to Aus for leave. So I have a job for you. I need an observation and ambush patrol done up here in the May Taos right on the Binh Tuy border with Long Khanh. You'll be operating close to Nui May Tao, but under no circumstances should you enter the village. It may be used as a staging point for the local VC. The little buggers are getting used to our tactics, so expect to get jumped soon after insertion. If the force you face is too much, pull out ASAP; otherwise continue with the job. Don't let that interfere with any ambushes. If you have the opportunity, kill and grab Intel and get out of the area until things settle down, then have another crack."

"LZ's, boss?"

Trader replied, "I can give you a couple to look at, but the recce will have to be done by chopper. The bastards see a fixed wing, they've learned we're going to be in the area soon after. I'll arrange that. Are you up to a recce tomorrow?"

I nodded my head. "Yes boss."

"Good man," he replied.

When I reached the tent, everyone looked at me, and I nodded. "Yep, we've got a job on."

That stirred everyone into questions, so I informed them I'd be doing a recce the next day and after that, I didn't want to waste any time before the insertion. "Apparently the Cong are getting used to our methods, so it could be a hairy one. It's going to involve ambushes, so Tag, get some claymores while I'm doing the recce."

"Copy that, boss."

The following morning I was at the chopper pad at zero ten hundred. I saw Tex and asked, "Don't you ever sleep?"

"Plenty of time for that when I'm toes up. No, your recce came up in the daily flight tasks, and I've decided where you go there's usually action. I put my hand up for the job."

I laughed and replied, "Sometimes, Tex, I think you have a death wish."

"Go on, get in and let's go perving." We both got into the chopper laughing.

We took some ground fire near the first LZ, but the second one seemed like the best option because the ground looked even and springy, which meant we could jump without the chopper actually touching down if needed. Plus if we did get into a fire fight on insertion, it could get in quick to lift us out again. Having made the decision, I told Tex, "I've seen enough, let's go home."

Back at base, after seeing Trader and telling him what I'd worked out, the patrol was arranged for a zero ten hundred insertion the next day. If we were lucky, it would be for only five days.

After getting the go ahead, I briefed the men while we split up the supplies in preparation. Tag managed to get a dozen claymores, which we split up into our gear, and Wires went to the communication unit to arrange sked times and frequencies to be used.

At ten the next morning we were coming up on the LZ. As the chopper lowered, I was standing on the skid and jumped the remaining two feet, as did all the guys. I was right in assuming that the ground was springy; it absorbed the shock of jumping. The chopper flew off but would hover for twenty minutes about five k's away in case we needed to get out in a hurry.

We moved into the jungle as soon as we cleared the LZ. We came across a natural depression in the ground a hundred yards into the jungle and used it as temporary LUP while I read the map to find our exact position. According to the map, we were about two or three hundred yards from a trail leading to Nui May Tao, so we would scout for it and lay off one side to see what sort of traffic used it. If it was enemy, then I'd consider an ambush site.

We started moving slowly through the vines and trees. Tag scouted ahead, and at one point we came up on him trying to extricate himself from the thorny clinging bush. The best part about moving in deep jungle is the ground is usually covered with damp, dead leaves, so any sound was minimal.

Tag spotted the trail, if you could call it that, and it was only wide enough to allow two people to move side by side. It was well used, and as we got near it, we spotted three VC moving along it. We slowly sank to the ground, and five minutes later seven more moved along the track. Only three of them had weapons.

It was easy to distinguish the enemy as opposed to local villagers because of the black pyjama pants they wore. Signing to Tag to stay put, I moved away looking for a place to use as an LUP and found a perfect depression big enough to shelter our presence about two hundred yards from the track on the side of a small hummock. I re-joined the team, and we looked slowly for an ambush point.

Within seventy yards of the Binh Tuy border, we found a perfect spot that allowed us to get right up beside the track. Because of the uphill rise on the other side of the track, the enemy would be boxed in. After making our plans to rig some of the claymores that night, we headed back towards where we'd found the track. I spotted a lone VC coming towards us along the track, and he was carrying a dispatch satchel. This was too good to pass up. Dumper and I walked to the bend in the track; I signed to him to trip the VC up. We readied ourselves.

Dumper sprang and tackled the courier around the legs, which made him fall onto our side of the track. I grabbed his mouth to stifle any cry as I slit his throat and dragged the body into the undergrowth. Dumper grabbed the satchel from his body while I searched his pockets. We made sure he couldn't be seen by any passer-by, moved back to the guys, and withdrew to the LUP.

As Tag passed me a coffee, I was wiped the blood off my knife and hand with a sweat rag and water from my canteen. I looked at the contents of the satchel; it was a goldmine, full of documents and maps. I put it all in his pockets, except the smokes, which I passed around to the guys, into a plastic bag and put them in the satchel. We made our plans to rig the ambush site after stand to and settled down for some sleep.

That night we rigged the ambush site with four claymores, and after hiding them well from any prying eyes, we marked spots where we would position ourselves to cut down anyone that survived the claymores. We returned to the LUP. After stand to the next morning, we had breakfast and headed to our ambush site to wait for a suitable target.

After we watched a few villagers pass by, Tag signaled that a large group of VC were coming down the trail. Dumper picked up the firing switch. As the main body entered the kill zone, I tapped Dumper. He hit the switch, and before the noise of the explosion finished, we fired at them. One survivor tried to limp in the direction of the village, but I shot him in the back. He must have lived long enough to crawl off because we never found his body. The men quickly searched and took anything worth something off the dead and wounded. The wounded were dispatched, and as we were about to withdraw, we were spotted by some VC coming from the village. We engaged in a fire fight. I killed one and maybe another, and Buzz got one as we withdrew into the jungle.

There were more VC than we'd originally assumed because for the next two hours we had to fire and withdraw; it became a game of dodgem. Every time we thought we'd shaken them, a shot would whizz by. We couldn't break contact with the enemy. We were close to the first LUP we'd found, so I decided we needed to bug out. But for that we'd need help, so I led the patrol to the LUP. We'd fort up there.

As soon as we reached it, Wires knew to send out a call for help. "Done. They're on the way."

I told Tag we'd have to get to the LZ, so he led the way. Just as we neared the LZ, I saw a flash of light and had the sensation of flying before being slammed up against something with my back.

I awoke to the sound of a lot of gunfire, but I couldn't open my eyes. My mind registered where my team were by the sound of their guns, and I could also determine a lot of AK47 fire, the slopes weapon of choice. My rifle was still in my hand, so I started firing towards the AK47 fire.

I heard Tag's voice. "Tiger, what's your condition?"

"Alive, but I can't see," I yelled over the sound of gunfire.

"Ok hang on; Buzz is trying to get to you. The choppers are in SR range and almost here. This is a real hot one."

Two gunships started tearing up the jungle with machine-gun

fire just in front of my position, but Buzz was beside me. "Boss, all I can do right now is get you closer to the LZ and get you on the chopper. Then we'll look at you. I'll guide you if you can run."

"Let's get to it," I replied, gritting my teeth against the pain.

He helped me up and said, "Ready? Let's go." I ran beside him, trusting his lead, and then I was pulled into the chopper. I heard Dumper yell go and I felt the chopper lift.

My head was on someone's legs, and I could feel something being poured on my face and wiping around my eyes. After a couple of times, I slowly started to see daylight and grinned.

Tag told me, "Don't do that boss, you look evil."

My sight was slowly returning as he wiped my eyes, and I said, "Boy am I glad to see you. What happened?"

"They hit us with a mortar and you went flying. I thought you were dead until you started firing. You've taken some shrapnel above your eye and near the top of your head that'll need stitching. You'll have a headache for a while. The blood you lost caked over your eyes. That's why you couldn't see."

"Yeah I thought I'd been blinded. My eyes wouldn't open," I replied.

When we arrived back at the chopper pads, Buzz took me to the hospital tent. One of the doctors came over and said, "We'll just put you under for a little while to take the shrapnel out. It won't take too long."

"No, you're not putting me out. Just give me a local and get it done," I ordered.

After a bit of argument, he finally agreed. "All right, but it's going to hurt quite a lot."

"Let's get it done, doc," I replied.

After being stitched and bandaged up, Buzz and I headed to the debriefing office and joined the rest of the team. There were cheers as I walked in. Trader had a smile on his face. "That case you brought back is a goldmine. You really got lucky with that."

"Thanks, boss," I replied.

Our next mission involved going back into the May Taos, only this time it was ten kilometres to the west of Nui May Tao in the mountainous terrain of the Long Khanh province and a ten day patrol. Due to the denseness of the jungle, and the mountainous terrain, we inserted by rappelling from the chopper skids, and would eventually make our way to a previously chosen LZ for extraction.

During this patrol we had better results. We setup three ambushes, which resulted in our body count rising and a wealth of paperwork for the intelligence section. We had numerous contact fire fights, but only during two were we really outnumbered. Luckily, we were successfully able to withdraw from the contacts. However, the scariest moment of the patrol was during our third day while climbing up a ridge. I was the forward scout that morning, and as I moved silently forward in a crouched position, I came face to face not more than five feet apart with a frigging white tiger. To tell you the truth, I don't know which of us got the bigger shock, it or me. It snarled and I thought "Uh oh" as I braced for the charge I expected.

The six hundred pound beast looked at me once more before padding downhill with only one backward glance, much to my sigh of relief. I shook my head as my heart started beating again, and I thought to myself, "No one's going to believe that."

Thankfully Tag later informed me that he and Dumper had seen the incident and had their rifles aimed and ready to shoot if it charged. The tiger incident became a talking point in the mess for weeks, and naturally I had to endure comments like, "Did you change your pants afterwards?"

After that patrol, we completed two more ten day patrols to the east near the coast in Binh Tuy province. By the time those were finished, the SRT team had racked up a total of thirty-seven enemies dead, and eight possibles, three possibles credited to me. While resting during the first week of November, I was summoned to Trader's office.

I walked to HQ and was taken into Trader's office by an orderly as soon as I arrived. Trader asked me to shut the door before I sat opposite him.

"What have you got, boss?" I was expecting to be assigned another patrol.

He replied with a laugh. "Surely I'm not that obvious?"

"Well, these days boss, it seems each time I'm called in we're assigned another patrol."

He laughed again and replied, "Yeah, I get your point, but this time it's some good news for you and your team. You're going home next week." I sat up and listened more closely as he continued. "Two of my advance troops will be rotated back next week, and your team will go with them. You'll be trucked down to Vung Tau to board the Herc bringing in the advance troops of two squadrons, and while it's refueling, you'll board the flight home."

"The boys are going to love this news," I told him.

"On a personal note, I'd like to give you the heads up that I've recommended you and everyone on your team for the Vietnam Campaign Medal, which automatically means you receive the Vietnam Medal as well. I will tell you that the boss back in Australia has also recommended you be awarded the Distinguished Conduct Medal for your exploits in May Taos, so please act surprised when they let you know. I haven't told you anything, ok?"

I was speechless about receiving awards just for doing my job. Trader reached across to shake hands and offer his congratulations. I stood before shaking his hand and said, "Thank you, sir. I don't know what to say."

Trader laughed. "Say nothing. You and your men deserve it. Now get out of here and go tell them the good news I'll give you dates and times as your departure gets nearer. Oh, and Tiger, thank you and good luck. By the way, I don't think you'll get away with your new rank pins at home; try it by all means, but be ready to change back to the traditional method." He was smiling as he said this.

"Thanks boss. Catch ya later," I replied, grinning at him.

What Trader had been referring to was the rank insignia that

I and the rest of the team had gotten used to. After being in close contact with some of the yank units, I had asked Jock to get six sets of eight US rank pins for sergeants, corporals, and lance corporals (the yank equivalent being PFC). We had worn them on our fatigue shirt collar lapels instead of the traditional sewn stripes. When questioned about this by Trader, the merit of my answer had swayed him to allow it. I explained that it made it difficult for the enemy to distinguish who led the patrol, and thus confused them about who to target as the leader. They'd worked out that if they killed the leadership, the rest would be easy prey.

I was smiling as I left HQ and walked to the tent. The guys had started cleaning their weapons and making up ammo requirements in anticipation of the coming briefing.

I burst out laughing when I saw them working. "What the hell are you doing?"

Tag answered with a quizzical look on his face. "Getting things in order before the next op."

"Well, there's not going to be a next op, guys. We're going home!"

There was a momentary stunned silence as I smilingly nodded my head. The reaction of stunned silence passed as my news dawned on them, and cheers and hugs were exchanged.

Over the excited din, I called, "Somebody get me a coffee and I'll tell you everything. You haven't heard the best part yet." The noise ceased immediately; they moved to the table to hear what I had to say, except Buzz, who passed me a coffee and sat down. "Do you want the good news first or the bad news first?"

No one responded, so I continued. "Ok, the rest of the good news: everyone has been recommended for the Vietnam Campaign Medal, which automatically comes with the Vietnam Medal" After the surprised gasps and smiles, I continued. "And now for the bad news: we won't be leaving until next week, so you've got a week to sort out what shit you want to take home. An even better bit of good news: it's my shout in the boozer tonight as a thank you from me to each and every one of you for a job well done. I hope

411

you will stay with the team, if you get the choice, when we get back home."

Tag reached out and shook my hand. "Thanks, Sarge, and I for one will be staying on the team." I nodded a thank you and looked around; everyone was nodding their heads in affirmation of staying on the team.

That night we all got well and truly hammered in the mess as we celebrated the decorations, the going home, and the main one, that we were alive and had been combat proven as a tight knit team.

CHAPTER 39

I suppose it was just as well we didn't have anything much to do the next day because we were suffering massive hangovers from about five hours of heavy drinking the previous night. The only dampener on our celebrations was when one of the eight RAR soldiers, who'd been waiting at the bar as I was buying a round, who had to wait longer when I changed my mind on drinks a couple of times, decided to comment to his buddies about waiting because of me. He called me a drunken, jumped-up short-ass with more money than brains. Wires was walking by and heard the comment and took exception to it. He grabbed the guy and smacked him in the mouth. Tag saw what was happening and quickly moved to intervene. I bought a round for them to patch things up.

We were a sad and sorry sight the next morning at breakfast, and things didn't improve much when lunch time rolled around. Considering all that, the day was pretty much a write off.

Over the next couple of days we sorted our going home stuff and decided to hold onto the ponchos that had liners in them. We each kept two of the cam blanket/liners as well. To fit all the better quality accumulated stuff, I had to leave out four sets of my green fatigues. Such a pity. I put them aside to go over to the Q. I also ditched the pair of boots I'd worn the most while in country.

Two days later, Trader informed me that we'd be leaving at zero nine hundred the following day with the truck convoy he'd arranged for his one squadron troops. The morning of departure, we had a big breakfast and crammed some travelling food into our ammo pouches. The six trucks were parked outside the HQ. I scanned the faces of the men returning to Aus and recognized a lot of them from my early days with the regiment. There were only a few still wearing the regular issue green fatigues; most of us were wearing the US cam fatigues and in full combat gear, except for our regimental berets instead of the cam bush hats.

Trader was saying good bye to his men and came over to us to shake our hands. "It was a pleasure having you around, and I hope we meet again back at base in Western Australia."

My first tour of Vietnam ended at golf zero sixteen hundred as the Herc lifted off on the journey home. I was dozing when we landed at Butterworth to refuel; we flew into Tindal at Katherine in time for breakfast at the mess while the Herc was refueled. We arrived in Western Australia at Pearce at thirteen thirty hundred hotel local time and at Swanbourne at fourteen hundred.

We were paraded and met and welcomed back by the boss, LT. Colonel Clarke, and Mark Ryan, the teams CO. After the arrival parade, we were dismissed, but the team and I were taken to the boss's office in HQ.

We stood at attention in front of the boss' desk. "I would like to take the time to congratulate you all on a job well done despite losing team members. You're each receiving the Vietnam Campaign Medal, and Sergeant Davis is also being awarded the Distinguished Conduct Medal. Now as to your rank insignia, I've been appraised by Major Teague of your reason for you wearing them, and I whole heartedly agree with him. You're a special team and exceptions can be made; therefore, I'm giving permission for you to continue wearing them only on your field gear. Dress uniform will comply with regulation rank insignia. I know your commanding officer wants to talk to you, so once again, thank you for proving the formation of the team was a good idea." He dismissed us with a nod.

Mark marched us out of his office and onto the veranda to retrieve our gear. "Smoke if you'd like." We lit our smokes while Mark talked to us. "As of sixteen hundred tomorrow, you're all on leave until February one next year, except for Sergeant Davis and Corporal Wilson. You two have until the eleventh of January, when I'll require you back here. We do have a couple upcoming missions. You both will be moving quarters. Tag, you'll be moving into Tiger's old room. Tiger, this might be hard on you, I know, but you'll be moving into Pep's room. Do the changeover tomorrow; for tonight stay in the rooms you have. If any of you require travel warrants, please come see me tomorrow. That's all, guys, go get squared away."

I stayed behind as the others moved off and pulled out the bag of equipment from my backpack. I handed it to Mark and said, "These are Pep's, and the others pagers and stuff, what'll I do with them?"

"I'll take them. You better go see your girl. I take it you'll be off base tonight," he said with a wink. "Oh and by the way, you better get used to drinking and eating in the Sergeants mess now."

After taking my gear to my room and changing out of combat gear, I considered the fact that I'd be moving house in the morning. I didn't put anything away. I opened my kitbag and placed all my washing and a spare set of cams into my spare bag. I looked at my watch, grabbed the spare bag, and locked the door on my way to the sigs OR's mess.

I passed Sharon's car and put my spare bag on the bonnet and continued to the mess. I realized I had a bit of a problem: protocol dictated that I couldn't enter the OR's mess without being invited. As luck would have it, I spotted a corporal I knew and stopped him. "Corporal Wallace, can you do me a favour and invite me into your mess?"

"You know you can just walk in, Tiger," he replied with a grin on his face. I pointed to my rank pin, and he said, "Oh, sorry Sarge. I guess we'll have to this formally." As we walked in, he called, "Attention the mess. I have invited this sergeant into the mess as my guest."

As we walked to the bar, no one paid any notice of me. At the bar I shouted Wallace a drink, saying "Thanks, I owe you one. Then the barman poured my scotch and handed it to me. I moved to the table where Sharon had her back to me and said, "I hope you don't mind if I put my drink here."

I placed my glass on the table when she looked up; she sprang out of her chair, threw her arms around my neck, and kissed me.

"Tiger! I'm so glad you're back!"

As she cuddled me without letting go of my neck, she started crying on my shoulder. I said into her ear, "Hi honey. Calm down, baby, we are in the mess darling."

"Oh shit." She tried to dry her eyes on my shirt before letting go. Before I sat down, she looked defiantly around at everyone who had been watching, and they put their heads down. Only then did she sit.

As I sat back, she started asking all kinds of questions at once that I didn't have a hope in hell of answering. When she asked me when I'd returned and I told her, she berated me for not letting her know I was back.

I interrupted her. "But this is the first chance I've had, babe."

"Right. Drink your drink. We're going home now."

I chuckled at her order, drained my scotch, and said, "Ready when you are." She finished her drink, got up, grabbed me by the arm, and we walked out of the mess.

When she saw my bag on the bonnet, she asked, "What's that doing there?"

"That was in case you weren't in the mess. You'd have seen it when you got to the car and would have come into the mess. Trust me; I had the devil's own job getting in,"

"Why?" I pointed to my rank insignia again, and she said, "Oh, so that's what that was about."

We got into the car and drove home. Once we were inside, she released the restraint she'd put on herself, and as I closed the door and turned, she wrapped her arms around me and kissed me long and passionately.

"Honey, do you think I can have a drink first? And maybe get some of this shit sorted out?"

She wrapped her arms around me. "Uh huh. It's just that I missed you and am glad you're back."

While she made the drinks, I opened the balcony doors and put my bag into the bedroom for sorting out later. I took my boots off

416

and joined her on the balcony. She gave me a kiss. I sat to drink my drink and lit up smokes for us both, passing the first one to her. I sat back and relaxed and told her that after tomorrow, I was on leave until January eleven. We discussed when she would be on leave for Christmas and if she'd arranged anything.

"I was thinking of driving home and possibly spending the Christmas week with my parents and family, but I want to be with you too. Do you think we could both go? You can meet my family. Or were you planning something else?"

My mind was racing with things that I needed to do. I asked, "Would there be enough room to stay at your parents' place, and more importantly, would they let us sleep together?"

She giggled. "Oh that's a thought, but I've spoken to them since we've been together. You know that. I've also spoken to them since you've been gone, and they know we live together when we're not on base."

I interjected, "How did that go down?"

She laughed got up. "I'll make you another drink, and then I'll tell you."

"That bad, huh?" I teased.

"No, of course not. Tell you in a minute."

While she was inside I lit another smoke. She handed me my drink and kissed me on the cheek. When she'd returned to her seat with her drink, she continued. "Well, the whole story goes like this. I was talking to my mum, and she was asking how I was, and inadvertently I told her I was fine but not sleeping too well because you were overseas. I told her how I missed not having your body next to mine in our bed. I realized what I'd said and tried to cover it up, but Mum's a quick one, so she knows, which means Dad will know also. She said it was ok as long as we loved each other, that it was fine by her. As for room at the house, since my sister moved out, they're the only ones there in a three bedroom house."

I nodded. "Ok, room at the house isn't a problem then. Let's get a calendar and work this out."

417

We moved inside and Sharon grabbed the calendar. I noticed she had already marked her leave, which saved a question.

"Here's what I've got in mind. I need to get my car, so with people to see and so on, I'll need a week to do that. If you flew into Brisbane, I could pick you up at the airport and we can go to your parents, have Christmas there, and drive back in my car."

Sharon liked the idea. "That would be wonderful, but how would you know which day to pick me up?"

I laughed and smilingly said, "I can see the boss tomorrow and get the travel warrants to return home. I'll use the return as a one way for you to Bris. I'll only be using them one way anyway because I'll be driving the car back. I'll drop you at work next week and go into the Ansett office. The only thing we need to work out before then is the day you want to leave."

She was nodding her head as she listened. "Sounds good. Let's work that out then."

"Mind you all this is only a rough guide. I won't have firm dates until I go into Ansett."

She leaned over and kissed me. "You're good at planning things. I'll start dinner cooking, and you can show me all your new stuff, and we'll wash it all on the weekend."

After dinner we sorted out my gear. The fresh set was put into the bedroom for the morning and the rest was put into the washing machine. We had a long shower together and an early night that involved a lot of love making and talking. We eventually drifted off to sleep after ten.

The next morning Sharon dropped me off at the quarters. We arranged for her to pick me up after she knocked off. I grabbed some of my gear and took it upstairs to Pep's old room, which was like mine but with an extra cupboard, larger fridge, and more space. It was an extra half a room bigger than the old one, and it had a double bed. I was taking the last load up as Tag came up with his first load. I told him I'd be back down in a minute after I took my last load up.

When I got back down, I showed him how to set the safe combination and how to reset it if he ever forgot his combination. I gave him the room keys, took my name slide out of the door, and took him up to show him my room. I slid my name into the door slide and told him not to forget his before he left his old room. He went back downstairs to sort out his room while I sorted mine.

Whoever had cleared Pep's gear had already reset the safe combination. I changed the combination and placed my pistols into it, along with all my ammo clips. After all my gear was hung up and squared away, I took both my dress shirts up to the laundry and asked for the corporal stripes to be replaced with sergeant stripes on both. I was told they'd be ready in fifteen minutes, so I wandered over to the Q store and asked about getting a shoulder holster for my colt. As luck would have it, they had one left in store. I signed for it and took it with me, picked up my shirts, and went back to my quarters.

At zero ten hundred, I went to HQ and asked to see Mark. I was ushered into his office five minutes later.

"What can I do for you, Tiger?"

"If possible, boss, I'd like to get a return air travel warrant to go home while on leave."

After asking where to, he said, "That means you'll have fly into Brisbane and get a connecting flight. I think we can do that, but unfortunately the only air warrants we have are booked as business class." Smiling at me, he asked, "Can you handle that?"

I replied with a laugh and smile, "I'm sure I'll be able to manage, boss."

He called out to the orderly to bring the air warrants and wrote the destination in and checked the return flight box. "When are going?"

"Not sure yet. I'll go into the Ansett office on Monday and see what they can arrange, but whichever way it goes I'll be back in plenty of time."

He smiled. "I know you will be. Have a safe trip and I'll see you on the eleventh of January."

"Thanks boss," I replied with a wave as I walked out the door.

Back in my room, I packed my travel bag with the civvy clothes I would wear while I was away, a set of fatigues, and after getting my gun out of the safe, put it into the shoulder holster, adjusted all the straps to fit me, and put them both into the bag with two spare ammo clips. I checked to be sure I had both my pagers and rang Sharon's direct line. I gave her my new room phone number and asked if I could borrow the car after lunch.

"Of course you can, sweetheart. You've got the keys, so just take it when you're ready. I'm not going to get away until normal knock off. How about we meet up at the mess?"

"Sure honey, but you'll have to wait outside for me. We'll have to go through the normal protocol thing. I do have a set of car keys, but I wanted to let you know first. I'm going into the city to the Ansett office to see what's available, and I'll let you know what happens. See you at the mess later. Love you."

"Love you too," she replied softly and hung up the phone.

This was the first time I'd been in the sergeants' mess, but it was the same as the OR's mess. The only new thing I would have to take part in was formal dining-in nights about once a month, which was completely silver service and meant I'd have to get a formal uniform that included a white jacket. I decided I'd wait until I was back from leave before going to the Q store to have a set tailored.

After lunch I returned to my quarters to make sure my stuff was ready to go and headed to the sigs company to pick up the Monaro. I drove back to the quarters and parked the car in the car park. I went inside to grab my gear. As I went up, I called into Tag's new room and told him I'd be out for the rest of the day. I gave him the numbers for my room, home, and personal pager in case he needed to contact me. He didn't have a personal pager, but I knew the number to the room phone if I needed him. He was on leave at the end of the following week, so after telling him I'd see him when I got back, I continued up to my room, grabbed my travel bag, dress uniform, and shoes, and took them to the car. I left the

420

base for the city.

At the Ansett office, I talked to a girl named Wendy, who was great. She was able to get me on a night flight to Brisbane, which would connect to my flight north after only a two-hour layover at the Brisbane airport. She also was able to change the return flights into a one way for Sharon into Brisbane that would arrive there at fourteen hundred kilo. I thought that would be perfect timing.

I said to Wendy, "Of course you know that as a serving member of my regiment, I'm required by regulations to always carry a gun with me. Is that going to be a problem?"

Wendy replied, "Of course not, Sergeant, as long as you won't be wearing it."

"No, it'll be in my travel bag, which is hand luggage," I explained.

"That's fine, I've made note on your ticket about it, so everything is good. Can I help you with anything else?" she asked with a smile.

I got up from the desk with the tickets in hand. "No thanks, Wendy. You've been great, thank you." I left the office, took my gear home, and headed to the base to meet Sharon.

We met at the mess for drinks. I handed her the ticket. "This is the best option we could come up with, honey. You'll arrive in Brisbane at fourteen hundred, and I'll be there to meet you. It's for Monday the twenty first. Unfortunately you have to travel business class." I smiled at her silly expression.

"I guess I'll have to put up with it. Wow, business class. I've never been able to afford that. When do you leave?"

"I'll have to get you to take me to the airport late Wednesday night, so I'll be home in the afternoon on Thursday. I'll have ten days to wind everything up there before I meet you at Brisbane airport on the twenty first. You just have to make sure you're at the airport in plenty of time for your early flight."

Instead of going straight home, we went down to Freo and had dinner at the Wharf pub because we liked it there and the seafood was excellent. During dinner, Sharon asked, "So do you think I can ring my mum and let her know we're coming and when now that we have the dates?"

I nodded my head. "Sure, go ahead. You can also tell them how we're doing it if you wish. Just don't let them come pick you up, that's my job. How long will it take us to get to your place from the airport?"

She thought for a second replying. "Twenty minutes top."

I replied, "Good. You can tell them we'll get there around three."

The following Wednesday night Sharon came to see me off. We'd made all the final plans, even down to when we'd leave her parents place and which way we'd drive back. Most of the drive would be inland, but after Adelaide, we'd stick to the coast road before joining up with the Eyre highway at Ceduna, for the trip across the Nullarbor.

After a lot of cuddles and kisses, I boarded the plane. The business class seats were great, as I'd learned on my trip to Adelaide. They allowed room to stretch out, and I was able to sleep most of the trip. After landing in Brisbane and finding out which gate I'd be using for the flight north and when, I went to the Ansett V.I.P. club, a perk of being a military person in uniform, and enjoyed a large breakfast without rushing.

I finally arrived in town at midday. I walked outside to the cab rank, opened the rear door of the front one, placed my bag on the seat, and climbed in front to tell the cabbie where to take me.

When the cabbie pulled up outside the shop on East Street, I paid him, got my travel bag, and walked into the store. There was a fresh face at the counter, and I wondered if he was as conscientious as I was in the day. It didn't seem so because he waited until I reached the counter before speaking to me. "Is there something I can do for you?"

I replied, "Where's that bloody little Norwegian that stole my car?"

The kid's face paled, there was a clatter in the back, and Eric's voice questioned, "Tiger?"

He rushed out from the back. I stood near the doorway to the back with my arms out, and Eric rushed into my opened arms. We embraced as close friends do.

"My god, it is you. And look at you! You look great and a sergeant already! Look at the ribbons! You've only been gone a year. You must have so much to tell me. Come, come sit down and tell me everything, John, go make coffee. Tiger likes his—"

I interrupted, "Black, no sugar. How've you been Eric?"

"Much the same, but let's not talk about me. What have you been up to? Wait don't say anything yet. I'm going to ring Doris and tell her we have a house guest tonight." After his call, he said, "That woman, no end of questions, but I told her it was a surprise and to make a good dinner for three. Now let's hear what you've been up to."

The new boy had come back with the coffees. Eric introduced us and raised his eyebrows, indicating that he wasn't all that good. I laughed when he told me, "John, this is the person whose shoes you're trying to fill, and as you know I've compared you to him so many times."

As I sipped my coffee, I gave Eric a quick account of what I'd been doing since the last time we last saw each other, which took nearly an hour.

After I finished, he said, "I think there's a lot you're not telling me. For instance, how did you get your medals, and how did you become a sergeant so quickly?"

"Yes, you're right. I haven't given you the full story yet. That I'll keep until we're with Doris because I don't want to go over everything twice. You know how she is; she'll want to know every detail."

We laughed together. He said with a smile, "You're right. Ok, we'll leave the full story for later."

CHAPTER 40

I told Eric I was back in town for the last time. I had no intention of coming back after this trip; this trip was to say goodbye to a lot of people. I was going to get a motel room and operate out of it because I'd probably be coming and going at odd hours for the short time I was in town.

That afternoon when we drove into Eric's driveway, Doris was standing there waiting. When I got out of the car, she ran down the stairs and into my arms, crying and laughing. "Oh Tom, it's so good to see you," she said between sobs. "Oh look at me. I must look a sight."

Eric carried my travel bag inside; unfortunately, I'd left the zipper unfastened, and as he placed the bag on the coffee table, he looked at me with a frown on his face and pointed into my bag. The butt of my forty five in the shoulder holster was showing. I looked at him and explained, "Regulations for me, Eric."

He nodded his head. "Ok, just this once."

I nodded and picked up the bag. "Let's put this in the bedroom I'll use, shall we?"

He replied, "Sure. I'll show you the way."

While we were in the bedroom, I said, "By rights, I'm breaking SOP's. I should be wearing it, so let's keep it quiet."

He nodded his understanding, and we went back into the lounge. He poured some drinks. Doris joined us and asked, "So what have you been up to, young Tom?" I laughed as I looked at Eric, who was smiling.

I told them in detail what I'd been doing, and my story continued through dinner and into the night, with pauses for drink pouring, smoking, and dish washing. Eventually my tale was finished and they were up to date. At times during my story, there'd been interruptions with questions.

When I told them about being wounded, Doris got up to look closely at my head. "My poor darling boy, how dare they!"

Eric and I laughed at that, and Eric asked, "So what are you going to do now?"

"Well, as I said earlier, I'll book a motel room, visit some friends and say goodbye, but first thing in the morning, I'll park my car at the shop, if that's ok. I want to go and see my father at work and have a talk to him before I even think of seeing the rest of the family."

They wanted me stay with them, but knowing I had to break ties, I said, "No. Most likely I'll be coming and going at all hours, but I will come and see you before I leave for good. Is that ok?" They nodded their acceptance, and we all had a drink before calling it a night.

The next morning, I put on my dress uniform and after saying goodbye to Doris, fired up the ford and followed Eric to the shop. When we entered the shop, I put the kettle on; old habits die hard.

After we had coffee, I walked up the street to see the old man. I got quite a few stares as I walked up the street and into Stewarts. I went up to the old man's office, and as the door to his office was open, walked right in. He didn't look up, so I said, "How's it going, Dad?"

He looked up then and sat back in his chair in shock. He got up, came around the desk, and hugged me. "Well, well. Let's look at you. My God, the army? And special forces too? A decorated sergeant, my God! You have been busy."

Just then Janice, his secretary, knocked on the door to see if there was anything he wanted before she started work. "Yes, coffee please, and one for ...." He gestured to me and I turned to face her.

She gasped. "Tom!"

I smiled and told her, "Black, no sugar. Thanks Janice. Oh, and hi, by the way."

Flabbergasted, she scuttled out to make the coffee while I sat opposite the old man.

"So you've come home," my father said to me, pride in his eyes.

"Shit no! Well, yes and no. I came to collect my car and say a proper goodbye to people. When I leave in a few days, I'm not coming back to this place ever again."

He sat back in his chair, a pensive look on his face. Janice brought the coffee in on a tray and closed the door as she left the office. "Are you going to come over to the house? If so, do yourself and me a favour. Don't wear your uniform. Your mother would have kittens. Why don't you come over and have dinner tonight? Where are you going to stay while you're in town?"

"I stayed at Eric's last night, but today I'm going to get a motel room somewhere. I need to pick up some of my gear, but yeah, I'll come over tonight."

"You could stay at home if you want," he offered.

"Oh yeah, I can see that happening. The old girl would go ape. Besides, I'll tell you what I told Eric. I intend to be coming and going at odd hours, and Mum would not take kindly to that. Not that she takes kindly to anything, so no; a motel is the best option."

He nodded. "So the Army? Is that what you were intending all along? How did you get in; you're too young? I'd say looking at the decorations you've already been to Vietnam?"

"I landed back a week ago, and I'm on leave until January. Yes, it was what I had intended on doing, and I copied and changed my birth certificate to the same year as my license. That's why I got them to put a different birth year on it. And yes, I was planning it way back then."

He shook his head in disbelief. "Why didn't you give me some kind of clue, or let me know what you were planning?"

"Because you would have tried to stop me. This way it's done and can't be undone. There were only a couple of people that knew what I was doing, and I've yet to see them. Even Eric wasn't aware of what I'd planned until the last moment."

426

He laughed loudly and said, "Sometimes you're too smart and devious for your own good. Come to the house at six. Now I'd better get some work done."

I wasn't sure whether his comment was a compliment or not, but I replied, "Ok, I'll see you at six. I've got some people to see, so I'll get going."

After telling Eric I'd see him later, I drove over to the other side of town to see if Skeeter still lived in the same place. I pulled up and Joan was sitting on the veranda. She said with some surprise in her voice, "Tiger, come in. How are you? Skeeter's at work."

After chatting for a while, I asked, "Please don't tell Skeeter I'm in town I'll come by tomorrow. Since its Saturday he shouldn't be working."

"No, he's not working tomorrow. We are having a BBQ at lunch. Some of the team are coming with their wives. Why not just turn up and surprise everyone? I promise I won't say anything," she invited with a wink and a smile.

"Thanks, love," I said, and gave her a kiss on the cheek. I headed back down the stairs and called, "I'll see you tomorrow."

Back on the other side of town, I booked a room at the Best Western Motel on Gladstone Road, sorted my gear out, hung up my dress uniform, and went for a swim in the pool. I showered and changed into civvies.

WA was two hours behind in time difference, so I phoned Sharon at work. Our conversation was over an hour long. Her leave started on Monday, and she'd be home most of the time next week, getting ready for the trip.

When I hung up, I walked across the road to the Ulster Arms bottle shop and bought a bottle of scotch and some dry ginger ale. I took it back to the motel room, figuring I'd probably be in need of a drink when I got back from the oldies place.

I pulled up to the house at six. The old man must have heard the car; he was waiting at the front door as I climbed the stairs. We shook hands and went inside. In the lounge room, I got hugs from my brothers and sister. My mother told them to go outside and play while the three of us talked, and as soon as they were out of the room, she said, "Well, are you back for good, or is this just one of your quick visits for a meal?"

Dad had poured us a drink, adding some dry to my scotch as she said this. He almost dropped the bottle. I took my glass and had a quick slug before I answered, "No, quite the reverse actually. I'm here to collect some of my gear, and then I'm leaving for good. When I leave tonight, I won't be coming back at all. In fact, I'm only in town for a couple of days to say goodbye to some friends, as I've already collected my car. I'm only here because my father asked me to come."

Needless to say, dinner was awkward; I was trying not to let my anger or temper get the better of me. After dinner and three scotches, I got the stuff I had planned to take together and put it into a large plastic bag. As I packed, my brothers and sister watched me. I told them I wasn't coming back anymore, so whatever I left behind they could share amongst them.

I put my gear into the car, and I went inside to say goodbye. My parents were in the lounge; the old man was fuming although not speaking. The old girl was sitting back in one of the armchairs.

Ignoring her, I shook my dad's hand. "You know my jobs dangerous, so don't be surprised if you get notified sometime in the future."

He nodded and embraced me in a hug. "Be careful."

The old girl wasn't about to let anything go. "Job? What job? It can't be any good if you're doing it."

That started it; Dad swung to face her and yelled, "Shut up!"

I exploded. "I'm not in the Navy, or Air Force, but I am in the Army. Special Forces, actually, and I've already done better than you. You were only ever a corporal. I'm a sergeant already and rising, so stick that up your jumper!" I stormed out to the car and left.

The next day I arrived at Skeeter's place at twelve thirty. He must have heard my car because he walked around the side of the house to look. He saw the car and looked at me. He rushed over and grabbed me in a bear hug.

With disbelief in his voice, he said, "Tiger!"

I smiled as he released me from the bear hug. "How you doing, buddy? Grab these and let's go in." I passed him a carton of beer.

He was stunned that I was there and wasn't sure what to say. "How…when did, yeah come on, let's go round the back." As we walked, he said, "Boy, you're a sight for sore eyes. Some of the old team are here. We're having a BBQ. They're going to love this! When did you get in?"

"I'll tell you the whole story soon. How did you know it was me?"

"Joan said she heard a car, and when I saw it, well, no one I know would be stupid enough to drive your car here without getting the shit pummelled out of them."

When we got to the backyard, Skeeter yelled, "Hey everyone, look what the cat dragged in!" The guys turned, saw me, and were out of their seats in a flash, some of the wives as well. I was welcomed back with handshakes and kisses.

So everybody got to hear the whole story of what I'd been up to. Of course there were plenty of questions and jokes. At the end of the afternoon, when everyone had departed, I stayed and talked with Skeeter and Joan well into the night. We knew we would most likely never see each other again, so we tried to prolong the inevitable by asking questions and reminiscing.

When I stood to leave, Skeeter embraced me for a long time before letting go. "There's always a home for you here, brother, whenever you need it."

I nodded, embraced and kissed Joan good bye. I whispered in her ear, "Look after him."

She whispered back, "I will, and you look after yourself."

I nodded again and walked to the car. I drove off without looking back, fighting back tears.

The next afternoon I went down to the team pub and walked in. It was off season so there weren't many in the pub. I did see Coach Dixon sitting at the bar. I went to the bar and stood beside him.

"What does a man have to do to get a drink around here?"

Bobby turned to ask his standard question. "What'll you...well I'll be, one VB coming up, Tiger!" His face lit up with a smile, and Coach Dixon looked up at me.

His face brightened. "Tiger, how the hell are you?"

As Bobby put the beer in front of me, he asked, "Are you back for good?"

I shook my head and answered after sipping my beer. "No guys, I'm still in the army. I'm just back on leave saying my final goodbyes. I won't be back after this trip. I live in Western Australia now."

I spent a couple of hours with them having a few drinks. With handshakes all around, I said goodbye to them.

The next morning, I rang the Finlay's. Betty answered, and I asked what Barbara was up to. Betty said she was on nights.

"So if I came up to see you and Ray at four, she won't be there?"

Betty replied, "That will be fine, Tom. It'll be good to see you."

That afternoon I changed into my dress uniform before heading up to see them. I figured they had the right to know what I gave up their daughter for. Ray answered the door, shook my hand and we went inside. I removed my beret as I entered.

We went into the lounge where Betty was waiting, and I kissed her on the cheek before sitting. Ray grabbed a couple drinks and made Betty one. As he passed it to her, he said to me, "So you did make it into the army. I didn't think you'd be able to do it, but look at you now and a sergeant as well. Well done, Tiger."

Betty invited, "Come and sit beside me Tom, and tell us all about it."

"Sure, but I don't want Barbara to see me. That's why I've come while she's at work. Has she gotten over our parting yet?"

Betty answered quietly, "Yes, she finally did, but it took nearly three months. I'm glad you did it the way you did, and you're right. Seeing you would probably give her hope again. Now let's hear all about what you've been up to."

I told them about everything that had happened, about my time in Vietnam, and that I would be going back again in the following year. I told them why I was in town, and what I was doing.

"So I promised I'd come and say my last goodbye, and this is it. I won't be coming back anymore. This is my last time in town. I wanted to tell you that you were more like parents to me than my own, and I'd like to thank you for that and much more. But when I go today, it'll be for the last time." Soon after that, I left amid handshakes, kisses, and hugs, before driving back to the motel.

The next day, the first thing I did was walk up the street to the dry cleaners and handed my dress uniform over for cleaning. The counter girl told me I could pick it up near lunch time, so I went back to the room and contemplated what I had left to do before I left town. Only two things were left for me to do; one was to visit my sister's grave, tree actually, because she had been cremated. I decided to visit her after my uniform was cleaned. The second thing was to say goodbye to Eric and Doris. Once I'd done those two things, I'd be free to leave.

I added a third thing: go and see my father at work before I left. I phoned the shop before I went to collect my uniform and spoke to Eric. We arranged to have dinner the following night. That would be it, all done with. I'd talk to my dad the next morning, so with that sorted, I went to collect my uniform.

I drove out to the north side of town to the crematorium and asked at the office for her plot number. After finding it, I sat and had a mental conversation with my sister, telling her of all the things I'd done and what I hoped I to do. I told her I had regrets, but that I wouldn't change any of the decisions I'd made and hoped she was having a good afterlife. I hoped I'd see her sooner than later, and I told her I'd not be back to visit her. I wished her well and hoped it was reciprocal. And with a final farewell, I got up. As I did, a wind gust out of nowhere made the rose bush that had been planted blow lightly across my face, and with tears in my eyes, I left.

The following morning, I drove down to the main drag. After parking, I went into Stewarts to see the old man. We spent the next two hours talking and having coffee, smoking a couple of his cigars. I stood and he shook my hand and embraced me in a farewell hug. I left his office, and I didn't see him for years afterward.

That night at Eric's was quite an emotional night. When I said goodbye to someone I considered a good friend and mentor and his loving and caring wife, a woman I considered would have been a very loving mother, because she was to me.

Note to the reader: As this is my story I reserve the right to leave out things, or not tell you things that happened at different times. Because this night was fairly intense, I use that right to withhold information about my last farewell to Eric and Doris. Please don't think ill toward me for this. To me it was quite gut wrenching.

The next morning I paid my bill at the motel office and left town forever. I had five days left before Sharon flew into Brisbane, and at most the trip down to Brisbane would only take me two days. I took my time and overnighted in Hervey Bay just for the hell of it and arrived in Brisbane at eighteen hundred the next night. I booked a room in a motel that was bit of a misnomer; it was called the airport motel, but it was nowhere near the airport, unless you were a crow. So I did some sightseeing in Brisbane for the next couple of days and was thoroughly bored. I was glad when Monday rolled around.

I was at the airport thirty minutes before Sharon's plane was due to land, so I whiled away the time in one of the cafes. I was quite jumpy while I waited for her to arrive. I came to the surprising revelation that I'd been missing her. Eventually her plane landed, and she flew into my arms as she got into the terminal. We had to wait for her bag to be offloaded. Honestly, anybody would think she was planning to stay here for six months considering the dimensions and weight of her suitcase.

Outside the terminal, we had long kiss and cuddle. She said, "God I've missed you."

"I've missed you too. You don't know how much."

When I showed her to my car, she was somewhat unimpressed. "Nice paint job, but don't you think it looks old fashioned."

As I opened the boot and put her case in with my gear, I replied, "This old-fashioned Ford would leave your little tin can Holden for dead. Don't judge a book by its cover, and if you don't believe me, you drive."

I unlocked the doors and handed her the keys. Surprised, she climbed into the driver's seat and started it up. The look on her face was priceless as she heard it rumble for the first time. I laughed and said, "You ain't seen nothing yet. Come on, let's go."

Once out of the car park, she put her foot down. The look on her face was enough to know she was in rev head seventh heaven.

She pulled over and started to get out. "You better drive. I'll get a ticket within five minutes. My God, what's under the hood?"

"Show you tomorrow," I replied and followed the directions she gave to the residence in Banyo.

I was given a warm welcome and made to feel part of the family. Later in the day, we had drinks while we were relaxing. I took Sharon out to the car and lifted the bonnet. Her father, Trevor, joined us.

"Lovely. Looks like a blueprint phase three," Trevor commented as he inspected what was under the hood.

"Four," I corrected.

"Top end?"

"Not sure but I've had it up to one eighty. I'm intending to find out on the Nullarbor."

He nodded and pointed at Sharon. "Just don't let this one drive. I've paid too many speeding fines for her."

Sharon leaned into him and said, "And I love you for it, Daddy."

I laughed and commented, "She does that with me too." We and I laughed as we headed back inside, with Sharon pouting behind us.

433

Trevor was ex-military and a plumber, so we got on rather well. Jenny, his wife, looked after the house and the business books. Wendy, Sharon's sister, came over on Christmas Eve with her boyfriend, Jim, and they stayed until after Boxing Day. Everyone had a good time. The only fly in the ointment was that Jim was a bit of a radical and opposed the war in Vietnam. At times he, Trevor, and I would have heated disagreements about the situation in regards to what was happening over there. At one point he made the stupid comment that South Vietnam would be better off if the communists won.

I took exception to that. "If you've never been there, how the hell do you have the gall to say that? I suppose we just pull up stakes and let them fend for themselves, is that it?"

"There'd be fewer atrocities being committed by our soldiers," he responded hotly.

I hit the bloody roof. "So you're one of those pricks that think that all our soldiers do all day is go around killing kids? Is that what you're saying?" My temper was up and my voice had lowered.

Sharon knew I was close to striking out, so she grabbed me and took me inside to calm me down. I went to the toilet. When I came out, I heard Sharon going to town on this moron, and by the time I walked out, Jim had stood up.

I said from the back door, "You even look like you're gonna touch my girl and I'll show you how we kill kids."

Sharon moved to my side, and Trevor looked at Jim. "You don't know how lucky you are that Tom didn't hit you. The only reason he didn't is that he has common sense and knows he's a guest in my house. I think it would be a good idea if you left in the morning."

The night before we left, I apologized to Trevor for my behaviour that night.

"You have nothing to apologize for, except for not letting me tear the little twerp to shreds. Now, which way are you planning on going back?"

"First out to Goondiwindi, down the Newell, and cut across to

434

Broken Hill. Then down through Renmark into Adelaide, and follow the coast road all the way to Ceduna and onto the Nullarbor."

"Yep, seems the best way to go."

The next morning Sharon and I said our goodbyes and started the drive back to Western Australia and whatever the future held.

To be continued...

AUTHORS NOTE:

This is where we leave Tom for the time being, as this is the end of book one of the Catalyst Trilogy.

In book two of the Catalyst Trilogy, entitled Divine Retribution.

We follow Tom's adventures into action again: with two more tours of Vietnam, followed by cataclysmic action in secret war zones, and how the job played havoc with his personal life.

The book ends as Tom receives an offer to leave the Special Forces and move into the clandestine world of government spy agencies.

www.ingramcontent.com/pod-product-compliance
Lightning Source LLC
Chambersburg PA
CBHW070306040726
47501CB00018B/225